W9-ADM-239

"Full of action, exotic characters, plenty of plot, and even a touch of romance. Outstanding."
— *Booklist*

"Space opera isn't just ripsnortin' adventure, though Lee and Miller give us plenty of that. The thing about space opera is it's more than nifty science, the clash of customs, the evolution of ideas, interesting planets, cool tech, and new pioneers, it's also and above all about character . . . and one cares about the characters, about their further adventures, and their families' adventures, and even about the villains. The Liaden Universe stories are very good space opera."
— Sherwood Smith, author of *Journey to Otherwise*

"Ambitiously creating a complex emotional environment, Mr. Miller and Ms. Lee pique our curiosity with an equally complicated plot development."
— *Romantic Times*

"No other authors can compare to their skill at bringing characters to full and robust life, half convincing me that there is a time portal to the future, hidden up in Maine through which Sharon and Steve have been watching and recording the lives of the Liadens for years."
— Jennifer Dunne, author of *Raven's Heart*

Praise for *I DARE*

"For those already addicted to Clan Korval, be warned: you had best be in a comfortable position when you sit down to read [*I Dare*], because you aren't moving until it's done. [Lee and Miller] consistently deliver stories with a rich, textured setting, intricate plotting, and vivid, interesting characters from fully realized cultures, both human and alien—and each book gets better."
—Elizabeth Moon, author of *Speed of Dark*

"In *I Dare* . . . Miller and Lee gather up half a dozen major story threads and weave them into, not only a complex and exciting whole, but a truly satisfactory ending. Or possibly beginning . . ."
—Tanya Huff, author of *The Better Part of Valor*

"Imagine Georgette Heyer crossed on James Bond in a universe of starships and psychic wizardry, and you'll have something like the Liaden novels of Sharon Lee and Steve Miller—nobody else in the field combines space opera and comedy of manners with the same deftness and brio as these two."
—Debra Doyle, co-author of the *Mageworlds* novels

"When I first met . . . the characters populating the Liaden Universe, their personalities were so sharply drawn and their adventures so breathtaking that I found myself thinking about them as if they were real. *I Dare* is a book I've anticipated for a long time. Now I can stop worrying about the characters I love, celebrate resolution in their lives, and begin nagging authors Miller and Lee. More please. And hurry."
—Maureen Tan, author of *Run, Jane, Run*

"Sharon Lee and Steve Miller have a marvelous ability to weave powerful characters, intriguing world-building, and swift action into a rich, compelling tapestry, and they're at the top of their game in *I Dare*."
—Mary Jo Putney, author of *The China Bride* and *The Spiral Path*

"Excellent and very satisfying . . . [*I Dare*] features colorful, likable, and occasionally improbably talented characters, some strange (but benevolent) aliens, barely sketched but highly evil villains, and plenty of combat and piloting where personal skills matter more than technology. There are humor, romance, courage, and incredible rescues."
—*Other Worlds*

continued . . .

"There's definitely a fantasy feel to parts of this exuberant space opera, with . . . wizards, a sentient tree, and even a cat who walks through walls, but it's a fun mix. Once the plot starts rolling . . . the fun snowballs, with a gloriously mixed ending that settles the current problem nicely—while promising more such entertainment yet to come."

—*Locus*

DON'T MISS THE OTHER THRILLING NOVELS OF LIAD

LOCAL CUSTOM
SCOUT'S PROGRESS
CONFLICT OF HONORS
AGENT OF CHANGE
CARPE DIEM
PLAN B

Praise for Sharon Lee and Steve Miller's novels of the Liaden Universe® . . .

"One of the never-failing joys of [*Local Custom*] is the crisp language, the well-turned phrases, the very exciting action, not to mention the confrontation of two vastly different cultures."

—Anne McCaffrey

"The stories have it all. Adventure, intrigue, romance. Loyal friendships and hidden treachery. The authors deftly weave plot elements that stretch across the known universe, while still remaining focused on the characters who drive the action."

—Patricia Bray, author of *Devlin's Luck*

"Sharon Lee and Steve Miller have imaginations matched only by the precision of their writing."

—Gerry Boyle, author of *Cover Story*

"Lee and Miller strike space opera gold."

—Robin Wayne Bailey, author of *Night's Angel*

"Val Con and Miri are the most romantic couple in SF!"

—Susan Krinard, author of *Touch of the Wolf*

i dare

sharon lee and steve miller

ACE BOOKS, NEW YORK

I DARE

An Ace Book / published by arrangement with
Meisha Merlin Publishing, Inc.

PRINTING HISTORY
Meisha Merlin Publishing, Inc. trade paperback edition / February 2002
Ace mass-market edition / August 2003

ISBN: 0-441-01085-7

ACE®
Ace Books are published by The Berkley Publishing Group,
a division of Penguin Group (USA) Inc.,
375 Hudson Street, New York, New York 10014.
ACE and the "A" design
are trademarks belonging to Penguin Group (USA) Inc.

PRINTED IN THE UNITED STATES OF AMERICA

10 9 8 7 6 5 4 3 2 1

MASTER JENN'S WORKSHOP
NEGLIT

They had doubted his skill. *Laughed* **at him, by Er-**lady! Took leave to believe him a once-was—a ten-thumbed, aging Terran, half-blind; incapable of bringing the table silver to luster, never mind to copy a ring.

That had been before the Liadens.

They were Liadens, right enough, with the pretty cantra pieces dandled like candies 'tween their slender elvish fingers and sweet words of flattery in their mouths.

Truth owed Erlady, it were the cantra pieces spoke loudest. A man and his grandson, with three cantra pieces to draw against, lived well, for a year or six, here on backworld Neglit.

And they promised him three cantra more, when they came to collect the ring.

The ring. Now, there was a beautiful piece of work. In his young days, he would have snatched the job up for the challenge of it, no thought of payment in his head.

He'd aged out of that nonsense—paid he would be. *Well*-paid. And still he had the delicate, brutal trial of the work, the result of which, polished and re-polished until the intarsia-work gleamed like water in the beam of his work-light, proved he was yet a master of his craft.

They'd sought *him* out, the canny Liadens. *Him*, Jen of Neglit Center, though they surely had all the fabled master jewelers of Solcintra to choose from. Yet they traveled to an outworld, sought out an old and fading *Terran* master, commissioned him to make—to remake—their ring. And why was that?

The tale they'd spun for Terran wits was simple enough. The original ring, a family heirloom, had gone missing, and must be replaced before certain elders of the house noticed its lack.

Such things happened, drain pipes and gambling games being

universally hazardous to jewelry. And mayhap the jewel-masters of Solcintra gossiped 'mong themselves, and a whispered word might waft to the ear of the stern elder, to the dismay of his pretty patrons.

Mayhap.

He was canny enough not to question them too nearly. He had no ambition to risk his six cantra, though he might have balked, if they had wanted paste or light-gold or glass.

But they were keen in their instructions: he was to use only pure-gem, true-gold and emerald. A *replacement*, that's what they insisted on: full duplication of the ring that was lost.

A replacement, exact in every detail, is what he had made for them.

He picked the ring up, turning it this way and that, admiring the simple power of the design. Caught in fluid perfection, a bronze dragon hovered, wide-winged, above a tree in full green leaf. Smiling, he set it against the holopic they had given him of the original.

"I witness ye'd deceive the master who made yon," he told the copy fondly.

"Indeed, it is remarkable work," said a strongly accented voice at his elbow.

The master jeweler started badly and jerked around on his stool, frowning down at the pale-haired Liaden in his costly leather jacket. "Enough to give a body his death, sneak-footing behind one!" He caught himself up, looked from his visitor to the workroom door, with the bell hung above it, that jangled when one of his rare customers came in from the street.

He looked back to the Liaden's smooth, emotionless face. "How came ye?"

The Liaden gestured behind him, to where the inner door stood ajar. "Through the house."

Fear—the tiniest spark of fear—flickered in the master jeweler's heart. The boy was his last treasure. He did not think these were child-thieves, yet—

"I have distressed you," the Liaden said gently. "It was not my intention."

"Well." Mindful of the three cantra yet to come, the master jeweler moved his hand, smoothing the fear out of the air, and spoke moderately. "Understand ye, it's late. The boy needs his rest."

"Of course," said the Liaden and a shadow moved at his shoulder. The master jeweler looked up, meeting the still eyes of the female Liaden.

"The child was asleep," she said in her soft, emotionless voice. "We did not wake him."

He ducked his head, relieved to look away from her eyes. "Thank'ee."

"Surely," she said, then moved forward. Her partner stepped aside, giving her clear view of the worktable. She paused, face as ungiving as ever, studying holo and reality, sitting side by side in the work-light.

"Excellent," she said at last, no faintest lilt of appreciation in her voice. She raised her cold eyes to his face, and went toward the table, her path forcing him to turn somewhat on the stool. The male Liaden had vanished into the shadows of the shop.

"You are indeed a master jeweler," the woman said. She extended a hand and plucked the ring up, turning it under the light, then lowering it to compare against the holopic. Trapped on his stool, the master jeweler watched her, seeing neither pleasure nor relief on her cold, comely face.

"Yes," she said finally, and dropped the ring as if it were a common trinket into the pocket of her jacket. The holopic went to the other pocket, from out of which came three cantra coins, shining across her palm like moons.

"You have earned your fee, Master Jen," she said, extending her hand, the coins glowing, murmuring comfort and ease and schooling for the boy. He leaned forward, felt a sharp pain at the base of his skull.

The Liaden woman stepped back and let the body fall to the floor. Her companion took the polishing rag up from the worktable and used it to clean the gore from the wire-blade before slipping it away into an inner pocket. From another pocket he drew forth a vial, and anointed the corpse with its contents. Then he recapped the container, and wiped it, too, with the polishing rag before returning it to its place.

The woman raised her hand and turned, walking unhurriedly down the dim, cluttered room. He followed her back into the house, past the still figure in the small bed, through the forced door and out into the night.

They were five minutes gone when the first flames licked to life, feeding on the lines of accelerant left to nourish them. Five

minutes more found house and workshop both engulfed in fire so
fierce the water from the firefighter's cannon sizzled and evaporated before it ever touched flame.

Five hours from the start, the fire was out, having consumed
house, shop and contents, leaving not so much as an ash on the
scoured stone floor of the basement.

**DAY 283
STANDARD YEAR 1392**

McGEE SPACEPORT
FORTUNE'S REWARD

"How many times you figure on firing me?"

Pat Rin yos'Phelium sighed. "Refresh my memory, Mr. Mc-
Farland. How many times have I succeeded in firing you thus
far?"

The big man grinned. "OK, that's fair. But, see, I thought we
had an understanding. I ain't only your pilot; I'm your backup.
This idea of yours—to cash up and go to ground—not a thing
wrong with it. In fact, it's a great idea, even considering how
much you bothered to tell me, which I really ain't dumb enough
to think is the whole story. Only thing wrong with it is you're
planning on going in without backup, and that just ain't bright.
How you go to ground—you go easy and smooth, making just as
few ripples as you can. But you go with the certain knowledge
that no matter how smart you are, or how low you keep your head,
something's gonna happen—most likely having to do with blind
stupid luck—and you're gonna be needing backup.

"You gotta suppose they're gonna find you, and be ready for
it. You go in thinking *anything* different and you might as well
take a pistol right now and blow your own brains out. Save everybody some trouble."

Such eloquence. Pat Rin raised an eyebrow. "You intrigue me,

Mr. McFarland. I wonder how you became such an expert in *going to ground.*"

"Someday I might tell you," the big man said, shortly.

It occurred to Pat Rin that he had annoyed his pilot quite as much as his pilot had annoyed him. He took a fresh hold on his temper and inclined his head.

"Forgive me, Pilot. I did not intend to cause you pain."

"You didn't," Cheever said, still tending toward short. "Unless you count a headache." He sighed, gustily. "Look, we been through this. Covering you is part of the deal between me and Shan. Do me the favor of believing I *ain't* dumb enough to go back on my word to a Liaden, OK? You got a problem with the arrangements, take it up with him next time you two are in the same room together."

"Ah." Pat Rin considered that. Such solicitude was . . . unusual; his cousins every one being younger than he, and accustomed all their lives to seeing him set his own course. What had persuaded Shan *this time* that Pat Rin might meet with difficulties large enough to warrant a Cheever McFarland? Unless . . .

Shan was a Healer, not a prognosticator. However, Shan's youngest sister, Pat Rin's cousin Anthora, was a dramliza of some note—including among her talents the ability to foretell event. Pat Rin had once witnessed Anthora in the throes of her gift, and did not doubt that the ability was genuine. Perhaps she had foreseen the cold shadow of the clan's danger even as he was preparing to leave planet, and whispered a word in her brother's ear?

And, in the end, what matter? Pilot McFarland was correct. It lay well outside the scope of Pat Rin yos'Phelium's melant'i to disturb an arrangement between Shan and another.

He sighed, and favored the pilot with a straight look.

"I am counted quite a good shot," he said, with what mildness he could muster. "I offer this as a point of information."

"Yessir, I don't doubt it. But you gotta sleep sometime."

And that, thought Pat Rin, *would appear to be that*. He inclined his head, granting the point as much to Shan as to Cheever McFarland.

"Very well," he said. "Since you insist upon remaining in my employ, I will tell you that I require a dawn departure."

The big man favored him with a stare. "You do."

"Yes, I do," Pat Rin said, rather sharply. "Have I made a demand which is impossible for you to meet?"

"No. Would've made things a lot easier on us both, though, if you'd've thought to call the tower and have us moved to a hot-pad."

It was Pat Rin's turn to stare. "In order to accept a hotpad hook-up, I would have had to file my license number with the tower," he said, wondering if the pilot had returned from his leave just a little drunk, after all.

Cheever nodded. "Yeah, but my card's already on-line. You could've filed the request manually, direct into the queue, an' nobody'd know it wasn't me on the board."

"Pilot McFarland—"

" 'Cause you know the protocol for accepting the hook-up, right? Just like you know the rest of the board? I tell you what, it beats hell outta me why you won't sit second. I don't think I ever seen anybody as hungry for the boards as you are—and I sure could use the help. Backup, get it?"

"Mr. McFarland, I am not a pilot. Placing my hands upon that board—"

"What's the protocol for accepting a hotpad hook-up?" Cheever demanded.

Pat Rin glared, goaded. "The keys to accept the hotpad hookup are twelve-green-right and the appropriate ship axis is north-south-east-west—that assumes one has a matching power-source, which we do else the power light would indicate blue-blue-red rather than the blue-blue-blue presently showing, and we would be using converters, at a cost of an additional half-cantra the Standard—prorated to the Terran minute—for the service." He drew a hard breath, and attempted once more to leash his temper. That a mere hireling should challenge him on so basic a drill! Did he *look* like a fool?

The Terran nodded. "Right. So you coulda done it, though they woulda likely hit you up for a higher charge unless you remembered to tell 'em to orient from ventral instead of dorsal, since this is a pre-1350 ship and they'd've mistook your protocol 'cause the lines look so new." He nodded again, possibly to himself.

"If you got that much, you can move us around when we're locked on to an outside bay in orbit somewhere. I'd right appreciate it if you'd sit second for me, 'case we might need an extra pair of hands or eyes somewhere down the road. *Boss.*"

Pat Rin sighed, chilly in the sudden absence of his anger.

"Mr. McFarland, I am not a pilot, and my hands on the board

would be sufficient to frighten any honest ship-handler into an early retirement. Yes, I know the protocols. Nearly all my kin are pilots. I was myself tested for pilot. And I failed. Repeatedly. I am at a loss as to how I might make this circumstance any plainer to you."

"Done just fine," Cheever assured him. "You're wanting me to understand that you know what to do, you just don't do it fast enough. That it?"

"Yes."

"OK. But there's stuff you could be helping me out with—to both our benefits. You know your equations, don't you?"

Gods, but didn't he. When he was a child, he had thought it a game—Uncle Daav, Cousin Er Thom—even Luken!—would throw out a partial piloting sentence and applaud lavishly when he completed it properly. On those occasions when he missed his line—often, at first—they would gently recite the correct response, and applaud again when he told it back without error.

He had done the same with his own child; teaching him the nursery rhymes of pilots . . .

Pat Rin looked up at the bulk of Cheever McFarland. *Master Pilot*, he reminded himself, and sighed. "I know my equations, Mr. McFarland. Yes."

"Good. I can't force you to do it, but I think it'd be best for the ship—my judgment as Master Pilot, while we're being clear on stuff—if you'd sit second for me."

The best interest of the ship must carry all before it. Pilot or no, the care and keeping of ships was bred into his bones. Korval, after all, was ships.

Pat Rin bowed, novice to master.

"Very well, Mr. McFarland, as you feel it is a matter of ship's safety I will sit in the second seat."

"Great," Cheever said, and stretched, arms over his head, hands brushing the ceiling of the ship. "I'm gonna go get a shower and some caffeine. Meanwhile, you call the tower and get us moved to a hotpad, OK? Don't forget to tell 'em about that orientation to ventral."

So saying he turned and exited the bridge, leaving Pat Rin glaring at nothing.

After a time, he sighed, and moved over to the board to input the request to the tower.

DAY 283
STANDARD YEAR 1392

LIAD
DEPARTMENT OF INTERIOR COMMAND HEADQUARTERS

Satisfied, Commander of Agents closed the field report.

Korval's strengths—that it husbanded—one might say, hoarded—ships; that it valued the skills and reactions of pilots above any other skill a clanmember might possess; that they deliberately bred for pilots, thus propelling themselves to a pinnacle of the type . . .

Those strengths had hidden a notable weakness.

Pat Rin yos'Phelium, heir to Kareen, elder cousin to Val Con, who should by all right of blood and kinship, now stand as Korval Himself—excepting only that he was not a pilot.

Crippled, in Korval's eye, he had been cast aside, dismissed to a wastrel life of spoilt self-indulgence.

The Department of the Interior, however, knew just how to value Pat Rin yos'Phelium, and his place within the Plan.

Commander of Agents smiled slightly and lay his hand on the closed folder.

Despite that the Department found it necessary to its own success to remove Korval from the board, yet it was true that the world, in some measure, required Korval. Lose a clan which held controlling interest in a triple-dozen industries on-planet, which controlled the pilots guild, funded the Scouts, which owned outright fifteen trading vessels and unnumbered smaller craft, not to speak of the yards which serviced them? The planetary economy trembled at the whisper of such calamity. Why, Korval owned the very dies from which cantra pieces were struck, only leasing them to the Moneyers Guild in twelve-year renewals stretching back to the time of the first Val Con yos'Phelium, Cantra's heir.

In any wise, it was no part of the Department's Plan that Liad should be made bankrupt. It was all to the Department's good that Liaden economy flourish and expand.

Thus, if the economy demanded a Korval, then a Korval there would be.

DAY 284
STANDARD YEAR 1392

DEPARTING McGEE

Cheever McFarland bulked large over the controls of *Fortune's Reward*, hands delicate and sure, nearly caressing in their motions. Despite his size he sat comfortably in the pilot's chair, which was locked at the rearmost limits of its track. At this stage in the flight his attention was securely on the board—with its dozens of lights, meters, knobs, and switches—and on the screens ahead.

The pilot's choice of screens for the main board was sparse: centered was local space forward, with radar ranging imposed over the combined straight visual and near infrared view; rear view was a super wide angle in radar encompassing everything not on the front screen at half-size below it. Some few of the screens were surprising—especially the left corner screen, showing a double-deck transcription of the last 144 syllables of Com One's radio communication in Terran—incoming on top, outgoing on the bottom.

The co-pilot's board was live, and Pat Rin yos'Phelium sat, ill-at-ease, in the chair before it. He scrupulously avoided the controls, concentrating instead on the Jump equations he was engaged in framing for the pilot's approval. As if in testimony to the fact that he sat second by the pilot's whim alone, instead of the proper view of space outside the ship, the screen above his board showed a mosaic of thumbnails: every system on the ship represented in an order known only to the pilot.

Pat Rin finished his last calculation and filed it. Leaning back in his chair, as far away from the board as he could reasonably sit, he watched the screens as Cheever McFarland threaded *Fortune's Reward* through the crowded spaceways of near orbit.

From time to time Pat Rin saw a pause, a decision point, pass through the pilot's hands. At the third such he glanced up and saw a new window open on the left.

"I'm watching for long-range interception," the Terran said, calmly matter-of-fact. " 'Cause in here, with all this mess, the normal thing to do is be worried about the next 72 seconds or so, then the next 720 seconds, and not much beyond because so many of the orbits are tight and the maneuvering's hectic. But if someone was looking for us to be Jumping from a particular point, more or less, they'd likely be close to an interception trajectory somewhere down the line, like three hours or so when a ship like ours might normally be expected to Jump."

A lesson in piloting, forsooth. Pat Rin moved a hand in acknowledgment.

"And so right now, there's a ship moving parallel, but that ain't a problem—I doubt anybody'd be trying to chase us with an oreship. There's also one summat behind that got underway from the repair docks about the time we hit orbit. Shows up fine on visual but the beacon on it's a bit funny and out of adjustment, I'd say. They been tuning their orbit something fierce, just like a ship right out of dock might."

Pat Rin moved his hand again as Cheever checked in with Control once more, confirming by voice his destination and learning that, "due to heavy traffic," the Portmaster requested all ships add another quarter planetary diameter to Jump run-up.

"Damn," Cheever said under his breath and hit the com button.

"Control, can we stay on original schedule? I've got a novice here calculating that Jump for all he's worth and we'll be in your way all day if he's gotta start over!"

The delay might have been due to more than the crawl of light across space; the answer was a half-chuckle. "Oh, aye, that's a stet then, *Fortune's Reward*. And I'm to tell you your novice owes a drink to the submaster next trip through."

"To hear is to obey, Control. *Fortune's Reward* out."

Pat Rin glanced at his pilot quizzically.

"I could have recalculated those equations—the quarter diameter is scarcely a—"

A Terran headshake.

"Sure it ain't. But now we got an excuse when we Jump a bit ahead of time with all the wrong energy levels, just in case we're being snooped."

And so they were prudent, on the off-chance that Korval's enemy had found him. Cheever McFarland was a man who took his own advice, then, and built plans upon worst-case projections.

"Tell you what," the pilot was saying, "once we Jump I'll adjust that side and you can shadow me inbound to Teriste. I'll probably ask questions to see if you're paying attention."

Pat Rin bit back a sharp retort. It was never good luck to argue with an elder willing to teach what was needed—especially with Plan B in effect.

DAY 50
STANDARD YEAR 1393

LYTAXIN
EROB'S MEDICAL CENTER

The names of their kin had gained them entrance to the house and a rapid and willing guide to the place where their sister lay, recovering from her wounds.

It was well, Edger thought, following Alys Tiazan Clan Erob, Cousin to Miri Robertson Tiazan Lady yos'Phelium, that they had not tarried, but had descended to the planet surface with all haste and come directly to this dwelling-place.

Truth, it had been Sheather's disquiet that had spurred them to seek their kin so speedily. Yet Sheather had studied Miri Robertson to a depth that none other of the Clutch had yet studied an individual of the Clans of Men, and Edger had been willing to heed his brother's impatience.

Nor was this impatience found to be excessive, once the door to Clan Erob's house had been opened to them. The news given by Alys Tiazan was alarming in the extreme and Edger hoped most stringently that they had arrived with speed enough, and skill sufficient for the tasks which bore their names.

Before him, the impossibly frail person Alys Tiazan ran. Her red hair, so like his sister's, was made into double braids that lifted a little in the wind of her own passing. Walls barred her way, then slid silently and swiftly aside, allowing her, and, quickly after her, themselves, into a short, quiet hall, where a single man wearing the clothing and sidearm of a mercenary soldier stood at guard before a door.

He looked up as they bore down upon him, frowned and moved a few steps forward, holding up his many-fingered hand, palm turned to them.

"Hold it," he said to Alys Tiazan. "You ain't taking them in there, are you, kid?"

"Indeed, I am," she returned, somewhat breathlessly. "They have kin-right. My cousin will wish to see them immediately."

He was a well-grown male of the kind which named themselves "Terran," yet he did have to look up quite some distance to survey both Edger and Sheather.

"Kin right?" he repeated, eyes squinted a little.

"The child speaks truly," Edger answered. "Miri Robertson Tiazan, Lady yos'Phelium, Captain Redhead, as she is known here, is sister to myself and this my brother. We are likewise kin to he who is named here Val Con yos'Phelium Scout."

The soldier frowned down at Alys. "Orders was, kin visits only, and as few of them as possible. Cap'n Redhead ain't hardly eight hours outta the 'doc, kid. She gets too tired, the techs'll stick her back in the box, and you can depend on it she won't like that."

"In fact," Sheather spoke up, with a forcefulness much unlike his previous diffidence, "we are here precisely because we have heard alarming reports of our sister's health. It would ease us, could we see her, speak with her, and make our own evaluation of her condition."

"Oh." The soldier chewed his lip, then appeared to take a decision with a sharp nod of his head. "OK, I can see where you'd want to make sure she's on the mend. I can let you in for a quick look, but like I said, there ain't no profit to anybody in getting her tired out to where the techs take an interest. Especially not with her partner in the state he's in."

Edger blinked. "We have heard that our brother's situation is dire."

"Well," the soldier said judiciously, turning to lay his hand on the door-plate, "he ain't as bad as he was six days ago, but I sure wouldn't want to trade places with him." The door slid open and he stepped aside, waving a casual salute.

"There you go. Remember what I told you, now."

"We will remember," Sheather said, and followed his brother into the room where their sister lay, convalescent among the song-less.

Red-haired Miri Robertson, lately captain of the Lytaxin Irregulars, lay against a mountain range of pillows, eyes closed. The room was full of sound—usual sickroom stuff: the bubble and babble of the machinery; the occasional rustle from the med tech there to tend them—and her. Funny, she thought, somewhat muzzily, how sickrooms always sounded just the same, Terran or Liaden, planetside or space based.

Sighing—quietly, otherwise the tech would be after her to take a nap, like she just hadn't spent six Standard Days unconscious in an autodoc—sighing, she marshaled her attention, deliberately blocking out the too-familiar sounds of the sickroom, and focusing on the place inside her head where she'd gotten used to finding the—ah, hell, call it the life force, call it the soul-shadow, or just call it the pattern, of her lifemate.

Previously, this edifice had been scintillant, brilliant with color, cunning in its complexity. A little more recently, she had observed it fading, the clever interlacings unraveling with regal, horrifying precision. Val Con had been dying, then, of various wounds, the most serious being the bullet he'd taken off an Yxtrang Elite Guard while in the process of stealing an atmospheric fighter craft the guard had considered, reasonably enough, belonged to his outfit.

Elite Guards used bullets with a smorgasbord of loads—explosives, hallucinogens, and other not-so-goodies. The bullet that had nicked Val Con had carried nerve poison. He hadn't taken a full hit, which was the good news, a full hit being something that could drop a full-grown Yxtrang soldier, and probably melt your basic "a bit over average height—for a Liaden" on the spot.

So, Val Con hadn't died, though at that his luck was mixed on the day. They'd managed to share his other injuries between them so that she ended up in the 'doc for days, being healed of wounds she'd never taken, and he was still sealed in a crisis unit, not quite out of danger yet. Shan had explained it to her—all right, he'd tried to explain it to her, but she had a feeling she was going to have to get him to go over the tricky bits again, like how exactly she came up with acceleration injuries when her body had been passed out cold on the ground, miles away and below the plane she'd brought in when Val Con—

Never mind, Robertson, she told herself. *There ain't any way to make sense outta it. Just stipulate it happened, OK? No use banging your head against the impossible.*

Banging her head against the impossible was also getting in the way of checking up on Val Con. She ground her teeth together and concentrated, feeling the sweat break out on her face. Chest tight, she craned inward, seeing nothing but gray, nothing but—it hadn't used to be this hard!

Abruptly, she had it—the pattern flared, bright and coherent, burning away the swirling fog.

Miri swallowed.

No doubt that this was Val Con. No doubt that he was alive. But there was—a division—a rift—interlockings sundered, portions isolated from the whole; here and there colors fluttered, pale, while other patches showed nearly translucent.

"Oh, gods," she whispered and bit her lip again. She absolutely did not want the attention of the med tech for the next while. She needed time to study this, to try to figure out just exactly what she was seeing.

And what, if anything, she could do to fix it.

Carefully, she brought her whole attention to one flickering sector, noticing what seemed to be fault lines—

"Cousin Miri!" a young voice shrilled, which would've been enough to get her attention, without the med tech doing her bit for peace and quiet by snapping a High Liaden order to, "Remove yourselves at once!" while a voice big enough to rattle all the aching bones in her convalescing body boomed, "The songs are all of discord, brother!"

Miri opened her eyes, took in nine-almost-ten Standards old Alys Tiazan, hair neatly braided and hands on her barely-existent hips, glaring at the med tech, while two large, shelled people moved with ponderous purpose toward the wall of instruments.

"Remove them immediately," the tech ordered, but Alys was having none of it.

"They are kin and have the right to be here! Yon lady is my cousin by blood-tie and I myself will—"

"PIPE DOWN!" Miri yelled, or tried to yell. The 'pipe' was pretty good, though not up to her best. 'Down' suffered from her voice squeaking out into a cough. Still, she managed to achieve the desired effect: everybody got real quiet and all faces turned to her. She glared at each in turn, trying to ignore the sweat running down the side of her face, and the way her pulse was pounding way too hard against her eardrums.

"What the hell's the matter with you people?" she snarled, somewhat faintly. "Don't you know there's a sick person in here?"

"Cousin . . ." Alys began.

"I said *pipe down*," Miri interrupted, then dropped into ragged Low Liaden, in case the kid hadn't caught it. "That means: be still, child, and don't dispute your elders."

Alys looked stubborn, but managed a creditable bow. "Yes, cousin."

The med tech was sputtering. Miri ignored her for the moment and looked up at the tallest of the two tall non-humans.

Eight foot high and bottle-green, the room's soft light waking gleams of malachite and cobalt among the tiles of his magnificent shell, eyes as big as dinner plates, yellow and slitted, like a cat's; four hundred pounds, if he weighed an ounce—her brother, Twelfth Shell Fifth Hatched Knife Clan of Middle River's Spring Spawn of Farmer Greentrees of the Spearmaker's Den, The Edger. May the gods have mercy on her soul.

"Glad to see you, Edger," she said.

"Sister, the song of my heart achieves fullness in your presence."

Wow. She looked to the second, smaller, and less grandly shelled Turtle. It struck her that he looked worried, though she'd've been hard put to say how she had formed that opinion.

"Sheather. What's bugging you?" She moved a hand against the coverlet. She'd meant to lift it and give him a high sign, but it was too much effort.

"Sister. The songs within this room irritate me. More, they interfere with the progress of your healing. If kin may say so, and with apologies, should I speak too briefly—I fear most strongly for you, wounded as you have been, and surrounded by discord. More, I fear for our brother, the mate of your heart, for it has been told us that his wounds are more serious than your own, leaving him more greatly vulnerable to the ill effects of wrong singing."

She blinked at him, sagging back against her battalion of pillows, the breath burning in her chest like she'd run an obstacle course with a full field pack on her back. She closed her eyes and wearily, warily, looked inside her head, at the broken, flickering pattern that was Val Con. The mate of her heart.

"Lady yos'Phelium," the med tech said, "allow me to call the House to your assistance. These . . . persons . . . tire you dangerously and—"

"One must be the judge of one's own danger," Miri said, more or less hitting the High Liaden mode from boss to hired hand. She opened her eyes and looked from Sheather to Edger.

"You're telling me that you got a better way to heal Val Con than the autodocs and the monitors can do?"

"Sister," Edger said solemnly, "we do."

"OK," Miri said, and took a couple minutes to chew on that, not that Edger or Sheather would notice. The Clutch did not lie. Especially, they didn't lie to kin, and they had the same rule as Liadens did about the duty of kin caring for kin. Which didn't mean that they couldn't do as much damage as the next guy in, all from good intentions. She moved her head against the pillows and sighed.

"Can you gimme a demonstration, before we move on to something life-and-death?" she asked. "Understand, I trust your word, but it seems to me there's room for reasonable doubt and honest error, especially since we're talking across species. Things just might not . . . match up," she finished, somewhat lamely.

"Our sister is prudent," said Sheather, and exchanged a longish, yellow-eyed stare with Edger, who eventually looked back to her and spoke.

"There are those among the clans of men who are more sightful than the common run," he boomed, his big voice shaking the bed she lay in. "These sighted ones may see into the soul of their fellows, touch the strands of their being and, sometimes, cure the ills that afflict the spirit. Should such a one be brought to us, we might show them our intention and our technique."

"That is quite ridiculous," stated the med tech.

"No it ain't," Miri said, way too tired now to deal with the tricksy modes of High Liaden. She managed to get her hand up and pointed at the kid. "Call Shan and get him down here."

Alys frowned while she worked her way through the Terran sentence, then she smiled, walked over to the house phone, and punched the call button.

LYTAXIN
EROB'S GROUNDS

They had passed the first sentry and were well on the way to raising the second, moving along the paths and wooded ways like the shades of dead soldiers. Not a leaf rustled, nor stone turned, not a branch broke by reason of their passing.

Nelirikk's heart soared with pride, that he walked at the head of such a group, equal, among peers. Swift and silent, that was how an explorer walked.

It was also, of course, how Liaden scouts walked, which his three companions were. They were an oddly matched trio, more gaggle than Troop, and very easy with banter among themselves—which reminded him forcefully of the manner often kept between the captain and the scout to whom he was sworn.

"How much farther to this house of yours, Explorer Nelirikk?" That was the shorter of the two elder scouts, called Clonak ter'Meulen, who wore a Terran-like mustache beneath his snub nose.

"We must be passed by one more sentry," Nelirikk told him. "Shortly after, the wood will surrender to field. From there, if we continue at the current pace, we will raise Erob's house in approximately twenty-five Standard minutes."

Clonak sighed gustily. "So far? Shadia, my delight, run ahead and beg the house to send a car. I am far too frail for all this traipsing about in gravity."

The youngest scout laughed. "Yes, of course. I can see the wobble in your gait. Poor old Clonak."

"Well, I don't know that I like that theme," the mustached scout commented. "I was thinking more along the lines of 'dear, delicate Clonak,' myself."

"I'm certain you were," Shadia said cordially, deftly ducking beneath a wickedly taloned branch.

"I don't see you running ahead to the house," Clonak pointed out.

"Nor will you," Shadia returned with spirit. "Send a car, indeed! Come, Clonak, it's a lovely day for a stroll. Even with the gravity."

He sighed. "What a desperate failure of discipline we see among the ranks of our juniors, eh, Daav?"

Daav yos'Phelium, he who bore the Tree-and-Dragon device that proved him in service to Clan Korval, raised an eyebrow. "Now, I'm puzzled. It seems to me that Shadia merely displays a—naturally regrettable!—lack of respect for an elder. How do you find a failure of discipline?"

"I outrank her," Clonak began—and between one step and the next fell both silent and still, the others doing the same, until they might have been three leather-clad boulders scattered along the pathway.

Likewise frozen, Nelirikk craned his ears, hearing the small sounds made by the sentry standing his post, just 'round the next bend in the trail. Nelirikk's regard for Clonak increased, even as he relaxed.

"It is well," he said, keeping his voice low. "Only the guard at his—"

"Halt!" the sentry shouted. "Who goes there?"

The brush to Nelirikk's left and slightly in advance of his position erupted into noise, as if some large animal was crashing back and forth, perhaps trying to free itself from one of the plentiful thorny bushes.

"Halt!" the sentry shouted again. "Give me the word or I shoot!"

The brush grew silent, then rustled more courteously, branches shivering as a large figure pushed through to stand in the very center of the path. He was holding a Soldiers General Duty Longarm in two hands, aimed up into the blameless sky. Slowly, he bent and placed the weapon on the ground. He straightened with even more care; went back two steps, and held his hands, palm out, at belt-level.

"Capan Meery Roberzun," he said, and Nelirikk felt the hairs on the back of his neck lift.

"Captain Miri Robertson," Daav yos'Phelium said in a stage whisper, loud enough to be heard ahead.

"Identify yourselves!" the sentry snapped, wisely remaining at cover. Nelirikk stepped forward, hands visible and very empty, one eye on the Yxtrang soldier who stood, patient and open-handed, in the path.

"Lieutenant Nelirikk Explorer, Lytaxin Irregulars." The soldier in the road did not react to the Terran words, as of course he would not. Troop were not taught Terran. Only squad leaders were given Trade.

"Aide," Nelirikk finished, for the benefit of the hidden sentry, "to Captain Miri Robertson. The word is *sardonyx*. I escort three scouts to my captain."

Out of the edge of his vision, he saw the soldier's lips move, saw his eyes go wide.

"Capan Meery Roberzun!" he repeated, voice too loud with excitement. He pointed at the rifle on the ground, and his next words were in Common Troop. "Sir, we have come to offer the Hero Captain our weapons and our lives." He swallowed as Nelirikk faced him squarely, possibly unnerved by the lack of *vingtai* on a face so plainly of the Troop.

"Have I the—the honor to address the Hero Nelirikk Explorer?" he stammered.

"What's that guy want, Lieutenant?" the sentry asked, but before Nelirikk could reply, Daav yos'Phelium stepped forward, claiming the soldier's attention with a hand-wave.

"We?" he snapped in the tongue of the Troop, his accent only slightly more rancid than Val Con yos'Phelium's. "Produce this *we*! Immediately!"

"Sir!" The soldier's fist hit his shoulder with a will and he spun on his heel to address the bushes, from which there issued no immediate reply.

"Dammit!" the sentry abruptly shouted. "Where did you come from?"

"The airfield, most recently," Clonak ter'Meulen replied in cheery Terran. "Before that—well, you'll appreciate that I can't tell you everything, even though you are carrying some very impressive fire power. I'm one of the scouts being escorted to Captain Robertson by the Lieutenant over yonder."

"He really is," Nelirikk called over his shoulder, anticipating the sentry's next question.

"Yessir. But what is he *doing* here?" wailed the sentry.

Clonak *tsk'ed*. "Why, only making certain you don't decide that it would be best for all to shoot the charming young person asking after Captain Robertson's health. It happens that the scout standing next to dear Lieutenant Nelirikk is kin to Captain Robertson, and very tender of her possessions."

"Possessions!" the sentry sputtered.

On the path, Daav yos'Phelium moved.

"Well?" he snapped at the bushes, crossing his arms over his chest. "Am I blind? Am I a fool?"

The bushes offered up no reply.

The scout snorted.

"Hero Captain Miri Robertson has no use for cowards. Lieutenant?"

Nelirikk came to attention and glared into the soldier's stoic face. "Captain Miri Robertson accepts only the bravest and most skilled into her troop," he snarled, taking up his cue with a will. "This is the captain who attaches a scout to her troop! *This* is the captain who keeps an explorer as her aide! The captain who broke the back of the Fourteenth!"

"Show yourselves," Daav ordered the bushes, and swept forward in a graceful lunge. He came up holding the long arm at ready. "Or die."

Still the bushes were silent, the branches melting away from the one who came forward, hands out and empty.

"There is one who is wounded," she said and looked over the scout's head to Nelirikk. He read the mark of an explorer on her cheek with a feeling of inevitability. Of course: a mere Rifle infiltrate the first line of guard, intent on giving his battle oath to Captain Miri Robertson? Common Troop did not behave—could not behave—in a manner so contrary to command. An explorer, however, like a scout, was required to think beyond the boundaries of the common. An explorer, like a scout, could easily claim the service of a Rifle, who would no more question her commands than he would the commands of any other officer.

"Hold!" he snapped at Daav, but the scout had already lain the rifle down.

"I do not shoot scouts," he said in calm Liaden. "Unless they give me cause."

The explorer looked down at him. "No cause," she returned, her Liaden halting and modeless. "Wounded, one's senior. Wounded—" She moved her hands in frustration and looked again to Nelirikk. "He is at glory's gate," she finished, in Troop tongue.

"Shadia?" Daav said quietly to the bushes.

"Here, Captain Daav." The youngest scout's voice came from the bushes at the explorer's back, a bit breathless in the Liaden mode called 'Comrade'. "He doesn't look the picture of health, truth told." There was a pause and a low groan. The explorer twitched, and stilled, her eyes down turned.

"Tell the sentry to send for a field 'doc," Shadia said flatly. "This man's dying."

"We need a 'doc, quicktime," Nelirikk heard Clonak tell the sentry. "There's a man down and critical."

"Mister, those're 'trang soldiers and all the 'trang I've seen lately *want* to die," the sentry argued.

"Yet you will observe that these particular Yxtrang soldiers appear to wish to live. They're behaving appropriately, aren't they? They've put down their guns like good children and they're being very seemly, by my standards, at least." Clonak's voice hardened. "Call for an emergency team. Now. You really don't want the scout over there on the pathway angry with you."

"Embroider my legend, do," Daav called, over the sound of a comm unit being engaged.

Nelirikk watched the explorer, seeing her eyebrows pull tight as she strained to follow the conversation.

"Medical assistance is being called for your senior," he told her in the language of the Troop.

"Yes." She shot him a look of challenge. "You are Nelirikk Explorer, lieutenant in the troop captained by Miri Robertson. Will you take our oaths and receive us into the Troop in the captain's stead?"

Certain as he was that the captain—and most certainly the scout—would welcome explorers into their service, and as well as he understood the dilemma behind the question, it was beyond the scope of his duty to stand as oathtaker in the captain's place.

"I will not," he said, wishing the Common Tongue possessed even so minor a word as "alas".

"What's amiss?" That was Daav yos'Phelium, speaking yet in the mode used between comrades, his bright black eyes darting from the explorer's face to Nelirikk's.

Nelirikk sighed. "She—they—came to give an oath and be . . . welcomed . . . into a troop, with a proper captain, to give their lives form and, and duty. We—the 'doc . . ." He stammered to a halt. Both of Daav's eyebrows were well up, but he waited with explorer-like patience for the matter to be made plain.

"It is cultural," Nelirikk achieved at last. "A matter of—appropriate behavior. They wish to—they must—offer their oath only to the captain or one who stands oathtaker in her stead. I—I cannot take oaths in keeping for the captain. And they cannot accept anything from the enemy."

"Ah." The black eyes gleamed. "And your own oath—to Line yos'Phelium, was it?"

"Yes."

"Yes. I believe we may contrive." He stepped toward the watchful explorer.

"I will have your name," he snapped in his awful Yxtrang.

She lifted her chin, "Hazenthull Explorer."

"So." The language shifted to Trade. "Hazenthull Explorer, I offer you compromise. I am kin to the Hero Captain Robertson—blood ties, eh?"

Her mouth tightened, but she gave a short jerk of the head. "I understand."

"Good. Understand that Captain Robertson's duties are manifold, including a position of command over the kin unit of which I am a genetic member. The name of the kin unit is Line yos'Phelium. Captain Robertson accepted the oath of Nelirikk Explorer in *the name of this kin unit.*" He tipped his head. "Do you understand this? I do not wish to trick you."

Once again, she jerked her head. "I understand."

"Excellent. Attend me closely, now: the customs of kin allow me to take from you an interim oath."

Hazenthull frowned. "Inter—a *temporary* oath?"

"Just so. In the service of your senior's life. The 'doc which has been called for is his only immediate chance of survival—Shadia does not use the word 'dying' lightly. I do not willingly watch scouts perish, as I believe I said. I require of you an oath that you and yours will serve Line yos'Phelium, in the person of Daav yos'Phelium—that is myself. In turn, I will give you my oath to bring you to Captain Robertson herself, so that she may make what judgment that a captain must, for the good of her troop." He paused, perhaps awaiting a question. Hazenthull remained silent.

"The term of our oaths," Daav continued, "shall be concluded when the captain has given her judgment. Can you agree to this?"

There was a long silence. Nelirikk saw the explorer's eyes narrow, as if she were turning the proposed oaths round in her mind, seeking the trap that she knew must be there.

Nelirikk could have pointed out the ambiguity attending the precise expiration of term, but it was to the Troop's benefit to acquire the services of other explorers, if it could be managed, and so he held his tongue.

Finally, Hazenthull Explorer gave another of her terse nods. "We are free to offer and to honor these oaths."

"Splendid." Daav waved at the patient soldier. "Explain the matter to him." He flicked a look to Nelirikk. "Assist her, please, Lieutenant."

"Scout." Nelirikk bowed slightly and stepped to Hazenthull Explorer's side.

Some distance up-trail, he heard the sound of a jitney engine, growing rapidly louder.

LYTAXIN
EROB'S HOUSE

"... grace of the Mother we came through well and whole," Priscilla was saying.

The transmission was remarkably clear, considering that it was a jerry-rig replacement for the planetary communication net the Yxtrang had shredded. And it was beyond joy to be able to hear his lifemate's voice, after these long, eventful days of separation. Still, Shan thought, wistfully, it would have been ecstasy to behold her face, to run his fingers into her curly black hair, to stroke her creamy cheek, to put his lips—

"Shan?"

He shook himself. *Do strive for some breeding, Shan*, he told himself, *will you scorn her voice because you may not have the rest?*

"Forgive me, Priscilla, I was entranced by the mental image of you doughty warriors, knives caught between your teeth—"

"Shan . . ."

"Priscilla, you really must spend less time with my sister," he told her earnestly. "You have her inflection exactly, there."

From their ship, high in Lytaxin orbit, she laughed. Shan, seated at the desk in the guesting room Erob had ceded him, smiled wryly and stroked the comm's plastic face.

"Let us make plans for your stay on planet," he said. "Leave now and I'll be at the spaceport to greet you."

The beam hummed empty for a moment, then gave him Priscilla's sigh.

"Love, you know I need to be with the ship. Ken Zel is able, but—"

"But Ren Zel is not of Clan Korval," he finished, knowing the necessities as well as she. "Gordy of course is of Korval, and also possesses all of nineteen Standard years. Too young by a year or so to stand command of a starship orbiting a world enduring postwar conditions."

"True," she said, her voice soft across the distance that separated them. "And you cannot leave Miri and Val Con while they are so ill."

"Miri is out of the 'doc," he said, suddenly recalling that he had not told her that. "Weak as a kitten, of course. Val Con . . ." His throat closed and he shook his head, as if she could see him.

"The techs still believe he'll be . . . impaired?"

"Impaired." He grinned without humor. "Yes, they do believe that, and quite ill-natured I find them for it, if you will have the truth."

"I'm sure you do," she said gently. "I—when he is out of the 'doc and an evaluation is made, perhaps—"

Shockingly, the portacomm on his belt buzzed. Shan jumped, swore, and thumbed the receive.

"One moment, Priscilla—yos'Galan," he snapped into the portable.

"Shan—Lord yos'Galan—it is Alys Tiazan. I am in the recovery room with Miri my cousin and two of the Clutch who are her brothers."

Yes, of course, Shan thought. *The situation had only lacked eight foot turtles.*

"How delightful for us, to be sure. I shall be down directly to make—"

"Their Wisdoms," Alys interrupted, with a refreshing lack of deference for his station; "Their Wisdoms say that the songs of the machines are harming my cousin, your sister. They say that the autodoc may be preventing Val—preventing Lord yos'Phelium—from healing completely. The med tech is—" she paused, apparently decided that he could judge the med tech's state of mind for himself, and finished in a rush. "Cousin Miri says to *get you down here*." The last four words were in Terran, pronounced in tones so authentically Miri-like that Shan grinned, even as his heart trembled.

"One moment," he said to Alys, flicking the 'mute' toggle. He glanced at the desk unit. "Priscilla?"

Her answer came slowly. "It is possible," she said, "that the rhythm of the machinery is interfering with total healing. It has been known to happen. Rarely." She was silent, then burst out, "Who knows what may harm them? They are linked, heart and mind, by that—edifice!—no more simple humans than—than the Clutch are. No," she corrected herself, more calmly. "More human than the Clutch are. And the Clutch may see truly—for their own kind."

"Then it appears my task has been laid out for me," Shan said and flicked the portable on.

"Please allow my sister to know that I am on my way to her side," he told Alys Tiazan. "Ask her, as she loves me, to stay her hand from the med tech until I arrive."

There was a small snort, as if Alys had half-strangled a laugh, then a demure, "I will so inform my cousin, sir." The line cleared.

"Priscilla, my love . . ."

"Until soon, Shan."

"Until soon. May your Goddess send it *very* soon."

He thought he heard a soft sigh before the connection light went out. Sighing himself, he stood and left the room at a brisk walk.

A short time later, he turned smartly into the hallway containing Miri's room, and nodded to the guard on duty.

"I am summoned."

The merc shook his head as he turned to put his hand against the plate. "They call this rest? She might as well hire a band and call it a party."

The door slid open and the guard waved an impatient hand. Shan strolled across the threshold and—paused.

Immediately before him, two very tall, green persons wearing a truly impressive quantity of tilework across their shoulders and down their backs, confronted an average-sized Liaden woman—which is to say, her nose was not quite level with the equator of the shorter tile-bearing person. That the woman was in high temper was obvious even without the abrasion of her passion against his Healer sense. The Turtles—were invisible to his Healer sight, in contrast to the rather irrefutable physical evidence. Shan glanced aside, locating Alys Tiazan, strategically placed between the med tech and the bed in which Miri wilted against an oppression of pillows, long red hair snarled across one shoulder, eyes closed in a face as white as salt.

Ignoring the med tech's anger, Shan focused on Miri, catching the shine of mayhem along her pattern, and a fear bordering on terror.

"Cousin Miri," Alys said. "Lord yos'Galan is here."

The woman in the bed opened fierce gray eyes and gave him a ragged grin.

"What took you so long?"

"I had to shave."

The grin widened, briefly, then one hand wavered more or less horizontally, index finger almost pointing at the taller of the two green persons.

"Edger," she said, hoarsely. The finger moved perhaps the width of a thought. "Sheather." Her hand fell back to the coverlet. "This is Val Con's brother, Shan yos'Galan. He's a Healer. Tell him what you told me."

"What they told you," the med tech snapped in a mode perilously close to superior to inferior, "is arrant nonsense! The machines are needful! Your heartbeat must be monitored! Your air must be filtered! Your blood pressure and body temperature must be monitored! Shut down the machines and risk doing yourself needless, preventable harm, Lady. To even think of removing your lifemate, damaged as he is, from the catastrophe unit . . ."

"Quiet."

One word, quavering on the broken edge of a whisper—terrifying from a woman who could make herself heard amidst the pandemonium of a battlefield.

". . . is to kill him outright!" the med tech continued unabated. "These—persons!—are not of Erob's house medical staff! They—"

"Silence!" Shan snarled, in all the force of Command. The

tech's anger flared and he countered it, barely heeding what he did; merely casting out a glamour of cooling, like a handful of snow flakes. The med tech fell silent, passion melting, bowed and went over to sit in a chair.

"Very good." He transferred his attention to the turtles, who were yet standing patiently, watching him out of yellow cat eyes.

"Shan yos'Galan," the turtle on the right—Edger, Shan remembered—boomed in what was recognizably the Liaden High Tongue, though exactly which mode was a bit difficult to determine at this volume. "It is a joy to speak with the brother of my brother."

"It is an honor to meet one of whom one's kin has spoken, often and with affection," he responded in the ritual stiffness of the High Tongue, in the mode of meeting the kin of kin.

"Allow me, also," said the turtle named Sheather, in Terran, "to express my joy at making your acquaintance, Shan yos'-Galan."

"I'm delighted to meet you, as well," Shan replied in the same tongue. He glanced over to the bed, saw Miri rigid against her pillows; once again caught the edge of her fear against his Healer sense.

"Please forgive me if I force the topic too quickly," he said to the turtles, in blessedly quick, modeless Terran, "but I cannot help but see my sister's distress. The med tech seems to believe that you would have her—and my brother as well—separated from the healing units."

"These devices are all in discord!" cried the turtle named Sheather. "They interfere with the truesong of my sister's self. We hear that our brother is more grievously damaged still. I fear—in my heart, I fear—that the machine which imprisons him, helpless and unable to communicate his own needs, may also slay him."

Shan frowned. "And yet our sister has come successfully out of a similar machine, healed of her injuries and only needing to regain her strength. Many—" What had Val Con said the Clutch called the family of humankind—aha! "Many of the Clans of Men do exactly that, every Standard Year. It is how we heal ourselves of physical wounds."

"Yet, as my younger brother will have it, we hear discord emanate from yon devices and know too well the damage that may be done. Our sister is surrounded by those things which leach her strength, and make her path to full vibrancy into a perilous journey, uncertain of a happy outcome." Edger blinked his eyes solemnly. "Our sister tells us that you are one who may see into the fabric of others, and who may reweave somewhat that which has become unwoven."

"I am a Healer," Shan said slowly. "But I have no skill in mending physical hurts—only common first aid, which this med tech will trump, without a single machine to aid her."

"It is your skill in seeing that we would harness, for the lives of our sister and our brother," said Sheather. "We have already observed the skill with which you silenced the medical technician and soothed her anger before she became a danger to herself."

He had *what*? Shan looked over to the med tech, sitting peacefully in her chair. Carefully, he extended his regard and brushed her pattern, encountering an overlay of cool patience, beneath which the rest of the woman's . . . essence . . . appeared to slumber.

Oh, gods, he thought in consternation. *Shan, you idiot, what have you done?*

"I will have to confess," he said, looking up into Sheather's enormous eyes, "that I am not entirely certain that . . . whatever . . . I've done to this person has been in her . . . best care."

Edger turned his massive head and—sang, one high, whispery note that was gone before Shan could quite—

"She takes no harm. She reposes in calmness and heals herself of her distress. It is well done," Edger stated.

"They said," Miri rasped from the bed, "that they could do a demo, like, and let you decide if what they thought was best would kill us or not."

He looked at her. "*I'm* to decide? How delightful for me! Val Con did mention to you that I'm his heir, didn't he? This is the perfect opportunity for me to murder you both and grasp Korval for myself."

"Sure it is," Miri said, agreeably. "Look, whyn't you turn off the monitors for a couple minutes while the tech's having her nap, and let Edger sing you a couple bars, OK?"

"My sister's plan has merit," Sheather said.

Miri turned her head on the pillow and addressed Alys, her voice almost steady in the mode between kin. "Cousin, you are wanted elsewhere. What we undertake now is Korval's affair, and nothing that should trouble the sleep of one who belongs to Erob."

For a moment it seemed that Alys would protest, then she

bowed, as kin, to the woman in the bed—"Cousin Miri"—and as housechild to the turtles and Shan alike—"Wisdoms. Lord yos'-Galan."—before walking away, with chilly dignity, and letting herself out into the hall.

Shan met Miri's eyes down the room. "You're certain you want to try this?"

She gave him a lopsided grin. "Hate to break it to you, but I've breathed unfiltered air before and didn't take no lasting harm."

He sighed. "I'll take that as a 'yes'." He moved over to the wall and threw the first switch, then the other five in quick succession. Across the room, the med tech sat, dream-eyed, in her chair.

The last unnatural hum faded from the air and the room filled up with quiet. Sheather filled his lungs, tasting the various scents on the confined air, soothed by the absence of discord. His work at the wall of instruments completed, Shan yos'Galan returned to them, his hair pale as the light of the homeworld's lesser moon; his eyes the color of the substance Men named silver.

"Very well," he said, his voice pleasing in its conservation of power. "I have a subject for a test, if you are willing, sirs."

One's brother blinked down at the man, tasting, Sheather was certain, of his power and his courage. "Say on, Shan yos'Galan."

The white-haired man bent and touched his right knee lightly. "I very foolishly wrenched my knee—it's too trivial a thing for the 'doc, but I will confess that it does irritate one." He straightened and looked from one to the other of them with his sightful silver eyes. "Is this the sort of thing one of you might put right, while I watch?"

One's elder brother signed that he would undertake this minor bit of healing. Thus released, Sheather moved away down the room, to stand by the bedside of his sister, Miri Robertson.

"Understand, this will be a very small thing, in comparison to what we propose on behalf of our brother and sister," Edger said.

"I understand perfectly, sir. What we wish to prove here is the concept. If my leg shatters under your care, it is an inconvenience, quickly put right by some time in the 'doc, and we have our answer without risk to either our brother or our sister, both of whom are as precious to me as I know they are to you." He paused and tipped his head. "I hope you won't be offended by my screams, if it should happen to occur that my leg does shatter."

"I believe you will not find it necessary to scream, Shan yos'-Galan," Edger said solemnly. "I ask you now to open your eyes and hold yourself to silence."

Shan yos'Galan straightened and closed his outer eyes. Sheather heard the song of his power intensify even as Edger opened his mouth and sang the two notes required.

Shan composed himself and dropped his inner shields, watching with Healer's eyes.

At this exposure, the turtles stood revealed as systems of all but intolerable complexity, informed by a method entirely outside of his understanding, stretching far beyond his ability to read, yet tantalizingly familiar, as if . . .

All at once he had it: himself, just home from Healer Hall and quite vain of his new-trained powers, striding up to Korval's Tree, the redoubtable Jelaza Kazone, and flinging his shields down like a dare.

Immediately, he had been swept into a long, slow, greenness that spiraled on—forever, or so it seemed to his shortsighted eyes. Every turn of the spiral was unique, rich with nuance and surprise. Ensorcelled, Shan hung, and watched, and was delighted—until Val Con knocked him into the sodden grass, and lay across his chest, shouting in his ear that it was ". . . *raining*, and our mother has been looking for you *every*where!"

Val Con.

Shan took another breath, deliberately imposing calm, sternly refusing the impulse to enclose himself in puny protections. This was for Val Con's life; he dared not make an error—of any kind. His knee ached, a little; Healer eyes saw the irritation as an angry red glow. He allowed the minor pain to remain within his consciousness.

Faintly, a note sounded. He heard it as the warm wash of rain against his naked skin; saw it as a bell tone, attenuating . . . The first note was joined, complimented, enlarged, by a second, inspiring the gentle shower to rain in earnest as the tone coalesced into a ball that grew dense, denser, dense to the point of implosion . . .

The music was ended. His knee was pain-free. A quick scan showed an entire absence of the angry glow of injury that had surrounded it.

Shan opened his eyes.

"Well?" Miri rasped.

He turned to look at her.

"Perfectly well," he said, and took a harder breath, deliberately strengthening his hold on the physical world. Slowly, he brought his protections up; and found himself saddened to lose sight of the turtles' vast incomprehensiveness.

If they can heal Val Con of the effects of the poison. If he can walk. If he can fly . . . he thought exuberantly; and then, more soberly. *If it fails, we may lose both.*

He stepped to the bed and bent down to take Miri's thin, cold hand between two of his.

"I give you the judgment of your thodelm, Korval," he said, in the mode used when addressing one's delm.

She blinked. "I ain't Korval."

"The Code teaches us that lifemates are one melant'i in two bodies. Val Con is nadelm—Korval-in-future. You are true lifemates, bound by the soul. My own father died of his lifemate's death-wound. You speak for both of your lives in this—and for Korval entire."

She paused, her eyes losing a little focus, as if she consulted her memory of the Code, which was ridicul—

Her gaze sharpened. "It is," she said, her voice pure and firm in the High Tongue, "as you have said. I decide as Korval in this, for the good of Korval. Let Thodelm yos'Galan render his judgment."

"I believe it to be—the best gamble for the clan, to allow these your brothers to attempt their peculiar form of healing. I say *gamble*. I have heard the judgment of the medical technicians; in best case, my brother will emerge from the 'doc able to care for himself, to speak, to reason, and to walk, for some limited distances. Your brothers offer a potential for a greater win—and a greater loss.

"I may not convey what I have seen, just now. However, as a Healer, I approve both the method and the results." He paused, then added in Terran, "It could work."

She was utterly still for a moment, limp and white-faced against the pillows, then nodded.

"That's a go, then," she said in Terran.

Shan released her hand and straightened. "As Korval wishes."

"It is therefore decided," Edger proclaimed, and fixed Sheather in his eye. "This my brother will remain and sing our sister into harmony. Shan yos'Galan and I will make haste to the side of our brother and discover us the song we must craft for his whole good health."

"Sounds like a plan," Miri said, and gave Shan another of her ragged, heart-stopping grins. "Take the med tech with you, and drop her someplace to sleep it off, OK? I don't want her waking up halfway through the proceedings and getting her nose outta joint all over again."

DAY 50
STANDARD YEAR 1393

LIAD
DEPARTMENT OF INTERIOR COMMAND HEADQUARTERS

Commander of Agents closed the file and leaned back in his chair.

He was not one to indulge optimism out of season; however, he allowed the plans lain for Clan Korval's confoundment to be . . . adequate.

Of necessity, the plans of action were several, for Korval presented several fronts to the offense.

There was, first, the on-going effort to recover Val Con yos'Phelium, rogue agent and Korval's delm-to-be. A breakthrough had been made on this front, in the form of a gene-match program run against the supposed "Terran mercenary," Miri Robertson. The odds that yos'Phelium was on Lytaxin, sheltering with Korval's oldest ally, Clan Erob, now approached certainty. Recent reports of Yxtrang activity near or on the planet, followed by a rumor of hurried retreat, and other rumors of a strangely behaving vessel seemingly carved from rock—these reports only added weight to the prediction of the odds.

So, a team of four full Agents of Change had been dispatched to Lytaxin, to recover Val Con yos'Phelium—alive. Alive, he yet had value to the Department he had betrayed. Alive, he would serve as both bait and bridle to the remainder of Korval, for surely his kin would do nothing to endanger the life of the one who would be delm? Surely, they would do all they were bidden, in trade for a guarantee of his safe return?

Commander of Agents was prepared to guarantee Val Con yos'Phelium's safe delivery back into the midst of his kin. Val Con yos'Phelium, after all, had been an Agent of Change, fully trained by the Department. And those who had once been trained could be retrained.

The second object of the Department's attention was Anthora yos'Galan, the sole member of Clan Korval remaining upon Liad. She had prudently withdrawn from yos'Galan's Line House, Trealla Fantrol, and established herself at Jelaza Kazone, Korval's ancient stronghold.

It was . . . daunting . . . that the masters of the dramliz, despite repeated testings, had failed to measure the limits of Anthora yos'Galan's abilities. According to one confidential guild report, she was not merely the best of the current depleted population of wizards, but the most puissant dramliza to manifest since Rool Tiazan's death, forty years after Cantra yos'Phelium brought her passengers safe to the planet they would name Liad.

Wizardly power, however, is but a matter of degree. The results of research done some years earlier and set aside for lack of relevance suddenly proved illuminating. It had been found then that certain modifications to a standard stasis box produced interesting reactions in a dramliza confined therein, not the least of which was an effective neutralization of wizardly abilities. Commander of Agents had ordered such a box constructed, and rendered mobile. It was even now in the final stages of testing. When it was completed, Anthora yos'Galan would give up her residence at Jelaza Kazone, from which base she might provide unknown, and potentially disastrous, assistance to her scattered kin, and live at the pleasure of the Department.

It was possible that Korval's wizard had value to the clan, though the clan left her alone and unguarded upon Liad while the rest fled to safety—somewhere. The Commander accepted that Anthora, too, might hold value as a hostage. It might be—should Val Con yos'Phelium not survive his recapture—that his half-Terran foster-sister would fulfill the roles intended for him, even to the ultimate destruction of the clan. Commander of Agents allowed himself some flexibility on this point of planning, pending clarity from the team sent to recover yos'Phelium.

Commander of Agents allowed himself a small smile before he pushed back from the desk and rose. Strike at the heart—once, twice, thrice—and Korval *would* fall.

It was well.

LYTAXIN
EROB'S MEDICAL CENTER

CATASTROPHE UNIT

Med Tech Per Vel sig'Zerba jumped to his feet as the door to the catastrophe unit slid open.

"Sir, I regret," he said to the white-haired man who entered. "This area is forbidden to—" He stopped, staring quite open-mouthed at the second . . . person . . . to violate the area—all two-and-a-half meters of . . . it—magnificently shelled and bottle green, luminous eyes as round and as yellow as moons.

The door slid closed. The med tech, with difficulty, returned his attention to the white-haired man.

"Sir—Lord yos'Galan. We had discussed this matter, sir. The catastrophe room is forbidden to all but medical technicians. The instruments are very delicate and the life of your kinsman depends upon their unimpaired function. It is natural to wish to stand close to kin who are in such desperate case, but, truly, sir, he cannot know whether you are here or elsewhere. You best serve him now by recruiting your strength and preparing yourself to show him a calm face when he emerges from the unit."

"These machines, also, sing of discord," the large green person rumbled. "Where is the device which imprisons our brother?"

Med Tech sig'Zerba blinked. "The catastrophe unit is there." He moved a hand toward the black rectangle, its domed lid bristling with readouts, monitors, alarms, and regulators. He looked again to Shan yos'Galan and bowed slightly. "Since you are here,

I will tell you that the latest data has been analyzed. Repair has been successful on many fronts. Cerebral function has been stabilized, so we may put the fear of seizures and random states of alt behind us. Blood systems and the functions of the organs are as they should be." He hesitated.

"And the damage to the nervous system?" Shan asked quietly, tasting the man's reluctance almost as his own. "How goes the repair there?"

The tech sighed. "Not well, alas. Repair may only occur where some system remains. Regeneration . . . has met with variable success. The latest analysis yields an estimate of forty-five percent function." He inclined his head.

"This means that your kinsman will not be able to pilot a spaceship, an airship, or a landcar. With practice, he will very likely regain his ability to walk, to grasp objects, and to throw them." He took a breath and met the white-haired man's intense silver gaze. "This is not so bad, if your Lordship will but recall the state in which his kinsman entered the unit. We had all despaired of his life, then. That he has regained so much is . . . cause for joy. That he has lost some things which he will never regain—that is . . ."

"Not to be tolerated," the large green person said, in a voice that made every dial in the room jiggle and jump.

Med Tech sig'Zerba jumped, too, and stared up into the huge, luminous eyes. "I . . . I beg your pardon, ah . . . ?"

"This is Twelfth Shell Fifth Hatched Knife Clan of Middle River's Spring Spawn of Farmer Greentrees of the Spearkmaker's Den: The Edger," said Lord yos'Galan. "He also claims kin-right to your patient. He has heard distressing reports regarding our kinsman's course of treatment, which your latest analysis supports. We had come here because of those reports. There is a . . . Clutch healing . . . that we propose to try."

"Propose—" Per Vel sig'Zerba took a hard breath, and retained his hold on calmness. "Lord—Sirs. The condition of your kinsman is precarious. This is not the time to 'try' alternate healings, but to allow the known method to stay its course. The time for alternative healings is when we have brought the patient safely out of his crisis and back into daily life. Then, after study and analysis, a regimen of rehabilitation and additional measures will no doubt be prescribed. Now, however, we must bow to proven methods, for the best eventual health of your kin."

"With all respect to yourself and your craft," Edger said, while the instruments jittered in their places, "the method now employed dangerously leaches my brother's strength." The big head turned.

"Open your eyes, Shan yos'Galan, and look at our brother. Does he seem to you to be mending as he should?"

Shan frowned and widened his perceptions, ignoring the orange and yellow flutterings of alarm that were beginning to infuse the med tech's pattern, and waited for the familiar and well-loved pattern of his brother to appear.

Moments passed. The med tech's alarm showed more orange, less yellow, and a spike or two of red.

Shan opened his shields wider still, caught a glimmer of Edger's seductive intricacy, but yet nothing remotely resembling Val Con's precise complexity or—

"Sir—" Med Tech sig'Zerba began and Shan held up a hand, hurling aside his shields entirely, desperate now to find his brother, his outer eyes on the readouts fixed into the roof of the sarcophagus, which told of him being alive . . .

Suddenly, he had it—a hint; nothing more than a faint touch of acerbic sweetness, as familiar to him as his brother's face. Sternly keeping himself to a Healer's discipline, he followed the hint, slowly, and with an eye to peril.

And found Val Con at last: diminished, lackluster and fragmented, surrounded by a sticky gray quag. Distantly, and engrayed, like a dirty rainbow, he could see the bridge that linked Val Con's soul to Miri's.

"No!"

"Sir! I really must insist that you both leave. Now. You are doing your kinsman no service by becoming overwrought on—"

"Stop." Shan opened his outer eyes and fixed them, with difficulty, on the med tech's face.

"What have you done to my brother—cerebral function has stabilized, you said. How was it found to be unstable?"

The tech blinked. "Why, there were—surges. One might almost say power surges. Also overactivity; extreme excitability, in what should have been an at-rest state. These anomalies led the seniors to suspect damage—not unexpectable, in light of other traumas. Steps were taken to normalize brain activity, and those efforts have been successful. We need no longer fear debilitating seizures or fatal lapses of attention."

"You . . ." Shan took a breath, for once at a loss for words.

"What distresses you, Shan yos'Galan? Does our brother not thrive beneath the known method of healing?"

"They have— In their care to normalize they have weakened the link between our brother and his lifemate—the same link which allowed him to survive his injuries until the field 'doc received him. They have—he is fragmented, without form . . ." He looked at the tech.

"I myself told the seniors that this man is lifemated," he said, his voice sounding thin in his own ears.

The tech inclined his head, nervously. "Indeed. It is so noted in the file. However, normal cerebration is not—"

"Out," said Shan.

The tech blinked. "Sir?"

"You will leave," Shan repeated and heard the power echoing within each word. "You will not return here until Val Con yos'Phelium has departed the area. You will not report this to your superiors. Go!"

The tech's face wavered, eyes going cloudy. He bowed, precisely, and walked briskly down the room and out the door. Shan slapped the lock up as the door closed and strode back to the brooding black unit and the enormous, patient turtle.

"I am able to end the healing cycle," he told Edger. "Some time will elapse before our brother may be removed from the unit, for systems need to cycle down in an orderly manner."

"I understand you," Edger rumbled and looked about him. He raised one three-fingered hand and swept it toward the wall with its profusions of equipment. "And are you able to silence those, as well?"

"Yes." Shan was already at the unit's control panel, flicking switches, turning knobs; withdrawing sensors, shutting down the flows of drugs and nutrients, canceling the muscle toners. When every light on the panel was dark, saving the master, he went over the wall of instruments.

Gods, gods—normalizing cerebral function? Fools! And if Val Con were crippled because they had denied him his lifemate . . . Shan took a breath, deliberately leashing his anger, and threw the last switch, then cast about him for—there.

He rolled the cot over to the healing unit, shook out the blanket, and took a moment to master an urge to pick up the nearest heavy object and have at the delicate instruments lining the walls.

"While we await our brother's release," the Edger's voice rumbled him out of his thoughts of mayhem and despair, "there is a matter we must undertake."

Shan looked up at him. "Yes? And this matter is?"

"A thing—you might perhaps call it 'fine tuning'," Edger said. "Your sight, your love and your understanding will aid me in what work I undertake, for the best health of our brother. You will guide the song—and deny it, should it wander from its purpose or reach beyond its bounds. Before we meet together in the field of mutual labor, it is prudent to test our partnership and strengthen that which may not be as strong as will be required."

"A dry run," Shan said, and nodded. "I understand the concept. What would you have me do?"

"Only listen, while I sing, with the scales behind which you shield your seeing eyes put aside."

Yes, of course. Shan took a deep breath in preparation, focused and brought down his shields, completely, as Priscilla had warned him not to do, his inner self exposed entirely, so that any with eyes—or other senses—to see might find him revealed in all his faults.

"Ah." A sound like the purr of an impossibly large cat. "You are a blade to behold, Shan yos'Galan. Who crafted you may be justly proud of his work. Hear me now."

The first note was an iron-tipped bolt through the living core of his heart.

The second note was a dash of acid across his eyes.

The third note flung his essence out into the snarling winds of Fortune and Mischance. Harried by their teeth of ice and iron, he struck back, willed *walls* and walls there were—stone walls and a stone floor on which he knelt, doubled over and sobbing, making no sense of the hand held down to him, until a stern female voice scolded him.

"This is no safe haven—and well you know it! Rise now and return. Quickly!"

Long strong fingers closed around his wrist. He rose, whether by her will or his he could not have said, and stood looking into the chill blue eyes of a raw-cheeked blonde woman no longer in her youth.

"Priscilla." How he was certain that this woman was she—but certain he was. "Priscilla, the song is changing me."

Her face softened. She let go his wrist and cupped his face in her two hands.

"The song changes us all," she said softly. "Do not fear it. Now go." She kissed him, the stone walls faded, and he straightened, his face wet with tears and his mouth warm from her lips, to face Edger the Clutch turtle in the room of catastrophes.

The turtle blinked his enormous eyes, once, and inclined his body as far as the shell would allow.

"All honor to you, Shan yos'Galan."

Stiffly, Shan returned the bow, equal to equal. "May our work together return perfect health to our brother," he said, his voice chill in the High Tongue, and turned to open the lid of the sarcophagus.

The interior lit itself, dimly, casting cool blue shadows across the slender, naked body of a man. Shan unsnapped the locks and lowered the front wall of the box. The pallet slid out of twilight and into brightness; the man was revealed as gold-skinned and unscarred; lean muscled, and somewhat longer in the leg than the average run of Liadens. His chest rose and fell with the blessed, unhurried regularity of deep sleep. His face was smooth—achingly innocent, in repose—the well-marked brows at rest, firm mouth tightly closed, long dark lashes smudging golden cheeks. And Shan saw with an absurd feeling of relief that the gash which had disfigured his brother's face had been erased by the 'doc's scar-cancelling program.

"Time passes, Shan yos'Galan," a big voice rumbled behind him. "And I fear that haste must be made."

"Yes, of course." Blinking away tears, he slid his arms gently beneath his brother's shoulders and knees and lifted him from the pallet to the cot. Val Con sighed and nestled his cheek into the pillow, his lips relaxing into what Shan dared to call a smile, but did not approach true wakefulness. Shan spread the blanket tenderly over the slim body and looked up into Edger's eyes.

"Now what?"

"An excellent question," the turtle said. "Let us ascertain. Your whole attention is required in this time and place, Shan yos'-Galan. Do you place your regard upon this our brother and guide me in my exploration."

"Guide?" Shan stared at him. "How am I going to guide you?"

"I subvert my will to yours: should the song go beyond its bounds, only will me nay and I will contain it. Should it quicken that which is best left sleeping, your touch will give it back to hibernation. It must be so, for the best health of our brother."

Shan inclined his head, glanced down at Val Con's sleeping face and, for the third time in a single day dropped his shields completely, focusing his entire attention on the murky disorder of his brother's once scintillant pattern.

"First, we question," Edger boomed, and formed a series of three short, interlocking notes. Watching with Healer's eyes, Shan saw fires sequentially awake and die within the murk, illustrating a pattern both broken and feeble—the damaged nervous system.

Edger sang again, and Shan saw a quickening of color, a sparking of passion, fading almost immediately back into the ambient grayness, displaying the med tech's proudly achieved normalized cerebration.

A third time Edger sang and the lifemate bridge blazed in glory, alive with the force of two willful, passionate souls, joining each to the other in—muddy melancholy.

"What," Edger inquired, his voice approaching a decibel level that Shan thought might pass for a Clutch whisper, "was that last?"

"The bridge that connects our brother and our sister, soul to soul and heart to heart."

"Those who heal by machine dared tamper with *this*?" Edger demanded, albeit rhetorically. "They are fools, Shan yos'Galan."

"I'm inclined to agree," Shan said, more than half of his attention still on Val Con's mired pattern. "They have forgotten what 'lifemated' means—what it had meant, in the past."

"This joining is not . . . usual among the Clans of Men, I know. Is it more usual among your Clan Korval, or among my sister's human clan of Erob?"

"Erob bred mighty wizards, once," Shan said, dreamily. "Korval has always been—Korval. Wild cards, pirates, and random elements. The luck moves roughly about us."

There was a pause, long enough for Shan to register as too long, in his stretched state astride two worlds, and then a gusty sigh.

"I am ever more in awe of these my kin, who live with such passion, creating thereby an artwork the like of which has not been seen in my lifetime! I am—I will seek the words, betimes; they elude me at this present. Mayhap I must learn new words to describe new art and encompass new endeavor. In this time and place, however, we have before us a work of love and artistry. May we sing as truly and with passion akin to those we would serve. Are you able, Shan yos'Galan?"

Gods, was he? Was *anyone*?

A flash of panic fragmented his inner sight. He took a hard breath, fighting for balance, and heard his father's voice from years gone by, stern and sweet and beloved.

"We do the best that we are able, my child. We make the best decision we may, dependent upon our experience and our training. It is what we owe to kin and to those who reside under our care. If it were true, I would tell you that necessity makes us wise. What I will tell you is that we all do our best; that we all make errors; and that those who love us will forgive us."

Shan gasped, and deliberately drew a calming breath into his lungs; another; and a third. Centered once more, he opened his inner eyes and beheld his brother, injured as he was and with only Shan to stand between him and a Clutch turtle's fearsome singing.

"I am able," he said, keeping his regard upon Val Con; only upon Val Con, whose future depended upon his brother Shan, and who would forgive him, if he failed.

Edger began to sing.

Miri lay back on her damp pillows and looked up at Sheather.

"Guess we better get dancing, in case the med tech comes back with her boss."

Sheather blinked his eyes, first one, then the other, solemnly. "Perhaps we will dance in a future time, you and I. It occurs to me that I would learn much from such an exercise. But, for now, I ask that you merely listen to the song I have crafted for you."

Right. Miri bit her lip, trying to remember that Shan hadn't looked like anything had hurt during the little song that Edger had sung his knee. Hadn't looked anything but surprised, really, and kinda . . . dreamy, like Val Con looked when he was deep into playing the 'chora.

"You need have no fear," Sheather said, in what passed for soft from Clutch. "I am your brother. Your heart has spoken to my heart. I will not cause you pain."

Which, come to think of it, sounded suspiciously like a Liaden promise. Miri sighed. *What's wrong with you, Robertson? Gettin' squeamish in your old age? If Sheather wants to cut your throat, his knife's way too sharp to hurt.*

"Sister?"

She grinned up at the long green length of him. "S'okay. You sing; I'll listen. Fair division of labor."

"Just so," said Sheather and paused. Miri sagged against her pillows and closed her eyes. Eventually, she heard something that might have been a note, or possibly just the wind, combing through leaves . . .

It was spring, and she was in a garden, strolling along a stone-lined pathway. It was a meandering path, all but overgrown in some places by effusions of flowers. In the branches just over her head, birds sang, oblivious to the passage of a stranger through their garden. The perfume of growing things was an intoxicant.

The path spiraled in, ending abruptly at a glade. She paused on the last stone, looking across a stretch of blue-green grass at the trunk of an enormous tree.

The glade was dim under the vast latticework of branches, and she blinked, then grinned as her adjusting vision made out the slim form of a man leaning against the massive trunk. Unhesitating, grinning wide enough to crack her face, she started across the springy grass.

The man stepped away from the tree and came forward to meet her. He was wearing a beat-up black leather jacket open over a fine white shirt, soft dark trousers and comfortable boots. His hair was dark brown, his eyes were green, and the grin that split the beardless golden face was every bit as wide as hers.

"Cha'trez." The soft, beloved voice caressed her ears and she laughed for the sheer joy of hearing it.

"Val Con." She grabbed his hand and stood holding it like an idiot, too damn happy to think of anything to say.

"You look good," she did say, finally—which sounded funny until she remembered that she knew he was in the catastrophe 'doc, being healed of injuries that should have killed him.

"Looks deceive," Val Con murmured, which was a joke. He tugged on her hand, urging her to walk with him back to the base of the monumental tree. "I am very glad you came here, Miri."

"Yah?" She slanted a glance at the side of his face. "Mind telling me where here is?"

"Not at all," her lifemate said. He stepped right up to the tree and turned to face her, laying his free hand against the trunk. "This is Jelaza Kazone—the safest place in the galaxy."

She'd've pegged that as another joke, normally, because neither one of them put much stock in "safe." But she felt a stroke of . . . certainty . . . come right out of the core of him and into the core of her.

It took her balance, as such things still did, though the gods knew the strands of them were so tangled together it was by no means certain which one would fall down, if either caught a pellet. She felt Val Con's fingers tighten on hers and she flung her free hand out to brace against the tree.

Welcoming gladness overfilled her, an embrace of green joyousness so vivid that she staggered, vision whiting, ears roaring—and might have fallen, except her partner was there to catch her and ease her down to sit with him on the soft grass, their backs against the Tree.

Slowly, the jubilation faded. Miri blinked the glade into focus, ears registering the racket of bird song once more. She sighed and closed her eyes, settling against the trunk that tangibly warmed her back in a sort of physical smile.

"Cha'trez?" Val Con's voice carried an edge of worry.

She shook her head and looked at him. "It behave like this often?"

His smile glimmered. "Only when it likes you."

"Lucky me," she said and leaned her head against the warm bark. "You know, of course," she said to Val Con's bright green eyes, "that all this is only a dream."

One eyebrow lifted. "As much as it must naturally pain me to disagree with my love and my lifemate—"

"A dream," Miri repeated, interrupting him ruthlessly. "I got out of the 'doc this morning. You—" She put her hand over his heart, feeling its firm beat against her palm.

"You're broke into six dozen pieces, Boss. They figure to get you outta the Last Hope sometime in the next week, Standard." She sighed.

"I wish you'd stop pulling these damn fool stunts," she said, trying to sound severe. "You're gonna get yourself killed."

"I'm sorry, Miri," he said meekly and she laughed, flinging forward suddenly to hug him.

"I'm sorry, too. Gods, I miss you. Miss you enough to dream you this hard . . ."

"This is not a dream, Miri," Val Con breathed in her ear, his arms tight around her. "This is Jelaza Kazone."

"The safest place in the galaxy," she said against his shoulder. "Right." She sighed and straightened out of the embrace. "We won, by the way."

He stared at her blankly for the beat of five before understanding dawned in the green eyes.

"Ah," he said, "the Yxtrang. That is good."

"You could say." She shook her head. "Happens reinforcements showed up in orbit just about the time we was finishing that business at the airfield. I ain't got all the details, but Shan and Beautiful sketched it in for me. Long and short—our backup is Suzuki and every merc who happened to be at liberty when the call came through, plus a Clutch rockship, captained by Edger." She grinned, remembering something else. "Edger and Sheather are here—there. Wherever. Got a serious problem with our course of treatment. Threw the tech outta my room and—hold it." She closed her eyes, trying to focus.

"Miri?"

"Wait, wait. I—" Her memory abruptly came through with the gruesome details of the last hour, and also a spike of pure terror. She opened her eyes and looked into his face, which she couldn't be doing, and there was more, worse, than him just being bust up . . .

"The techs say you're not going to be able to pilot," she said, hearing her voice waver. "They say—the nerve damage—you might not be able to walk, at first, and there's something the matter with—with my . . . seeing . . . you. They—"

"No." He caught her hands in his. "Miri, think: Edger and Sheather are come, and they have thrown the med techs out. And then?"

"Then . . ." Then what? Right, she had it. "They sung Shan's knee better and said they could fix us up all right and tight. Edger and Shan went off to sing at you. Sheather—Sheather must be singing to me right now" She sighed, sharply. "My head hurts."

He grinned at her. "No, it doesn't."

"Know all about it, do you?"

"More than I had used to do," Val Con said seriously. "I—whatever happened that . . . allowed you to pilot that craft after my body failed me . . ." He reached out and touched her cheek, eyes shadowed. "Miri, I don't know what we are become."

"Greater than the sum of our parts?" she asked and saw him frown.

"That is—?"

"The whole is greater than the sum of its parts," Miri recited. "Maybe what happened—however it happened—is that we built an *us-pattern* which is . . . stronger than either you or me alone."

The green eyes gleamed. "Together," he murmured, "we are hell on wheels."

Miri grinned. "Like that. Maybe. Least it gives us a theory to play with."

Val Con tipped his head. "It does not distress you, this . . . new intimacy?"

"Person can get used to the damnedest things," she said, shaking her head. "I wouldn't trade what we got—whatever it is—for a Class A Jumpship."

"There's no need to make that trade," Val Con commented. "Korval owns several Class A Jumps. Only tell me which you choose to reserve for your use and it is done."

She stared at him, then grinned, slightly lopsided. "I keep forgetting how rich you are."

"Now, there, you are out. yos'Phelium is not nearly so wealthy a line as yos'Galan—they being traders, you see, and yos'Phelium tied to administration."

"And mayhem," Miri added.

"From time to time," he agreed. "One must do something to relieve the tedium. However, Clan Korval itself is . . . influential. We own yards, and ships, houses, businesses . . . dea'Gauss will reveal all, when we are arrived home. My information is several years out of date, but I don't expect that Nova has run us off our legs."

"We going back to Liad?" Miri asked, watching him.

"Eventually, we must. The Department of the Interior—that must be Balanced, and not only on Korval's account. I have a duty, as the Captain's heir, to keep the passengers safe from peril. The Department preys on all of Liad, and on all Liadens. That will end."

Miri frowned. "Captain's heir? What captain?"

"Eh?" He blinked, then shook his head, rueful. "I have forgotten that you have not yet read the Diaries. The *Passage* carries a complete transcription. Ask Shan, when you are returned, to provide them to you. You will need to know our history and the decisions which have gone before ours, when we are delm."

Right. "We likely to be delm soon?"

He sighed and took her hand. "Soon, yes. Nova holds the Ring in trust, and has proved herself able on many paths. But she cannot Balance the Department of the Interior. That, cha'trez, is for us." He glanced up suddenly, brows pulled together, as if he had heard someone call his name.

"Ah. I must return." He stood, and bent to offer her a hand. She slid her fingers into his and rose smoothly, then stood looking into his eyes.

"Val Con—" Her throat closed, and it was all she could do to blink the tears away.

He stepped forward and slid his arms around her, hugging her tight as her arms slipped 'round his neck.

"It will be well, Miri," he whispered in her ear. "Gods, time runs—give me your kiss to bear away."

She raised her mouth, hungrily. Scant heartbeats later, they relinquished the embrace with equal reluctance, and Val Con turned toward the pathway.

"Until soon, Miri," he said.

"Until soon, Val Con," she whispered, and watched him move away across the grass, quick and silent and graceful. She turned her face aside for a moment, and when she looked up, he was gone.

Alone, she stood in the glade, listening to the birds and to the wind, gently combing the moist, spring leaves.

They had seeded the fragmented nervous system with a double-dozen crystalline notes, and turned to the larger problem of weaving the unraveled pattern whole. Shan saw himself within a gray, ill landscape, Edger's song ranging somewhat before him, seeking, as would a hunt-beast, and wherever it passed, color took root and began to glow.

Up ahead, the song snagged on a sullen, dusty outcropping, disturbing murky complaints of burnt sienna and umber. Shan extended himself and caught the note, holding it frozen while he examined this anomaly.

It had the taste of something constructed, yet it reacted when he put his will upon it, hissing in a febrile hostility that said *wrongness* to his Healer senses.

He widened his area of perception, seeing how it was laced, haphazard, into his brother's soul—laced *twice*, now that he looked more closely, with some of the original rough bindings broken and replaced by stuff somewhat finer and recognizable as the same material of which the rest of the pattern was formed.

Carefully, he put his will against the edifice, felt it snarl and jerk, like a half-tamed dog, straining against the newer, finer lacing. Wet red numbers flared, foretelling doom and dire consequence. Shan reached forth and shushed them.

Once more, he brought his attention to the newer bindings, recognizing Val Con in the knots and redoubled lacings. So. His brother valued this thing, whatever it was, but did not care to trust it. Well and good.

He cast his will over the edifice, calmed its hostility with a kiss, ran his hands along the shape of it, smoothing away the kinks of falsehood, closing the access ports of strangers, draining off the poison pooled at its core. Then he withdrew to the place where Edger's note reposed in patience and contemplated the results of his efforts.

Its color was better—richly topaz, with glints of copper—its shape more pleasing, less intrusive, nor did it snarl when he touched it with his will, but merely held itself in readiness. It would do.

He hoped.

He removed the compulsion from the note in progress, allowing it to swell forth and encompass the thing—whatever it was—and mold it irrevocably into the totality of Val Con.

DAY 286
STANDARD YEAR 1392

TERISTE MIDPORT
PANAKE HOUSE, FIELD OF FIRE, SPECULATOR'S TRUST

As it transpired, Cheever McFarland knew Teriste, though not the side that Pat Rin knew. Cheever knew the repair shops, both large and small, and had offered to arrange to have the modest Tree-and-Dragon sigil on the ship removed, or covered; which offer Pat Rin refused after some moments of consideration.

Fortune's Reward already appeared on the day-board, and was registered with the portmaster, and while it was true that it would very soon be desirable for it to become another ship entirely, registered to a fictional owner from a far outworld, it would perhaps be best to have those adjustments made in a place somewhat less . . . popular . . . than Teriste.

Pilot McFarland also knew numerous local eateries catering to Terran or mixed crews, and it was to one of those they repaired before they moved forward with the various tasks of the day.

At the Panake House, Cheever's jacket—or perhaps his face—won them entry into the roomy and more comfortable inner sanctum with a cheerful, "This way, pilots!" from the beaming host.

The menus were on the table and coffee poured before Pat Rin could refuse.

The offer to "stow those bags" was waved away, politely acknowledged, and followed by a "back in two" as the waiter hurried to refill the cups at another table.

The menu, for all that it was in Terran—a language Pat Rin read well—was next to incomprehensible. The "slabs" and "stacks" offered for his delectation were meaningless, as were the supposed qualifiers: *thick, short, full* . . .

He needn't have concerned himself. His companion intercepted the waiter with a wave of his big hand.

"Two Morning Specials; double medium slices, and c-juice."

This repast, when it arrived, proved to be a stack of flatbreads which one—taking Cheever McFarland as one's model—doused with various liquids and jams; recognizable eggs; and several patties of ground or pressed meat, each about the size of one of the flatbreads.

Warily, Pat Rin sampled the various offerings. The juice drink was familiar enough; the other flavors pleasantly spicy. He had a bit more of each.

"This here," Cheever said, around a mouthful of flatbread. "This is a hard-working port. This place here is always open, and pilots always get the best tables. Take whatever they got on special and you'll get a good, cheap meal."

Pat Rin glanced up from his plate. "However, I am not a pilot."

McFarland forked a meat patty into his mouth and chewed thoughtfully.

"You can pass though," he said eventually. "We get you a jacket and nobody'll doubt you know Jump."

He emptied his coffee mug, waved it in the general direction of a waiter, then shook it gently at Pat Rin.

"If we're going low or something, you're gonna have to learn to drink this stuff like you mean it."

Pat Rin raised an eyebrow, looked at his nearly untouched mug, and smiled slightly.

"I see that I face greater hazards than I had thought," he said in quiet Terran. Deliberately, he picked the mug up and took a long slow sip of the dark beverage. He sighed slightly, wishing for some quiet morning tea, and sipped again as the waiter hove into view, bearing an oversized carafe.

"Nah, now this isn't too bad," said Cheever. "If we get to a place where *I* only drink a sip, you can pass . . ."

"Pilot, I see many lessons ahead for both of us!"

Cheever only nodded as the waiter warmed both their mugs from his pitcher, and offered news of fresh pastries and doughnuts to finish the meal.

Pat Rin's name gained them entry at Field of Fire, where the hostess was pleased to find them a place in the members only section as guests of the house.

The hostess also offered to waive the range fee in return for his signature in the guest book. It was seldom that a Liaden shooter of his caliber called on a Terran establishment such as this, and the signature of the reigning champion of Tey Dor's would enhance the melant'i of the house. Whether he could afford to indulge the house in this, Pat Rin left for later, merely bowing polite acknowledgment of the offer.

They were then walked down a long, transparently walled hall, the hostess intent on convincing Pat Rin of the joys of the establishment. As they passed several dozens of lanes, some lighted and occupied, some lighted and empty, and some dark, all with a variety of targets visible, she continued her spiel, explaining that Field of Fire was not the largest range in number of shooting lanes on planet—no. But it was the best equipped, certainly, holding a complete set of house weapons from light to heavy, including dueling pistols of many calibers. There were also tuning and repair smiths on duty at all times, and instructors.

She paused there, recognizing a potential faux pas, and covered by extravagantly sliding a keycard into a section of wall marked "Club Members Only."

Beyond the door there was better lighting, upgraded carpeting, and a small canteen, manned by an alert looking young man. The individual lanes fanned away from this concourse, eight on each side of two small central shooting theaters capable of accommodating four marksmen at once.

Only one of the single lanes was occupied, and through the thick plastiglass a man could be seen laboriously packing an armored travel bag with an array of small pistols. On the floor next to the shooting stand was an identical bag, sealed.

Their hostess escorted them past the semi-circle of observer's seating to the theater on the left, activating the keyplate and lights with a card and—after the door slid soundlessly aside—motioning them down the ramped entranceway to the sunken shooting floor with its equipment benches and controls. She made no attempt to descend to the floor herself: only shooters were allowed in the fire-zone.

"I think you gentlemen will be comfortable here," she said. "The range isn't scheduled until this evening. You're cleared for up to three hours of shooting; the timer starts with the first shot or when you invoke the tracking computer, whichever comes first. Once again, we will be pleased to waive all charges, should Lord Pat Rin care to sign our guest book."

Pat Rin accepted the keycard and the code as she left, and in short order he and Cheever McFarland had arranged their equipment, donned the club-supplied ear protector headsets and began the straightforward testing-and-truing of what the Terran termed "the hardware."

On Cheever's bench sat two massive chemical LaDemeters and several dozen cartridges, a much smaller and also chemically powered double-barrel derringer-style boot-pistol with its bright shells next to it, and a brace of standard pellet pistols, three extra charges for each sitting by. In his hand was what appeared to be a large—even for a Terran of Cheever's not-inconsiderable size—survival knife. Before each of his three shots with it he turned and glanced over his shoulder to make sure no one was watching, and as soon as he finished the third shot he carefully reloaded it, sheathed it, and immediately slipped it back into his boot.

He moved on quickly, though not as stealthily, to the derringer, squeezing off shots quickly and accurately, the gun almost hidden in his big hands. The noise of its firing—like that of the knife-weapon—was a sharp *snick*, even through the ear protectors. The chemicals left a slightly smokey haze and an acrid odor, which was quickly cleared away by the air filtering system.

Pat Rin was still working with his first weapon, a standard caliber Liaden dea'Nobli pellet pistol. While the caliber may have been standard, the pistol itself was a work of art, with filigree metal work, a custom jay-bead quick-sight, and grips of lovingly hand-shaped kreel-horn. Each shot produced a quiet *whap* through the ear protectors, though the accompanying magnetic whine seeped through without hindrance. His "show gun," the dea'Nobli was more accurate than many clans' dueling pistols and more costly than most.

The targets varied from stationary bull's-eye, to gallery-like mythic creatures, to moving human silhouettes, chosen by the shooter's whim. Satisfied with the dea'Nobli against the bull's-eye, Pat Rin was about to bring up something more challenging when the rhythm of his companion's shots altered—and stopped.

The big man's hand motion was discreet but clear. Lowering his gun, Pat Rin turned and saw that they'd drawn a pair of observers, who were lounging in the chairs on the other side of the plastiglass, mugs and food on the table before them.

The man was certainly Terran—not quite perhaps of Cheever's size, but larger than the average male of the race, with the dark and beginning-to-wrinkle complexion of one who has been overexposed to solar radiation. An ex-mercenary perhaps, or a native of one of the back-worlds, his face was strong-featured, square jawed, and not overly intelligent.

The woman was . . . most likely . . . Terran, and also dark, though it appeared her complexion was of birth rather than burn. Her hair made a black silken cap 'round her neat head, her features were fine, and she had quick ebon eyes, which at the moment rested upon himself with more than casual interest.

"Just sat down," Cheever said, sotto voce. "He's muscle, but if she ain't a pilot I'll eat my license. They both got bags, but she's . . ."

"She is carrying a gun under her right arm," Pat Rin finished for him, "which is why the vest seems a bit bulkier than one might expect on so warm a day. The man is, as you say, a bodyguard."

The woman raised her hand, perhaps indicating that they should feel free to continue with their practice.

"I believe it is time to take a break, Mr. McFarland. Please do me the honor of saving our records. Then we shall see what we may discover of our visitors."

"Gotcha."

Pat Rin engaged the safety on the dea'Nobli and left the pretty gun lying ostentatiously on the bench, feeling the accustomed weight of the hideaway in his right sleeve as an unexpected comfort. Cheever McFarland at his back, he touched the keypad and stepped out into the concourse.

Cool air assailed them, and the increasingly familiar odor of coffee.

"There was no need to disturb yourselves on our account, Master," the woman said in lightly accented Liaden as they approached.

Seated, she bowed, gracefully approximating the mode of novice to master, which was surely flattery. "We will be using the other theater in a moment, but it is rare for us to see such shooting here."

Pat Rin inclined his head. "We had not intended a demonstration, and I fear the shooting may not have been up to our best. We have been some time traveling."

"Ah, all the more impressive!" The dark eyes measured him, then she turned, motioning to her companion, bespeaking him in Terran no less mannered than her Liaden—"Julier, my manners have failed me. Please—fetch our guests coffee and a snack—or perhaps tea for the master."

Pat Rin eyed the woman speculatively, and held up a hand. "Allow me to send Mr. McFarland, as well," he said, following her into Terran. "He understands my taste in coffee."

She gave him a half-smile and shrugged a proper Terran shrug. "Of course you will wish to send someone to attend your interests."

Pat Rin glanced to Cheever.

The pilot nodded, waiting for the bodyguard to rise. They walked side by side to the canteen, not quite bristling, like two strange cats thrown together on unknown turf.

The woman leaned toward Pat Rin, inclined her head in a motion that became a formal bow.

"Master, it is urgent that we speak—alone. I am Natesa. I believe our interests coincide."

•   •   •

The two big men fidgeted, uncomfortable in their sudden roles as spectators, as the door sealed with a slight hiss.

"They are nervous of this," Natesa said as she walked with him down the ramp to the shooting floor. "It speaks well of them."

"I suspect we all four have some concerns," Pat Rin murmured, picking the dea'Nobli up from the bench. "Mr. McFarland tells me that you are a professional shooter and likely a first class pilot."

"Ah, and my guardian informs me that you are a better shot than you appear."

Pat Rin sent an exasperated glance toward the two-man audience, and Natesa laughed, soft and musical.

"I thought you might appreciate the level of assistance I am equipped with when the locals insist. Julier is a good man in a barroom brawl—as I suspect Mr. McFarland is—but he is perhaps in the second tier, both of shooters and of intellects, unlike Mr. McFarland." She smiled, and pointed. "I shall take the blue side." Pat Rin appraised her coolly as she finished unloading the weapons from her bag. These disposed to her satisfaction upon the bench, she turned to face him fully, raising one hand, fingers spread wide, in the old, old gesture of peace.

"By your leave, Master. I should test these as well."

From beneath her vest she pulled a palm gun, laying it carefully on the bench, its muzzle aimed, without a doubt, down the lane. The design was not familiar; and it was unclear from its lines whether it was a chemical weapon. Natesa reached beneath her vest once more and brought forth a tiny and strange weapon— which was immediately recognizable, despite that he had held one only once, and that many Standards in the past.

He raised an eyebrow, and she inclined her head, not without irony.

"I thank you for your care; you may rest assured that I know this is *not* a toy. It is best that we be plain with each other. I am called Natesa the Assassin—among other things—and that"—she pointed—"is a triple caliber pellet weapon. A single shot. Very high energy. Perhaps the equivalent of one of Mr. McFarland's special loads."

So. Pat Rin drew a careful breath, conscious that the stakes had risen, though not, or so he thought, out of all reason.

"I am not," he said to the woman's intelligent dark eyes, "a professional. Certainly I carry nothing to . . ."

She raised her finger to her lips with a sibilant Terran *shush*.

"You are correct, of course," she said, with a brisk nod. "Neither of us can be expected to display all of our weapons and backups. However, you should know that I see two of your hideaways."

He inclined his head, coming the lofty lordling. "My thanks."

Her lips twitched, and she bowed once more.

"Shall we say best of fifty?" she asked. "Mixed targets? I have here a match in caliber for your pellet pistol."

"Of course." He checked the charge on his weapon as she checked hers.

"Shall we alternate? Use the same targets? Or shoot duo?" he asked, automatically looking at the floor to be sure of his footing.

"Duo," she said promptly, and moved a hand toward the targeting switch. "I choose this. You choose the targets."

And that, Pat Rin thought, was a gambit. The gamester in him rose to the challenge: the best refutation of a gambit is acceptance.

He reached to the controls, punched his choices in, and held his finger on the presstab as he looked over to her.

"We shall have duplicate heavy game. The pace to be energetic. The distances to vary identically. If you agree."

She nodded rather than bowed, her face merely comely. "Indeed, heavy game. An excellent choice."

He raised five fingers to indicate the delay to start, activated the presstab, and stepped back to the line.

Numbers flickered on the ceiling, counting down. The lights dimmed. The targets came up.

Heavy game.

The first target swung out of the floor, at the far end of the alley, a crouching image of a man bringing a sighted rifle to bear. Pat Rin's shot was quick, and automatic. One shoots between the arms, below the stock, as close to the throat as one can. The target spun away, replaced by something out of the left wall—two men, side by side, with pistols, followed by a young girl with pistol, skip the young boy with the flowers in his hand, try the head shot on the figure with a gun sheltering by a tree trunk.

He was aware that in the other lane the targets came out at the same time, and that it seemed the sound of her gun was overlaying his . . . but the targets came on.

Pat Rin was sweating, the dea'Nobli's charge near exhausted, the targets each taken down in their turn, allowing the boy with flowers, the old man with his broom, the couple with their ice-licks, and the two tiny creatures—perhaps they were dogs?—to hold their ground.

In a moment, the scores.

Natesa whistled lightly. Blue side: 297 points. Green side: 298.

"May I?" she asked, reaching toward the controls.

Pat Rin bowed, and the assassin brought up the fine scores.

"So, Master. We each have fifty live targets. We each score fifty respectable hits. My times were—see here—slightly faster. Your shots were exceedingly accurate, if slower. Mine were all good enough."

Pat Rin bowed. "Your shots were all quicker than mine, and with heavy game, this is important. I will tell you that I noticed you overcorrecting a drift to the left at the end. Without that, you would have certainly had the three hundred."

She laughed then, and bowed lightly.

"Master. You see well enough to watch both our targets. And why the drift to the left, if you can tell me?"

He looked at her carefully, raised a finger and indicated that she should spin about. She shrugged and did so, coming to rest facing him, dark eyes quizzical. He moved his finger again, miming a slower spin, which was perhaps an error: he was momentarily distracted by her shape; and the tilt of her shoulders and head made it plain that she had noticed.

"I believe it is clear," he said in Liaden—in the mode of master to master. "Your vest bound you slightly as you worked. It is that very flat item above your left kidney that is the problem."

"Ah." For an instant only was Natesa the Assassin nonplused, then she bowed, deeply, in the mode of novice to master. "I am instructed."

She straightened and gave him a serious look.

"Let us inspect weapons a moment," she said, "and speak looking down the alleyway so that none behind us may read our lips."

Now it was come. Whatever it was. Pat Rin bowed agreement and proceeded to field strip his pistol.

"Master of Tey Dor's," she said softly, her hands busy and sure at her own weapon, "please consider me at your disposal. If you have need of transport, or a safe house; for additional bodyguards, for a cash advance—" She shot him a quick, dark glance. "Understand, I have discretion. More. I have jurisdiction. Much may be contrived, if you have need."

"And you offer from the goodness of yourself, no doubt . . ." he murmured, glancing across to her.

She raised her head and looked fully into his face.

"If you like, you may consider this a formal offer of the Juntavas—an extension of the aid-and-comfort you may perhaps have heard." She paused.

That she was a Juntava did not surprise him—he had supposed as much. That she came to him with this generous and open offer of aid was—distressing. Still, it was best to hear her out, so that he might know what protections he might need to find—elsewhere.

Bland-faced, hands steady on his weapon, he inclined his head—courteous invitation to continue.

Natesa sighed. "Ah. I feared you would see it thus. Master, hear me—I repeat it: *our interests coincide*. I know, I know—the old agreement. But many things are . . . not as they have been." She held up a hand, her face earnest.

"So, I will tell you: the Juntavas discovers that there is something very wrong on Liad. Korval-in-person disappears from the breadth of space, but for you—perhaps you are the bait in a trap?—and the silly young cousin. Korval ships ply their routes, but we note the changes in long-established patterns, the captains redistributed, the crew-members put ashore, the heavy weapon pods mounted.

"In other sectors, confusions begin to grow, which seem to our analysis related to the . . . alterations in Korval's behaviors. We hear of—certain people one is wise to avoid; of some of those who have dealt with particular Liadens turning up—not ruined or shamed—but dead."

Plan B, thought Pat Rin, and then said it, softly: "Plan B is in effect. Korval is beset, Natesa the Assassin. We have gone into hiding."

"Yes?" Her eyes gleamed. "But *you* have not gone into hiding, Master. And the Juntavas has made a study of Korval. We do not expect that the dragon is meek in its exile. We anticipate decisive action, from an unexpected quarter—and that soon." She paused, her eyes yet on his face.

"Understand me, Pat Rin yos'Phelium. As a Sector Judge I am able to provide what you may need. *Whatever* you may need. And if you should lead us to your kin, that the Clutch turtles may be satisfied that the Juntavas treats with honor, so much the better for us all."

"Sector Judge?" He repeated the unfamiliar title quietly, slowly fitting his gun back together.

"Yes, yes." Impatience was evident in her voice. "I am—a power. When there are disputes over territory, or of proper ownership of particular objects or properties, I am called in to find the answers, to make things smooth again. And if there is a problem which cannot be solved by discussion, I am empowered to solve it as I may." She paused as she concentrated on something finicky within her weapon.

"This is why I walk with Julier, who is a gift of the local boss while I am on planet. The boss wishes to be certain that I will agree with him when need be."

She glanced at him as the *snick-click* of the new charge going home broke the silence.

"The old agreement—that the Juntavas does not meddle with Korval. That Korval does not meddle with the Juntavas . . ." Pat Rin said, softly, so softly. "You counsel me to set it aside, you argue—persuasively!—that circumstances have altered so entirely that the boundaries of wisdom—the boundaries of mutual survival—have been re-drawn, placing the Juntavas and Korval side by side in the face of a common enemy." He moved his shoulders, of a sudden very weary.

"You know who I am. It is not within my scope to set aside clan policy. Certainly, not this, of all possible clan policies. No matter what the need."

She was silent. He stood and backed away from the work bench, his gun pointed specifically away from her. He glanced along the alley, and moved to the target console.

"Shall we shoot?" he asked, fiddling with the settings. "One hundred targets, descending from standard size and distance to one sixth size and double distance."

"You are certain?" she asked, and, indeed there was a tentative note in the soft, cultured voice.

Pat Rin glanced over his shoulder, saw her standing, gun reassembled and aimed at the innocent floor, slim and deadly and very comely, indeed. "Why should I not be certain?" he asked lightly. "A cantra to you, should you best my score."

She laughed then. "You *are* a gamester, aren't you? But no, I'll

not put you out of pocket. Rather let us agree to part amicably."
She bowed, lightly and with whimsy.

"And yes, Master, I would be very pleased to shoot again."

They disposed of the hundred targets in short order, failing yet
again to find one of them ascendant over the other. Natesa had left
him, then, with a graceful bow. He let her out of the theater to rejoin her gift bodyguard, and re-admitted Cheever McFarland.

"We will be departing Teriste earlier than anticipated, Mr. Mc-
Farland," he said as the big man loaded his second LaDemeter
and stepped up to the line. "When we finish here, I will call at the
bank. It would be best if you take leave this evening."

The pilot looked at him, wearing an expression between a grin
and a grimace. "Got a date?"

"Mr. McFarland, I do. I must to the casino, else we arrive at
our destination without enough cash to buy into a game."

"Oh. Yeah. But she's something, ain't she, Boss?"

"Pilot?"

"That Natesa. A bit of a looker and she shoots like a champion.
She ought to, 'cause she's the reigning champ in *this* club."

"I am informed, but not surprised." Pat Rin stepped up to the
line and squeezed off his first shot.

"Juntavas, huh?"

"You are apparently aware."

"The boy she was with had a half-dozen tell-tales on 'im. Tattoo here, 'nother one there. Carries official Juntavas ordinance—
what that Natesa *don't* do—even wears the damn ring! Got no style
at all. I gotta tell you, if he's a friend of that lady I'll be surprised."

"Indeed. I believe her to hold you in much higher esteem than
that enjoyed by Julier."

"I sure hope so. He's about as subtle as a drunk merc at a nude
beach."

"Mr. McFarland, if you think to spoil my aim by distracting
me or by making me laugh, you're quite off the mark."

"Well, a guy's got to try. You're two whole shots up on me
with twenty to go."

"Shoot, Mr. McFarland. If you continue, you may match
Natesa's score."

"Guess *she* was distracted, huh? I think she likes you, Boss."

"Mr. McFarland. . . ."

"Yeah. Right. Gotcha. My shot."

• • •

The private accounts manager was new since the last time Pat Rin had accessed his funds at Teriste Speculator's Trust. The former manager had been male, soft-spoken and respectful.

The new manager was female, breathless and provoking.

"I very much beg your pardon, sir," she dithered, her fingers stuttering over her keyboard. "I don't seem to find that account. I—oh, here! Ah, no. No, that's not it."

Pat Rin swallowed a caustic comment, counted to twelve and pointed out that the paperwork he had provided listed not only his name and his account number, but the first of his two pass phrases, which really should be all she needed in order to locate his funds.

"Yes, yes, of course, you are quite correct, sir!" she babbled. "It is only that—well! I see that I will need to bring the branch manager in. Only a moment, sir, of your goodness. I will return immediately—" She leapt up from her chair and fled, the door sealing behind her.

Pat Rin bit down on his annoyance. Really, this was preposterous. There should not be the slightest difficulty in accessing his account. The manager had very likely miscoded the request; indeed, it was a rare wonder that she had been able to type at all, as badly as her hands had been shaking.

And why had her hands been shaking? he wondered abruptly. He was hardly a fearsome individual, after all; and his request had been merely commonplace.

Frowning, he got up and walked 'round the desk. The screen was still active, awash with red lines and danger-signals. In the center of it all was the code for his private account, showing a balance of some ninety-six cantra; followed by an unfamiliar code, also in red.

Just so.

Absolutely calm, he retrieved his paperwork from the desktop, folded it into the inside pocket of his jacket, rounded the desk and lay his hand against the door. It slid open at his touch, which surprised him somewhat, but he rather thought that the new manager was unused to dealing with dangerous clients.

Walking quickly, he went down the hall and through the discreet common office, heading for the door to the street. Behind him, he heard a clatter of heels and a gasped, "Sir? Sir, a moment, please!" He did not turn his head, but swept out the door.

Gaining the street, he strode on, despite the fact that his knees had developed a disconcerting wobble. He had scarcely gone six steps before he was joined by a large man carrying a pair of gun bags.

"Business concluded, Boss?" Cheever asked.

"Concluded," he said, rather breathlessly, "but not to our advantage. I was not able to withdraw funds. Worse . . . Mr. McFarland, I fear I may have alerted someone . . . unsavory . . . to my presence."

"Bound to happen, I guess," Cheever said philosophically. "Time to lift?"

Pat Rin walked on, somewhat less quickly now, and forced himself to focus. Panic was never a winning hand.

"No. I must attempt the casinos. With the ship's fund and my personal accounts beyond reach, the need for money becomes desperate."

"If they know you're here, they'll be watching the casinos," Cheever pointed out, reasonably enough.

Pat Rin moved a hand in agreement. "They will. But the casinos have security on-staff and an investment in maintaining the safety of their clients. I may be seen, but it is unlikely that I will be importuned." He sighed. "The risk must be accepted in any case. We must have cash."

There was a short pause, then a sigh.

"If that's the way it's gotta be, then we go with it," he said. "I'll be coming with you."

It was perhaps indicative of his state of mind that Pat Rin felt not annoyance at this presumption, but relief.

"Thank you, Mr. McFarland," he said. "I will be glad of your company."

TERISTE CASINO DISTRICT
THE PRACTICAL STATISTICIAN

"Lord Pat Rin—a moment, if you will!"

The beautifully dressed gentleman did not look up at the hail. He received the dice, shook them briefly and threw with an expert's snap of the wrist, rings flashing richly in the table lights. The dice struck the felt-covered end wall, rebounded, rolled twice and stopped; the first and second die each showed one pip, while the third displayed five. The gentleman stood quietly, dark head tipped, calmly awaiting the House's judgment.

"Seven called and seven rolled!" the croupier announced, deftly separating three coins from the bank and placing them before the winner. "House pays three gold to the gentleman with the blue earring." The dice rattled to the cloth beside the coins. "Roll again, sir?"

The gentleman took a moment to consider, as well he might, gambling at gold level, with the House's three and his own two riding the toss.

Jewels flashed as shapely fingers spread above the coins. "Hold."

"The gentleman with the blue earring holds his line," the croupier cried. "Who rolls against the House?"

The dice passed to a brassy-haired lady in an inexcusable scarlet coat, who shook them with great energy. The gentleman with the blue earring deftly palmed his five gold and left the table, moving away from the area from which the most unwelcome hail had come, and toward the table at which Cheever McFarland had last been seen.

No sooner had he cleared the crowd surrounding the dice table than his sleeve was snatched and held by a sharp-faced man of extraordinarily nondescript dress.

"Lord Pat Rin?"

He lifted an eyebrow. "Yes?" he murmured, and glanced significantly down at his mangled sleeve.

Alas, his captor was wholly intent upon his own business and failed of taking the hint.

"Sir, there is one who would speak to you. Most urgently." The man's fingers tightened. Pat Rin frowned.

"You will," he said, softly, and yet unmistakably in the mode of Command, "release me."

Startled, the stranger did just that, dropping back a step, his dead eyes leaping to Pat Rin's face.

"Your pardon, sir. I meant no disrespect. But there is one who has—"

"Urgent need to speak with me," Pat Rin finished, all of his attention seemingly upon smoothing the creases out of his abused sleeve. "Just so. I do not desire to leave my amusement. If your—employer—must speak to me as urgently as that, he will come to me."

The stranger gaped, then bowed, abruptly and muddy of mode, spun on his heel and vanished into the crowd, leaving Pat Rin to stare at the place where he had been and damn himself three times for a fool.

Careful to display neither haste nor concern, he crossed the room to the Smaller Wheel and insinuated himself into the crowd 'round the table. There, sheltered on all sides by tall Terrans, he tried to think.

That the sharp-faced man belonged to the Juntavas, he doubted, though the possibility could not be rejected out of hand. It was conceivable that the local boss sought to gain advantage over the Sector Judge who had been thrust upon him. And yet . . .

The sharp-faced man had been Liaden. Plan B specifically warned him away from Liad—and from Liadens. And, truth told, there was that about his recent captor which made the Juntavas—most especially the Juntavas in the person of Natesa—show honorable, wholesome and foursquare for clan and kin.

There was a disruption in the crowd of spectators to his left. Pat Rin half-turned and looked up into the very welcome face of Cheever McFarland.

"Well met, Pilot," he murmured, for his companion's ear alone. "I believe it is time for us to leave."

They were not—not quite—taken unaware.

They left together by a side door, at Pilot McFarland's insistence, and made rapid progress toward the distant shine of a taxi stand.

The night was busy with wind, damp with the threat of rain; and it had taken Pat Rin a few moments to be certain that the small noises and the motions of shadows were concerted action and not simply the random pattern of people on the town.

And by then, it was clear that they were both shadowed and outnumbered. Cheever flipped his pocket lightly and Pat Rin muttered under his breath, "Not yet, we have no plan."

They had continued moving in the direction of the transport kiosk, hoping against the odds for the timely appearance of a taxi or a shuttle, but the interception went smoothly.

"This way, please," the pale-haired man who drifted in beside them said in Liaden, and then in accented Terran, "There is no need for alarm."

The place to which they were taken was not far from the casino district, down a windowless alleyway and into a court where several vehicles were parked. Surprisingly, there were a smattering of trees and bushes here, as if some effort at landscaping had been made.

They were ushered past the trees, into a somewhat smaller and dimmer alley. Several of their escort peeled off to take up what Pat Rin thought must be guard points. A few more steps along the second alleyway and they came to a rough-walled building. The door stood open; the pale-haired man bowed them within. He entered after, his bodyguard sealing the door behind all.

The man led them down a thin and lowering hall, then, and into a sparsely lit, irregularly shaped room.

The room smelled of old dust and the floor was uneven, as if the building had shifted and created tectonic ridges in the tiles.

The leader motioned toward a rude table attended by two ruder chairs, set near the center of the gloom. He took for himself the chair nearest the door, his second standing behind him.

They took this as a model: Pat Rin in the chair; Cheever McFarland behind.

"We are messengers," the pale-haired man murmured, soothing the air between them with a gesture one might more reasonably expect to encounter at a High House dining board than at a rough plastic table in a badly lit, abandoned storeroom. "Merely messengers, sir. Bearing news from those who wish you, not harm, but only well."

"News," Pat Rin repeated, liking the matter no better, and fervently grateful for the formidable bulk of Cheever McFarland standing behind his chair. He took a breath, keeping his face calmly neutral—the old, the familiar, gambler's mask—and inclined his head.

"Of course," he said, matching the man's soft tone, "one welcomes news, when one has been heedless upon holiday."

The man across inclined his head gravely, his gun-sworn standing at stiff attention behind his chair.

"Of course," he agreed, and put his hands palm down against the table, meeting Pat Rin's eyes squarely.

"I bring news of your clan."

Yes? Pat Rin flicked a glance downward, looking for the Tree-and-Dragon token held discreetly between two of the man's quiet fingers. He was not . . . entirely . . . surprised to discover it invisible.

He looked again at the man's bland, mannerly face. "One is ever joyful to have news of one's kin," he said softly.

"As who is not?" the other replied according to the proper formula and leaned forward abruptly, his curiously flat eyes pinning Pat Rin's gaze.

"Your kin are dead," he said, as if it were the merest pleasantry; as if he imparted nothing more startling than an unlooked-for change in the weather.

Behind the gambler's mask of calm neutrality, Pat Rin froze, hearing again that calm, uninflected sentence, not quite making sense—His *kin*. His kin—*dead*? *All* his kin? Quin? Luken? Nova? Shan? His mother? Dead? Ridiculous.

"Ridiculous," he heard his own voice state, dispassionately.

The other man inclined his head. "I understand," he murmured. "So large a change in Korval's fortunes—in your own fortunes. Of course, so skilled a player as yourself would wish proof. As it happens, we have proof." He dropped his eyes deliberately to the tabletop.

Pat Rin followed his gaze, saw the sinewy golden hands lift up and away, leaving alone upon the scarred plastic a smallish thing that glittered even in light so low; a thing he had reason to know well, having seen it upon the hands of several of his kin, most lately on the hand of his cousin Nova, who held Korval in trust for Val Con.

And who would have surrendered Korval's Ring to the man who sat before him only in the extremity of her death.

He forced himself to blink, to look up from the impossibility on the table before him; forced himself to speak calmly to the man opposite, who sat watching with his flat, predator's eyes and his curiously immobile face.

"There are," he observed, as if the thing upon the table were the merest bauble, "others before me. Indeed, I believe that there are children not yet halfling and at least one Terran far-kin to whom the Ring would fall before ever it came to me."

The man smiled gently. "They no longer impede you. Nova yos'Galan, Anthora yos'Galan, Shan yos'Galan, Kareen yos'Phelium, Luken bel'Tarda, Val Con yos'Phelium, even Gordon Arbuthnot. All have been swept from the board."

Hearing the names of his kin—his *dead* kin—but the man had not named the children! Pat Rin grasped that thought, insisting that his mind work. The pale-haired man had not named the children, but his mother and Luken—by every iteration of Plan B he had ever memorized, Luken bel'Tarda and Kareen yos'Phelium were responsible for the safety of the children. If his mother and Luken were—dead . . .

No. It—they could not—it was not possible . . .

Blindly, he reached out, plucked the Ring from the table and stared at it, eyes tracing the familiar lines of Korval's Tree-and-Dragon, the bright enamel-work, the perfect emeralds framing the boldly scripted *Flaran Cha'menthi*.

"Who did this?" he asked, eyes on the dragon, on the emeralds. Two *perfect* emeralds . . .

"It is necessary," the pale-haired man said in his soft, mannerly voice, "from time to time to remove from play those who impede the work of the Department of the Interior. Thus it was with those who had been your kin. And, now, through the efforts of the Department of the Interior, you rise to your proper estate."

With an effort, Pat Rin lifted his eyes to stare at the man opposite, who inclined his head deeply—a seated bow of profound respect.

"*Korval*," he said.

Pat Rin could not quite control the shudder as he placed the ring back in the center of the table. He took a breath.

"The Department of the Interior will require some . . . service, in payment of its efforts on my behalf," he suggested gently.

The pale-haired man moved a hand in that curiously soothing gesture. "You need only mind the Department's interests with the Council of Clans. Advisories and information will be delivered to you at the appropriate times." He smiled. "Small enough payment. You will find the Department is a staunch defender of its allies."

"Ah." He took a hard, sudden breath, raised a hand as if to shield his face, and all at once recalled himself, snapping the arm down as he glanced aside. "Your pardon," he gasped, as the hideaway slid from his sleeve into his hand.

"Of course," said his enemy. "You will wish time to assimilate—"

Pat Rin brought the little gun up and shot him through the right eye. The body of the man collapsed forward, face flat on the table, his gun-sworn snatching at her sidearm as he fell. The boom of Cheever McFarland's weapon and the rain of blood from the gaping hole in her chest were simultaneous.

"You OK, sir?"

Pat Rin took a breath which failed to fill his lungs, and tried another, finding his voice at last, remarkably steady, though somewhat light.

"I am perfectly well, Mr. McFarland, thank you." Absently, he slid the hideaway back into his sleeve and stood.

"You'll have to leave your jacket," Cheever said apologetically. "The blood."

"Of course." He unfastened the seal and stripped the garment off, dropping it into the merciful shadows along the floor. For a moment, he stared uncomprehendingly at the square of cloth Cheever silently held out. Clean-silk. It came to him, then, that his face might not be . . . perfectly . . . clean. He plucked the cloth up and used it thoroughly, then dropped it, too, into the shadows.

"Is that Nova's ring?"

He looked up at the big pilot, then turned and plucked the thing off the table. Two *perfect* emeralds. Fools. And yet . . .

"Mr. McFarland, I fear we're in a scrape." He held up the counterfeit. "This is *not* Korval's Ring, though those—" he swept his hand at the dead without looking at them—"claimed that it was. They also claimed that all of my kin are—are dead." His voice was not doing so well, after all. He swallowed and forced himself to go on.

"They named names, Mr. McFarland. And—we are neither of us children. Or fools. We both know that a man who tells one lie does not necessarily tell two."

Cheever's face in the dim light might have been hewn from wood.

Pat Rin inclined his head. "Just so. Balance is owing." He slid the bogus Ring onto his left hand—onto the *second finger* of his left hand—and held it up to catch the sullen light.

There was a brief silence before Cheever nodded his big head. "Gotcha. Now, let's get outta here before their buddies wonder what all the noise was about."

•   •   •

At the door to the alleyway, Cheever held up his hand. Pat Rin obediently slipped into the shadows at the edge of the doorway, gun ready, as the big Terran moved silently out into the dark.

Shivering in his thin silk shirt, Pat Rin counted to twelve, to twenty-four—to thirty-six, and the alley gave up neither sound nor light nor Cheever McFarland. Forty-eight, and Pat Rin began to consider the likelihood of alternate exits and how they might be guarded. Fifty-seven—and gravel scraped in the alleyway, as if purposefully scuffed beneath the heel of a boot.

A heartbeat later, Cheever McFarland himself materialized, showing empty palms.

"We're clear, sir. The guards are accounted for."

Soundlessly and quickly. Pat Rin slipped his gun away. "Your work?"

Cheever grinned and lowered his hand. "I ain't that good." He jerked his head to the right. "Your girlfriend did us a favor."

Girlfriend? There was the very slightest of motions in the shadows at the right. Pat Rin turned, and Natesa the Assassin allowed him to see her, bowing profoundly in her dull black leathers.

Behind her Pat Rin caught glimpse of a face, a body in the weeds—the man who had accosted him at the casino . . .

"Master. I hear there was a disagreement inside. Perhaps we may assist you."

She straightened, showing him a face expertly darkened, in which her eyes shone like ebony waters.

"I understand that you have already assisted me," he replied, and bowed in acknowledgment of the debt. "Have you taken any harm from it?"

Amusement, rich and subtle, was conveyed in the curve of one leather-clad arm. "No harm in the least. They were unwatchful and arrogant."

He moved a hand, describing the building behind him. "There are two dead persons in the room at the end of that hallway. It would be best if they were not found."

"Housekeeping will deal with it," she said calmly, and bowed once more. "Again, I offer transport and whatever you might require." She straightened, eyes gleaming. "Master, there was no need for you to be in that room at all."

"There was every need," Pat Rin corrected, and raised his hand. What light there was skidded off the bright enamel work, and Korval's ancient sigil flared like a star in the alley. The assassin drew a breath, pulled the most obvious weapon from its holster and offered it to him across her two palms.

"Service, Korval. I would stand at your back."

Pat Rin closed his eyes. Cantra's own words, from the very Diaries of Korval, burned bright against the inside of his eyelids: *In an ally, considerations of house, clan, planet, race are insignificant beside two prime questions, which are: 1. Can he shoot? 2. Will he aim at your enemy?*

Pat Rin opened his eyes and bowed, acknowledging his receipt of her oath.

"Service accepted," he said, and turned to his pilot. "Mr. McFarland, we are enroute."

The big man nodded and touched the butt of the gun thrust through his belt. "Yessir. I see that we are."

DAY 287
STANDARD YEAR 1392

DEPARTING TERISTE

There was a Juntavas safe-house somewhere on Teriste; Natesa had wished to take him there. Which offer he of course refused, insisting that they—or at least he—return to *Fortune's Reward*.

"I will not leave my ship untended when there are enemies to hand," he said, reasonably. At least, he thought he was speaking reasonably, survival dictating that one *ought* to speak reasonably—in fact, with all courtesy—to a Juntavas assassin.

She considered him for a moment in silence, black eyes unreadable in her darkened face. She bowed then, honor to the delm, and Pat Rin felt a frisson run his spine, which she certainly saw—and it would not do to show weakness before such a one, when he must display only strength and absolute certainty—when he must be ruthless in the pursuit of his Balance . . .

"After all," Natesa murmured, "Korval is ships." She looked to Cheever, who nodded.

And so they three had returned to *Fortune's Reward*, though in an order dictated by Cheever McFarland, who took to himself the task of ascertaining that enemies had neither subverted the ship-codes nor awaited them within the shadows of neighboring vessels. When the all-clear came, Pat Rin went forward, Natesa slightly behind and to his left, and thus they entered his ship.

Cheever was already at the board, chatting with the tower as if the entire universe had not been altered in its course over the last hour—but, of course, for Cheever, the universe maintained. The two of them had been beset by cut-throats, whom they had dispatched with speed and efficiency. They had thereby gained a rather . . . irregular . . . ally, but Cheever seemed to hold the Juntavas in neither awe nor loathing, regarding them simply as another fact of life. And life went on.

So it did.

Standing in the center of the piloting chamber, Pat Rin took a careful breath, and turned toward the waiting assassin. His oathsworn.

"I was unfortunately naive prior to raising this port," he said, speaking in the mode between equals. "I seek now to correct an error."

She inclined her head. "Master, I am at your service."

"Then you will tell me if it is possible—or when it will be possible—to alter the name, ID, and port of origin for this vessel."

She pursed her lips, considering; indicated the busy pilot with a subtle move of her head. "Pilot McFarland already files an amended flight. He is wise in this, I think. We have this evening discommoded a player of whom I am insufficiently knowledgeable. Ignorance being an active threat to survival, it is wisdom to retire to a less volatile location.

"So. If you will allow me, there is a station within this sector where the modifications you mention may be made, easily and professionally."

"And the price?" he asked, which was only prudent, when buying from the Juntavas.

Natesa's dark eyes gleamed with amusement. "I have jurisdiction there. The legitimate expenses of a Judge on assignment are charged on account."

"I see." He had taken her service, he reminded himself—necessity. And if, through her, he had also taken service from the Juntavas entire?

Necessity.

He took a breath, deep and calming, and looked down at his hands. Bright and bogus on the second finger of his left hand—the finger on which Korval-pernard'i had worn the true Ring, and, gods willing, wore it still—his newest adornment quite cast his usual jewels into the shade, as if they were mere paste, instead of . . .

Instead of cash. Pat Rin shook himself, recalling that his earnings on the evening were slight, and all accounts closed to him. He looked up, to find Natesa watching him closely.

"Something else," he said, showing her his right hand, all aglitter with gemstones.

She inclined her head. "It would be most profitable to sell those here. If you will, I may summon one to conduct the appropriate transactions. The money will await you at the service station we spoke of."

And he had only to trust her, he thought, and very nearly laughed.

"Of your kindness," he said, instead, and had the things off, jumbling them into her waiting palm. He hesitated, then, and raised a hand to the blue earring. His trademark, by which he would be known.

"Hold," the woman said, softly. "The rings are enough for now, Master. That—it is worth too little, if it must be sold without provenance."

He considered her, both eyebrows surprised into lift, but she only smiled, and bowed, and moved to the board, murmuring a request that the pilot open a comm line for her.

"We got lift scheduled inside the hour, sir," Cheever McFarland said over his shoulder, face as calm as always. "Any idea where we're going?"

"First, we must undertake certain renovations too long ignored—Natesa has the coords for the . . . preferred shop in the sector."

Unflapped, Cheever nodded. "And after that?"

Well? Pat Rin asked himself, interestedly. *And after that?* He looked at the big man steadily.

"After that shall depend upon necessity, pilot." He moved a hand toward the hall leading to his quarters. "If you have no need of me, I shall retire now, and meditate upon my . . . requirements."

"Right." Cheever nodded again. "I'll give you a heads-up when we raise the station."

"Thank you, Mr. McFarland," Pat Rin said, softly. He inclined his head, and walked away from the busyness of the piloting chamber, down the hall and into his quarters.

Asked, if any were bold enough to do so, Pat Rin would have said that he was not a fond man. Of course, one had preferred acquaintances—even preferred kin—but one was not, after all, clanbound. Certainly, he was no such weeping heart as might overload his personal databank with images of his kin, in all their faces and seasons.

Indeed, a most thorough search of that same databank produced precisely six images, all unsatisfactory in the extreme.

Six.

Carefully, he arranged them on the screen, side by side, top to bottom; enlarging each as if he would read every line and nuance of the digital faces.

Here: Shan, Nova and Anthora grouped, laughing, around the ubiquitous Jeeves. The picture was not recent—Shan was wearing Korval's Ring in trust, which he had assumed upon Cousin Er Thom's death; Anthora looked the merest halfling, and Nova—Nova scarcely looked older.

Here was Quin, his own heir, caught in the midst of a race against his cousin Padi, Shan's daughter. This image was of more recent vintage, though still some years behind the calendar.

The next picture—that was recent, and Pat Rin spent some time looking into the faces of the two most dear to him in all the worlds. Luken bel'Tarda, his foster-father, sandy hair gone to gray, shoulders square in his second best coat, and Quin, who had gone from hooligan to young gentleman in the space of one image, standing before the hand-knotted Pasiryki carpet which was Luken's pride and sole extravagance. Fortunes had been offered Luken, in exchange for that rug. Alas, fortunes interested Luken—not at all. Quin was dressed in traveling clothes, his dark hair painfully neat, the opal blue eyes which were his legacy from his mother wide and guileless. A kit-bag sat at his feet. After the picture was taken, Pat Rin recalled, finding it suddenly difficult to breathe, he had escorted his son to the excellent private school that now—that had had him in its keeping.

Another: Not recent, though not as old as the image of his cousins and their housebot. His mother at study, various editions of the Code laid open on the table around her workstation; her face intent upon the screen.

Another: His cousin Val Con, slouched in a chair before the fireplace in Trealla Fantrol's family parlor, his legs thrust out before him and crossed at the ankle, a glass of wine held loosely in his left hand. He was looking directly into the camera, and gently smiling, eyes as brilliant as the emeralds in the counterfeit ring on Pat Rin's finger.

The last image was the oldest of all, blurry with the photographer's lack of skill. It showed four persons in formal tableau, paired two-by-two. On the left, tall Anne Davis, kind-faced and smiling, her hand resting on the shoulder of a yellow-haired man of extraordinary beauty—Er Thom, her lifemate. Beside Er Thom, lean and dark and diabolic—Uncle Daav himself, holding the hand of a slight and elegant lady, her tawny hair caught back from her face by a carven comb, her green eyes aglow with joy. Aelliana, Daav's lifemate. Val Con's mother. Dead—they were all four dead; had been dead long before Plan B had been called. It was a portrait of ghosts he studied so intently, and had been so for years . . .

Six images, incomplete and old—which, if the representative of the Department of the Interior was to be believed, was all that he had now, of his kin.

He sat for some time, staring sightlessly at the screen, trying to think of a way—any way—to gain news of his kin without endangering those who might yet remain unmurdered.

Fortunes Reward carried a pinbeam. He was in possession of a beam-code, meant for use in the irregularly scheduled roll calls, as well as other codes, which in happier times would rouse Luken; the *Dutiful Passage*; Nova; dea'Gauss; and the master computer at Jelaza Kazone.

He dared invoke none of them, he decided after a period of cold and close reasoning. The Department of the Interior had located him, offered their preposterous deal, and their messenger had died as a result of their impertinence. These facts in no way guaranteed that the Department's interest in himself had likewise died. Indeed, he rather thought that their interest might grow significantly warmer, when it was discovered why their messenger, and his team, had not reported in.

Certainly, the Department of the Interior was monitoring his accounts. Certainly, they monitored Korval's known bands and, perhaps, if only one adult had fallen to them, the lesser known bands, as well.

Pat Rin shivered, closing his eyes. He dared attempt to call— no one. More: he dared not be taken by the Department alive, to then be compelled to betray whomever yet remained at large.

And, above all, he must not allow his desperate desires to blind him to the possibility that the Department's messenger had indeed told him nothing more than the plain truth, and that he, Pat Rin yos'Phelium, was the last of his clan.

He opened his eyes, blinked several times to bring the faces of his kin into focus, and pulled the keyboard to him.

He left the images on the primary screen, opened a second screen and, typing uncertainly with fingers that were none too steady, began to compile a list of . . . Korval's . . . necessities.

They heard him out—the pilot and the assassin—as he outlined his requirements and his plan. When he had finished, the pilot whistled, long and low.

"So, you're gonna vanish, and build up reserves?"

Pat Rin inclined his head. "In essence."

"It is a bold plan—and difficult," the assassin said in her turn, her slim fingers woven together upon the table. "I wonder, Master, about the necessity of a working spaceport. I wonder—will a primitive port—even, a very primitive port—serve you? You might then shape it to your needs."

He thought about that. A spaceport was necessary—he would need ships; he would need to build, dock, and maintain ships. And yet, spaceports invited the galaxy, and it was equally imperative that he remain beneath the range of Korval's enemy. Until he should reveal himself, at a time and place of his choosing.

"A primitive spaceport has some advantage to us," he told her. "But not so primitive that it may not be upgraded—quickly."

"I understand." She looked down at her hands, then into his eyes, her own as deep as starless space.

"Let us then posit a world which is primitive in many ways, yet its barbarism allows—opportunity for manipulation. A strong-willed person, capable of conceiving and·implementing a plan, might do whatever he wished, eventually." She sighed, which he thought was not like her. "I know of such a world."

Pat Rin glanced at Cheever McFarland, who waved a big hand, indicating that he was attending the conversation, but had nothing to add.

So.

He considered Natesa the Assassin, her quiet hands and unquiet eyes.

"I believe you are not entirely pleased with this world," he said softly. "Why not?"

She moved her shoulders—closer to the fluid and ambiguous Liaden gesture than an honest Terran shrug. "I have—no jurisdiction there," she said, matching him soft for soft. "I—perhaps—have contacts there, tenuous contacts, at best. I know the language, as do you. I know of a . . . relatively secure landing place, so that we need not alert the port to our presence—but jurisdiction?" She met his eyes squarely. "*No one* has jurisdiction there."

"Ah." A world that was alike protected from the so-called Department of the Interior, and the Juntavas—perfect.

Pat Rin inclined his head.

"I believe that is—desirable."

She nodded, as if she had expected no other answer. As perhaps, Pat Rin thought, she had not.

"What's the name of this place?" Cheever asked from his corner of the table.

Natesa turned to look at him. "Why, Surebleak, pilot. Have you heard of it?"

Surprisingly, the big man threw back his head and laughed. "Oh, I heard of it, OK." He transferred a wide grin to Pat Rin. "She's right, Boss. If there's a world where anything can get lost and never looked for, it's Surebleak."

"Good," Pat Rin said, and inclined his head to both. "Then it is settled."

DAY 50
STANDARD YEAR 1393

DUTIFUL PASSAGE
LYTAXIN ORBIT

The shift was more than half done. First Mate Ren Zel dea'Judan finished the last report in the queue and leaned back in his chair, reflecting that it was odd that the paperwork of war and the paperwork of trade should be so similar.

Though, he thought, reaching for his cup, to be precise, they were no longer at war, but rather stalled in some halfling state between the usual and the unthinkable, waiting for the gods knew what.

Ren Zel sipped, found the tea tepid, sighed and drank it anyway.

The reports provided by the mercenary forces on the planet below spoke of the "mop up phase" of the on-going military operations, and indicated that the present hostilities between the mercenaries and those Yxtrang soldiers remaining were sporadic and disconnected, ranging over considerable geographic area. Clan Erob's airfield, which had been a point of contention before the Yxtrang warships had abruptly withdrawn from orbit, abandoning thousands of soldiers to their deaths, was secure. What was left of Lytaxin spaceport was also secure.

The captains and mates of the ships now surrounding the *Passage*—officers old in warfare—gave as their expert opinions that it was extremely unlikely that the departed Yxtrang would return with reinforcements to retrieve the soldiers they had left behind.

Ren Zel shuddered, and not because his tea was cold. To be abandoned by one's ship among hostile strangers, the last duty remaining one to die well . . .

It struck too close to the heart, that, and set uneasy memories snarling. To have one's death recorded and made fact before ever one had lain down and—

"Have done!" he told himself sharply and stood.

He wanted tea. Fresh, hot tea, and an end to the nattering of ill memory. He was clanless—dead to kin, outside the laws of Liad. Dead in truth, had Shan yos'Galan not put forth his hand, and declared that he and his crew welcomed pilots of ability and steady will. Here, on *Dutiful Passage*, Ren Zel dea'Judan, deceased of Clan Obrelt, had comrades, and a place, and work—as pilot and, now, as first mate, under Shan yos'Galan's lady lifemate, Priscilla Mendoza. His wealth exceeded, by many orders of magnitude, anything another clanless might hope to achieve—aye, and many who were clanned, as well.

Tea. He moved to the refreshment console—and the comm unit on his desk beeped.

Pilot-quick, he was across the room, finger on the button.

"First Mate."

"Hi there, First Mate," Radio Tech Rusty Morgenstern said brightly. "Got a call on the priority channel for the officer in charge. Want it now?"

Priority channel? "Certainly."

"All yours," Rusty said. There was a click as of a second line being opened, then Rusty's voice again, almost painfully respectful. "Here's Pilot dea'Judan, ma'am—officer on shift."

"Thank you, Mr. Morgenstern," said a cool feminine voice. "Pilot dea'Judan?"

"Yes, ma'am," Ren Zel agreed in his careful Terran. "May I know to whom I have the honor of speaking?"

There was a slight pause, as if the lady were taken aback to find one who did not know her.

"I have the honor," she said, abruptly and icily in the High Tongue, in the mode of announcement, "to be Korval-pernard'i. My personal name is Nova yos'Galan. I will be arriving at Docking Bay Two in one-half hour, Standard. My necessity is to meet with the captain immediately upon my arrival. Am I plain?"

"You are extremely plain, my lady," Ren Zel answered in the mode of oathbound to lord, which was precise, as even the laws of Liad must acknowledge, while disputing his right to speak at all to a living Liaden lady. "Arrangements will be made to welcome you at Bay Two in one-half hour, Standard."

"That is well," said Nova yos'Galan and signed off. Ren Zel frowned.

Nova yos'Galan, first speaker in trust for Clan Korval, was the sister of Shan yos'Galan. He had met the lady once, standing protected and anonymous within the shadow of his captain's melant'i. That same captain who casually brought his sister's reputation a whisper from ruin by introducing Ren Zel, in Terran—"Pilot dea'Judan, sister. Ren Zel, my sister Nova, also a pilot."

Now she came, Korval-pernard'i, riding a double wave of danger, and demanding to see the captain of *Dutiful Passage*. By whom she could only mean her brother, who was . . . no longer aboard.

Ren Zel leaned over the desk and punched in a quick sequence, barely glancing at the keypad. The second remote trill was cut off by the deep, resonate voice of Priscilla Mendoza, who had been first mate before him.

"Mendoza."

"Pray forgive me for disturbing your rest," he said in formal Liaden, scarcely heeding his own speech. "Circumstance requires."

"Appalling circumstance, apparently, to have kicked you back into the High Tongue," said Priscilla in light Terran. "What tragedy has overtaken us, friend?"

Ren Zel smiled slightly and amended his language. "I pray forgiveness," he said carefully. "One has just now closed conversation with a lady of high mode, indeed." He glanced at the clock on the wall beside the refreshment unit. "In precisely twenty-eight minutes, Standard, Nova yos'Galan, Korval-pernard'i, will arrive at Docking Station Two. Her desire is to enjoy an interview with the captain, immediately upon her arrival."

Priscilla said three hard-edged words in a language neither Terran nor Liaden. Ren Zel blinked.

"I beg your pardon," he said, as gently as Terran allowed him.

Her sigh came clearly out of the speaker. "No, I beg your pardon," she said, equally gentle, "for I must send you into peril alone, and for no better reason than I cannot face the upcoming interview with Korval-pernard'i on an empty stomach."

She sighed a second time. "Please do me the favor of meeting Lady Nova at Docking Bay Two and escorting her to my office."

"I?" Ren Zel bit his lip. "Priscilla, I am—"

"Pilot, first mate, and crewman of good standing on this ship," she interrupted. "Lady Nova knows how to value such things."

And he had, after all, Ren Zel reflected wryly, received his orders from his captain. He inclined his head, as if she could see him—and who knew that she could not, dramliza that she was? "I will meet Lady Nova and bring her to you in your office."

"Good," said Priscilla.

His hand moved toward the disconnect—and stopped as she spoke his name.

"Yes?"

"It will not be necessary," she said, "to tell Lady Nova that her brother is not presently aboard."

The ways of the dramliz were mysterious, Ren Zel thought, but the ways of Korval were stranger still. Again, he inclined his head.

"I understand," he said, and the connection light went out.

The status light went from red to green, and the hatch slid open, revealing a tall blond woman wearing the leather jacket of a Jump pilot over serviceable dark shirt and trousers. Her face was comely, as he had recalled, and fell easily into a frown, though he had taken care to be in place several minutes beforetime, so that she would find him neither tardy nor breathless.

He bowed, oathbound to lord, which might have waked a question in her mind, had she been less focused upon her own business. As it was, she returned his courtesy with an inclination of the head, and a brief, "Pilot."

"Lady," he murmured, straightening in proper time and keeping his gaze decently averted. "I am sent to bring you to the captain."

"So I surmised," she answered drily, the accent of fabled Solcintra gilding her words. "If the captain has likewise desired you to lead me the long dance, I pray you will allow yourself to be persuaded otherwise. I do know the shortest route, and will have no difficulty escorting myself."

Well, and Captain yos'Galan had been known, upon occasion, to issue such orders to those sent as escort, Ren Zel allowed, and bowed again.

"The captain was off shift," he offered, softly, "and required time to prepare."

"Of course," said Lady Nova and swept a slim hand toward the corridor. Korval's clan ring flared briefly in the light, silver and green. "My business with the captain is urgent."

"Certainly. If your ladyship will accompany me . . ."

•   •   •

All honor to the lady: she did not insist on the shortest route, through the narrow service corridors. However, the pace she set through the public corridors was swift enough to discourage conversation, which Ren Zel could only feel was to his benefit.

Soon enough, the bright red door of the captain's office came into sight. The lady broke her step, courteously allowing Ren Zel to lay his palm against the plate. The door slid silently open and he preceded the guest across the threshold, as protocol required, saw his captain sitting tall and proud behind the desk and swept a low bow as Nova yos'Galan stepped past him.

"I bring—" he began, and then halted, as Priscilla's voice overrode his, speaking mild Terran.

"Well met, sister. Will you have wine?"

Ren Zel straightened. *Sister.* What came next was between kin. He had no business here. He moved one careful step forward. Both women looked at him, but he kept his eyes on Priscilla's face.

"Captain, shall I take your place on the roster this shift?"

She smiled. "That will not be necessary, first mate. Please, pursue your rest shift."

He bowed—"Captain"—again—"Lady"—and resisted the impulse to back out of the office.

The door slid shut behind the brown-haired pilot. Nova took a deliberate breath, and glared at the woman behind the desk. "So. Sister and captain, is it? Where is my brother?"

"Planetside," Priscilla said in her deep, calm voice, and raised a hand as if she felt Nova's cry of protest rising. "It was an accident, I swear. We had taken damage and he insisted on being part of the repair crew. The enemy attacked and separated him from the ship." She paused, then added, "Seth Johnson gave his life to protect his captain and his ship in that action. I think you knew him."

Nova bowed her head, recalling with the vividness that was her gift and her curse the long, rat-faced Terran pilot. "Who are we, that people die for us? All honor to him."

"All honor to him," Priscilla repeated softly.

Nova looked up. "First mate rises to fill the void in command, when the captain is separated from the ship. It is understood. Now—sister?"

"Shan and I have declared lifemates."

Nova closed her eyes. "With recourse to neither law nor first speaker."

"The clan was scattered; our enemy in pursuit," Priscilla murmured. "I refused to leave the ship to be safe, and he was too wise a captain to order his first mate away."

Nova opened her eyes. "Ah, I understand! A sacrifice upon the altar of duty! How like Shan, to be sure!"

Priscilla threw back her head and laughed. After a moment, Nova sighed and moved forward to take a chair. "I believe I will have a glass of the white, if you please. Sister. And then you may tell me how my brothers fare, planetside."

"Shan," said Priscilla, moving gracefully across the room to the bar. "Fares well. Val Con fares . . . less well." She poured two glasses of white wine and carried them to the desk. She handed Nova a glass and sat again behind the desk, her own glass cradled in long, slender fingers.

Nova's mouth tightened. "How much . . . less well . . . stands my younger brother?"

Priscilla raised her glass and almost laughed again, to catch herself employing one of Shan's delaying tactics.

"Val Con was desperately wounded in the strike that broke the back of the Yxtrang on-world. He remains in the catastrophe unit at Erob's medical facility. The med techs there are divided in their predictions of the final percentage of his disability."

The color drained from Nova's face, leaving it a sticky beige color; her distress slammed across Priscilla's inner senses with the shrill force of a scream.

"Nova—"

Her lifemate's sister raised a slim, golden hand, and turned her face aside. "A moment, of your kindness. Val Con—" Her breath caught. "If he is not able to fly . . ."

If Val Con were not able to fly, Priscilla thought, following Nova's logic effortlessly, then he could not, by Korval's own law, be delm. And Korval needed its delm now as never before, with Plan B in effect, and enemies on all sides.

"Val Con's lifemate is out of the 'doc and by all reports will make a full recovery," she said to Nova's stricken eyes. "She will be able to fly. Korval has its delm."

"Lifemate," Nova repeated flatly, and had recourse to her glass, eyes half-closed.

"Lifemate," Priscilla asserted. "Shan says—lifemates in the fullest sense, shadowing the link that your parents shared."

Nova closed her eyes. "Gods be merciful," she murmured. She had another sip of wine and opened her eyes. "I will be leaving for the planet surface as soon as I have cleared descent with the appropriate commanders," she said, with a forced and brittle calm.

"There are Yxtrang on the planet surface," Priscilla pointed out, though she had very little hope of turning Nova from her course. "You will be placing yourself in peril."

The other woman stared at her for a long moment, violet eyes unreadable.

"I acknowledge the possibility of peril," she said, slowly. "However, the report I have from the mercenaries is that Erob's House is no longer in immediate danger of attack and that the Yxtrang have lost heart. I am Korval-pernard'i. Necessity exists."

And that, Priscilla thought with an inward sigh, *was that.* She knew better than to try to talk any Liaden out of an action that had been found, by some fey balancing of duty, desire, and melant'i, to be "necessary."

"May I ask you a thing," Nova said suddenly, "as captain of this vessel?"

What now? Priscilla wondered, but kept her face and voice serene. "Yes."

"I wonder how you came to name a clanless first mate?"

"Ah." Priscilla leaned back and sipped her own wine, her eyes drawn upward, to the glittery frivolous mobile Anthora yos'Galan had given her brother Shan. "Ren Zel is able; mere hours away from master pilot. He is respected by his shipmates, and—" She brought her eyes down to meet Nova's gaze. "And, he is not . . . entirely . . . clanless. This ship—this crew—are his kin. He will fight to keep both safe, with his last gasp of life."

Nova sat for a moment, then inclined her head. "It is well-reasoned. I thank you." She stood, leaving her empty glass on the corner of Priscilla's desk. "If I may have the use of a comm?"

Priscilla rose. "You may use this one, and welcome," she said. "I am wanted on the bridge."

"Thank you. Sister." She smiled, then, sudden and genuine. "I am glad to be able to say it."

LIAD
DEPARTMENT OF INTERIOR COMMAND HEADQUARTERS

The box was approximately five foot square, matte black and, on casual inspection, seamless.

Commander of Agents, completing an inspection that was not at all casual, paused before the door and looked to the hovering technician.

"I would examine the interior."

"Certainly, Commander." The tech removed a cylinder no longer than his forefinger from a pocket and depressed a section of its black surface. There was no sound, but when Commander of Agents again faced the box, it was to discover that one wall had slid away. The interior was very dark. Commander of Agents produced a hand light from his pocket, flicked it on and stepped into the box.

Its interior dimension was somewhat less than the outside led one to expect; the ceiling short enough that Commander of Agents needed to duck his head and round his shoulders. A taller person would not have been able to stand at all, but would need to kneel upon the ungiving metal floor.

"The apparatus," the technician murmured from the doorway, "is enclosed in the floor and the sidewalls. If one braces oneself against a wall, or kneels or lies down on the floor—the lethargic effect is far greater. The test subject has been able to experience the weakening of his abilities, which was not expected, but which may prove useful. In the short term, the perceptible ebb of power has been observed to awaken panic to the verge of hysteria in the test subject."

Commander of Agents played his light around the interior of the box, noting with satisfaction the smooth, nearly featureless metal walls. There were a series of small vents—33 holes altogether, the report had said—on the immovable wall. These were for ventilation, or for the introduction of gasses, as necessary. On the very center of the "ceiling" were several indentations—these the microphone and speakers for communicating with the inmate, or for introducing sounds as might be required. An uncomfortable place, altogether, in the normal way of things, but for those of the dramliz—a torture.

"You lost a subject, I believe?" he said over his shoulder to the technician.

"Commander, we did. The first dramliza understood her circumstance very quickly and was able to raise sufficient power to hurl a fireball at the apparatus beneath the floor."

The Commander's little beam of light danced across the floor, found a black smear rather like a grease stain on the floor nearly at his feet; a similar stain ran halfway down the wall he faced.

"Did the mechanism take harm?"

"Tests immediately after the incident indicated that the apparatus remained fully functional," the technician said. "The material, you see, is highly reflective of that energy utilized by the dramliz. The bolt was thus sent back to the subject from the floor and all the walls, immolating her. An unfortunate loss of an interesting subject. I very much regret the waste."

"There is some waste in all experiments. You have found the second subject less volatile, I understand."

"It was understood that proper testing required that we utilize dramliza of greater rather than lesser ability, and the present subject, like the first, is very strong. He is, however, young; and we hold his cha'leket hostage to his cooperation. Also, I took care to show him the stains you have found, sir, and explain in depth how they came to be there." The technician paused. "There was, of course, some danger that he would attempt to suicide, using this proven means, but he is, as I have said, young, fond of his cha'leket, and inclined to believe in the possibility of rescue."

Hunched, the Commander backed out of the box and flicked off his light. Straightening his cramped shoulders, he looked again to the technician.

"You planted the belief that he might expect a rescue?"

The tech inclined his head. "It seemed the best strategy, given the need to conceal our development from the dramliz."

The Commander took a moment to consider this. Ordinarily, he did not tolerate such innovations from mere technicians. In this case, however, given, as had been said, the need to conserve resources . . . He inclined his head.

"You have done well," he said. The technician bowed profoundly. "I will wish to speak with the subject in"——he glanced at his

chronometer—"four hours, Standard. I suggest he spend the time
before our meeting in there." He flicked a negligent hand at the box.

The tech bowed again. "Commander, it shall be done."

LYTAXIN
MERCENARY ENCAMPMENT

Clonak was on the camp, engaging in poker with as
disreputable a half-dozen card sharps as Daav had been privileged
to behold in at least twenty years. He hoped, though without much
optimism, that Clonak would allow them to retain their dignity, if
not their pay.

Shadia, sensible woman that she was, had retired immediately
after their release from Commander Carmody's dinner party.

Nelirikk—or Beautiful, as Commander Carmody had it—had
chosen to remain with the fearsome duo he referred to, with no
irony that Daav could detect, as "the recruits." The Rifle—one
Diglon—appeared of a phlegmatic nature and would very likely
follow Shadia's sensible schedule. However, the winsome and
biddable Hazenthull had been another kindle of kittens entirely.
She had been most displeased to find that she was not to be allowed to sit sentinel by the autodoc enclosing—and gods have
mercy, healing—her senior, and had only reluctantly accompanied Nelirikk and Diglon to quarters.

Which left Daav, wide awake and content to be alone, sitting
cross-legged on the bench by the 'doc containing the wounded
explorer, eyes closed against the darkness.

It was at times like this that he could feel her sitting next to
him, her knee companionably pressing his; her silence sanctifying
his disinclination to talk. Aelliana, his lifemate. Dead these last
twenty-five Standard years.

Daav sighed in the dark, and felt Aelliana lay her hand, com-
fortingly, on his thigh.

It came to him that he was as much a ghost as she: his brother was dead, and his brother's lifemate. Who of Clan Korval would remember Daav yos'Phelium, so long absent from kin and hearth? Certainly not the so-formidable son referred to, by explorer and mercenary commander alike, as "the scout"—as if there were only one in all the galaxy. The small boy he had given, weeping, into the care of his cha'leket had in some way become a man revered as a lesser god by the Yxtrang soldier he had bested in single combat; lifemate of a red-haired rakehell no less beloved of Jason Carmody.

"What may we bring to these feral children, our kin?" he murmured into the darkness.

"Why a working Rifle," Aelliana answered, her voice warm inside the whorlings of his ears, "and a brace of explorers. It seems a gift they will know how to value."

Daav smiled and resisted the temptation to pat the hand that could not be touching him. "Why, so it does. And how fortuitous to have met them upon the road, to be sure."

Aelliana laughed softly and it was all he could do not to open his eyes and turn to look at her. Instead, he smiled for her, and sighed, just a little.

"Commander Carmody has promised to send a message to our son's lady, desiring her to visit at her earliest convenience," he said. "Perhaps we may meet her soon."

"Will she accept the Yxtrang, do you think?" asked Aelliana.

Daav sighed again. "Commander Carmody thinks it. . . . possible. And we see that she has allowed our son to persuade her to one Yxtrang already . . ."

"Singularly persuasive, this scout of yours," she teased him.

"You will hardly blame him whole cloth upon me," he said, with mock severity. "Not only did I find you an enthusiastic participant during construction, but saw you thoroughly besotted with the result."

"You, of course, never named him 'Little Dragon', nor recited nonsense verses for hours on end to lull him to sleep."

"A man of my honors and position? I should think not."

"False, oh false, van'chela! A man of your dignity indeed."

"Oh, and now I have no dignity?" He forgot himself and spoke aloud, rousing the tech on duty.

"Everything OK over there?" she called.

"Yes—" Daav began, opening his eyes, and then came to his feet, staring at the 'doc, which ought to be—which had been—aglow with readouts, and status lights.

"Something's wrong," he called to the tech.

She ran to his side, took one look at the somber 'doc and shook her head with a sigh.

"Nothing wrong," she said. "He's just dead, is all."

THINGS THAT GO BUMP IN THE NIGHT

The house lay shrouded in pre-dawn, its rooms at rest. Abovestairs, a woman slept uneasily in a bed beneath a silvering skylight, her hair a dark wing across the pillows. A gray cat, his pre-dawn nap disrupted by the lady's restive habit, sat at the foot of the bed, meticulously washing his whiskers.

"Necessity," the woman said clearly, her voice full of unshed tears. The cat paused in his ablutions, paw poised by cheek, ears ticked forward, as if reserving judgment on the truth of her assertion until he had heard the whole.

"Necessity, captain," Anthora yos'Galan moaned, twisting beneath the knotted blankets. She gasped and abruptly sat up, silver eyes wide, staring toward the cat, but seeing something entirely else.

"Yxtrang," she gasped. "Suicide craft. Gods, oh gods—the *Passage* . . ." She blinked, eyes focusing at last on the cat; who met her gaze, looked away, and completed the suspended pass at his whiskers.

Anthora threw back the blankets and swung to the floor, the ribbons of her bed shirt fluttering with the speed of her movements. Barefoot, she went across the room, snatched up a white silk robe and shrugged it on, knotting the sash as she moved.

"Lord Merlin," she called as she passed from the room.

The cat shook out his paw, jumped to the floor and followed.

He had barely closed his eyes when the battle-dream formed, horrific as ever, shaking him out of slumber, as it did every third or fourth sleep shift. Lina, the ship's Healer, assured him that the memory would fade in time and leave him in peace. Until that time, however, Ren Zel was left to devise his own strategies for outwitting the demon and gaining his rest.

With the room lights cycled to their brightest, he pulled a bound book of Terran poetry from the cache next to his bed.

The volume was a collection of lyrical poetry on the theme of sensual delight; a gift from one Selain Gudder, with whom he had enjoyed a liaison of pleasure three trade trips back. He smiled with remembered fondness and, opening the book at random, soon lost himself in the rich, evocative language.

Eventually, lulled by images at once alien and comfortable, he caught himself nodding and waved a hand to extinguish the light.

He fell immediately into sleep. At once his sleeve was snatched by—well, he was not precisely certain who, save that the touch and the voice seemed—familiar—and whose evident distress had root in the same horrific incident which haunted his own sleep.

"Peace, peace," he soothed her, for she was crew—she must be crew, mustn't she, who had such a memory upon her? It was no less than his duty as first mate to ease her.

"Peace," he said a third time, as she thrust the dream forward, shrilling a warning of disaster to come.

That brought him up for a moment, then he saw that she must be caught yet in the throes of the thing, where past and present were as one.

"We are beyond it," he told her, in the mode of Comrade. "We are safe. The battle is over. The war is ending. All is well." He extended a hand and touched her shoulder, lightly, as a comrade might. "Sleep now; you have no cause for worry." And with gentle firmness, he pushed her away.

He half-woke, then, sighed, and subsided into dreamlessness, the book slipping from his fingers to the floor. A few hours later, he drifted toward wakefulness once more, roused enough to feel the cat kneading his chest. Drowsily, he raised a hand and stroked the creature, feeling the plush fur warm against his palm, and the vibration of a purr—his eyes sprang open in shock.

"*Cat?*"

The room lights came up at the sound of his voice. There was no cat on his chest; no cat glaring at him reproachfully from the floor, or the comm shelf or the desk. There was, however, a long white whisker caught in the weave of the coverlet. Ren Zel worked it loose and stared at it for several heartbeats before throwing back the covers and swinging out of bed.

There was no cat under the bunk. There was no cat in the 'fresher. Truly, his cabin was catless. As it should be.

And yet . . .

He held the whisker up to the light, admiring its length and its sturdiness, then went over to his locker. A moment's rummage produced a thin glass sampling vial—another reminder of Selain—with a re-sealing top. The whisker slipped easily into the vial. He resealed it with care and glanced ruefully at the clock.

Two hours 'til the start of his shift; too late to court sleep a third time. Well, then, a shower and an early start, he thought philosophically, moving toward the 'fresher.

He showered longer than was usual for him, invoking the cold, needling cycle twice, but the cat whisker was still in its vial when he emerged.

The song was everywhere; it filled the room, the planet, the infinite cup of space itself. At once a single note and wholly aside the song, Shan observed the bold, improbable and eminently *correct* pattern that was Val Con yos'Phelium.

In the course of the Healing, they had come across other leavings of the interloper responsible for the insertion of the calculation program. When they did, Shan had reached forth his will and made the interloper subservient to the greater pattern of his brother. Now, as the song rested within itself, he inspected the work, tested the bindings and the connections, observed the brilliant shine of integration, and was satisfied.

Shifting his regard, he considered the arc of living power flowing in unending waves of iridescence to and from the guarded center of the pattern, where Val Con kept his soul—and found it beyond anything he had ever before observed.

The thing is done, he decided; and it is good.

Gently, he brought his attention to the song, signaling completion. The note stretched, altered, quickened, and stopped.

Shan shook his head and blinked his eyes, focusing first on Val Con, covered with a thin blanket and deeply asleep, and then across and up, into the luminous eyes of the enormously old being called Edger.

"It is done," he said, feeling his voice rasp in a dry throat.

"It is done," Edger returned, and lifted a three-fingered hand in what seemed a salute. "And done well. All honor to you, Shan yos'Galan." He blinked. "Our brother sleeps now and will wake when the time is appropriate. We two should likewise seek our beds."

"That," Shan said, abruptly aware of his aching back and the grate of exhaustion immediately behind his eyes, "is a wonderful idea." He hesitated, glancing at the figure asleep upon the gurney. "Should we—?"

"I believe we may leave him here in all safety," Edger boomed, moving toward the door. Shan hesitated a moment before bending and kissing his brother on the cheek.

"Sleep well, denubia," he murmured, and followed the turtle down the room.

Once, in a teasing moment, Anthora had asked her brother Val Con how scouts were able to persuade savage persons to divulge sometimes quite secret information about their world and culture, all without being ritually murdered and eaten.

"Oh, there's nothing to that," Val Con had assured her, green eyes dancing. "It's only a matter of asking the right questions."

She had laughed then, as she had been meant to do. And it had only come to her slowly, over a course of years, just how often success in any endeavor hinged upon asking the right questions. Even when one was a dramliza at the height of her not-inconsiderable powers.

Especially when one was dramliza.

Now, as she sped along the path to the garden's center, horrific visions of the *Passage* beset by countless numbers of mine-bearing Yxtrang in tiny craft, she berated herself for her stupidity. Every evening since she had removed to Jelaza Kazone, just before retiring, she had gone out to the heart of the garden. Leaning thus cozily against the Tree, she had, bumblebrained, asked the question, "Are those most dear to my heart alive?" and flung her mind out into the void.

Every evening, she counted the fragile, brilliant flames of her kin, and was thereby comforted.

And never once had it occurred to her to ask who—if any—reposed in danger, who was their enemy and if there were any means known to the dramliz, or hidden in her own untapped talents, to aid them.

Of course, it was true that they all reposed in danger, with Plan

B in effect. To Anthora's mind, however, there was danger and there was *danger*, into which latter category attacks by armed and desperate Yxtrang plainly fell.

The stone pathway ended at a glade dimly illuminated by the night-blooming friatha. Anthora did not slacken her pace, but sped across grass that chilled her feet and soaked the hem of her robe, straight to the faintly phosphorescent enormity of the Tree. She lay her hand against the warm bark.

"Good morning, Elder," she said, though she hardly needed to speak aloud. "I'm an idiot."

Above her head, leaves rustled in a light chuckle, though the air elsewhere in the glade was still. Anthora sighed.

"Yes, all very well. But the *Passage* will be—or perhaps already has been!—under attack by an Yxtrang force. I must warn them, or—" She broke off, biting her lip. What if the attack were past? If the *Passage* was already an Yxtrang war prize; Shan— and his Priscilla, too—dead or dying of unspeakable tortures?

She felt a soft, reassuring pressure against her shin and glanced down, finding Merlin in the shadows at her feet. She looked up into the dark, attentive leaves.

"I must warn them," she said again to the Tree. The leaves directly over her head were still, though there was a commotion higher up, as if a squirrel had thrown a small stone forcefully groundward. Anthora stepped back and a seedpod struck the turf by her right foot.

"Thank you," she murmured, warmed. Bending, she gathered up the gift, skritched Merlin's ear and straightened. She cracked open the nut and ate the kernel, savoring the minty taste. Then, she set her back firmly against the trunk of the Tree, closed her eyes, and brought before her Inner Eye the construct of emotion, intelligence, and power that was uniquely in this galaxy known as Priscilla Delacroix y Mendoza. Priscilla was a Witch, with talents and abilities uncannily close to those Anthora held, as one of Liad's few remaining wizards. If any on the *Passage* had the ears to hear her message, Anthora thought, it would be Priscilla.

Thought was swept away in the tide that drew her from herself into timelessness. Light flickered in tongues like flame, and there was wind, upon which souls strange and unsought swirled like so many alien leaves. Within the maelstrom, Priscilla's pattern flared, brilliant.

Anthora exerted control—but, instead of making the expected

contact, she hurtled past her target, tumbling out of control—no. Control was there, abrupt and rather startled, as if she had some way stumbled and landed in the arms of a stranger, who now took care to set her gently upon her own feet. Puzzlement emanated from the one who had caught her; puzzlement and a dim, sweaty horror, doubtless the residue of an ill dream.

Anthora snatched at that hint, trapped it, wove it to her own dream—and even as she wove saw it shaken into another image entirely, accompanied by a brief, warm touch of comfort.

Contact was broken then, and not by her will. Blackness swirled, thick and comforting as a favorite blanket.

Anthora sighed, opened her eyes and discovered herself all atangle at the base of the Tree, her head resting on a moss-covered root, and Merlin staring down into her face.

Painfully, she sorted her limbs into seemliness and sat up, her back against the Tree. Across the glade, sunlight touched the bank of night-bloomers, which were folded tight in daytime slumber.

She had been asleep, Anthora thought in disbelief. Asleep for *hours*.

Beside her, Merlin settled, chicken-fashion, atop the moss-covered root, his eyes slitted in satisfaction.

Anthora let her head fall back against the Tree and spoke aloud, her voice breathless.

"It was not a foretelling—it was a memory. I don't know who—held like a babe!" She bit her lip, hard, curbing her baffled indignation. To be held like the merest novice, and then dismissed—*put to sleep*—as if her will were nothing—

"The battle is over," she continued, more or less calmly. "The enemy has been vanquished. The *Passage* is safe, and I—" Her voice broke here and not even she was certain if the cause was hysteria or fury—"I am not to *worry*!"

LYTAXIN
MERCENARY ENCAMPMENT

They were granted quarters by Commander Carmody;
good quarters, with a shower in one corner and a corporal before
the door.

Nelirikk, who knew the order of the Gyrfalks and how the soldiers were distributed in camp, understood that they were well-
contained, surrounded by watchers, in case there should be
trouble.

He did not anticipate trouble, himself. Less so, after watching
the gusto with which the recruits wolfed the sandwiches sent from
the mess tent—explorer no less ravenous than Rifle.

It was, largely, a silent meal. After, the recruits made use of the
shower, brushed out and put on their battle leathers.

Clean and fed, Diglon Rifle sat unconcernedly on the floor, his
back against a cot, and rolled out his kit, preparatory to stripping
and cleaning his weapon. Nelirikk approved—it was a common
soldier's duty to care for his weapons, as much among Terrans as
among the Troop. More, the familiar task would soothe the Rifle,
who must know as well as Nelirikk did that he was a single soldier, surrounded on all sides by those not of his troop, who had no
reason to trust him.

No, thought Nelirikk, sitting on his own bunk, a piece of fan-
cywork in his hands, the Rifle was not his most pressing problem.
His problem was Hazenthull Explorer.

She had argued against Daav yos'Phelium's order that she
bunk with her troop, leaving her senior alone and vulnerable, in
the care of those who had been their enemies. It spoke much for
the abilities of the scout's father, that he had been able to enforce
his will and see his order carried out, however reluctantly, while
raising neither his hand nor his voice.

Now, denying herself the simple solace of caring for her
weapons—or even of sleep, though he could read exhaustion in
the muscles of her face—Hazenthull Explorer, dressed and ready

for combat, prowled the quarters from end to end and corner to corner.

On her third circuit Diglon Rifle looked up from his task, tension growing. "Explorer?" he said, respectful and soldierly. "Duty?"

Hazenthull checked.

Head bent above his work, watching from the side of his eye, Nelirikk saw her understand the danger. Surrounded by those who had defeated them in battle, oathbound to a Liaden, soon to offer oath to another—it was unthinkable that these things be so. And yet, incredibly, they were so. It was the duty of command to accept these impossibilities as commonplace, with no breath of unease. For the good of the troop—large or small.

So. "At ease, Rifle," she said, firmly, but not too firmly.

Comforted, he saluted, and returned to his weapon.

From the corner of his eye, Nelirikk saw the explorer take a breath, turn cleanly on her heel and walk down the room, to where he sat, setting careful stitches in the gift he was making for Alys Tiazan.

For seven or eight heartbeats, she stood over him. Nelirikk continued his work without looking up. At last, she moved soundlessly back, folded her legs and sat on the floor before him. He raised his head and met her eyes.

Surrounded by the tattoos describing her honors and accomplishments, her eyes were dark brown; the shade, Nelirikk thought, of his captain's favorite beverage. She jerked her chin at his hands. "What work?" she demanded, in the tongue of the Troop.

Nelirikk smoothed it on his knee before holding it up for her to see. Her eyes widened as she recognized the device he was working into the patch—the device of the troop that had broken the back of the Fourteenth Conquest Corps.

"There is a young soldier in the House of the captain," he said, also in the Troop tongue, "who is worthy of this."

Hazenthull's mouth thinned. "Soldier."

Nelirikk returned to his work, plying the needle with care. "As much as I am. Or you are." He glanced up, switching to the dialect of explorers, in consideration of Diglon Rifle's comfort. "Why do explorers march with common troop?"

Her eyes shifted. "Command had left planet. We fell in—"

Nelirikk tied off the green thread. "I meant," he said, interrupting her ruthlessly, "why were explorers fighting alongside common troop?"

She glared at him. "That is for the senior to tell."

As chain of command went, she was correct, Nelirikk allowed, threading his needle with crimson. It was . . . useful . . . that soldierly behavior made it impossible for Hazenthull to answer a question she would rather not; explorers not being always at one with soldierly behavior. Still, Nelirikk did not begrudge her the stratagem.

Needle at the ready, he glanced up.

"The captain will require things. Things that run counter to the order you know." He moved his head, a short jerk toward the busy Rifle. "Far out of the order that one knows."

Hazenthull sighed. "She will take us out of context," she said, sounding as weary as she looked. "She is fortunate. Half her work has been done for her."

For what context was there, Nelirikk thought, for being abandoned to the enemy—the *victorious* enemy—while Command ran to save itself? He bent a moment to his work, concentrating on keeping his stitches small and even.

"The captain will require that the *vingtai* be erased." He raised his head again, giving her a plain sight of his naked face. "As you see. The healing units have an erasure program." He stopped short of telling her that the procedure was painless, though that was the truth as he knew it. Acquiring *vingtai* was excruciating; it seemed somehow wrong that they could be effortlessly and painlessly wiped away during the course of one brief sleep inside the healing unit.

"The captain requires this because her troop is the enemy of Yxtrang," Hazenthull said slowly, working out the process of Command's thought, as explorers were taught to do. "Soldiers who think they are Yxtrang, who wear the rank marks and hold the traditions of the Troop, will not fight strongly against Yxtrang." She frowned.

"Explorers can backtrack the captain's thought and understand the requirement. But, he—" she cocked her head toward her Troop—"he is only a Rifle. He will not understand."

"You are second in command," Nelirikk told her ruthlessly. "It is your duty—or the duty of your senior, if he is able—to make him understand. I suggest that the best strategy is to lead by example." He saw her draw a sharp breath, but did not allow her to speak.

"Captain Miri Robertson does not accept mediocrity. She expects superior performance. Occasionally, she demands more. You will adapt—"

"Or die," Hazenthull snarled, as if it were a challenge, and not a truth they both knew in their bones.

"Or die," Nelirikk repeated, calmly.

Hazenthull looked down, possibly at her hands, folded tightly together on her knee.

"The senior . . ." she began, and paused, throat working. "Protocol linked us, junior and senior—you know how it is done. Before it did, he had been twice across the sea of stars, marking many worlds for the future conquest of the Troop."

"He brought much glory to the Troop," Nelirikk said, when he had set an entire row of stitches and she had not spoken again.

"Much glory . . ." she repeated. "I am junior to him in all ways—in glory, in knowledge, in understanding. When the order came down that we should accompany the Fourteenth as . . . when we had the order, he first sharpened his grace blade, and had me sharpen mine, and while we sat together over this task that we hold in common with all soldiers, from creche to command, he talked to me of battle. He said that a soldier must always be prepared to die, that—that duty demanded that the death not be wasted, but served the living good of the Troop." Another silence, not as long as the first, then a rapid burst of words.

"The senior—that he has not received the Starburst—regardless, he is a Hero. To allow him to . . . just die, when Command had betrayed us, would be to go against everything he had taught me. It is not to the good of the Troop that such a soldier die, uselessly and in defeat, when there is so much more . . ."

From outside the door came the sound of the corporal's voice, issuing challenge.

"Scout Captain Daav yos'Phelium," came the reply.

Hazenthull came to her feet, face toward the door, muscles betraying eagerness. Nelirikk put his work aside and had also risen by the time the scout's father entered.

His face was bland, his muscles betraying nothing more than a reasonable alertness, yet Nelirikk felt compelled of a sudden to move within restraining distance of Hazenthull Explorer.

The scout paused, and looked up into Hazenthull's face, his hands folded together at belt level.

"I'm sorry, child," he said, in Terran. "He's dead."

DAY 307
STANDARD 1392

BLAIR ROAD
SUREBLEAK

It was Insurance Day in Boss Moran's streets, and Jim Snyder, the boss' new second-hand man, made it a point to hit the pavement early, collar turned up against the cold morning wind. He'd been third-hand man last Insurance Day and while the events of that day had resulted in Jim's elevation, he was determined to learn from the downfall of his predecessor.

And what he had learned, first and above everything, was that the boss expected Insurance Day to go easy and smooth, no problems, no short-pays, and no excuses.

Bosses in general were a touchy breed, which only made sense, when you thought about it. Bosses had all the responsibility of keeping order on their turf, collecting the insurance, putting the bouncers on the borders, setting the tolls—*and* seeing that collected tolls was turned in—it was a job of work being a boss, no argument there, and anybody who took it on, in Jim's opinion, had a right to be a touch irritable.

It could be that Boss Moran was a thought touchier than most. Jim couldn't precisely say: he'd been just a tad when Boss Tourin owned these streets, and Boss Randall hadn't lasted long enough to make much of an impression. Boss Vindal had held on a couple, four years—Jim'd run a toll-booth under Boss Vindal. It hadn't been bad; he couldn't off-hand remember her shooting anybody for shorting on the tolls. But, push come to shove, maybe she hadn't been such a good boss, 'cause when the smoke cleared off their meeting, it was Boss Moran standing and the late Boss Vindal being carted off to the crematory.

Sometimes, all the fatcats would meet on neutral ground and rework the boundaries, trading around this business street for that manufacturing block. It was important to have a strong boss protecting your interests when that happened—even though it hadn't happened lately. Give her a couple beers and Jim's Aunt Carla could tell stories that would raise your hair right straight up on your head, about the days when *she'd* been just a tad and lived on Boss Henrick's turf. That was before the fatcats had one of their meetings. Boss Tourin had got made at that meeting, and everything from Blair Road over to Carney—part territories from Boss Henrick and Boss Tiede—got swopped out and called his turf. There'd been a period of shakedown, and one of the bosses— Aunt Carla switched between Henrick and Tiede when she told it, depending on how much beer she'd had—got to thinking he'd been cheated when he sat down after the meeting to do the math. Lot of guns on the streets back then, as Aunt Carla had it, and the crematory'd done real well.

But they didn't have them kind of problems no more. Not on these streets. Boss Moran had held the turf for going on three years and if he occasionally shot his second-hand for a minor screw-up in addition, or made a public example of some shopkeeper who'd got behind on his insurance payment—well, that showed he was a strong boss. And you needed a strong boss to protect your interests, else some other boss would make a move on the turf—and there wasn't no percentage for anybody in that.

First stop on the morning was Wilmet's grocery. Jim opened the door with a shove, and the bell hung on the wire overtop clanged in protest. Old Wilmet came hurrying out from the back, and stood twisting his fingers together while Jim made a leisurely circuit of the place, on the spy for any improvements to the premises, or new equipment. He helped himself to a pretty good apple, and kept on inspecting, 'til he'd eaten all the fruit expect the brown spots. He dropped the core to the floor and nodded at Wilmet like he'd just noticed him.

"Insurance Day," he said, hooking his hands in his belt. He saw the other man's eyes dart down, following the motion, saw him look real hard at the gun on Jim's belt, before he looked up and nodded, quick and sort of jerky.

"So it is," he said, and his voice sounded a little jerky, too, Jim thought. That was good. It was important that the streeters kept a healthy respect for the boss—and for the boss' 'hands.

Making a show about it—stretching it out just a little—Jim reached into his pocket and pulled out the Book. The grocer was looking a little gray around the mouth. Jim licked his finger and leisurely leafed through to the right page. It took him a couple minutes to review the payment schedule—Jim could read, but it wasn't a strong point—nodded, and looked up. The grocer was sweating now. Jim let himself smile on one side of his mouth, like the boss did when he wanted to make you squirm. Useful tactic; and Jim knew personally that it worked a treat.

"So," he said to Wilmet, "'at's twelve, cash, this month, and the boss'll have the rest in chocolate, sugar, 'toot, and pot meat. Case lots—you know the play."

The grocer's face was so gray now that Jim kind of wondered if the man was going to pass out. He did pull a stained rag out of his pocket and mop his forehead with it.

"Twelve cash, sure, yeah. Just a sec." He scurried into the back. Jim helped himself to another apple, not as good as the first one, but the best he could find in the basket.

Wilmet was back, bills clutched in his hand, and counted them out, one through twelve, right there between the carrots and the potatoes.

"The kid'll take the goods to the boss' house," he said, looking down at his money. "Everything delivered before lunch, Mr. Snyder."

Jim nodded, dropped the unfinished apple to the floor, fished the pencil out of his other pocket, and made a tick-mark on Wilmet's page. Then, he put the book and the pencil away, picked up the cash and stowed it in the folder the boss had given him, slid that away, gave the trembling grocer a cheery nod.

"You're covered 'til next month, Wilmet. Profit to the boss."

"Profit to the boss," the man repeated, at a whisper.

Jim grinned and strolled out, slamming the door so hard the bell tore off its wire.

By mid-morning, Jim had called on and collected from all the streeters listed in the Book, except for the hardware store, which he'd deliberately left 'til last because it was just a couple doors up from Tobi's, where he figured he'd grab a bite and a brew before taking the day's receipts back to the boss.

In no real hurry, feeling kind of warm and peaceful in the pit of his belly, Jim strolled 'round the corner, heading on down to the hardware store.

Something bright and colorful pulled at the edge of his vision and he glanced across the street, expecting to see maybe one of Audrey's Scarlet Beauties, out on an early job.

What he did see rooted his feet to the ground and left him staring.

It was—a store. Jim guessed it was a store. But it was like no other store he'd seen in his life. The big front window was not only unshuttered, it was clean, so you could see right into the brightly lit insides, and count—one, three, eight, nine, *twelve* rugs, some hanging around the walls, some laying down on the scrubbed plastic floor. Rugs in colors Jim had no name for. Rugs woven in patterns so complex his eyes crossed trying to look at them.

As if that big, bright, risky window wasn't enough, the door to the joint stood wide open and a thin little rug showing vines and flowers in dark red, bright blue and yellow was laying half on the store's floor and half on the crumbling walkway, where anybody who went into the store would walk on it. Standing just inside the doorway was a man Jim might have mistaken for one of Audrey's, if he'd seen him maybe at Tobi's: dark-haired and on the short side, almost girl-slender, he was dressed in a pretty blue jacket, with a gleaming white shirt under it. His britches were a darker blue than his jacket and fell smoothly to the break of his shiny black boots. He was standing with his hands behind his back, gazing out at the street as if the view of the crumbling tarmac and shuttered, dusty storefronts was—interesting.

Looking at him, Jim found himself counting backwards, trying to remember exactly when he'd changed his shirt last.

As if he'd felt the incredulous weight of the stare on him, the little man looked up, meeting Jim's eyes across the street. Jim clamped his jaw and glared, so the guy would know he was lookin' at somebody important on the turf.

The little man—he sort of bowed, inclining from the waist an inch or two, then turned and walked into his store.

His impossible store.

•   •   •

"**How** the sleet long has *that* been there?" Jim demanded of Al, the hardware guy, a couple minutes later, jerking his thumb over his shoulder in the general direction of the rug store.

Al shrugged. "Couple days."

"Couple *days*?" Jim boggled, remembering the storefront as he had last seen it—empty, 'course, its previous occupant having been a streeter Boss Moran had used as a public example, three, maybe four Insurance Days ago. As third-hand man, Jim had been in charge of the clean-up crew that stripped the joint—shoe store, it had been. He remembered, now. He glowered at Al, trying to regain some of the vanished feeling of warm accomplishment.

Al shrugged again, and looked up at the ceiling, like maybe the date the rug store had opened was written on one of the blackened beams above Jim's head.

"Yeah, let's see. Day before yesterday, him and the big guy come in right while I was opening. Needed board, hammers, nails, paint, brooms, soap, buckets, wet mops, cleaning cloths, heavy gauge wire—didn't I have a time digging that out!—and a buncha eye-hole bolts. Talked soft, paid cash. Went back over there and started in. Looked out around lunchtime and they had the shutters off the window and he was out there with a wet mop an' a bucket of soapy water, scrubbin' away. Heard some hammerin' from inside and saw a couple of the extras in and out—guess he had 'em runnin' errands for him. Anyhow, they was still at it when I locked up. And when I come in yesterday morning—well, there it was, just like you see it now, and the big guy, he was out front sweeping the sidewalk."

Sweeping the sidewalk. Jim closed his eyes.

Now, strictly speaking, the situation was out of his hands, the rug store not being notated down in the Insurance Book. Jim having come up through Toll, instead of Insurance, he'd never even seen a store set up, much less done it himself. But one of the couple hundred things that Boss Moran didn't have no patience with was 'hands who were light on *initiative*. Set a high price on initiative, did Boss Moran, and as Jim was as eager to show well to the Boss as he was to *not* follow the previous second-hand man to his final ash-pile, he considered that he had no choice but to cross the street after he had concluded his business with Al, and demonstrate to the fancy little man in his pretty blue jacket just *who* was a big dog on the turf.

So thinking, he pulled out the Book and read off Al's premium—fifty, cash, and nothing in goods. Al pulled the bills outta his drawer and paid without comment.

Jim made the tick-mark in the Book, folded it and the pencil and the money away, turned—and turned back.

"So, what's his name?" he asked.

Al shrugged for the third time on the visit, trying for deadpan, but Jim thought he saw the man smile.

"The big guy calls him 'boss'," he said.

The bright-lit showroom was empty when Jim swaggered in through the open door a couple minutes later. He had just enough time to figure out that the big rug hanging on the back wall showed a bunch of naked people, doing things to each other that Jim felt pretty confident even Audrey's Specials hadn't mastered, when it was pushed aside, revealing a doorway and the pretty man entering the main room with a slight smile on his face.

"Good morning, sir!" he said, and his voice was soft, like Al'd said it was, but clear, for all of that, and not at all jerky. "Doubtless you have come to take advantage of our grand opening sale."

Jim stared at him hard, and hooked his hand in his belt near the gun. The man glanced at the gun, but didn't seem exactly bothered, which a man who was naked—that is, who wasn't carrying—really oughta been. Up close, his blue jacket showed a nubbiness that Jim vaguely associated with silk, having seen a silk pillow upstairs at Audrey's, once. The shirt beneath was white enough to hurt a man's eyes, and he was wearing a blue stone in one ear—it matched the color of his jacket.

"In what way may I serve you?" he asked, and there was something funny about the way he talked. Not that he was hard to understand, or anything like that, but there was a smooth kind of feel to the way he said the words, like he'd carefully polished each one and taken all the burrs and sharp edges off.

Jim frowned and did his best to harden his glare.

"It's Insurance Day," he said. "You owe Boss Moran for the month."

The man inclined his head, gravely courteous. "Thank you, but I have my own insurance." He moved a hand that glittered from the big ring on his second finger, showing Jim the clusterfuck rug. "I see that you have some admiration for this specimen here. Now, this is a very interesting carpet, of a type not normally found beyond the world of its weaving."

Following him to the back wall, Jim stared up at the frolicking people. "Why not?" he asked.

"Ah, because they are done as penance, you see. The weaving of the carpet is imposed by the temple upon adjudged sinners, who are required to weave in an open square, where all may see them and know their shame. After the carpet is completed—and a value affixed to it by the temple—the penitent is required to purchase it and display it in the public room of their home for the rest of their life. So, you see how rare it is to come across one of these. Look!" He lifted the edge of the rug, and turned it over to display the underside.

"See these knots? One hundred twenty to the inch! Truly, sir, this is a carpet that will give you many years of enjoyment." He flipped the edge right-side-up and ran his fingertips over the projecting backside of an amazingly curvaceous lady.

"Feel this nap. Imagine walking barefoot on this carpet."

Jim extended a hand—and jerked it back, pulling his glare on, big-time.

"I ain't here to buy no rugs. This is Insurance Day. You're on Boss Moran's turf and you owe on the month."

"No, no, please," the little man said, rubbing his fingertips over the lady's bottom once more before looking up at Jim. "Put yourself at ease on that account, sir. My insurance is entirely adequate." He moved a hand, drawing Jim's eye to the corner of the room. Jim looked—and blinked.

He thought he knew every pro gun in the surrounding three territories, but she wasn't nobody he'd ever seen before. Not all that much taller than the guy, she was slim, except for some really interesting curves, her skin dusky and soft looking. She wore a dark vest, dark shirt and dark trousers. A pistol with silver-chased grips showed in the holster on her belt—and she stared at him outta black eyes as cold and as pitiless as a dead winter night.

It took some effort to look away from those eyes and back to the guy, but Jim managed it.

"Boss Moran don't let nobody else sell Insurance on his turf."

The man inclined his head. "I understand. There is no difficulty. This lady is in my employ."

What that had to do with the way business was done, Jim couldn't have said. He was beginning to think maybe the little guy was a couple snowflakes short of a blizzard. Not that it mattered. Insurance was Insurance, and it had to be paid, every first of the month. That was how business was done under Boss Moran, no exceptions, no problems, no short-pays, and no excuses. Unless somebody had an ambition to be made a public example of.

Any case, the situation was outta Jim's hands. He'd tried—even the boss would have to admit that—and done as much good as anybody could, trying to reason with a nut-case. It was up to the boss to decide what to do with the little guy now.

Jim frowned regally down at him. "I'll be reporting to Boss Moran right after I leave here," he said. "You got a present or something you wanna send along?"

A good present—say, something along the lines of that amazing rug on the back wall—might actually help keep the boss' temper down to a non-life-threatening level. Which you'd think even a nut-case could figure out.

Not this one, though. He wriggled his shoulders under his pretty blue jacket and murmured.

"Alas, I have nothing that would be . . . appropriate, I think." Jim shook his head.

"OK," he said, ominously. "If that's how you wanna play it, it ain't no skin off my butt."

It struck him that this was a pretty good exit line, so he did, stamping hard on the little rug in the doorway. Once on the sidewalk, he turned right, toward the boss' place, rather than going down to Tobi's for lunch, like he'd planned.

Somehow, he wasn't real hungry.

From behind him came a sound remarkably like a hiss. Pat Rin turned and looked at Natesa, both eyebrows up in inquiry.

She shook her head, black eyes snapping.

"There was no need to provoke him."

"No? But, as I understand it, our whole mission here is one of provocation, with violence as the pay-off."

That Natesa knew this, he had no doubt. They had planned as best as they were able, choosing the victim and the turf with care. For Pat Rin to succeed—for his Balance to succeed—he must establish himself as a power—a "fatcat"—and the territory he annexed must be on the Port Road.

There were two paths by which one might arrive at the pinnacle of fatcat. One might, for instance, perform a service for an existing boss which required territory and status to balance it. This was a potentially bloodless path, but time-consuming.

Natesa herself had argued, persuasively, for the quicker way—elevation by assassination. This was the traditional path, and one of the primary sources of Surebleak's multitude of ills. Cheever McFarland had offered it as his opinion that the sooner Pat Rin established himself, the quicker the real job could get done, which had also been persuasive—and so Pat Rin had allowed himself to be persuaded.

Now, however, the Juntava appeared to be having second thoughts. Pat Rin spread his hands, averting his gaze from the false glitter on his left hand.

"We will shortly have callers, if all goes according to plan," he said, softly. "We have provoked, wisely or no, following the plan—wisely or no. If you have found a flaw in my intentions, now is the time to speak."

For a moment, Natesa stood silent, her eyes on his face. Then, she bowed in the mode of student to master.

"I would ask that you not expose yourself," she said, slipping into High Liaden. "Master, it is not needful. There are Mr. McFarland and myself to receive and . . . entertain . . . these callers."

"Ah, I see. My oathsworn are expendable, but I am not."

Again, she bowed. "Master, it is so."

"I disagree," he returned, his tone rather more acidic than the mode allowed. He sighed, and moved his hand soothingly.

"Come," he said, going back into Terran, "let us not argue. The trap has been set, and we as much as Boss Moran are caught in its unfolding."

She appeared to consider this, sleek head slightly to one side, then shrugged.

"As you say." Light as a dancer, she glided out of her corner, using her chin to point at the rug hanging on the back wall.

"Is the manufacture of this carpet truly as you described it to the boss' hand?" She asked.

"Of course," Pat Rin said, walking toward it with her. "Surely, you don't think I would misinform a customer regarding the value of his potential purchase."

"But . . ." her brows pulled together. "How did—it come to be at Bazaar?"

"I suspect that someone who did not like warmth retired from the kitchen," he murmured, extending his hand to sample the pleasant nap again. "I paid a cantra for this carpet. Were we selling out of Solcintra—and with certification from a merchant more experienced than myself . . . There are customers of—that I know, who would offer twenty cantra, sight unseen—not because of its subject matter, but because of its rarity." He moved his shoulders, considering what he had thus far seen of Surebleak. "Here, we will be fortunate to recover our cantra."

He stood for a moment, the Juntava—his oathsworn—at his side, considering the thing that had come to him, over the weeks of their association, weighing his necessity against the likelihood of erring against custom. He had performed this exercise more than once, over the last few days, and had learned that his necessity was greater than his natural wariness of Juntavas custom.

So.

"I am doubtless lacking in courtesy," he said, very gently, "but I wonder if you will tell me your name."

Beside him, he felt her shift, and quickly turned to face her, schooling himself so that he neither stepped back nor went for his weapon, but only faced her, and met her eyes, equal to equal.

Her face was composed, her eyes bottomless.

"You know my name, Master," she said, matching his gentle tone.

"I believe I know your gun name," he replied, wondering at the strength of his need to know this thing. "I ask that you honor me with your personal name."

There was a brief silence; the composure of her face unbroken, then, a quiet, "Why?"

He inclined his head. "I hold your oath, which means that I have certain obligations toward you. As I am certain you know. The path we embark upon is chancy. Should there be need, I would wish to . . . properly inform your kin."

"Why, as to that," she said, lightly—too lightly. "You need merely inform the Juntavas that Sector Judge Natesa, called The Assassin, has ended her career under conditions described here-under." She extended a hand, as he had done, and stroked the nap of the Sinner's Carpet. "To file such a report is to fulfill your obligation as oathholder, completely and with honor."

So he was rebuffed, Pat Rin thought, as he might have known he would be—and very gently answered in his impertinence, too.

"Very well." He bowed slightly, to show that the subject was closed. "Will you join me in a cup of tea before our visitors arrive?"

•   •   •

Boss Moran counted the take while he listened to Jim's report. He put the bills down when Jim got to the sudden new store and the streeter who had his own Insurance, and sat staring at him, his face starting to take on that purple tinge that meant somebody, somewhere, was gonna get hurt.

"Who's the Insurance?" he asked; Jim shook his head.

"Don't know her. Pro, though." He frowned, trying to remember what the little guy'd said.

"Told the streeter he couldn't buy nobody else's Insurance, but he said everything was warm, 'cause she worked for him." Jim remembered something else. "Hardware guy says the rug-man's 'hand calls him 'boss'."

"Yeah?" The boss' face was the shade it had been when he'd up and shot his former second-hand, his eyes all glittery and narrow. Just about the time Jim started to have some serious concerns about the length of his own lifetime, the boss slammed both hands down flat on the table and shouted for Tony.

Jim relaxed. Tony was head of the publicity committee.

The pretty little man—and his pretty little store—was about to become a public example.

Five of them walked across the red-yellow-and-blue rug and into the brightly lit store, Jim and Tony first, then the boss, then Veena and Lew. Barth and Gwince took up position outside, showing serious weaponry.

The store was empty, just like it had been earlier in the day. The boss looked around, walked over to the rug hanging on the right-hand wall, picked up a corner, and let it drop.

"Rugs," he said, and shook his head. "How much is he sellin' these things for?"

Jim bit his lip, suddenly aware that not having asked the little man this question demonstrated a lack of initiative on his part. He was about to blurt out a number—four hundred cash seemed expensive enough—but the smooth, rounded voice of the streeter who owned the joint cut him off.

"That particular carpet is a little worn toward the center, as I am sure you have noticed," he murmured, walking forward with his empty hands in plain sight. "However, such wearing must not be thought a defect, rather, it is a badge of authenticity. We do, of course, have its papers on file. So, this carpet," he extended a hand and stroked his palm across the material, like he was gentling a restless dog. "This carpet, I am able to sell to you for one thousand cash."

"One thou—" Boss Moran stared at the little guy, who stared right back, cool as a water-ice despite the presence of five armed people, any one of whom was bigger, heavier and meaner than he was.

"You know who I am?" the boss asked. The guy moved his shoulders in that snaky shrug of his.

"Alas. However, I feel certain that you are about to tell me."

"Damn straight." The boss used his extended fingers to hit him, hard, in the shoulder. "I'm Moran. I'm the boss from Blair clear on over to Carney. You set up on my streets, you follow my rules. Got that?"

"I confess to having had a similar tale from this gentleman, here—" The hand sporting the big, flashy ring swept gracefully towards Jim. "I believe he also wished to sell me insurance. I was unfortunately not able to accommodate him, as I have my own insurance, which is entirely adequate to my needs."

"You set up on my streets, you take my Insurance," the boss told him, and brought a rolled weed out of his pocket. He snapped his fingers and Jim jumped forward to light it with the industrial strength flame-stick the publicity committee had loaned him.

The boss drew in a deep lungful of smoke and blew it down into the little man's face. Give the guy credit, Jim thought, remembering his first face full of the boss' smoke, he didn't flinch and he didn't cough, though he did fold his hands, neatly, in front of him.

"Could be you don't understand about Insurance," the boss was saying, conversational-like. "Lemme 'splain it to you." He waved the weed at the thousand-cash rug, its business end hovering above the cloth by no more than a baby's hair. "Now, see, without Insurance, somethin' terrible might happen to your stock here. You got nice stuff—it'd be too bad if it all burned up, say, in a fire."

The little guy inclined his head. "Thank you, I understand the concept of insurance very well."

"Good," said the boss. "That's good. But there's worse things could happen, if you wasn't to have Insurance. You—you could get hurt. Happens alla time—guy falls, breaks his leg. Or his neck." He brought the weed up and had another long draw. The smoke this time missed the little man's face, though Jim couldn't have exactly said how—or when—he'd moved.

The boss looked around, eyes squinted at the rugs on the wall, on the floor, counting . . .

"I'm figuring your insurance payment is ten thousand cash. Per month. You can pay Mr. Snyder, there."

The little guy spread his hands. "Regretfully, I must once again point out that I hold my own insurance, with which I am perfectly satisfied."

The boss nodded, looking serious. "Right, you did say that. Not a problem. Bring her out. I'll get rid of her for you."

"Ah." He turned his head slightly and spoke over his shoulder. "Natesa."

"Sir?"

Jim whipped around, staring—and sure enough, there she was, all in black, like before, the fancy gun glittering in its holster. Behind her, standing just in front of the clusterfuck rug, was a big, rugged looking guy, his arms crossed over his chest, eyes half-closed, looking slow and sleepy and stupid, like really big guys usually were. If he was armed, his vest was covering the weapon.

"Natesa," the little guy was saying, moving his hand to show her the boss. "Here is Mr. Moran. He represents himself as someone able to be rid of you."

"He is," she said composedly, "in error."

"Are you certain?" the little guy asked. "I wish us to be plain, Natesa. I had understood that our contract was exclusive. If I find that you are also in the employ of Mr. Moran, I shall be most displeased."

"I have never seen Mr. Moran in my life," the pro answered, still in that completely composed voice. "Nor do I wish to see him again."

The boss' face went purple, but he only nodded again, and said to her, real serious, "We can deal. Tony."

Tony was the quickest shot on the boss' staff. Jim saw him go for his business piece—and 'way too many guns went off.

There wasn't any time to draw, no time to really understand what had happened, before it was all over.

Jim was standing, arms held out from his sides. Natesa the pro was standing, too; her pretty pistol pointed at him. The big guy was standing, not sleepy-looking at all, holding a cannon in one hand, the business end covering the street door. The pretty man with the blue earring was standing, palm gun also pointed at Jim. There wasn't a mark on any of 'em—the little guy's jacket wasn't even wrinkled.

The publicity committee hadn't done so good.

Tony was on the floor at Jim's right. There was a neat little hole centered between his eyes. His gun was still in the holster.

Boss Moran—former Boss Moran—was in a heap under the rug he'd threatened to burn. His weed was crushed, like somebody'd stepped on it, a couple sad little curls of smoke twisting up from it.

Jim swivelled his eyes, made out an arm and a loose gun on the floor, which was probably all that was left of Veena and Lew.

"Your compatriots are dead, Mr. Snyder," the little guy said, and his voice was kinda breathless, like maybe he'd run a couple blocks. The gun, though, that stayed steady, and even if it hadn't, the pro wasn't havin' no trouble at all with her aim. "If you attempt to draw a weapon, you will join them. Am I plain?"

Jim licked his lips. "Yessir."

"Good. Now, I have a proposition for you—"

"Company," the big guy interrupted quietly. Jim turned his head cautiously, and saw Gwince in the doorway. It didn't take her long to figure out what'd happened. Jim saw her take stock of the three holding guns, her own pointed peaceably at the floor. She nodded at the big guy.

"Boss?" she said.

He jerked his head to the left. "He's the boss."

If Gwince thought she'd never seen anything in her life lookin' less like a boss than the fancy guy in the blue jacket, she didn't say so. Instead, she nodded to him, and said again, real respectful, "Boss. I'm Gwince." She frowned at the mess on the floor. "You want we should get rid of that for you?"

"Shortly, perhaps." The boss' voice was back on the smooth, not breathless at all. "First, however, you and your partner have a choice to make. Please bring him inside and close the door. Take care not to rumple my carpet."

"Yessir," she said, and leaned outside, keeping one foot in the store. "Hey, Barth! Boss wants ya!"

He came quick enough, which is how you stay alive in the employ of bosses, checked on the edge of the doorway, eyes flickering around the room while Gwince moved behind him, closing the door real slow, so as not to muss the boss' rug.

Gwince was no dummy, and Barth was some quicker than her. He wasn't in the room two heartbeats before he had the situation scoped and the little guy pegged, with a nod and a soft, "Boss."

"Barth," the boss returned, softer. Then, considerably sharper. "Please tell me if any of the deceased had kin."

Barth's forehead rumpled and he shot a look at Gwince. "Kin?"

"Family," the boss said, even sharper. "Brothers, sisters, mothers, fathers, children—anyone who valued them—and who will miss them, when they are discovered to be absent."

"Well . . . ," said Barth, "Tony had a girl, I think . . ."

"Not anymore," Gwince interrupted. "Smacked her around once too often, and she went and found somebody else to pay the rent." She frowned down at the bodies on the floor.

"Veena—unnerstand, I don't know if it's her or her money he'll miss—but she always sent some of her draw to her brother. Lew—" she shrugged. "Lew ain't got nobody that I ever heard about. The boss . . ." Her eyes flicked to the little guy's face. "Beg pardon, sir. I meant to say Moran—might be some of the other fat-cats'll miss him. I don't run at that level."

"I see," the boss said. "Do you know how to contact Veena's brother?"

"Yeah, I do. You want I should break the news to him?"

"Eventually, perhaps I shall. We will also wish to take her possessions to him and to discover the sum he was accustomed to receiving from her, so that a payment schedule may be arranged."

Gwince blinked. "Payment schedule? Boss, unless I read this wrong, Veena went down shooting at you and your crew, here."

"Indeed. She died in performance of her duty. Her pension shall be assigned to her brother, as her surviving kin. These others . . ." The boss glanced to Natesa, who inclined her head. "We shall publish their names in the newspaper, and also an announcement of the . . . change of administration."

"Newspaper?" Jim shook his head, keeping a careful eye on Natesa's gun. "We ain't got a newspaper."

"We did though," Barth said, excited. "Sleet, musta been eight, nine years ago. Only thing Randall did before Vindal come along and promoted herself was shut down the gab-rag and make the guy who owned the print shop into a public example. Vindal, she got busy with building up the border guards an' all . . ."

The boss held up a slim, pretty hand, his big ring glittering like something alive. Barth gulped into silence.

"Is there a printer in this territory?"

"Oh, well, sure," Barth said, nodding. "Sure, there is, Boss. Just she ain't never done a gab-rag, is all."

"But she may be able to adapt herself to the concept. Very well." The boss lowered his hand, and moved his eyes. "Mr. Snyder."

Here it come. Jim squared his shoulders and tried not to look at the pro holding the gun on him. "Yessir."

"I believe that you are a man who values his life, Mr. Snyder. Am I correct?"

It took Jim a second to figure out what he was hearing, but once he did, he nodded enthusiastically.

"Good. Then this is what we shall do. You and I are going into the back room. I will ask you questions and you will give me truthful answers. When my questions are satisfied, I will arrange for you to be escorted across the border."

Jim goggled. "You're sending me outta the territory?"

"I am. I don't wish to seem discourteous, but, since the two of us are dealing in truth, I must confess that you are not at all the caliber of citizen I wish to tenant my streets. However, you did not draw on us, and so you have earned your life. Conditionally."

The boss sure did talk a twist. Frowning, Jim worked out his meaning, and arrived at the theory that the new boss valued *initiative* just like the old boss had, and that Jim hadn't shown all that well.

"Hey, it ain't so bad over on Deacon's turf," Gwince said cheerfully. "You'll do just fine, Mr. Snyder."

Easy for her to say, Jim thought. Nobody was talkin' about throwin' her off the turf she'd grown up in. On the other hand, looking at Natesa's gun and cold, patient face, it didn't look like he had much of a choice.

"OK," he said to the boss, trying to sound like moving turf was nothing. "We can deal."

"I am delighted to find it so," the boss said, and pointed at the back wall. "Please go with Natesa. I will join you very soon."

Natesa moved her gun, inviting him to walk ahead of her. He did that, and the big guy lifted the rug away from the door so they could pass.

"Mr. McFarland," the boss said when the big man had dropped the carpet back across the doorway.

"Sir?"

"You will please ascertain if Gwince and Barth have value to my administration. If they do not, or if they choose not to remain in my employ, they may also be escorted to the border and passed without toll. If they wish to remain, and you find them valuable, please consider them attached to your department."

"Yessir," the big man said easily. "I'll get right on it."

"Thank you, Mr. McFarland," the boss said, and left them.

"OK," the big guy said. "My name's McFarland, like you heard. Which of you don't wanna stay on? Sing out, now; don't be shy."

Gwince looked at Barth and Barth looked at Gwince. They both looked at the deaders on the floor and then back to big Mr. McFarland. Neither one said anything.

"Right, then." He put his hand-cannon away in its holster and nodded at the floor. "First job we got is to clean out those pockets. Then, we'll straighten up and put everything back neat, the way the boss likes it."

"Yessir!" they said in unison, and in matching tones of relief, and moved forward to tackle their first job for the new boss.

The woman Gwince was the key that gained them entry into the late Mr. Moran's so-called 'mansion', much more than those on the ring retrieved for him from the dead man's pocket.

By the time Pat Rin had met and taken provisional allegiance from the house staff; spoken to the printer, hastily summoned from her shop, covered over with ink and ill-concealed terror, regarding the necessity of a newssheet and the contents of the first issue, which would—"yessir, Boss, no problem at all"—be available on the street tomorrow at no later than one hour beyond dawn; and located the boss' private office, it was dark on the—on *his*—streets. Natesa and Cheever McFarland were engaged in other parts of the house—Natesa on a "security check" and Cheever interviewing others of the staff. Well enough: duty awaited him as well.

The office was on the second floor, a dank and dismal chamber—cold, as it was cold everywhere on this wretched planet—the walls of which had once, perhaps, been painted white. The desk was rust-colored plastic, the filing cabinet was red plastic, the two chairs—one behind the desk, one in front of it—were blue plastic and yellow, respectively. The floor was also plastic, and in need of a scrubbing. The rug—for there was a rug in this room that otherwise showed him neither books, nor comm unit, nor teapot, nor potted plant, nor any other human comfort—the rug was nothing short of astonishing. Merely, it was a primitive of tied and woven rag, rectangular in shape, yet made with some artistry, so that it was cheerful without being over-bright; pleasant and easeful on the eye.

Pat Rin gasped, his vision suddenly clouded. There was someone—someone within the few ghastly blocks of this wretched, filthy city that he was now pleased to call *his*—someone of his people had heart enough to have produced a thing of beauty. He shook his head, banishing ridiculous tears, and walked, somewhat unsteadily, over to the file cabinet.

He pulled open the top drawer with difficulty, and stood staring, confronted not with a row of neatly labeled files, nor even a disorderly mess of papers. No, the top drawer of Boss Moran's cheap, unlocked filing cabinet was filled to capacity with cash of every denomination, mixed all helter-skelter, as if it had just been flung within, and the door slammed shut.

The second drawer held a similar outrage. The bottom drawer held coins.

Pat Rin closed it and straightened. *Idiot*, he thought. *Not even a safe?* Sighing, he crossed the room to the desk.

The blue chair was grubby, the plastic mesh seat stretched, the plastic legs bowed alarmingly. Pat Rin pushed it to one side.

There was a small book lying in the center of the desk; for one mad instant he thought he had discovered Moran's personal debt-book—but, there, Terrans did not keep debt-books. Most especially, he suspected, recalling his researches into the place—not to mention the tales he had from Natesa and Cheever—did the worthy citizens of the planet Surebleak fail of keeping debt-books.

He picked the thing up and opened it, frowning as he riffled the pages. Very quickly, he ascertained that what he held was Moran's Insurance Book, listing all the businesses in the territory, what they owed and what they had paid.

It was a singularly frustrating document, written with some blurred and blurry charcoal-like substance; the notations ranging from barely lettered to indecipherable. Pat Rin emerged from his study not much informed on the topic of the profit to be had from Insurance sales on Surebleak, and with a nasty ache over his eyes.

Sighing, he rubbed his forehead and deliberately sought out the cheery, unassuming little rug on the dirty plastic floor.

The pain in his head flared, and he was seeing—not the floor in the office of the vanquished Moran, but the floor of his store in the aftermath of the gunplay, the gleaming plastic surface littered with the bodies of—the bodies of his kin.

There—Anthora, her arm blown off at the shoulder; here, Shan, a pellet hole between his frost-colored eyebrows; there again! Quin, half of his face torn away—

Retching, Pat Rin raised his hands before his eyes, blocking out the horrific sight; and hearing again the pale-haired man's inflexible, emotionless voice: "Your kin are dead. Nova yos'Galan, Anthora yos'Galan, Shan yos'Galan, Kareen yos'Phelium, Luken bel'Tarda . . ."

There was a sound in the doorway, audible even over the voice of his enemy, chanting the names of his dead. Pat Rin spun, the gun coming neatly into his hand, and in one smooth motion, he raised it, aiming—

At Juntavas Sector Judge Natesa, called The Assassin.

It spoke well of her skill, that she neither went for a weapon nor drew his fire by assuming the attitude of prey. Merely, she paused in the doorway, black eyebrows arched above black eyes, and inclined her head.

"Master," she murmured in the mode of student to teacher. "It pleases me to find you so well guarded, as I was just now coming to scold you for deserting your oathsworn."

Pat Rin lowered the gun, heartbeat roaring in his ears, stomach roiling. He fussed over the placement of the palm gun in his sleeve, and answered her without looking up, in Terran.

"I had thought my oathsworn intent upon their own business."

"Certainly, Mr. McFarland and I were performing our various duties, to insure that the house would keep you safe," she said, keeping to the High Tongue. "Yet Mr. McFarland tells me he had left Gwince at your back."

Another word from her in the language of home and he would—he would do something irreparable. Pat Rin took a deep breath and found the courage to meet her eyes.

"If you please. I prefer to converse in Terran."

Something moved in the black eyes; she inclined her head before he could identify it and murmured, "As you wish."

"Yes." Pat Rin cleared his throat. "Gwince stood her duty well. When I had done speaking with the staff and with the printer, I dismissed her to her meal, and perhaps to her bed." He glanced away, resting his eyes cautiously on the rag rug. "She has taken losses today."

"To hear her tell it, perhaps not," Natesa said drily. "However, you may be pleased to learn that she rose to meet Mr. McFarland's expectations of her. It could not be expected that she would refuse a direct order from the boss, but she did seek out her department head to inform him of her dismissal."

"Whereupon you were dispatched to scold me," Pat Rin concluded, and moved his shoulders. "Well, I am pleased that Gwince proves herself able. But I do not intend to live with a constant guard at my back."

"Then you do not intend to live," she said, leaning gracefully against the doorframe and crossing her arms beneath her breasts. "I am disappointed."

He inclined his head, eloquently ironic. "I am, of course, grieved to hear it."

Natesa sighed, sharply. "Illuminate my error, that you draw on me twice inside a single conversation."

And it was not, he thought, her error, but his own. Error understood too late, with his feet irrevocably upon a path that demanded he deal violent death to people who had never heard of Liad, or Clan Korval, Plan B, nor even the Department of the Interior. People who had brothers. People who might live well for several years on the profit made in selling the piece of trumpery he wore upon his finger—provided they weren't murdered for gain in the meanwhile.

"I beg your pardon," he said to his oathsworn, being certain that his tone was inoffensive in offering the unaccustomed Terran phrase.

"That is no answer, Master," she chided, her eyes intent upon his face.

Indeed, it was not—and Natesa was wise enough in custom to know he owed his oathsworn more than pettishness and ill-temper. And yet, what might he tell her that would not reveal he who held her honor in his hands as the madman he undoubtedly was?

Sighing, he showed her empty palms. "I beg your pardon," he said again. "I—people have lost their lives today, for nothing more than my necessity. Shall my Balance go forth as it must, more will die—and those before ever I lay hand upon my enemy." He moved, suddenly restless, pacing 'round the desk to stand staring down at the rag rug. From Natesa he felt a vast patience, which soothed him oddly, and moved him to speak more fully.

"Balance—you understand that Balance *must* go forth. This—Department—must be answered."

"Certainly they must," she said, softly, from the doorway. "Your kin have died at their hands."

Almost, he laughed.

"Yes. But that is not why the Department must be stopped," he said to the rug and looked up to meet Natesa's eyes.

"I am old enough to know that Balance does not bring back the dead. If I murder worlds—slay the galaxy—yet my kin will not arise—" Tears, however, were arising, and he had been—must continue to be—very careful not to weep before his oathsworn. He closed his eyes, breathed deeply and calmingly, and again met Natesa's black gaze.

"However, Korval has—a contract. An ancient and explicit contract, which requires the one who wears this—" he showed her the ring on his finger, "to protect the population of Liad. Such assumptions as the representative of the Department of the Interior made, such policies and procedures as he revealed to me—Liad is in danger. If Balance does not go forth—and that with precision—innocents will be enslaved or worse." He found it somewhat easier to breathe, thus retracing the chain of duty and right action he had laboriously forged in the aftermath of the Department's . . . offer . . . to himself.

The silence stretched, not uncomfortably, then Natesa spoke in her quiet, sumptuous voice.

"I understand—and I thank you." She straightened, and stretched, cat-like and supple.

"Last seen, Mr. McFarland was attempting to convey the notion of *vegetable* to the cook," she said. "I doubt he succeeded, but it is not unlikely that we have some sort of meal awaiting us."

Food. Pat Rin's stomach clenched—and yet he must eat and remain healthy, so that he might see his Balance precisely placed. Once again, he looked up at Natesa.

"I have taken your point regarding the necessity of a guard. I bow to the wisdom of my oathsworn."

"Ah." She smiled. "We will endeavor not to leave you too often with strangers." She moved an arm, gracefully inviting him to precede her out of the room. "We mustn't keep the cook waiting."

There were vegetables—a mess of indeterminate green leaves boiled with a piece of fat. As a dish, it was a failure—even Cheever McFarland scarcely ate more than a forkful—yet at that it was not the worst of the offerings brought forth for the new boss' delectation.

The meat was old—a fact that the cook attempted to disguise by using a heavy hand with hot-tasting spices. Cheever didn't even manage a forkful there, and neither Pat Rin nor Natesa bothered to take a portion onto their plates.

On the other hand, the rice was quite good, and the butter not, as Pat Rin had certainly expected it to be, rancid. He satisfied himself with a plate of rice, well-buttered, smiling as he saw Natesa do the same. Cheever manfully worked his way through the table, a forkful here, a half-spoon there.

The choice of beverages were three: a uniquely undrinkable hot brew that the serving girl had whispered was, "Tea, Boss;" beer, which Cheever drank without gusto; and plain cold water. After one disbelieving sip of "tea," Pat Rin had water, Natesa again following his lead.

"What they're calling coffee ain't no better," Cheever said. "Worst excuse for 'toot I ever smelled in my life. Didn't even bother to try and drink it." He shook his head at Natesa. "We're gonna have to figure out something about provisions."

"Security first," she said, and he grinned at her, good-humoredly.

"Boss, this woman don't know how to live high. OK—security." His big face got serious.

"We ain't in too bad a shape, everything considered. The old boss put a high price on his hide, so we inherited some good systems." He used his fork to point at Natesa. "Not as good as she can do for us, but we don't got to be worried about being overrun while she's doing the upgrades. People . . ." He put the fork down and reached across the table to break off a piece of hard brown bread, the meal's other outstanding success.

"Got some decent people. What I mean by that is, they can be trained. Old boss doesn't seem to have made himself real popular with the hired-ons, so we're going in with them feeling grateful to us for doing them a favor. Gwince has the instincts of a pro. Barth's probably steady as long as we don't ask him to do too much work." He buttered his bread.

"Any one of 'em'll sell us out to a high bidder, 'course—that's the way they do business here. But we ain't gonna see a high bidder 'til folks catch their breath—longer, if we don't give 'em any reason to feel abused." He grinned. "Which Boss Moran also made real easy for us."

Pat Rin pushed his empty plate away and reached for his water glass. "How—" he began, and the door opened to reveal the doorman—one Filmin—and a young red-haired woman enclosed from throat to ankles by a tolerably good black velvet cloak. To her feet were strapped the daintiest of silver sandals.

"Girl's here, Boss," Filmin announced, and, obviously feeling that he had fulfilled his duty with utmost propriety, departed, closing the door loudly behind him.

The girl, rather quicker than Filmin, checked, her eyes sweeping the room. Pat Rin raised his hand, the ring glittering in the dull light. "I am the boss," he said. "May I know your name?"

Her eyes were ginger brown, her gaze straightforward and not at all afraid. "I'm Bilinda, Boss. From Audrey's House."

Audrey, so he had gathered from the excellent Gwince, was the owner of the most profitable business in Pat Rin's new territory. He thought that whorehouses were often so.

"I see," he said gently. "But, do you know, I did not request a companion for this evening."

"No, that's OK," Bilinda told him easily. "It's all written down on the schedule. I can write it out for you, if you wa—" She stopped, her rather pale face suddenly ablaze, and her gaze not quite—so fearless.

Pat Rin frowned at her, wondering what the difficulty might be, then recalled the unlettered entries in the book he had found above stairs.

"I can read," he told Bilinda, and saw the fear edge out of her eyes.

"However," he continued, "I am not thin of company this evening. Nor do I foresee a need to follow the former boss' schedule."

Bilinda frowned. "You don't want me?"

Pat Rin raised his hands soothingly. "It is a matter of business," he said gently, "and nothing whatsoever to do with you, yourself. I regret that I did not know of the existence of the schedule and thus exposed you to the dangers of traveling at night." He glanced at Cheever, who was sitting almost absurdly still.

"Mr. McFarland will escort you to Audrey's House. Also, if there is a fee—"

Bilinda blinked. "Fee? For me? Nossir, Boss. That's all part of the arrangement. This is how Ms. Audrey pays her Insurance." She hesitated, then said, rather breathlessly, "I don't mean no offense, but—if you ain't gonna hold with the arrangement, does that mean Ms. Audrey's outta business?"

Across the table, he heard a slight sound, as if Natesa had sneezed. Pat Rin gave the girl a slight frown. "That is between Ms. Audrey and myself." He inclined his head. "I apologize for the inconvenience, to yourself and to Ms. Audrey. Have a pleasant evening, Bilinda. Mr. McFarland?"

"On my way." Cheever came to his feet and grinned at the girl. "OK, Bilinda, time to go home."

There was, as the vernacular went, no percentage in arguing, which Bilinda was quick enough to understand. She gave Pat Rin a nod, and, on reflection, Natesa, too, and allowed Cheever to usher her out. The door closed—softly—behind them.

Pat Rin closed his eyes, abruptly very, very tired.

"Master?"

He opened his eyes. "I believe I will retire for the evening," he said with a languid wave of the hand. "The exertions of the day have quite exhausted me."

It was meant to ape the manner of the more insular and annoying High Houselings, but Natesa did not smile. Merely, she inclined her head and rose.

"I will escort you to your bedroom and make certain that all is secure."

Someone had been at the bedroom. Here, as nowhere else in Boss Moran's narrow, tawdry house, the floor was clean, the walls washed, the bed linens spotless. There was a rag rug akin to the one in his office next to the bed. He stood near it, watching Natesa make her circuit about the room.

When at last she was satisfied, she moved to the door, paused

on the threshold and inclined her head. "Master. Sleep well. One
of us will be close by."

"Do not cheat yourself of sleep to guard mine," he said, and
she did smile, then, by which he knew she would not obey him.

"Sleep well," she said again, and stepped into the hall, pulling
the door behind her. Within an inch of closing entire, the panel
paused, and her voice wafted to his ear.

"My name is Inas Bhar."

DAY 50
STANDARD YEAR 1393

LYTAXIN
EROB'S HOUSE

The breeze subsided so gradually she couldn't have
said when it quit completely. She noted its absence; in so noting
decided she had slept long enough—and awoke.

For a moment she lay, eyes closed, listening to the silence,
feeling the jubilant singing of blood through her veins, the sweet
passage of air through her lungs. She stretched, luxuriating in the
smooth slide of well-toned muscles. Sensuously, she stretched her
mind as well, reaching out in that undefinable, definite way, to the
pattern that was her perception of Val Con's self.

The pattern blazed with lucent purity, its byways and inroads
fully integrated, absolutely, entirely and unmistakably Val Con,
joyously intact. Throat tight with the beauty of him, Miri extended
herself and stroked him, raising a crackle of startled lust, and a
flicker of the particular bright green she understood to be laughter. Then, slowly—very slowly, as if relishing every instant of
contact, she felt his fingers stroke down her cheek, and across her
lips. Miri sighed, reached—and found him abruptly absent,
though she saw his pattern as plainly as she ever had.

Regretfully, she opened her eyes to Erob's sickroom. The wall
of medical gizmos was dark and silent, the tech's noteboard stand-

ing blank and ready in its place, though no tech was in evidence. Nor was there any sign of the large-ish green person known to them both as her brother Sheather.

Throwing back the quilt, Miri bounced out of bed and strode over to the door to check the lock. Locked, all right, and from the inside, too. She tried to figure out if that worried her, or ought to, then decided the hell with it: the door was locked from the inside, and Sheather, who had presumably arranged for that circumstance, was conclusively not in the room with her. Therefore, Sheather was on his own inside a Liaden clanhouse. That might've been worrisome, had the House in question not recently survived both a civil uprising and an Yxtrang invasion. At this stage in the proceedings, nobody was likely to get too upset about a little thing like a Clutch turtle wandering the halls.

Which, come to think of it, sounded a whole lot more entertaining than sticking around a deserted sickroom. She wasn't sick. If she'd ever felt better in her life, she couldn't at the moment recall the occasion.

She did feel a trifle grubby, which could be remedied by a shower, after which she intended to go for a walk, unless somebody came up with a compelling reason why she shouldn't.

Decision taken, she moved briskly—in the direction of the 'fresher, stripping off her nightshirt as she went.

The shift had thus far been quiet. Ren Zel had run routine systems checks, and done some general housekeeping. His mind did wander, now and again, to the impossibility of the cat in his cabin and the irrefutable evidence of that long, white whisker. At last, knowing what he would find, he pulled up the current roster of the pet library.

As he had expected, there were no cats currently on file in the library. Certainly, there was no ship's cat, free to wander the vessel, earning its passage by dispatching vermin. Useful as such creatures were, they had a tendency to get into unchancy places, resulting in fouled machinery and, more often than not, a dead cat.

And even if the *Passage* did harbor a cat, who had let the creature into his quarters?

He sighed and closed the roster.

It was a puzzle, certain enough, and the only other possibility that occurred to him was that a crew member had smuggled a pet aboard. Though how they had kept it secret from all was another, just as knotty, puzzle.

He sighed again and considered taking the whisker to the ship's Healer, to see what she might scry from it. Lina was a Healer of no small skill, her lack of success with himself having to do with some sort of 'natural shielding' that he possessed. He understood that this was not entirely unknown. Unhappily, the shielding prevented him being Healed of the nightmares of battle, and the pain of his dying. Though he thought he was healing of that last wound on his own, if slowly.

So, then, he thought. At shift-end, he would take the whisker to Lina. That was the best course, surely.

Someone had been kind enough to lay in a couple shirts in her size. The same someone, Miri supposed, newly showered and thoroughly air-dried, who had been forethoughtful enough to shine her boots and make sure that her leathers were clean.

The arrangements had a certain feel of Beautiful to them—the Compleat Captain's Aide, Miri thought with wry gratitude, sealing the cuffs of her shirt. She stamped into her boots, put her hand against the plate and left the dressing room. Half a step into the main room, she checked, turned and frowned at the man lounging in the chair next to the tech's station, his legs thrust out before him and crossed neatly at the ankle. He was dressed like she was, in working leathers, and boots buffed to a mirror finish. One irrepressible eyebrow rose at her frown.

"The door," she said, trying to sound severe, "was locked."

"It was," Val Con admitted. "And it is locked now. I hope you don't think me lax in such matters."

It took a major effort of will not to laugh out loud, which was, of course, what he wanted. Instead, Miri managed quite a credible sigh while she surveyed him.

He looked like his pattern, she thought—new-made and shiny; so beautiful it made a body's throat close up and her heart start acting funny. In fact, he looked miraculously well for a man she'd been told was going to have to devote some considerable time to relearning how to walk. Val Con raised his other eyebrow.

"Is there something wrong, cha'trez?"

"Depends," she said. "We having another one of those dream sequences?"

"Dream—Ah. Jelaza Kazone." He smiled. "I believe it safe to

assume that we are now both present in . . . contiguous reality." He tipped his head, considering. "Mostly contiguous reality."

"Mostly's more than we had last time," she allowed, drifting over to his side. She cleared her throat. "You don't happen to know where Edger and Shan are, do you?"

"Alas. Must we locate them immediately?"

She looked down into his face. "You got anything better to do?"

"Yes," he said. She saw familiar lightning weave through his pattern, and shivered.

"Yes, is it?" Her hand rose, not entirely on her order. Softly, she stroked the well-marked, mobile eyebrows, ran her fingertips along the high line of his cheek . . .

"Cha'trez?" His voice was not quite steady. Miri stroked his cheek again.

"Scar's gone, boss," she murmured, tracing the place where it had been.

"Many scars are gone. I am—Miri . . ." He took a hard breath. "Miri, let us make love."

"Here?" she asked, teasing him, like her own blood wasn't hot with desire.

He reached up and captured her hand. "Why not?" he murmured, and kissed her fingertips before slanting a glance of pure mischief into her eyes. "The door is locked."

It was the custom of Emrith Tiazan, Erob Herself, to take a turn or two through the atrium prior to seeking her bed. As this had also been the custom of her father who had been delm before her, the room's cycle had long been set opposite the day-night cycle of the outside garden, where the seedling of Korval's Tree held dominion.

Here, there were more convenable plants, mild-mannered and conducive of an easy sleep. Korval's Tree promoted madcap dreaming, of a kind unsuitable in an old woman who had lost a third of her House in the late warlike disturbances.

Alone with her thoughts and her dead, she ambled along the sweet-smelling ways, pausing now and again to admire the progress of certain favorites. Her shoulder muscles began to loosen under the suasion of the mock sunlight; her houseboots made a soft shuffling sound against the shredded bark path; the first notes from the singing waters wafted 'round the next curve, teasing her ears. Comforted by all that was gentle and usual, Emrith Tiazan's face relaxed into a smile.

She followed the path around, and the full song of the waters rushed to greet her. She paused, as she always did, face turned up toward the false sun, eyes closed in pleasure, before moving across the little stone bridge to her especial spot, a stone nook, surrounded by simple rock plants, enchanted by the joyous waters.

Which was this evening filled very nearly to overflowing by two large, green . . . things.

Emrith at first thought them twin boulders, brought in and disposed by some well-meaning but mad gardener. Then she saw the extended foreleg of the smaller, culminating in a three-fingered hand. She walked closer, discovering other details—beaked faces with nostril slits, horny green hides, and a shell-like substance partially encasing each large torso. Both appeared asleep. Or dead. Emrith Tiazan stared at them a long time, by her lights. She didn't even wonder where they had come from—to whose orbit, after all, did any of the strange, uncomfortable or dangerous oddities of the universe attach themselves?

Eventually, she sighed and did something that she had done only once before in this garden—she reached in her pocket and thumbed on the remote.

"My delm?" An Der sounded startled, as well he might, she thought, sourly.

"Find Shan yos'Galan," she said, striving for an appropriate calmness. "Bring him to the singing waters in the atrium. I believe I have found that which belongs to his House."

As agreed, the majority of their party waited in the side garden while Nelirikk went ahead to alert his captain to the presence of both scouts and recruits.

The hour was far advanced, and he was certain that the medical technician currently in a position of authority over the captain would find his visit unseemly. Had he been in pursuit of an Yxtrang commander in similar straits, Nelirikk would simply have put the technician aside and given his report; a soldier's duty came before all: illness, pleasure, sleep, or food.

Liadens held to another ordering of duties, and the necessities of soldiers were not always at the top of the list. Which is how it came to pass that a mere medical technician could order a captain.

Nor was it appropriate, according to the complex net of rule and custom in which Liadens ensnared themselves, for a captain's aide to lay hands on a med tech for the purpose of gaining his captain's side.

It was thus necessary to have a reason for speaking to the captain *at once* that the tech would accept as sufficiently urgent to disturb her rest.

Wrestling with this conundrum, Nelirikk turned a corner—and slammed to a halt, staring.

Two people were walking toward him—two people he had reason to know well. The woman was none other than his captain, who he had last seen that morning, lying pale and weak against pillows; med tech on the hover. The man was no one less than the scout himself, who certainly should not be walking—not so soon, if ever again.

Regardless, here they came, strolling hand-in-hand down the center of the hallway, to the uninformed eye, as vulnerable and as guileless as children. Nelirikk frankly stared.

"Hey, Beautiful," the captain called. "How was your walk?"

"Captain." He recalled himself and came to attention, saluting. "My walk was . . . interesting."

"Yeah? You didn't see any Clutch turtles, did you?"

Clutch turtles? Nelirikk managed to stifle the shiver, while fervently hoping never in his lifetime to see a Clutch turtle, enemy of the Troop, slayer of fleets.

"Captain," he replied, somewhat stiffly, "I have not. I have, however, seen scouts, and together we have—"

"Scouts?" the man murmured. "Are you certain?"

Nelirikk frowned. "Are there others among Liadens who walk silent and woodwise and arrive on-world in a scout class ship?"

"Actually," the scout said surprisingly, "there are."

Nelirikk thought about that, then looked to the captain, who was watching him out of ironic gray eyes.

"Two represent themselves as scouts: Clonak ter'Meulen, scout commander; Shadia Ne'Zame, scout lieutenant, first in. The third . . ."

He looked from gray eyes to green. "The third did not say he was a scout, though the others treat him as a peer—and at times defer to him. The lieutenant addresses him as 'captain'. He bears a Tree-and-Dragon—" he touched the matching symbol on his collar, "and gives his name as Daav yos'Phelium."

The scout's eyebrows rose. "Does he?" He glanced at the captain.

"Odds he's the genuine article?" she asked. He moved his shoulders.

"It would be difficult to fool Clonak, even at this remove; he and my father trained together. Later, he was a member of the survey team of which my father was captain. Uncle Er Thom said the two of them were great friends—even though Clonak had been in love with my mother." Again, he moved his shoulders, and smiled into the captain's eyes. "If it's *odds* you're after, my lady—then I am compelled to say that I have too little data and must see the man for myself."

"Sure you are," she said resignedly. The scout grinned and Nelirikk gave a start, the sense of wrongness about the other man's face crystallizing all at once. The green eyes moved, pinning him.

"Yes?"

"I—" Nelirikk cleared his throat. "Scout, your *nchaka* is—gone."

"Ah." The smaller man inclined his head. "The Troop remembers."

"The Troop remembers," Nelirikk affirmed and looked back to his captain.

"Captain. In addition to scouts, my walk produced recruits."

She shook her head. "The Irregulars are outta business; ain't taking recruits. Point 'em at Commander Carmody."

"Commander Carmody has given medical care, food and quarters, so winning himself a place in the camp-tales. However, if the captain pleases, these recruits will give their oaths and their weapons only to Hero Captain Miri Robertson, who vanquished the Fourteenth."

She sighed. "You're talking about *Yxtrang* recruits?"

"Tales of your prowess echo throughout the ranks of two armies," the scout murmured. "A hero to Yxtrang and mercenary alike, you—"

"Can it," she told him and frowned up at Nelirikk.

"How many?"

"If the Captain pleases. One Rifle and an explorer—two in total. The third—a senior explorer—has gone to glory's reward."

"Yeah? Two of you have an argument?"

"Captain. I had not the honor to know Gernchik Explorer before he died. He was wounded in a rear-holding action, to allow the officers time to escape. Seeing that his condition was serious, and unwilling to use the grace blade, his junior—Hazenthull Explorer—attached Diglon Rifle to her command, and marched the three of them here, to present their weapons and offer you their oaths."

"And to get her senior into an autodoc, quicktime." She nodded. "How's she taking his death?"

This was the joy of serving a captain wise in the way of the common troop. Nelirikk saluted. "Captain. She is at the moment . . . docile. Daav yos'Phelium gives it as his opinion that this condition might change, quickly and catastrophically."

"He does, huh? Then I hope you got her someplace where she can't do too much damage."

"Captain. She is in the garden attached to the side of this wing."

The captain blinked. She looked at the scout, who lifted an eyebrow.

"Nelirikk," she said, mildly.

He swallowed and came to full attention. "Captain."

"Have you lost your mind?"

"No, Captain."

"You're sure about that?"

"Yes, Captain."

"Right." She looked up at him. "You want to tell me what you was thinking?"

"Captain. It was the thought of Daav yos'Phelium that Hazenthull Explorer should be brought immediately to give full battle-oath to the captain. He fears that the interim oath he holds from her is not strong enough to bind, if her grief overcomes her reason. He was supported in this by the scouts."

"Daav yos'Phelium holds temporary oaths from an Yxtrang common trooper and an explorer?" she asked.

"Yes, Captain."

She shook her head and looked again at the scout. "This has got to be your father."

"He does appear to have something of the familial sense of humor." His face was bland.

"Is that what you call it?" She sighed. "What else, Beautiful? Might as well spill it all."

"Captain, there is no more. Your recruits await you, accompanied by scouts."

"The Irregulars're out of business," she repeated, but it was the scout she was speaking to. "I don't guess it would be good form for Line yos'Phelium to hold a private troop."

"There is," murmured the scout, "some precedent."

"Great. I suppose the House routinely hires Yxtrang soldiers to guard its piggy-bank. No—" she raised a hand—"*don't* tell me."

"As the captain wishes."

"No respect, that's your problem." She fell silent then, frowning at a space somewhere between Nelirikk's left elbow and infinity. Eventually, she looked up.

"OK. Get on back. We'll be there soon."

Nelirikk saluted. "Captain. Thank you, Captain."

"Think you'd know better than to thank me by now," she said, and her voice sharpened. "If the explorer decides her oath ain't binding, shoot her dead. If her trooper's reasonable, you can stop there and wait for me. If hell breaks, I expect you and the scouts to be standing when it's done. This is an order."

Nelirikk saluted once more. "Yes, Captain."

"Right. Get outta here."

Another salute and he was gone.

Miri waited until the sound of his footsteps had faded to nothing before looking into her partner's speculative green eyes.

"How much precedent?" she asked.

The child is going to break, Daav thought, stifling a sigh. Behind his eyes, he felt Aelliana stir, though she offered no comment.

To casual—that was to say, non-scout—eyes, Hazenthull was the picture of well-mannered docility. She sat where she had been directed, on a wide stone bench beneath a fragrant tree laced with fairy lights, Diglon Rifle at her side.

The garden was largely shrouded in night, pierced gently here and there by the spangle of decorative lights. Shadia was invisible between the bench and the outside gate, on the alert for trouble. Clonak had disappeared into the shadows nearer the house, guarding the door against the possibility of an Yxtrang rush.

As oath-holder, Daav occupied the position of greater peril, leaning against an artfully placed boulder directly before the stone bench occupied by his oathsworn. He crossed his arms over his chest, which put his right hand on the butt of the pistol riding hidden in his vest.

Gods, he thought, *I don't want to waste a scout.*

"Nor ought we to endanger the House." Aelliana's tone was more than a little acerbic, which was, Daav owned, no less than he deserved, who had placed Erob's House in peril by insisting upon this mad course.

If the captain comes quickly . . . he thought. Yes, and if Hazenthull could but hold scout-sense against the rising tide of rage—that the solution which was to have bought her senior's life had failed, leaving her and her dependent trapped and in the power of the enemy . . .

"She depended upon her senior to find the way clear, once he was healed," Aelliana said. "She did not plan fully."

How could she? He replied, reading the change in Hazenthull's muscles, malleable under the growing warmth of her rage. *His survival was the essence of her plan.*

On the stone bench, Hazenthull shifted, her muscles bunching as if for the charge. Daav's hand closed around the hidden pistol.

"Explorer." Unexpectedly, Diglon Rifle leaned forward. "Explorer, the captain comes."

She turned on him, face set in a snarl, and started badly when the house door snapped open, admitting the person—and the voice—of Nelirikk Explorer.

"Prepare for inspection!" he commanded, in the Yxtrang common tongue.

Diglon Rifle rose at once, marched over to the pool of light spilling from the open door and dropped into parade rest.

Hazenthull Explorer sat, as a woman turned to stone, staring, her face beneath the tattoo work beginning to crumble.

"Explorers kept discipline, when I was in the corps," Nelirikk said, acidic in the extreme, and then snarled, "Prepare for inspection!"

The command voice sent a little thrill even along Daav's scout-trained nerves. Diminished as she was, Hazenthull was in no condition to resist.

Sullen, but obedient, she stood, walked out into the light and assumed parade rest slightly in advance of Diglon Rifle, as befit her higher rank. Nelirikk placed himself to the right and slightly forward of both, eyes front.

Daav sighed and stood away from the boulder, hands at his

side, pistol nestled yet in its secret pocket, and wondered how soon the captain might arrive.

Wonder was speedily answered.

"Troop! Attention!" Nelirikk bellowed, and all three straightened as the empty doorway framed a slender woman in working leathers, her white shirt laced with silver cord, her red hair neatly braided and wrapped three times around her head, like the crown of a barbarian princess. At her back, not immediately noticeable, walked a man, dressed as she was, in working leathers, his shirt black, his hair dark.

Daav took a careful, quiet breath. *The scout, is it*? he thought. *Aelliana, behold our son.*

His vision slipped, the images going ghostly, as it did when she was actively using his eyes, rather than merely depending upon the data he gathered for both of them.

"A scout sublime," she murmured. "No more substantive than a thought, and the edges of him so sharp he fairly glows. Though I think that he would not be quite so invisible if his lady did not deliberately draw the eye to herself." She paused. "A formidable pair of children, to be sure, van'chela—and aptly joined, leaf and root." His eyesight blurred; became his own once more. "We may be proud."

Or terrified, Daav amended, and heard her laugh before she vanished from his awareness.

Straight up to the waiting troops walked the red-haired lady, and stood before them, hands behind her back, chin up. She took her time considering them; the man at her side glanced casually 'round the garden, unerringly picking out the positions of the three scouts.

Apparently satisfied with what she saw, the lady deigned to speak. "I am Captain Miri Robertson, field name Redhead." Her voice was firm, her Yxtrang slow, but robust, her accent, Daav noted wryly, neither native nor quite as ghastly as his own. "I am in command here. Lieutenant, present the recruits."

"Captain." Nelirikk saluted, showily, and barked out, "Candidate Hazenthull Explorer, stand forward for inspection!"

For a marvel, she did so, and saluted, somewhat faintly, her stance eloquent of disbelief as she gazed down upon a captain two-thirds her height and less than half her mass.

"Captain," she said, warily.

"Explorer." The captain's tone was cool.

"Candidate Diglon Rifle!" Nelirikk ordered. "Stand forward for inspection!"

He did, saluting with energy. "Captain!"

"Rifle." Slightly warmer, there, accompanied by an infinitesimal nod of the head. "Why do you want to enlist under me?"

"Captain." He saluted, looking bewildered, as well he might, thought Daav. *Why* was not the concern of mere Rifles.

"Captain, soldiers need command. We are . . . abandoned in place, without orders, except to resist the enemy until we die." He paused, brow furrowed, tattoos rumpling. "Captain, I would rather live than die."

Captain Miri Robertson, field name Redhead, smiled. "So would I." The smile faded.

"Hazenthull Explorer."

"Captain."

"Why do you want to enlist under me?"

There was a pause, possibly longer than was quite considerate of the captain's honor.

"Captain. Soldiers need command."

The captain shook her head, Terran-style. "But explorers—like scouts—chafe under too much command. As I well know." She paused, then snapped in full command mode.

"Explain!"

Hazenthull jerked, and saluted, hastily. "Captain. It was known that the Hero of the Battle for the Airfield had recruited an explorer. It was thought that such a captain might attach more explorers to her unit. The Fourteenth Conquest Corps has deserted us. Without command we are dead and without honor. Under a Hero captain we may serve with honor and die with glory. For the good of the Troop."

There was a small silence before the captain nodded. "Better." She glanced at the silent scout, perhaps gaining some information from his face that was invisible to Daav. She brought her gaze back to the two Yxtrang.

"Before I ask for your oaths," she said slowly, "I will tell you that the troop you came to join, the Lytaxin Irregulars, was a field troop, its ranks filled by survivors from the first wave of the invasion and a few old soldiers who had been separated from their home troops. Having done duty, the Irregulars have—honorably and without prejudice—been disbanded. The survivors have returned to rebuild their homes. The old soldiers, many of them,

have been reattached to their home troops, which came in as part
of the counterattack. Those who have not are temporarily attached
to mercenary units here. They will take transport when the mercenary forces lift and will rendezvous with their home troop out
of headquarters. Understand this. I hold rank as a captain of mercenary soldiers, commissioned by Commander Carmody himself,
but at this time, I have no command."

She paused. Neither recruit made a sound.

"In addition to my rank as captain," she continued, "I owe allegiance to a kin-group—Clan Korval. This kin-group has acquired a worthy and cunning enemy. In order to fight this enemy,
we will need soldiers. The sub-group Line yos'Phelium stands
ready to receive your oaths, if you wish to give them, but you
must understand that this service will be different. You will be required to learn languages other than the tongue of the Troop; cultural study will be required. I expect this of explorer and Rifle,
alike. Worse, you will serve not one captain, but the leaders of the
sub-kin-group, who are two and equal." She put her hand, palm
flat, against her chest; then likewise touched the man beside her.

"This is Val Con yos'Phelium Clan Korval. He is, among
many other things, a Liaden scout and my lifemate." She tipped
her head, and asked a question in Liaden. "Do you understand
'lifemate', Hazenthull Explorer?"

"If the captain pleases. As we are taught, it is an arrangement
of sexual convenience, with implications of exclusivity."

"Oh, my," Aelliana murmured.

She's young, Daav countered. *And I will own, my lady, were we
both embodied . . .*

"True."

The captain's eyebrows had lifted. She glanced at the man beside her.

"Hear that?" she said in Terran. "*Convenient.*"

He moved his shoulders. "The interpretation of custom is
uniquely subject to error, as even the most careful scholar will
confess."

Hazenthull stirred. "If the captain pleases," she managed in her
ragged Terran. "Does this mean that 'lifemate' is not a sexual ar-
chitecture?"

"In general, it is," the captain said slowly. "In specific, it's a lot
more. Nelirikk'll fill you in, and you can mince it up into Rifle-
size pieces. If you wanna go through with it, that is. I wouldn't

blame you if you didn't want to have nothing to do with swearing to Line yos'Phelium. Nelirikk can fill you in on that, too."

Hazenthull's eyes moved, questioning.

"The scout who stands beside the captain is of Jela's own blood," Nelirikk said in the tongue of the Troop. Daav saw Diglon start and lean forward, face intent.

"The Line the captain asks you to give oath to is the Line to which I have myself given oath. When the captain and the scout go against the enemy of their blood, I will be at their backs. If there is a place or a service of greater glory in all the galaxy, I have not heard of it."

There was silence. Hazenthull looked to Diglon Rifle, not as if she were seeing him, Daav thought, but as if she were weighing the burden on her soul. She sighed, and saluted.

"Captain. We came to offer ourselves and our weapons to Captain Miri Robertson. That has not changed. If a captain so wise in war will accept our oaths and weapons, we will serve her until our last bullet is spent."

The captain nodded, glanced aside—and Daav found himself pinned in a feral gray glance.

"If Scout yos'Phelium will relinquish the short-oaths he holds in my name, this man and I will take your oaths to Line yos'Phelium."

yos'Galan had been roused from his bed, Emrith Tiazan surmised, not without a certain satisfaction. Not that he was rumpled, misbuttoned, clumsy, or in any way unseemly; but the silver eyes were heavy, and the charade of the voluble fool was missing entirely. Indeed, one might almost say the bow he accorded her was . . . terse.

"Erob."

"yos'Galan." She inclined her head, merely, not bothering to rise from her seat on the edge of the stone bridge, and pointed at the giants slumbering in her quiet place.

"Those are yours, I believe?"

He sighed. "In fact, they are not, though they stand kin to my brother and his lifemate."

She sighed in her turn. "How else? Well, no matter. Korval's kin-lines are not mine to tend. Thank the gods. Remove them. Immediately."

The thin white eyebrows lifted. "I failed to notice the location of the pneumatic hoist when I came in. Perhaps you would be good enough—?"

"Or perhaps I would not. *Wake* them, yos'Galan, and remove them. Understand me, I would not require it of you, were your cha'leket or his lifemate able. However, my information is that both are convalescent, so the duty falls to near-kin."

"They are," he said slowly, "guests of your House."

She stared at him. "I beg your pardon? Who admitted them?"

"Surely that information is in the door-log."

Well, and so it would be—later just as much as now. And she was far too wily an old woman to be found in doubt of an assertion made by one of Korval. She sighed again and looked at the large, unmoving bulks of them, sprawled all over her comfort place.

"And I suppose this is just like home?" She raised a hand. "No, leave it. Only tell me how long they will sleep."

"Forgive me, but I am ignorant of their customs and their habits. It may be that my brother's lifemate will know the length of their sleep cycle, though I hesitate to disturb her own rest."

"Yes. Well." Creakily, she began to rise from her seat on the edge of the bridge, and was agreeably surprised to find a large brown hand extended to her service. She slid her hand into his and allowed him to help her rise, then walked with him, companionably side-by-side back across the bridge and toward the door.

"This is a pleasant garden," yos'Galan said, smiling at a colorful bank of gladoli.

Well, and it was that, Emrith allowed, when it wasn't being invaded by giant turtles. She inclined her head.

"I thank you," she said calmly. "It is one of the joys of—"

The remote in her pocket gave tongue. She snatched it out, thumbed 'receive' and snarled, "Who dares?"

There was a moment of terrified silence, or so she devoutly hoped, before An Der spoke, respectfully.

"Your pardon, my delm. I relay a message from the door. Lady Nova yos'Galan has arrived claiming guest-right and requesting the comfort of her close-kin."

"Has she?" said Erob, and directed a glare at the lady's brother. "Pray conduct Lady Nova to the guesting suite in the garden wing. Her brother will be with her shortly. Should she have any other requirements, the House exists to serve her." She closed the connection.

yos'Galan spread his big hands. "Surely you can't blame me?"

"Oh, can I not?" Emrith Tiazan snapped. "She is your sister!"

"But more than that," he said soothingly, "she is Korval-pernard'i, in which face she strongly represents a force of nature. A brother—a mere thodelm!—hardly commands her arrivals and departures."

She drew a deep breath, but he was bowing, gracefully, and with more than a touch of irony.

"However, since the House has promised my sister the comfort of her close-kin, I should betake myself to the guesting suite in the garden wing with no further delay. Good evening, ma'am." And so he left her, seething.

"Lieutenant, please take the troops to the staff cafeteria inside and wait for me there," Captain Robertson ordered. She turned her head, looking out across the dark garden.

"Shadia Ne'Zame."

The darkness shifted, and coalesced into a woman in scout leathers, bowing the bow between equals. "Captain Redhead?"

"Do me the favor of lending your countenance to the troop," the captain said, and her Liaden bore the very accent of Solcintra. She switched to Terran. "Stay out of trouble, got it?"

Shadia grinned. "Got it." She waved a hand at Nelirikk. "After you, Lieutenant."

"Troop, about! Single file! Follow me!" Nelirikk marched into the House of Erob, followed by an explorer, a Rifle, and, lastly, skipping, a scout, who lightly touched the control as she passed over the threshold. The door slid shut behind her.

Daav shifted, and found himself caught in the regard of two pairs of eyes—one gray, one green.

"Clonak," the scout said, without turning his head. "Grant us half-an-hour."

There was no reply, merely a subtle disturbance in the air, then the slight sound of the gate at the end of the garden, opening—and closing.

Daav waited.

Surprisingly, it was Miri Robertson who spoke.

"Any ideas what we ought do with you?"

The tone was more than a little ironic; the dialect street-rat Terran. Daav shrugged, deliberately Terran.

"I don't know that you need to *do* anything with me," he said, in his most finicking, professorial accents.

She snorted. "Got the proper respect for command," she told the green-eyed man at her left shoulder.

"Ah," he said, eyes and face bland. She shook her head and looked back to Daav, an expression of mingled exasperation and amusement informing her mobile features.

"Wanna tell me under what authority you took those oaths?"

"Blood kin," he said, more sharply than he had intended. "I couldn't very well take oaths for the House, you know—especially as I rather think my name has been written out of the roster of lives and into the lists of Korval's dead."

"No," the scout said in his soft, murmuring voice, "it has not." Daav met the green gaze and waited.

The scout's left eyebrow slipped upward a fraction. "Surely, you don't think your brother gave over hope of your eventual return—or that your son did?"

"My brother," Daav said slowly, "perhaps not. What my son might do is—alas—beyond my ability to predict. He was so young when we parted, you see."

"Precisely," the boy murmured. "It will perhaps amuse you to know that your son did not strike your name from the book of the living, nor did he ever give over hope of your eventual return. He had several pointed questions to ask you, as I am certain you will understand."

"My understanding is perfectly engaged," Daav assured him, "since it was the very need to ask pointed questions which drew me out of my Balance and sent me back toward Liad."

Something flickered in the green eyes. The boy inclined his head. "I regret to inform you that Er Thom your brother has died during your absence. He survived his lifemate by only a Standard."

It still sent an electric chill along his veins, the knowledge that Er Thom was gone; that he would never again see his brother's face, or hear the rare, sweet music of his laughter. Daav took a hard breath, inclined his head in turn, and dropped into High Liaden for the perfectly correct response.

"I thank you. Clonak had previously informed me of these things, but I had not yet had it from kin."

He straightened to find the captain looking over her shoulder at the scout.

"Well?"

"Well," he returned.

"Right." She looked at Daav, gray eyes serious now. "You want back in or is this just a visit?"

He had discussed this very choice with Aelliana, several times. *She* was of a mind to become re-clanned, pointing out that he could not reasonably expect to resurrect Professor Kiladi on Delgado and would thus need to establish another character elsewhere, over another period of years, before he might take up his Balance once more.

"And truly, van'chela," she had said, "I believe this phase of Balance complete. Now it is time to gather allies and to pool what is known."

Sound advice it was, and well-argued, yet there was a certain disinclination to return to the confines of Liad after having for so many years enjoyed the easy customs of the Terran worlds.

Miri Robertson grinned. "Tough call, ain't it?"

"Surprisingly so." He smiled at her. "I am guided in this by my lifemate, who I am persuaded would wish me safe among kin."

"Safe among kin ain't what we're offering this quarter," she told him, very serious indeed. "Be sure you know that."

Daav raised his eyebrows. "I know it now, I thank you. The condition is not so different from my life away."

"OK, then. First things first." She moved one step back, which put her shoulder to shoulder with her lifemate.

Daav took a sharp breath, and felt Aelliana, awake and aware, and very interested in the matter at hand.

Miri Robertson lifted her chin and looked him in the eye before spreading her arms in the ritual gesture.

"We see you, Daav yos'Phelium," she said, the High Liaden phrase ringing against the darkness. "Come forward and be reunited with your House."

Throat tight, and eyes misted, he stepped forward. He had to bend a trifle to accept his Thodelmae's kiss; not at all to receive the Thodelm's. He did not entirely anticipate the embrace that followed—as perhaps his son had not, judging by its abruptness and the rough, anguished whisper in his ear: "Father, where the *hell* have you been?"

BLAIR ROAD
SUREBLEAK

Despite a natural desire to please one's oathsworn, Pat Rin did not sleep well. Indeed, his exertions toward a restful slumber were so little rewarded that he arose from his celibate, sagging bed after only a few hours of tossing and turning, and made hasty use of a shower which could at best be coaxed to produce tepid water. Thereafter, Natesa at his back in defiance of a direct order to seek her own couch, he had another tour of his new property, yanking open every drawer in every room, ending—unfulfilled, frustrated, but considerably warmer for the exercise—in the so-called "parlor," where he was in good time to greet the printer.

That worthy came, as she had last evening, ink-stained and breathless, with the addition this morning of a fistful of flimsy gray sheets, which she thrust at Pat Rin with a broad grin.

"On the street, Boss. Got a couple of mine from the shop and some of Audrey's on the corners, reading 'em out, with extras to give the ones who can read themselves."

"Well done." Pat Rin shook one sheet loose and passed it to Natesa, took another for himself, and put the rest atop the chest of drawers he had been, fruitlessly, exploring.

It was, he saw at once, the paper that was gray; the printing itself was remarkably crisp and resisted smudging. The announcement of the change in administration was set top-and-center, with no alteration in his original text. That was good. At the bottom of the page was a boxed advertisement, announcing the grand opening sale at the Carpet Emporium on Blair Road, directly across from Al's Hardware.

"We will want one of these put out every morning," he said to the printer. "I will give you news from the boss' office. It would please me, however, if this effort were to develop into an . . . honest . . . publication, imparting news of interest and importance to everyone who lives on these streets."

The printer nodded. "I was talking to one of mine last night, while we was setting the type on this. Old fella. He remembers 'way back, and he says we usta have a—a daily gab-rag. Told me how to set it up. We're gonna need couple people on the street, finding out what's up and who's doin' which. They'd write it up and we'd set it—and every morning, early, it's on the street, free. *Free*," she said again, emphatically, though Pat Rin had made no demur. "Reason we can give it away is we sell these boxes like you got here to the joint-owners—like Al and Tobi and, hell, Ms. Audrey. Sounded weird to me, but Laird—that's the old guy— Laird says the owners paid up, and were glad to do it. The percentage is that they got more traffic through their joints, especially if they'd do a—a *special* on something everybody needs—sugar, say. Sell it low instead of high to—"

Pat Rin raised a hand, and the printer chopped off in midsentence, eyes showing white in her ink-smudged face.

"I am familiar with the concept. It is precisely what I propose and I am delighted that you have an advisor to hand. Do you find yourself able to undertake this project?"

"I'm in," she told him. "I need to know what your piece is so we can price up the boxes right."

Pat Rin frowned. "My . . . piece. I—Ah." It was expected that he take a profit from the printer's endeavor, while absorbing nothing of the risk. Gods, what a hideous place. He sighed.

"My piece will be taken in advertising space," he said, showing her the flimsy sheet. "A box, precisely as you have it here, with words that will alter at my discretion. Three times a week, I will have such an advertisement from you."

She blinked. "That's it?"

He lifted his eyebrows, consciously adapting a High House hauteur. "It is sufficient."

"Yessir," she said hastily, and cleared her throat, looking around her. "Well, if you're not—"

"Hold." He extended a hand, and she froze as if he had turned her to stone. "There may be another service you may perform for me. I will pay," he said sternly, "for this service."

The printer glanced aside, possibly trying to gain something from Natesa's face. In this, she was apparently frustrated, for she looked back to Pat Rin with a jerky nod. "Sure, Boss. What can I do for you?"

"Pens," he said.

"Pens?"

"To write with. Ink pens. Black ink, by preference, or blue. But any color will do—I apprehend that I may not be able to afford to be proud. Have you such access to such things?"

She swallowed, her eyes sliding toward Natesa again, before being forcibly brought back to his face. "Yessir. I can get you pens. Black ink *and* blue. Got red, too, and green. Purple . . ."

"Black," he said firmly, and added, after taking thought. "And red. A dozen each, if you have them in such quantity. If not, as many as you can bring me today, with the balance due when they are available."

She nodded, jerkily. "Right, Boss," she said, her feet sliding against the plastic floor, preparatory to taking her leave—and froze once again when Pat Rin raised his hand.

"One last thing," he said. "A—a log book."

"Log book, Boss?" There was genuine puzzlement on the woman's face.

Pat Rin sighed. "A bound book, with the interior pages blank, so that one may—may make notations. Of a good size . . ." His hands moved, squaring it out in the air between them. "The binding of some durable material—leather, perhaps or—"

"Got it!" The printer's face lit. "Can do, Boss. Got just what you need. I'll send it over with the pens."

"And an invoice," Pat Rin cautioned her. "I *will* purchase these from you."

"Sure, Boss. Whatever you say." She moved her feet again, clearly aching to be gone.

"Thank you," Pat Rin told her. "You have done well. Natesa will see you out."

"Right. Uh—you're welcome. Boss." She darted after Natesa and Pat Rin closed his eyes, wishing most heartily for a cup of tea.

Pat Rin put the tin down on the kitchen table, not quite able to repress the shudder, and stood, head bent, striving for patience. Once, the tin before him had contained a perfectly unexceptional blend of afternoon tea. Now . . .

The cook, who had been hovering, hands twisting in his apron, sighed.

"Bad, huh?" He said it almost wistfully.

"On several counts," Pat Rin told him, with really commendable calmness. "First, it is old. Second, it is damp. This sort is a dry leaf tea." He took a careful breath. "Well. We shall have to purchase more. When—"

The cook was shaking his head vigorously. "No, sir. Or, at least, not if you're after more that look like that tin there. Got a bunch of 'em in the pantry."

"Which are of like age?" Natesa murmured.

Pat Rin moved a shoulder. "The age perhaps does not matter so much," he said. "This tin had been stasis-sealed. If the others have not been breached, there may actually be something in this house worth drinking." He waved a languid hand at the cook. "Take me to the pantry."

The man blinked. "Ain't no need of that, Boss. Won't take me a minute to fetch 'em out for you."

"Yes, but you see," Pat Rin explained gently, "eventually I will wish to partake of a meal, and I am afraid that the quality displayed last evening must improve. Rapidly. So, I am interested in what else might be in the pantry in addition to tea, and if any of it is eatable, or may be made to be eatable." He fixed the man in his eye and frowned. "In short, I wish to ascertain whether I need a new pantry or a new cook."

"Oh," the cook said. "Gotcha." He unwrapped his hands from his apron and pointed. "Right this way, Boss."

Pat Rin followed, Natesa at his back. The pantry was at the end of a narrow hallway, behind a heavy wooden door. The cook pushed this portal open and brought up the lights, revealing half a dozen orderly shelves of tinned stuff, and bags that announced their contents in letters and pictograph: salt, sugar, flour, rice. To the right of these were a few bins, covered over with old blankets. Above, suspended by cords from the center beam, were perhaps a dozen round, waxy balls.

The cook stood respectfully aside as Pat Rin toured the room. There were more empty shelves than full, which struck him as odd in the house of a supposed Power—but, then, much about the late Boss Moran's house struck him as odd. He perused the stocks leisurely, finding first ten stasis sealed tins of the same unexceptional blend as that which had been spoilt. He picked one up and stood with it cradled in his hand, reading the labels of the other tins.

It appeared that he was wealthy in tinned fish, tinned crackers, and two or three varieties of tinned soup. Next to these things were perhaps half-a-dozen glass jars, vacuum-sealed, each bearing a hand-lettered label: *Jam*. He took one of those, too, and carried it and the tea-tin in the crook of his arm as he moved over to inspect the contents of the bins, Natesa to his right, and a step behind.

Further to the right, within the shadows cast by a row of empty shelves, something moved; at the door, the cook gasped, and stiffened. Beside him, Natesa drew, fierce and fluid.

"Do not!" He flung a hand out, and she whirled, staring at him out of obsidian eyes that must surely have done damage—*had* done damage . . . He shook away the wound and pointed. "It is only a cat."

She looked down the line of his finger and the cat obliged him by strolling out into the greater light, sparing the two of them a yellow-eyed glance of utter boredom before trotting off down the room, to be lost once more in the shadows.

"I . . . see," Natesa said, on a long sigh, slipping her weapon away. She looked back at him, eyes considerably less sharp, and inclined her head. "Master."

"Surely, merely lucky?" he responded, deliberately flippant, and looked over to the cook, standing clenched and slightly pale by the door. "I have some . . . familiarity . . . with cats."

"Yessir, Boss. Boss Moran, he liked to shoot cats."

"Yes, well. I prefer not to have mice." Taking a deep breath, he continued to the bins.

Leaning over, he flicked back the blankets. Bin One contained a goodly number of some sort of tuber, still wearing their native soil. Bin Two was wholly given over to pungent-smelling bulbs—possibly the local equivalent of onion. Bin Three was filled near to overflowing with large orange fruits, which appeared to be of a robust habit.

Pat Rin turned to face the cook, and pointed up at the center beam.

"Cheese?"

"Right you are, Boss. Best cheese in the city."

"Ah. As it happens, I am partial to cheese."

The cook smiled. "We'll getcha a slice off the one in the kitchen, when we go back. Man who likes cheese'll find it a friend."

Pat Rin eyed him. "I infer from this that Mr. Moran did not care for cheese?"

"Nossir. Boss Moran, he didn't like much, 'cept to hoard his money. And makin' his 'hands crawl—he did get a heapin' cup o'pleasure outta that."

"I wonder that you stayed with so unsatisfactory a master," Pat Rin commented, but the man only stared at him. Sighing, he jerked his head toward the bins.

"Those tubers—are they a local specialty?"

The cook nodded. "Jonni grows 'em up on the roof. He takes care of 'most all the vegetables."

"I see. Yet when Mr. McFarland particularly desired vegetables for last evening's meal, you sent in a mess of leaves. I wonder why?"

"After *greens*, is what he told me. We're too early in the season for greens. Froze some stuff, end of last growin' season, but it's gone now, too."

"I see," Pat Rin said again, and used his free hand to motion the cook out into the hallway. "Let us repair to the kitchen. I am very much in need of tea, and perhaps some of your excellent bread, with jam on it."

They were seated 'round the kitchen table sometime later when Cheever McFarland arrived, all three supplied with a beer tankard filled with a gently steaming pale green liquid. Plates before each bore the sticky remains of toast-and-jam sandwiches. Pat Rin and the cook had their heads together, apparently engaged in producing a grocery list, while Natesa looked on, her eyes heavy, and faintly amused.

"Mornin'," he said to her, and pointed at the wreckage. "Any more of any of that left?"

She moved her head in a subtle nod toward the counter. "There is tea, and there is jam, and there is bread. Toast is made on the grill."

"Right." He considered her. "Long night?"

The fingers of her left hand flickered in the sign-language known as Old Trade, letting him know the boss hadn't slept—and neither had she.

"Right," he said again. "I'm on shift now. Get some rest. I'll sit on him."

She smiled faintly. "I wish you good fortune, but I believe you will find yourself bested," she murmured, easing out of her chair.

At the sink, she emptied what was left of her tea, rinsed the beer mug and set it to be washed.

She looked back as she left the kitchen. Pat Rin yos'Phelium and the cook were still deep in their plans, the cook laboriously writing down the boss' suggestions.

"Don't look like the ad's drawing so good," Cheever commented at about half-past lunch. "What say we shut the store for an hour and go on down to Tobi's for a bite?"

Pat Rin glanced up from the battered notebook he'd been studying for most of the morning. "We do not appear to be awash in customers," he allowed, courteously. "Nor have I properly attended the hour. By all means, Mr. McFarland, provide yourself with lunch."

Cheever sighed mightily and shook his head. "I thought we'd got the concept of 'security' through to you. I ain't leavin' you here on your own, even if you probably are the best shot on the planet." He swung a hand around, impatiently. "Think about it! What if five guns come in through the front door right now and you was alone?"

The Liaden smiled, politely, like Cheever'd maybe told him a slightly off-color joke. "Why, then, Mr. McFarland, I should immediately be out the back door."

"If I believed that—which I don't—how'd you plan on dealin' with the two they sent 'round to watch the alley?" He frowned, as ugly as he knew how. "You ain't making things easy for your security, Boss. My copy of the plan don't include the part where your head gets blown off."

"Ah." He closed his eyes. Cheever considered him, letting the frown go, and allowed as how he was worried. The plan—because there was one, hammered out between the three of them long before they raised Surebleak—was only good to a point. Taking over Moran's territory—that had been according to plan. They had to have a planetary base, and while Moran's streets weren't exactly convenient to the spaceport, they had been the nearest most accessible target. From here, they could consolidate, and figure out how to get past the more powerful fatcats who controlled the territories surrounding the port.

He'd considered that they'd be using their guns more than once, 'cause that was how business was done on Surebleak, and didn't think much more about it.

Since yesterday, though, he'd thought about it a lot.

Pat Rin . . . Pat Rin wasn't a pro. Oh, he was a good shot; he walked the walk, and that cool, pretty face of his didn't give away much, but that was gambler bravado—plus a measure of pure cussedness, give the boy his due—and nothing like what marked Natesa out as a gun to fear.

Pat Rin had a revenge to accomplish. Cheever understood that. In fact, he sanctioned it. And he didn't doubt—if the boss had to personally shoot every fatcat and loyal 'hand on Surebleak to do it, that the job would get done. What worried him, considerable, was the question of what would be left of Pat Rin yos'Phelium at the end of the campaign. He'd already taken a hit that would've unhinged most Liadens, as Cheever understood it. Pat Rin hadn't come unhinged—at least, not so you'd notice—but he was starting to show some strain. Even as he sat there in his chair, eyes closed and restful looking, Cheever could see the tension in his muscles, and new lines starting to etch in around his mouth. The success of the game depended on this man, Cheever thought—and came suddenly to the realization that nobody—maybe not even Pat Rin himself—knew what Pat Rin would do next.

"Well." The Liaden opened his eyes and slipped the little book away into his jacket. "One does not build an entire day's labor upon a jam sandwich." He stood, a shade less graceful than his usual, which Cheever thought was the sleepless night starting to show.

"Let us have lunch, Mr. McFarland."

Come down to it, Cheever hadn't expected to win the argument, and he wasn't sure he liked the idea of the boss in Tobi's surrounded by workaday streeters, now that he had the victory. Still, they had to show their faces around town—that was the point of the rug store, after all. As if to enforce this line of reasoning, Cheever felt his stomach rumble an order for a brew and a sandwich.

That being settled, he followed the boss into the store proper just as the first customer of the day walked in off the street.

She was a sight to behold—on first glance as out of place on the street as Pat Rin himself. Second glance found the silk to be second-grade synthetic; the jewelry light-gold set with mine-cut stones. Still, she bore herself as would a person of melant'i, come to call upon an equal.

Accordingly, Pat Rin bowed.

The lady considered him out of clever blue eyes, and shook her pale, elaborately coiffed head.

"I won't even try to duplicate that," she said, and her voice was high and sweet. "Let's just consider that I done what was polite."

"Indeed," Pat Rin said, smiling. "Let us do so. Have I pleasure of addressing Ms. Audrey?"

She nodded, unsurprised. "Expecting me, were you? Well, I guess you shoulda been, after last night. I was out on business, or I'd've tried to set things straight then. I'm hoping we can come to an accommodation today, if you got time?"

"Mr. McFarland and I were on our way to lunch. If you would care to join us . . . ?"

"Great minds think alike," she said, with a grin. "I was hoping you'd see your way clear to having a bite at my place. Not as public as Tobi's, and the food's better."

Pat Rin considered her, noting a certain tension—which was certainly expectable in one come to call upon the new and unknown quantity to whom one owed allegiance—as well as a certainty of her own worth. The clever eyes met his with frankness, which was rare in this place where he found himself. She was not by any means in her first youth, and struck him as both competent and commanding.

In fact, she was just such a one as he would need by him, if they were able to forge an alliance built on mutual profit.

He inclined his head. "Almost, you persuade me," he murmured. "Mr. McFarland?"

He felt rather than heard the big man sigh. "Sounds great," he said. "Tobi's ain't the kind of place to do business, Boss."

So, Pat Rin thought grumpily, *I have cleared the matter with 'security.' Behold me, virtuous.*

"Well, now, that's—" the lady began, and cut herself off, frank gaze going over Pat Rin's shoulder.

"Will you *look* at that," she breathed, reverently. "I ain't *ever* . . ." She brought her eyes back to Pat Rin's face with a visible effort. "That is one hell of a rug."

"So it is," he agreed smoothly, slipping into his merchant's role. He moved a hand, inviting her to make a closer inspection. Nothing could have been more to her liking.

At his direction, she sampled the nap, her fingers as reverent as her voice, and obediently inspected the underside, admiring the precious, hand-tied knots.

"Who'd make something like this?" she asked, when he had done and stepped back to allow her to commune with the carpet.

"Certain . . . members . . . of a particular sect," he replied, with perfect truth. "It is very rare to find such things for sale."

She looked at him, blue eyes shrewd. "Why's that?"

"Because, upon its world of origin, this carpet is a religious artifact, and the rules of the sect did not allow of them being sold."

"So, how'd you get this one?"

He smiled, liking her more and more. "Naturally, I must protect my suppliers. Let us say that it was offered for sale from a licensed dealer, who had paperwork sufficient to convince me of the carpet's authenticity."

She sighed, stroked the carpet one last time and moved a regretful step back, her eyes still on the pattern of the joyous revelers.

"How much does something like that put a body back?"

"That carpet—being a uniquity, you understand—may be purchased for eight thousand cash—" He raised a hand, smoothing away the protest he saw rising to her lips. "Or, it may be leased, by the Standard month, or the Standard year."

"Leased." She frowned, the clever eyes showing puzzlement. "What's that?"

"Ah. It is an arrangement whereby a customer will agree to pay a set sum which is significantly lower than the cost of the carpet, plus a refundable amount of earnest money, in order to have the use of a particular carpet for a month, two months—a year." He moved his shoulders, and raised his hands, showing her empty palms. "In that case, there are papers to be executed—agreements to be made. The customer would pledge to protect the carpet from spoilage, to keep it safe from theft, and to return it, intact, upon the day specified. If the customer failed of meeting the terms, he would be seen to have purchased the carpet, and the full retail price would then be due."

Audrey considered him with interest. "So, how much to lease it, say, for a month?"

Pat Rin frowned slightly while he did several lightning calculations. *Of all the mad starts*, he scolded himself—and yet he was certain that he needed this woman's goodwill. Not that he would buy her—in fact, he doubted that he could buy her—but that he would show good faith, and a willingness to negotiate—yes, that he must do. Equal to equal. So . . .

"I ask two thousand cash, plus earnest money of an equal amount. But, you see, it is not efficient—for either of us—to lease for a month. I must ask a higher rate, because I must move it, twice, in a very short time. The most efficient arrangement for both is one that allows the carpet to rest in one place for a period of a few months. Should you wish to contract for three months, for instance, the monthly rate falls to one thousand cash; six months, and the rate falls again—to eight hundred cash. A year's lease may be had for a mere six hundred cash per month, plus the deposit of earnest money."

She grinned at him. "That's quite a scheme. Let's see . . ." She was quick at her numbers. "If I lease from you for a year, you'll see a return of seventy-eight hundred cash—two-hundred cash less'n the full selling price."

"Precisely so. However, the carpet will not be available as an item for sale during the period of its lease, and I must cover my potential loss."

It was a laugh this time, full-bodied and attractive. "Sure you do! And you get the rug back at the end of it to sell. Or lease. Seems to me that leasing's more profitable."

"On certain items, of course it is. I am fortunate that the carpet under discussion is durable as well as difficult to stain or to singe. However, it *is* a unique item and thus vulnerable to theft. And if it were stolen, I should not have it to sell ever again."

"There's that." She looked at him thoughtfully. "OK, I came to invite you to lunch, and your 'hand there's lookin' about ready to eat one of the rugs, which *can't* be good for business. Let's go over to my place, and talk."

"Certainly." He inclined his head. "After you."

Smiling, she turned and led the way out, though she did pause for a moment on the threshold, to look back over her shoulder at the Sinner's Carpet, and sigh.

Ms. Audrey's house quite cast the late Boss Moran's "mansion" into the shade. Most likely, Pat Rin thought, as he followed his hostess through wide rooms and broad hallways, before embarking upon its career as a whorehouse, it had been three connected houses, and had required extensive remodeling to achieve its present state of relative sumptuousness.

It was a well-occupied residence, to judge by the number of brightly dressed young people they passed on the way to the "private dining room." The urge to understand it as a clanhouse was very nearly overmastering—and a temptation that he must at all costs resist.

The "private dining room," achieved at last, proved to be a cozy interior chamber. A long table at the far wall supported various tureens and platters. A smaller, round table sat on a rag rug of a kind he was coming to know well, in the center of the room. Three places were set with what appeared to be silk napkins and silver utensils. A glass at each place was filled with a faintly amber liquid. In the middle of the table sat an artful and modest bowl of flowers.

"Here we are," Audrey said, cheerfully. "Gotta serve ourselves, but we can talk private."

She ushered them to the buffet, removed the lids from the tureens, and proceeded to serve herself, which was certainly her right, in her own house. Pat Rin picked up a plate, as she had, and followed her down the table, taking a mite from every unfamiliar dish. When he reached an end, he followed his hostess to the round table, situated his plate, pulled out his chair and sat.

"Elegant little thing, ain't you?" she said wistfully.

In the act of unfolding his napkin, Pat Rin froze. *How dare*— Slowly, leisurely, he turned his head, and met her eyes, frowning.

It could not precisely be said that a frown of disapproval from Pat Rin yos'Phelium caused seasoned gamers to swoon. However, it was generally agreed among those who had reason to know that it was no easy thing to bear, that frown, nor that it brought forcibly to mind the recollection that Lord Pat Rin shot first at Tey Dor's—and had done so for a number of years.

Ms. Audrey laughed, quite merrily, and shook her napkin out.

"Now, no offense meant—it's a habit of business, like you doing a quick-and-dirty assess on my poor old rag rug, first thing you walk in the room." She sighed, and looked up to bestow her pleasant smile on Cheever McFarland and his well-filled plate.

"That's right," she said comfortably. "Man your size has got to have his food. Enjoy yourself."

"I intend to, ma'am, thank you," Cheever answered easily. He shook his napkin onto his knee, picked up a fork and fell to.

Not entirely mollified, Pat Rin finished with his own napkin, extended a hand to his glass, raised it and essayed an exploratory sip.

It was a new wine, and a sweet one, with a faint, enchanting note of something reminiscent of ginger beneath. Pat Rin had a second sip and set the glass aside.

"The wine is pleasant," he said to his hostess. "May I know the vintage?"

Audrey smiled. "We just call it Autumn Wine. It comes in from the country in lots of six, and I generally buy a couple dozen, if that many pass through. Some of our clients are partial, and some of the staff. We've got a few left from last season's buy; I'll be pleased to give you a bottle."

A gift of wine. Pat Rin felt absurdly pleased as he inclined his head. "Thank you, I would like that."

She nodded, and had an appreciative sip from her own glass. "That's good," she murmured, and shook her head. "Understand, this wine'll turn, if you keep it too long into spring, and what you'll have then is some nice smellin' paint remover."

"Ah, then I will remember to enjoy it soon, with warm memories of your hospitality."

For a heartbeat, she stared at him, her mouth half-smiling, then she shook her head and returned to her meal.

At long last did Pat Rin address his own plate, and found the unfamiliar viands good—even very good. Nor did he wonder when Cheever McFarland rose from his place to refill his own plate.

"I wonder," Pat Rin said softly, "if you know who makes the rag rugs. I have several in . . . my . . . house, and would be pleased to have more—or even to purchase some for trade."

"Well, for that, Ajay Naylor makes 'em—has for years. But buying 'em for trade—there's no profit there, Boss. The rugs is how she pays. Strictly barter, is Ajay."

"Is she? But the trade I had meant was not necessarily local."

"Gonna sell 'em at the port?" Audrey frowned at her plate consideringly. "Might do, I guess."

"Do no ships come through the port?" Pat Rin murmured.

"Oh, well, ships. Sure they do. Once in a summer snowstorm. The trouble with trying to sell things to the *ships* is you gotta deliver the full order on time. Which means you need a safe road from here to there. Which you ain't got."

"And yet there is the Port Road, which runs through this territory and straight to the port," Pat Rin pointed out.

"That's right. And there's six different territories between here and there. That's a lot of toll—and assuming there ain't a turf war goin' on in one—or more!—when you gotta pass—*not* the way to bet, not with that bunch. Also assuming that somebody up an' comin' don't decided to knock you over and make your profit his."

"I see." Pat Rin sipped his wine. "Then we will need to work to secure the Port Road, so that all may have equal access to trade."

Audrey blinked at him. "Sure we will," she said politely, and Cheever McFarland laughed.

"Don't egg him on, ma'am," he said, pushing his plate aside and reaching for his glass. "He'll do it just to prove you wrong."

"Thank you, Mr. McFarland," Pat Rin said coolly, and turned back to his hostess.

"You will understand that I have not had much time to go over such records as I have . . . inherited . . . from the late Mr. Moran, so I wonder if you might tell me if there is a bank within my territory?"

Her eyebrows pulled together in a puzzled frown. "Bank?"

It was seldom that Pat Rin had cause to question his abilities in Terran, but she was so plainly at a loss, and that over an inquiry after an institution that must surely be well known to so astute a businessperson . . . Hurriedly, he sifted his vocabulary for the correct word to convey his meaning—and the word was "bank."

"Bank," he said again, softly, certainly—but her puzzlement did not abate. "Forgive me. An . . . institution . . . which keeps large sums of cash in trust for customers, which makes capital loans, receives collateral, pays out interest—"

"Oh!" Understanding dawned. "Gotcha. Pawn shops. Sure, you got two established and one making a start." She frowned, briefly. "Pays *out* interest, now—that's opposite the way it's been done. The shop charges you interest, see, to keep your item instead of selling it. No percentage in them paying *out* interest, when they gotta store the stuff, too."

Beside him, Cheever McFarland shifted, but when Pat Rin looked, the pilot was found to be gazing raptly at the artful arrangement of flowers.

"A pawn shop is a different enterprise entirely," Pat Rin said carefully. "The institution that I envision holds cash in trust for members, and loans cash to other members, to whom it charges interest. The institution then pays interest to its depositor-members, in payment for its use of their funds." He was about to go on to elucidate the more arcane functions of banks, but he saw from her face that he had said quite enough. Audrey obviously thought he was raving.

She had recourse to her glass, and sat holding it in her hand, looking at him out of considering blue eyes.

"OK," she said at last. "Just who would be running this joint—this *bank*?"

Pat Rin raised an eyebrow. "A board of trustees."

"Uh-huh. And the reason they don't take all the free money and leg it for Deacon's turf would be?"

Ah. *You have forgotten where you are*, he told himself, and sighed ruefully.

"Ordinarily," he answered Audrey, "I would say, because of the contracts and laws binding upon them. I quite see that such contracts and laws would be unenforceable under . . . present circumstances."

"It'd be tough," she allowed. "We don't have much to do with contracts and laws—not here, an' not on any other turf I ever heard of." She frowned and had a bit more of her wine.

"I like the idea," she said slowly. "I can see how it could work. But these trustees of yours—they'd have to be people who weren't tempted by big stacks of cash, and that ain't anybody I ever met."

"Many people are tempted by large sums of money." Pat Rin frowned. Surely, he thought, there was something, some mechanism, aside from law and honor, which would insure the safety of the investors, and the honesty of the trustees?

"How if," he murmured, his eyes now on the flower arrangement as well, but seeing something rather different—Mr. dea'- Gauss seated in his office, holding forth on the structure of a particular fund that Pat Rin had wished to invest in, outlining the various failsafes and protocols . . .

"How if the procedures required the keys of at least three trustees in order to access the money itself? If the trustees are all businesspeople of consequence . . ."

"And, better yet, if they all hate each other," Audrey said, suddenly smiling. "This could work. It *could* work. It'll take some planning and some finagling, but it might be possible." Her smile widened into a grin. "Just moved from the Impossible pile to the Maybe pile. You'll be a trustee, yourself?"

"Indeed I will not. The bank—best call it a—a *mercantile as-*

sociation—it should have nothing to do with the boss or the boss' office. Ideally, it should be a separate entity, protected by those laws and contracts we have both agreed are unenforceable at the moment."

She stared, then laughed, and looked aside to Cheever McFarland. "He like this all the time?"

"No, ma'am," Cheever said seriously. "Some days he's downright ornery. He sleeps, occasional. And, from time to time, he likes a game."

"Does he?" She looked back to Pat Rin with interest. "Cards?" she asked, then corrected herself, "No, you're a boxman, ain't you? Dice."

Pat Rin sighed, and spared a glare for Cheever McFarland, who was once again studying the flowers. To Audrey, he inclined his head, slightly.

"I am . . . familiar . . . with most types of gaming and gambling practiced in the galaxy."

"Well." She finished her wine and put the glass down. "What're you doing here?"

He raised an eyebrow. "Rusticating."

She didn't smile. "Plan on sticking around?"

"Surely that's my business."

"Was," she said, her voice almost stern. "But then you set yourself as boss. That changes the rule of play." She raised a hand, as if she'd felt his outrage.

"Hear me out, just hear me out. Nort Moran was a stupid, selfish animal, and the whole territory's best off without him. Vindal—that was the boss before—she was smart, but she wasn't tough. Word was she didn't even try to pull when Moran walked in on her. You—you're smart *and* you're tough—and we need you. You're gonna be good for business—this bank idea of yours, for one; and putting the gab-rag back on the street. That's for day one. Who knows what you'll come up with by the time you're on the street a week?"

"Who, indeed," Pat Rin said politely, sternly suppressing the shiver. For the second time in his life, he was being offered a Ring. Gods. At least, this offer was made with honor—or so he thought—perhaps leavened with a healthy dose of fear.

Audrey nodded. "Right. Right. You're the boss. An' I'm outta line." She sighed, and pushed back from the table. "Just—think about it, OK?"

Apparently, their luncheon business was concluded. Pat Rin inclined his head and rose. "I will think about it. My thanks for a most delicious and convivial meal."

"You're welcome," Audrey said, matching his formality. "I hope it'll be the first of many." She glanced up to Cheever McFarland. "Mr. McFarland, my pleasure."

"No, ma'am. *My* pleasure," the pilot assured her, gallantly, which won him an easy laugh before she led them back through the hallways and spacious rooms to the main entranceway.

There were rather more people about now, the clients obvious by their less grand—and more concealing—clothing. That several of the clients took him for a new addition to the house was plain from the stares of interest he intercepted. He sighed to himself, and followed his hostess, coming up to her side when she stopped a sleek young man dressed only in a pair of scarlet synth-silk trousers, and a purple sash. The young man favored him with a wide smile.

"Villy, love, run down to the pantry and bring a bottle of Autumn Wine up for the boss," Audrey said, quite loudly enough to be heard across the room. In fact, several heads turned in their direction—clients and residents alike.

The young man's smile dimmed considerably, but he nodded briskly enough. "Sure thing, Ms. Audrey. Back in a sec." He was gone, running lightly on bare feet.

"He's a good boy," Audrey said comfortably to Pat Rin. "Your wine will be here in a flash."

"Ms. Audrey," he said, softly, but with genuine feeling. "You must remind me never to dice with you."

She laughed, and patted his arm. "Let them get a good look at you," she said, her voice as soft as his. "Your security's right behind you. Besides, it's been a long time since anybody was stupid enough to draw in *my* house."

There was a light patter of feet against floorboard, and Villy was back, bottle in hand. He presented it to Ms. Audrey with a flourish and prudently faded away.

"OK." Audrey presented the bottle with a similar flourish, smiling as he took it from her hands.

"Thank you," he said, pitching his voice to be heard.

"Glad to be able to oblige," Audrey assured him, also in carrying tones. She smiled impartially around the room and they went on.

In the entrance hall, Cheever opened the door and examined the street.

"Clear," he said, over his shoulder. Pat Rin bowed to Ms. Audrey—the bow between equals—turned.

"Oh," she said. "One more thing." He looked back, eyebrow up.

"I'll lease that rug from you for six months. Can you have it here tomorrow?"

Throughout the afternoon they entertained a steady trickle of customers—most, so Pat Rin thought, come to look the new boss over. It was peculiarly unnerving, to be thus on display, and it required every bit of his considerable address to carry through, moving unhurriedly among his customers, answering questions with gentle and attentive courtesy.

Beside himself, the Sinners Carpet was the item of most intense interest. He lost count of how many times he displayed the knots; elucidated the fabric; told over its curious history—and revealed that, beginning on the morrow, it was on lease to Ms. Audrey, for a period of·six months, Standard. Often enough, this led to a discussion of the concept of "lease," as it had with Audrey.

When at last Barth arrived to take up his post as night guard, Pat Rin felt he had been, in the idiom of Shan's mother, *spin washed and hung out to dry*. His head ached, and he wanted the study of his house in Solcintra, with its comforts of books, and comm screen, and a chair that cherished the contours of his body—wanted it so fiercely that his sight misted and he bent his head, biting his lip.

It is gone, he told himself, grimly. *Everything and everyone— gone, dead, destroyed, unmade. Believe it. Make your Balance your focus, or you will surely go mad.*

"You all right, sir?" Cheever McFarland's voice was soft, for a wonder, and carried a strong note of concern.

Pat Rin straightened. He must not display weakness before his oathsworn. He took a breath. "I am perfectly fine, Mr. McFarland," he said coolly and strode up the sidewalk, toward the "mansion" he called his home.

The door was opened to them by Gwince, grinning good-naturedly.

"Evening, Boss. Mr. McFarland. Natesa said to tell you, Boss, that the work you wanted done is in process. Cook asks when you want to eat supper. Printer's boy brought a package for you. Natesa put it in your office."

Pat Rin closed his eyes, there in the tiny vestibule of his house, and tried to recall what tasks he had particularly wished Natesa to accomplish. Ah. That would be the upgrading of Boss Moran's security arrangements. Very good. News of the delivery from the printer was also welcome—he had two persons of honor on the day, which surely found him richer than yesterday. What had been the—yes. Supper.

"Please tell the cook that Mr. McFarland, Natesa and I will dine in one Standard Hour. Mr. McFarland has a bottle of wine, which we will wish to drink with the meal."

She took the bottle from Cheever, eyebrows twitching in what might have been surprise, but she merely murmured a respectful, "Yessir, will do."

"Thank you, Gwince," he said and began to turn away, then swung back. "I wonder, do you know Ajay Naylor?"

Gwince looked surprised. "Sure, Boss. Everybody knows Ajay."

"Alas, not everyone," Pat Rin murmured. "I have not had the honor, an oversight that I wish to rectify. Do you think you might ask her to call on me at the store tomorrow, mid-morning?"

Now, Gwince looked puzzled, even faintly alarmed. "Sure, I can do that." She sent a glance into Cheever McFarland's face, but apparently found nothing there to ease her distress.

"Um, Boss—just so you know. Ajay's like four hunnert years old. She ain't—well, she ain't—" Gwince stumbled to a halt, regrouped, and produced a rather faint, "She makes rugs, see? And trades 'em out for stuff she needs."

Gods, what a filthy place! Pat Rin thought, furiously. *As if I would murder an old woman*—His fury flamed out, leaving him cold and shaken. While it was true that he had not yet murdered an old woman, who could say where the necessities of his Balance might take him? Gwince was within her rights to be wary of his reasons for wanting Ajay Naylor. He sighed and met her eyes.

"I have business to discuss with Ajay Naylor," he said, mildly, and was absurdly pleased to see the alarm fade from her eyes.

"Right," she said, briskly. "Mid-morning tomorrow, at the rug store. I'll tell her, sir."

"Thank you," he said again, and walked down the short hallway, Cheever McFarland a large and ridiculously comforting presence at his back—and paused on the threshold of the front parlor.

Last seen, this chamber had been very nearly as grubby as the printer he had interviewed there. This evening, while the furnishings must still dismay any person of taste, other matters had undergone a change for the better.

The floor, for instance. This morning, it had been a dull and slightly sticky gray. It now flaunted its true color for all to see—a pale, and not unbecoming blue—and showed a small, repeating pattern of a darker blue—flowers, perhaps, or some sort of decorative insect.

The walls, which had this morning been of a dinginess in competition with the floor, had been washed, revealing that they had, at some all but forgotten time in the past, been painted a blue to match the floor. The ceiling, likewise relieved of several years of grime, was discovered to be white, the central globe-shaped light fixture yellow. The effect was unexpectedly pleasant—rather like walking into a sunlit sky.

"Well," he murmured, and heard Cheever McFarland grunt behind him.

"Thought she was going to sleep."

Pat Rin glanced at the big man, eyebrows up. "You think Natesa did this?"

"Well, sure, don't you?"

"No," said Pat Rin, looking 'round the room and considering its possibilities. "I think she had it done. I wonder what else has gone forth, as we were whiling our hours in pleasure?"

"Guess we could take the tour and find out."

"We could," Pat Rin conceded. "Or we could ask Natesa, which would be much less fatiguing." He turned to look up at the big man.

"Mr. McFarland, I am going to prepare for dinner. I don't doubt that you are heartily sick of the sight of me and wish a few moments to yourself. I give you my word that I will not be assassinated before the dinner hour."

Surprisingly, Cheever grinned. "Dismissed!" he said cheerfully and nodded. "See you at dinner."

Blessedly alone, Pat Rin took one more look at the blue room, reminding himself to congratulate Natesa on the result, and went upstairs to dress for dinner.

•   •   •

The meal arrived in a surprising two courses. The first consisted of a plate of tinned soup for each, and a communal platter of crackers and cheese. This was removed by a main course of baked tubers under a spicy brown sauce accompanied by thin slices of meat braised with onion; fresh bread, butter, tea, and Autumn Wine.

"Much improved," Pat Rin murmured, and heard Cheever Mc-Farland chuckle.

"Improved ain't the word. I'm thinking that the cook was after poisoning us last night, eh, Natesa?"

"Possibly," she answered. "Just as possibly, he was frightened enough to have been thrown off his skill." She sipped the wine cautiously, and Pat Rin saw her eyebrows lift.

"This is pleasant," she said. "Have we a winery?"

"Alas. The bottle is a gift. And we are instructed that it is a fragile thing, not to be held far into the spring." He moved his shoulders. "We are further told that this vintage originates in the country, and that sometimes as many as two dozen bottles make it into this territory, whereupon they are purchased by Ms. Audrey."

"Ah." Her face lit. "You called upon Ms. Audrey?"

"Rather, she called upon us. We had a very pleasant discussion over lunch in her house."

"Where the boss here sweet-talked her into startin' a bank—no, hold it, a mercantile association—since pawn shops ain't good enough for him, and she tried to get him to promise to be boss for life." Cheever forked a slice of tuber and looked at it meditatively. "'Course, that's how it works here, anyhow, but she seemed of the opinion that his life was gonna be longer than most. Right taken with him, she was. Thought he was elegant."

Natesa laughed.

"We have also," Pat Rin murmured, "placed the Sinner's Carpet at lease for six months, Standard, at a rate of eight hundred cash per month."

"Ms. Audrey, of course," Natesa said. "No one else could afford it." She paused, her head slightly to one side. "Indeed, I am surprised to hear that *she* can afford it."

"A test of trust," he said softly, finishing the last of his meal with real regret. "She must know if we can work together—which is what I must know, as well. Also, I believe that her smuggling operation is profitable." He moved his shoulders. "So, we have progress upon the day." He pushed his plate aside and reached for his wine.

"I have noticed the improvement in the front parlor," he said, which phrase would have been entirely appropriate in the High Tongue, but struck the ear oddly in Terran, almost as an accusation.

However, Natesa, who spoke Liaden, seemed to have heard the commendation he intended to convey. She inclined her head politely and murmured that she would inform the staff of his approval.

"How's house security?" Cheever asked then.

Natesa turned to him. "Like the meal, much improved. We are not impregnable, of course, but we are difficult. If tomorrow's work goes as well, we will be formidable."

"That's good. What about the overheads? I can help out tonight, if you need it."

"Thank you; assistance would be most welcome. There is also a . . . device . . . in the sub-cellar that I would like to have your—" The door to the dining room opened just enough to admit a thin person dressed in what appeared to be the street standard: ill fitting trousers and shirt, with a second shirt worn over the first, as a jacket. This particular specimen also had a shapeless cap crammed down over his ears. He came two steps into the room, a flicker of shadow at his heels, and froze, eyes stretched wide in a pointed brown face.

Pat Rin tipped his head, considering this apparition. He was young—a boy only; at a guess, several Standards younger than Quin—and bore himself with the tentativeness one might expect of a smaller and weaker "extra"—those who loitered in crowds on street corners, and were available for such day-labor as might manifest.

"Good evening," he said gently to the wide, frightened eyes. "I am the boss."

The boy nodded vigorously, and abruptly reached into his pocket. Pat Rin tensed and forced himself to relax, which was wisdom, for what came out of the pocket was a tuber. The boy held it up, and then touched it to his chest.

"What the—" began Cheever, but Pat Rin held up a hand, watching the wide eyes watch him, watch his *face*, with such intensity that—

"Wait," he said. "I think that this is Jonni, who gardens on the roof."

The boy nodded so vigorously this time that his cap came off his head and tumbled to the floor between his boots. He made no move to pick it up.

"And I also think," Pat Rin continued, "that Jonni is deaf."

The boy nodded again. His snarled black hair, released from captivity, flopped in his face.

"Deaf?" Cheever blinked. "But they can implant—" He cut himself off on a sharp sigh. "Right. Surebleak."

"Indeed." Pat Rin frowned. There was something he had heard, once—perhaps from Val Con?—that the deaf on lowtech worlds often developed a sign language for use among themselves, which, while diverse as to culture, were each built along the lines of Old Trade, with its emphasis on the concrete over the philosophical.

Tentatively, he moved a hand in the ritual greeting.

Jonni cocked his head, his eyes suddenly on Pat Rin's hands, rather than his face. His own hand—the one not holding the tuber—rose, touching fingertips to lips and descending, palm up, and stopping at chest level.

Not the sign he had used—not quite. He repeated the boy's truncated version, and earned himself another enthusiastic nod.

"So." He sighed, and moved his hand again, showing first Cheever and then Natesa. He said their names, clearly, keeping his face turned toward Jonni, so the boy could read his lips, then drew a circle in the air with his index finger, signing "protection." Jonni frowned briefly at that, then suddenly grinned. He dropped the tuber into his pocket and used both hands to mimic pistols.

Diverse as to culture, indeed, Pat Rin thought, and tried the sign for "service."

But this proved beyond Jonni's ability to translate; and after a few frowning moments, he gave it up with an exaggerated shrug.

"Just so," Pat Rin said, slowly and distinctly. "Why have you come to me?"

That met with comprehension, and produced a veritable storm of signs, the single one Pat Rin recognized having to do with growing—or growing things. Quite possibly the unfamiliar signs were technical terms, invented to describe specific plants.

Pat Rin held up a hand, palm out. Jonni's hands faltered; fell.

"Tomorrow morning," he said. "We will go to the garden and you will show me. Is that soon enough?"

Jonni nodded.

"Good. Tomorrow morning at . . ." He ticked the time off on his fingers and heard Natesa sigh behind him.

Once more, Jonni nodded, then offered what was apparently his version of "good-bye"—a mere reversal of "hello"—recaptured his cap with a swoop, and vanished out the door before Pat Rin could return the courtesy.

"Tomorrow morning at two hours past dawn?" Natesa asked, resigned.

"It would be best to tend to it before I leave for the store," he told her earnestly. "And tomorrow will be an early day because of the necessity to deliver the Sinner's Carpet to Ms. Audrey's house." He tipped his head. "You needn't come with me, you know. He scarcely looks able—or inclined—to hurl me off the roof."

"True. However, he may easily have friends who are very able and desperately inclined." She rose, and sent a meaningful glance at Cheever. "Mr. McFarland, if we are to tend the overheads, now is the hour."

"Yes'm, I see that's so." He frowned at Pat Rin. "Gwince is your security this shift. Try not to do anything to scare her, OK?"

Pat Rin inclined his head, stiffly. "I will do my humble best, Mr. McFarland. Within reason."

The big Terran just shook his head, and followed Natesa out of the room.

On the verge of following, Pat Rin paused, his eye drawn . . .

The cat was sitting upright beneath one of the extra plastic chairs, tail wrapped neatly 'round its toes, ears forward-pointing and interested, eyes glowing like molten gold.

"Well," said Pat Rin and went gracefully to one knee, extending a finger in greeting.

The cat considered options, leisurely, and at precisely the moment Pat Rin thought to withdraw his hand, stretched up onto its toes, walked from beneath the chair and touched the proffered fnger with a flower pink nose.

It was, Pat Rin saw, the precise cat that had startled Natesa in the pantry that morning: brown, with several broad, uneven stripes of black down its washboard sides, and another down its spine. Its tail was slightly fluffy, as was the rest of the cat, and also striped brown and black. It was not by any means a handsome cat; rather a brawler, if its ears were to be believed, and Pat Rin all but wept with joy to behold it.

"Well," he said again. "I don't doubt but that you've come to thank me for protecting you from Natesa's skill."

The cat blinked, strolled forward and stropped forcibly against Pat Rin's knee. Lightly, prepared to snatch his hand back at the suggestion of a claw, he stroked the brown-and-black back. The tail went up, the cat arched into the second stroke, and there was heard a momentary grinding sound, as if someone were drawing a whetstone down a blade. Pat Rin smiled, stroked the cat a third time and, reluctantly, arose. The cat looked up at him, yellow eyes molten.

"Duty calls, and her voice is stern," Pat Rin told it. "I must to the office. You may come with me, if you like, or you may return to your own duties, in the pantry."

So saying, he departed the dining room, collected Gwince from the other side of the door and went upstairs to his office, where Natesa found him, some few hours later, having resolved both the overheads and the matter of the device in the sub-cellar.

He was slumped over the desk, his head resting on an open book, pen fallen from lax fingers, an ugly brown-and-black cat curled on the floor by his knee, eyes slitted and yellow. Natesa drew a sharp breath, heart squeezing, then saw his brows pull together in a frown at some upstart dream, and sighed. He was asleep, nothing more. Silent as an assassin, she went forward.

He had been writing—black ink across the grayish pages of his so-called log book. She glanced at the left-hand page, expecting to see code-words, or some arcane language of symbol and nuance . . .

He had chosen to write in Trade, very simply, the smooth lines of his hand drawing her eye even as she told herself that this was not hers to read.

Surebleak, Day 308, Standard Year 1392

My name is Pat Rin yos'Phelium Clan Korval. I write in Common Trade because I do not know who you will be, or from what world you will hail, who will come after me. I will begin by describing the circumstances immediately preceding my residence upon this planet. I will delineate the Balance that must go forth, and the reasons for its going forth. I will put down, as best as I am able, those things from other log books and diaries that may illuminate my actions and necessities.

Let it begin.

On the planet Teriste, in Standard Year 1392, Day 286, a messenger of the Department of the Interior brought me word that the entirety of my kin were killed—murdered by agents of this Department.

I will herein name the names of my kin, lest they are forgot, and I will say to you, whoever and whenever you may be, that it is only I, Pat Rin, the least of us all, who is left now to carry Balance to fruition . . .

DAY 50
STANDARD YEAR 1393

DUTIFUL PASSAGE
LYTAXIN ORBIT

Lina had agreed to meet him over tea in the library at the end of his piloting shift. The necessity of retrieving the whisker from his quarters put Ren Zel a few moments behind the appointed time, and he found her at table ahead of him, teapot steaming and two cups standing ready.

"Well-met, shipmate," she said with a smile, that having become a joke between them, over the years of their acquaintance. Despite the concerns he brought with him from his shift, Ren Zel felt his mouth curve upward in response.

"Shipmate," he responded, slipping into the chair opposite her, and inhaling the fragrance of the tea. "Ah." His smile grew wider. "Shall I pour?"

"If you please. I find myself remarkably indolent this hour."

To find Lina indolent was to find an impossibility. Ren Zel filled a cup, and passed it to her. She cradled it in her hands and lifted it to sample the aroma. Ren Zel poured a cup for himself, and leaned back in his chair, likewise enjoying the sweet steam, and then taking a bare sip, teasing his tastebuds with the complex notes of the beverage.

"So," said Lina eventually, putting her cup aside. "How may I assist you, shipmate? Have you been dreaming again?"

"In fact, I have," Ren Zel murmured, setting aside his own cup and reaching into his pocket for the sampling tube. "And, when I woke, I found that dreaming had produced—this." He placed the tube before her on the table, then sat back, with an effort.

"I . . . see." She picked the tube up and turned it this way and that in the light. "A singularly handsome specimen. Found in a dream, you say?"

"In the aftermath of a dream," Ren Zel said, slowly. "I woke—or dreamed I woke—and felt the weight of a cat on my chest. I raised a hand to stroke it—and realized of a sudden that a cat was—not possible, so that I woke in truth." He waved a hand at the tube. "And found that whisker caught in the coverlet."

"I see," Lina said again, her eyes on the whisker. "And was there a dream before the dream of the cat?"

"Two," he said promptly. "First was the battle-dream. I woke from that and read until I nodded. There was another dream, then. Within it, a . . . shipmate had come to me with the same dream, of the fleas and the—solution we undertook to save ourselves. I soothed her as best I might and sent her to her own rest. And then—"

Lina raised a hand. "Did you recognize this shipmate?"

Ren Zel considered that, then shook his head, Terran-wise. "Indeed, it was only that she had the memory upon her, and stood so very distressed, for ship and crew . . ." He moved a shoulder. "But, after all, it was a dream."

"Just so." Lina touched the tip of her forefinger to the tube's seal. "May I?"

"Certainly."

And so she had the whisker out, and settled back in her chair with it held close between her two palms, and her eyes closed. Momentarily ignored, Ren Zel retrieved his teacup and sipped, recruiting himself to patience.

"I know this cat . . ." Lina murmured, her voice slightly slurred, as if she spoke in her sleep. Ren Zel froze, cup halfway to his lips, unwilling to break the Healer's trance.

"I know this cat," she said again, barely more than a whisper. "It is . . ." Her face changed, tightened; her eyelids flickered, flew open. She sighed and shook her head gently. "To my knowledge, this cat has never been on the *Passage*."

With which, she picked up the tube, reinserted the whisker, resealed the top, and leaned forward to place the whole before him.

Ren Zel lowered his teacup, looking from her careful face and opaque eyes to the tube and its captive wonder.

"It had seemed," he said eventually, and with utmost care, "that . . . trance had produced more information regarding this cat."

"Had it?" Lina recovered her cup and sipped.

And whatever that information might have been, Ren Zel dea'Judan was not to be made a gift of it. He bit his lip, staring down at the tube, concentrating on breathing. He had counted Lina among his friends . . .

"You think me cruel," she said. "Friend, acquit me."

He looked up, saw sympathy in her eyes and raised a hand. "Then, why—?"

She shifted, setting her cup down. "Tell me, has there been a return of that phenomenon such as Shan reported, when he found you on Casiaport?"

He blinked, bought a moment of thought by putting his cup down.

"Certainly not. Why should there have been?"

She moved a hand, soothing the air between them. "Forgive me; I meant no offense. It was merely that Shan had said you were in trance, and foretelling . . ."

"I was wounded," he said, more sharply than he had intended, "and raving."

She was still for a moment, then inclined her head. "As you say, Pilot."

Ren Zel flinched. "Lina . . ."

"Ah, no—" She bent forward and put her hand over his where it rested next to the damned tube. "Peace . . . peace. Friend, you must understand that it is . . . difficult to know the correct path to take with you. We have on this ship three not-inconsiderable Healers—one a full dramliza—and you remain beyond the touch of all, shielded so well that none of us may so much as reach forth and give you ease of ill dreaming." Gently, she patted his hand and withdrew.

"With you, we must—we must pilot blind, trusting our training and an honest regard for yourself to win us through to safe landing." She sighed and picked up her teacup to sip. Ren Zel, curiously breathless, did the same.

"So," Lina continued. "I will tell you that the trance did produce more information. Not," she said wryly, "as much as I would have desired. Yet more than I will give to you. My training—and my sincere regard for yourself—tells me that it would be best to allow you to proceed . . . unencumbered by preconception. The cat may never come to you again—or it may reappear often, at the times it chooses. Cats are like that, after all."

"So they are." He picked up the sampling tube and slid it into a pocket, rose and bowed, respect to a master. "My thanks, Healer."

She smiled, wistfully, and inclined her head. "Pilot. Good lift."

"Safe landing," he answered, that being the well-wish pilots exchanged before a journey.

He walked back to his quarters slowly, wondering what sort of journey Lina supposed him to be on.

DAY 309
STANDARD YEAR 1392

BLAIR ROAD
SUREBLEAK

Natesa had perhaps been correct to protest his choice of hour for this meeting, Pat Rin thought, as he followed Jonni on a tour of the rooftop garden. The air was frigid, and the light breeze soon had him a-shiver and longing for the temperate climate he had been born to.

Well, he would have a cup of tea soon enough, and in the meanwhile he was in a fair way to learning the sign-names for rather a number of vegetables.

It appeared that Jonni's purpose in the tour was to elicit Pat Rin's advice on the crops to be planted this season. The unraveling of this would doubtless have proven tedious, if not impossible, as the beds had lain fallow over the winter beneath tarpaulin shrouds, long since stripped of their visual aids to communication. But here Jonni revealed unexpected resources.

Showing Natesa empty hands with fingers spread wide, he opened a plastic tool chest and pulled out an object inexpertly wrapped in oilcloth. A few moments later, Pat Rin was holding a spine-shot paper book entitled *How to Grow Food in Small Spaces*, and trying to simultaneously read the descriptions appended to the pictures Jonni pointed out and attend the boy's hand-talk and pantomime.

So, in the end the planning was only laborious, leaving Pat Rin feeling that he had personally turned every bed and hand-set every seed.

"That is good then," he told Jonni, closing the book. "With care, we will be comfortably supplied through next winter. I depend upon you to do well for us."

The boy smiled and nodded, and reached rather anxiously for the book Pat Rin cradled in his arm.

"A moment." He held up a hand, and the boy stopped, smile vanished and eyes anxious.

Pat Rin sighed. "Only a question, child. Can you read?"

The pert nose wrinkled, and the right hand wobbled in a sign which was most perfectly plain: *So-so*.

"Ah." He glanced to Natesa. "I suppose it is too much to hope that there is a school in this territory?" he asked, foreknowing the answer.

But she surprised him. "Gwince tells me she learned to read at Ms. Audrey's house. I do not believe that she was ever employed as a Scarlet Beauty, so it seems at least possible that Audrey sponsors a school." Her mouth twitched in a faint smile. "For some definition of school."

"Well, since I will be seeing Ms. Audrey today, I will make inquiries." He held the book out. Jonni pounced on it with visible relief and went over to stow it in the tool chest, first re-wrapping it in its sheet of waterproofing.

A blade of wind sliced across the rooftop; Pat Rin gasped, shivering renewed, and turned toward the rather fearsome metal staircase which ascended from the attic to the garden.

"Come," he said to Natesa. "There will be tea in the kitchen."

"Beautiful," Audrey breathed, some hours later, gazing raptly at the Sinner's Carpet.

It did look well, Pat Rin thought, standing at survey by her side. He had been at pains to impress upon the extras hired to carry and lay it that it did indeed matter how the carpet was oriented in the room, that the edges be straight, and that there be no unsightly wrinkles. In fact, it had taken rather longer than he had estimated to finish the thing properly. But the result was well worth the labor.

"I got it all planned out," Audrey was saying, with what sounded to be genuine happiness. "Real special deal, only for the, you know—connoisseur."

"I hope that it brings you profit," he murmured politely and she chuckled.

"Oh, it will. That rug is gonna be *good* for business." She turned to him with a smile. "Thank you. Now, let's step along to my office and I'll hand over the deposit and the first month's rent."

"I wonder if you might assist me," he murmured, as they walked through halls and rooms much less busy than yesterday. Audrey threw him a quick blue glance.

"Well, I can try," she said, with appropriate caution. "What's up?"

"There is a child of my house who requires tutoring. He reads, but poorly. I would have his skill increase."

Both of Audrey's eyebrows were up. "If he reads at all, he's better off than most of the streeters."

"True. However, he bears the burden of being deaf, and thus it is doubly important that he learn to read and write well." He tipped his head, considering. "It would also be good if he were able to learn basic mathematics."

She snorted, half a laugh. "What d'ya think this is, a nursery school? Who's the kid?"

"His name is Jonni. He is employed as my gardener."

She stopped, there in the middle of the hall, and turned to stare at him. Perforce, Pat Rin also stopped, wondering.

"Kid about—what?—thirteen? fourteen?—with a kinda pointy face and a head full of black hair that just makes you itch to take a comb and a pair of scissors to it?"

A fair description. Pat Rin inclined his head. "It sounds the very child."

Perhaps she heard him, perhaps not. Certainly, she continued on as if she had not—"And deaf. Blizzard, it's gotta be the same kid!"

"I am to understand," Pat Rin ventured when several moments had passed and she said nothing more, "that Jonni is known to you?"

"Known—" She looked at him, her face set in grim lines. "Look, that kid used to live here—we taught him what he knows about reading, and he used to be pretty good at his numbers, too. Not that he cared about the reading or the sums—but he did care about growing things, and so he learned what he needed for that. Then—it's been maybe two years ago, now—an'—well, you don't need the details. Short of it is a customer walked in here one night higher'n a spaceship on somethin' that wasn't doin' him no good, and when the smoke cleared, he was dead, which he deserved—and so was two of mine, which they didn't." She sighed. "An' o'course one was Jonni's mom. Kid come strollin' in from somewhere, took one look and screamed—first time I ever heard him make a sound—turned 'round and ran out the front door. A couple of the boys went out after him, but they lost him in the dark. And, you know, we thought he'd come back, after he got himself in hand." She sighed. "Hasn't yet."

A bitter tale, indeed, and if the boy could not bear to return to the place of his mother's murder, who was Pat Rin yos'Phelium to call him a coward? Yet, he must have his letters and his sums, if he were to profitably make his way into adulthood. He looked up at Audrey.

"I will speak with him," he said, and saw her brows lift slightly, possibly in amusement. "If he will not come here for lessons, perhaps lessons may come to him." He tipped his head. "If, of course, you are agreeable to providing tutoring for this child, in return for a reasonable fee."

She waved her hand, a shapeless, meaningless gesture. "Oh, sure—got a pregnant girl right now who reads like a house afire. She'd be glad of the work and the cash. Don't know how she is with her numbers, but there's Villy to do it, if she ain't able. Patient as glass, Villy, and real good with the kids."

"Then it is decided in principle," Pat Rin said, with a feeling of entirely ridiculous relief. "That is good. I will speak with Jonni this evening and see if I might persuade him here tomorrow. If not, I will send word and you may dispatch his tutor."

"Suits," she said, and suddenly grinned her wide, infectious grin. "There you go again, pitching changes into the wind! Let's make that settlement before you decide it's too cold and install central heatin' on the streets!"

It was mid-morning when he and Cheever McFarland returned to the store to find a bent and tattered person at the front window, her hands and nose flattened against the glass.

So rapt was she that Cheever McFarland needed to clear his throat three times before she stirred and looked up, blinking, but unafraid.

"I'm Ajay Naylor, Boss. Gwince said you wanted to talk to me." Cheever shook his head. "I ain't the boss," he said, and pointed. "He's the boss."

She peered along the line of his finger, and there came over her face an expression Pat Rin was beginning to know well—raw astonishment mixed with disbelief.

He inclined his head. "Indeed, I am the boss. Thank you for taking the time to come to me. Will you step inside, so that we may talk in comfort?"

Disbelief increased by a factor of six. She turned back to Cheever.

"This is for real? He's the boss? The one took Moran and the publicity committee out, like Gwince was tellin' me?"

"This is for real," Cheever assured her. "He's the boss. I'm one of his 'hands."

She shook her head. "Damn." Her gaze drifted back to the window. "Pretty things you got there. Boss."

"Thank you. Would you like to examine them more closely? As a rug-maker, yourself, you will perhaps be interested."

She grinned at that, showing toothless gums. "I'm interested, OK. Though you can't hardly put my rugs in the same room with them."

"Ah, but I intend to," Pat Rin said, moving to unlock the door. "If the two of us are able to reach an agreement."

Gwince opened the door with a grin and a nod.

"Evening, Boss. Mr. McFarland. Natesa sends that the work progresses, Boss. Cook asks when you want to eat supper."

"We shall dine in an hour," Pat Rin answered. "Please ask Jonni to attend me in my office in three hours."

"Yessir, will do."

"Thank you, Gwince." He moved down the hall, and paused to look up at Cheever, who grinned.

"Got it. See you in an hour." He strode off, whistling. Pat Rin continued, more slowly.

The business with Ajay Naylor had been concluded to mutual satisfaction; she was not adverse to providing him rugs on commission, though she was less sanguine, even, than Audrey regarding the possibility of shipping off-planet. The road was the thing, as he understood it. As recently as Ajay's young womanhood, the Port Road had been neutral territory, and free passage guaranteed. That was not to say safe passage, even then, but caravans had regularly formed to bear items for sale or trade to the Port and most, if not all, won through.

On the subject of what had changed, Ajay was unclear. There had been a rumored falling out among several of the bosses of the larger territories, which resulted in the road being closed, and abandoned to bandits. Another rumor had the Port itself closing, the ships withdrawing entirely. But that rumor, Ajay had allowed, with a certain dryness, had likely been air-dreams—as he doubtless knew better than she.

Ajay departed, and there had come Al, the keeper of the hardware store, and their near neighbor. He had chatted for a while, admired the carpets without displaying the least desire to understand them, and finally brought the conversation around to Pat Rin's proposed Insurance rate structure.

Upon being informed that Insurance payments were for the meanwhile suspended, Al looked less pleased than one might have supposed, and pulled his long chin thoughtfully.

"Gotta have a scheme for makin' money," he said. "No offense meant, Boss."

"Nor any taken," Pat Rin assured him. "My scheme for making money is entirely straightforward—I intend to sell carpets. For cash."

"Yeah, OK," the man said. "Though you might wanna get in some low-end stuff—I'm not sayin' cheap, just affordable to somebody—well, sleet, to somebody like me. These 'uns are pretty, but they're pricey. But that's just the store. You're the boss—need to get cash somehow."

"For what should I receive funding?" Pat Rin had demanded, rather heatedly. "Does the boss mend the holes in the street? Does he fund clinics? Libraries? Schools?"

"Well, no. Not lately. Audrey, she grabbed what she could of Vindal's clinic and library before Moran torched 'em. You get nicked, or break a leg or an arm—like that—go to Audrey's house; they'll take care of you. Can't do much if you're sick with something high-end, but they're pretty good with the usual. Same way, you wanna learn how to read—go to Audrey's. Somebody there'll teach you."

"It appears to me," Pat Rin commented, "that if there is Insurance—or street tax—to be paid, that it ought to be paid to Ms. Audrey, who is doing more for the residents of this territory than any boss."

"Naw, naw, that ain't fair. See—done right, now—forget Moran; he was a pig—done right, the boss is the one who fixes the problems. Say I got a problem with Tobi and we ain't been able to work it out. So we come to you and we say, Boss, we got this problem and we can't fix it—tell us what to do. And you maybe study on the case for a while and then you tell us what to do. Oughta get something for havin' to do everybody else's thinkin' for 'em. Right? An' then, see, the boss is the one who keeps the turf together, and makes sure no other bosses annex us. Ought to get something for that, too. An', if you was thinkin' about bringing a clinic, or maybe a library out on the street, to kinda ease the load on Ms. Audrey—you oughta get cash for that, too." He'd paused here, perhaps a little startled at his own eloquence, then did his summing up.

"Tell you what, Boss—this little store ain't gonna support alla that."

Nor would it, Pat Rin thought now, climbing the long, chilly stairway to his room. Properly done, as Al described it, a boss on Surebleak was near enough to delm. He sighed, irritated with himself. He had allowed the information that this was a Terran backworld, brutish and barely-governed, blind him to the fact that persons of honor naturally strove to form into clans, if not precisely kin-groups.

Sighing again, he pushed open the door to his room, saw a shadow move and heard a burble the instant before the brown-and-black cat hurled itself into his legs, tail high and purring fit to deafen him.

Smiling, Pat Rin bent down and stroked the animal. Impossibly, the purrs increased, and the cat threw itself against Pat Rin's legs in an ecstasy of welcome.

"All very well," he said with mock sternness. "I suppose you've been lying abed all day, neglecting your duties to the cook?"

The cat burbled again, shifting from side to side and it lifted first the left front paw and then the right, kneading air.

Pat Rin laughed softly and straightened. "Flatterer. Now, by your leave, I must prepare for dinner."

Dinner was simpler that evening—a jam pastry removed by a casserole which took advantage of the pantry's abundance of tinned fish. Despite its lowly beginnings, the dish pleased.

The conversation was mostly between his oathsworn, on the arcane lore of security. Pat Rin listened closely, astonished at those things they considered merely prudent, and marveled at the tale of protocols and devices that had been put into place, solely for the purpose of protecting his life.

Pushing his plate aside, he sat quietly sipping tea. There was eventually a lull in the discussion of protections and defenses, offensives and attacks, and Natesa turned to him, her eyes dark and luminous, her face subtle in shadow and nuance.

"Has Ms. Audrey a place in her school for Jonni?" she asked, with every appearance of interest.

"Curiously, she does, though she doubts he will come to her. He had used to live in Ms. Audrey's house, until his mother got her death there, whereupon he ran away. We left it that I shall speak with him, and if he will not go to her, she will send a tutor here."

"That is well, then," she said, approvingly.

"Well enough," he agreed, and hesitated on the edge of mentioning his conversation with Al. But—no. That was something he wished to examine thoroughly himself, weighing his melant'i well, before he sought the opinion of a Juntavas Sector Judge.

So. "We have a contract with Ajay Naylor for rugs on commission. She doubts the spaceport, as well, though she tells me the Port Road had been open and neutral in her youth."

"It had been, until several concurrent tragedies changed the rule," said Natesa. "First, there was a turf war between two neighboring bosses, which ended, not as might be expected—in one boss annexing the other's territory—but in the subdivision—in the several subdivisions—of both territories. From there grew chaos, which might have eventually settled, had it not been for the arrival of an epidemic virus. There was a vaccine at the Port—

Surebleak belonged to the Health Net in those days, too—and it was to be delivered by Port personnel. But the Port was short-handed, and, rather than sending Port personnel, in an armored car, with appropriate weaponry, they sent several natives, who were employed at the Port, with a list of territories and the number of vaccines to be left with each boss."

Pat Rin put his mug down. "They were robbed?"

"Ah, no. But that was only because they sold the entire shipment to the boss just next to the spaceport, and disappeared." She moved her shoulders, eloquent as a Liaden. "Perhaps they were clever enough to keep vaccines for themselves. One rather hopes they forgot that detail. It was, by all reports, a horrible disease, and thousands died for lack of the cash to purchase the cure."

He closed his eyes. Gods. What sort of world produced such people? And yet, Al and Audrey Gwince, Jonni, Ajay, Villy . . .

"Master?"

He opened his eyes, seeing what appeared to be honest concern for himself reflected in her face.

"I wonder," he said, changing the subject brutally. "What are our options of communication devices? I find no radio, for instance, among Mr. Moran's former possessions. How do the bosses keep contact among themselves? Worse, I find no local radios, so that we might communicate between ourselves—myself to you from the store, for instance."

Cheever grunted. "Been tryin' to crack that nut," he said. "Got a couple people on staff who say there's a native equivalent of a portacomm, but the trade's controlled by one of the bosses out from here. I'm going down to check on the ship, day after tomorrow. Thinking about making a side trip to check out the porta-comm trade while I'm over that way." He paused. "Speakin' of which, the emergency talkies off the ship'll do fine to keep us three in touch. I'll bring them on back, if you want."

"Yes, do that," Pat Rin murmured. He finished his tea, put the mug down, and looked up to find Natesa's eyes yet upon him.

"*Do* the bosses communicate between themselves?" he asked her.

Her eyes narrowed slightly. "My information indicated that the more powerful bosses, who control larger territories—that there had been communication between them, arrangements of trade, alliances. Whether this is still so . . . I doubt. Matters seem to have deteriorated badly since the report was written." She sighed, sharply, and leaned forward, eyes and face intense.

"The difficulty with Surebleak is that the boss system is rotting from the core. There is no orderly transfer of authority when bosses are often murdered by a wild gun who aspires only to their power. Such guns rarely have any notion of responsibility or of administration, never mind compromise and mutual profit. So, the territories are proliferating in number while they dwindle in size, and chaos has become the order of the day."

"Chaos is what we wanted," Cheever pointed out from his end of the table.

Natesa nodded. "Indeed, chaos serves us very well in what we propose to do. But it hardly serves those who live here, and who cling to survival amidst the slow disintegration of their world. Nor is it good for business."

Juntavas business, that would be. Pat Rin considered her. "I would think the Juntavas a supporter of chaos."

"Not so—not so, Master. The Juntavas is a champion of order. We require certain things so that business may go forth: safe and easy access; safe and easy egress; steady supply; an economy. And a consistent structure of command, with which profitable associations may be forged. Surebleak offers none of these things. It is a bitter waste—and not only for the Juntavas."

"But if a boss arose who was able to consolidate and hold the territories—and train a successor to do likewise?" Pat Rin asked.

"Perhaps the rot might be excised," she said slowly. "Perhaps. But we must first ask if Surebleak is able to produce such a boss."

"Surely, there are honorable people in other territories, as we have found here?" he said.

"Surely, there are," she agreed. "But, consider the present system, if we may dignify it so. Did a person of honor and integrity arise, yet she must take the path to power which is open to her— cold murder. To unite all—even most—of the territories, she will need to murder much more than once. And, upon achieving her goal of one cohesive territory, she must transform herself into a statesman, capable of compromise, slow to slay even the most intractable dissident." She shook her head. "I do not know that one individual could successfully encompass both roles, and yet they are inseparable."

"Yet, you are yourself both judge and assassin."

She smiled. "I am *called* Assassin," she said, amusement rippling her voice. "Would you like to know why?"

"Yes," Pat Rin said seriously. "I would."

But Natesa merely laughed and came lightly to her feet. "Perhaps I will tell you one day." She glanced aside. "Mr. McFarland, if I may have a few moments of your time?"

"Sure thing." The big man got to his feet, and looked at Pat Rin, who raised a hand.

"Gwince. I will try not to frighten her. Thank you, Mr. McFarland."

"Good night, Boss."

Alone in the dining room, Pat Rin sighed, closed his eyes and simply sat for the space of a dozen heartbeats. He was tired, gods. Already he was tired—and there was so much yet that he must do.

"The shortest way to finish is through begun," he murmured, which was what Uncle Daav had used to say. The Liaden words felt odd in his mouth, after even so few days of speaking only Terran. Would he be able to speak Liaden at all, when he at last returned to the homeworld to destroy Korval's enemy?

Well. One thing at a time—and that was Anne Davis advising him now. "Er Thom's Terran," according to his mother, but never in Uncle Daav or in Cousin Er Thom's hearing.

Pat Rin pushed back from the table, gathered Gwince from her post at the door and went down to the kitchen.

The cook was polishing a soup pot; he set both rag and pot aside when Pat Rin walked in and nodded politely.

"Evening, Boss. What can I get you?"

"Nothing just now, I thank you. I merely wished to tell you that I am pleased with the standard of cooking displayed since yesterday's dinner."

The man grinned, and shuffled one foot. "That's—thank you, Boss. I mean to keep the standards high."

"I am delighted to hear you say so," Pat Rin assured him, and turned to go, his mission accomplished.

Two steps toward the door, he recalled something else and turned back.

"The brown and black cat," he said to the cook's suddenly anxious face.

The anxiety deepened. "Yessir. He ain't bothering you, is he?"

"Not at all. I merely wished to know his name."

"Name?" the cook repeated, hands twisting in his apron. "Well . . . Cat, I guess. I mean—who names cats?"

Pat Rin paused, then inclined his head. "A personal idiosyncrasy. Good evening."

"See ya," said the cook.

The office was the next order of business. He left Gwince guarding the door and went over to the file cabinet to retrieve his log book.

He had written perhaps three pages when Gwince put her head in the door.

"Jonni's here, Boss."

He glanced up. "That is well. Send him in, please."

She vanished, and a moment later Jonni stepped tentatively within, his pointed face showing wariness.

"I'm not going to eat you, you know," Pat Rin said mildly, and motioned at the yellow plastic chair. "Sit a moment. I have a proposition for you."

Still tentative, Jonni sat.

"Thank you. Ms. Audrey has said that she will teach you to read better, to do sums and to write. I wish that you will undertake these things. Do you understand me?"

The boy nodded, insufficiently exuberant—his cap remained on his head.

"That is good. Now Ms. Audrey tells me that you may not wish to go to her house for lessons. If this is so, then she will send a teacher, and you will have your lessons in this house." He fixed the child with a stern eye, much as he had done with Quin, by way of enforcing his filial authority. "The lessons are not negotiable, but the location is. Which do you choose?"

The boy held up a hand, fingers rippling—*wait*.

Fair enough; it was bound to be a weighty choice, between honor and horror. Pat Rin leaned cautiously back in his own chair, prepared to wait for some time, if necessary.

It was unnecessary. Jonni sat for several moments with his head bent, contemplating, perhaps, the hole in the right knee of his trousers, then looked up, eyes bright. He made a sign as appropriate as it was lewd.

"You will go to Ms. Audrey?" Pat Rin asked, to be certain.

Jonni nodded, placing his cap in peril of a tumble.

Pat Rin smiled. "I am pleased. Be in the front hallway when I leave tomorrow morning, and you may walk with me as far as Ms. Audrey's house."

The boy grinned, and nodded again.

"Good. Is there anything else?"

A headshake, grin unabated.

"Then our business is concluded. Good night." He made the sign that he knew as "farewell".

The boy rose, hesitated and—bowed. It was in no discernible mode, though it was done with grace and good intent—and surprised entirely.

Before Pat Rin could clear his throat, Jonni was gone, ghosting out the door.

Another victory upon the day, he thought, picking up his pen and returning his attention to the log book.

It was well.

He was running down cold and twisting hallways, gun in hand. The ones who pursued him also had guns—as he knew to his dismay—and there were many more of them than his pellets could account for. He could not do this on his own. He needed help. He needed kin.

The hallway twisted, right, left, right, and spilled him into a dingy gray room, where a lone man sat in a chair, legs thrust out before him, holding a glass of wine. Pat Rin's heart leaped and he ran forward.

"Val Con! Cousin, you must help me—" He extended a hand, touched his cousin's shoulder—and leapt back, an unvoiced scream choking him.

The man in the chair was a skeleton, grinning death into his eyes.

Gasping, Pat Rin awoke. Slowly, he oriented himself, and brought his labored breathing down. He turned somewhat in his twisted nest of blankets, and his knee bumped something solid.

Carefully, he put his hand down—felt warm fur and the beginning vibration of a purr—the nameless brown and black cat.

Smiling, he put his head back down on the flat pillow, his hand still on the cat.

The rest of his night passed, dreamless.

BLAIR ROAD
SUREBLEAK

The cat dogged his heels from the bedroom to the kitchen, sat by his knee while he broke his fast with bread, cheese, and tea; and trotted, tail high and jaunty at his side down the hallway to the vestibule.

It was a strangely crowded vestibule. In addition to Cheever McFarland, who was entirely capable of filling the small space without assistance, there was Jonni, and the slender subtlety that was Natesa.

"Good morning," Pat Rin said to his oathsworn, simultaneously offering the same greeting in sign to the child.

"Mornin', Boss."

"Good-day, Master."

The child likewise returned his greeting; paused and signed something else, not, Pat Rin thought, to himself, but to—

The cat.

"Good morning, Boss Silk," he murmured, reading—and captured Jonni's attention with an interrogative wave.

"The cat's name is Silk?" he asked, imitating the soft, smoothly flowing sign.

The boy nodded, grinning, and tossed a spangle of sign off his fingers.

"Ah, did he so? I had thought him a cat of discernment."

"What does he say?" Natesa wondered softly.

Pat Rin shook himself. "Why only that this cat—this Silk—had the good sense to scratch the late Boss Moran very thoroughly not too long ago, to the vast amusement of one barbaric and bloodthirsty child." He tipped his head. "Forgive me if I pry, but am I to understand that you will be accompanying us today?"

"My business today is on the street, and I thought to walk with you and Mr. McFarland—and one bloodthirsty child—until my way turns from yours." She bent her head gracefully, suggesting a full bow in her favorite mode of student to master.

"Perhaps I am inconvenient."

"Or perhaps you are not," he said dryly. "One merely—inquired."

"Cat comin', Boss?" Cheever asked lazily from his lean against the door.

"I believe that his duties keep him at home," Pat Rin replied, and looked sternly down at his attendant feline. Silk blinked molten gold eyes, then turned and flowed away down the hall toward the kitchen.

"Now is the hour," Pat Rin said. "Mr. McFarland, the door, of your goodness." He moved a hand as he spoke, alerting Jonni to the door's opening, and they exited the house a veritable army: Cheever, then Pat Rin, the boy at his side, and Natesa, silent and graceful, walking slightly to the rear and the right.

He heard the pellet sing by his ear and Natesa's shouted *"Down"* in the same instant, and dropped to the street, gun to hand, a target in his eye.

It was target practice then—heavy game, and when the targets stopped showing, he blinked, disoriented, and with a high buzzing in his ears.

"Stay down," Natesa hissed, from somewhere behind him. "Do not move. We are awaiting Mr. McFarland's sign."

It was the word "sign" that jerked him back to the reality of the street, where he lay in the half-frozen mud, staring at the dead man crumpled at the base of the wall opposite, his blood shockingly bright on the dingy walk.

"Where . . ." he began, but Natesa's voice came again, louder this time.

"We have the sign. I will stand first. Count slowly to twelve. If I have drawn no fire, stand, but hold your weapon ready."

He sensed her movement and counted to twelve, slowly. Silence reposed upon the street. Pat Rin rose, gun held ready. Across the street, a door somewhat down from the dead man opened, and a woman peered out, then hastily withdrew, the door slamming into place.

More action across the way. Cheever McFarland slipped out of an alley that should have been too thin for him, and waved.

"All clear," he shouted and strode toward their position.

Released, Pat Rin spun, looking first at the ground near at hand, but there was nothing there, save the mud.

"Master?"

"The child," he said, remembering the pellet whine and Natesa shouting—and of course Jonni could not have heard either. Though, surely, seeing all of his house going to the ground, he would—

"The child," he said again, to Natesa's black, black eyes. *Where is the child?*"

Her gaze shifted over his shoulder. He turned and saw the ragged huddle of cloth, not so very far away, really.

"Gods."

He knelt next to the still, small body and turned the boy in his arms. No breath, no heartbeat, no wide, glad smile. *Gods, gods . . . no.*

"Master?"

"Who did this?" The High Tongue felt like ice in his mouth. "Master, Mr. McFarland has found Jim Snyder among the fallen," she answered softly. "He believes the others come from Boss Deacon's turf."

Pat Rin knelt, holding the dead child in his arms, and if he wept now before his oathsworn, he was lost to shame, lost to all but a vast and frightening coldness.

This ends, and ends now. No more of mine will be shot down in the streets.

He raised his face to Natesa, and saw her eyes widen.

"Fetch Audrey," he said. He heard his voice shake—and did not care. "I will know the name of my enemy. They will answer me. Fully."

Natesa hesitated at the entrance to the garden, an unaccustomed shyness rooting her feet to the top stair. Midway across the roof, she saw him, silhouetted against the starry glow of Surebleak's nighttime sky, seated on the edge of a shrouded garden patch, shoulders bowed, the cat crouched at his side. Neither seemed to note the wind, intermittent from planetary north, which added to the evening's chill.

The child's death—she recalled the face he had shown her then, mud-streaked and slick with tears, icy with a purpose that surpassed mere revenge by an order of magnitude, and shivered with something more than the cold.

"Inas, why are you come?" His voice was soft and mannerly. He did not turn his head. And who knew what the invocation of her personal name might mean?

Natesa gathered her courage, lifted her feet and entered the garden.

"It is cold," she said, matching his tone. "I have come to bring you a blanket."

"Ah."

Gently, she moved among the shadows of the dormant beds, and came to stand before him, the blanket draped over one arm.

He looked up at her, his face a golden mask in the starshine.

"Thank you," he said, but made no move to take the blanket from her. Beside him, the cat straightened from its crouch and settled into a sit, fuzzy tail wrapped neatly 'round its toes.

Natesa sighed lightly. "Ms. Audrey bade me say that her house is open to you."

The golden mask displayed no emotion. "I am grateful to Ms. Audrey, but I do not seek distraction."

The wind gusted, bitter enough to dismay her, though she had taken care to don a jacket. This close, she could see that he was shivering, though she doubted he knew that himself.

"Pat Rin." Surely, she might dare his name, when he had established the mode himself? "Pat Rin, you are cold. The night is not temperate. At least the blanket, if I cannot persuade you to go inside." She bit her lip. "You serve no one, if you sicken."

"Very true," he said politely, yet still he made no move to take the blanket.

Wondering at her own temerity, she stepped forward and draped it around his shoulders. The cat Silk, sitting tall at his side, blinked golden eyes in approval.

Something moved in his face. Indeed, he sighed, and lifted a hand on which Korval's Ring glittered, to touch the fabric of the blanket and pull it more snugly about him.

"Thank you," he said again, and it seemed to her that there was more than mere ritual in the phrase. "I am grateful for your care."

"You are welcome." She hesitated, unsure of what now she should offer, reluctant to leave him here, alone, but for his cat and his dead, inside the freezing night.

"You will wish to know," he said surprisingly, "that I have decided to take up the roles you doubt may be acted by a single individual."

She frowned. "I beg your pardon?"

"I will unite the territories," he said, sounding altogether sane. "We shall have laws and contracts. We shall have free and easy travel between streets, even to the spaceport itself. We shall rejoin the Health Net. There will be schools, libraries and clinics. Children and adults will take advantage of these benefits without fear for their lives. I will accomplish this thing."

"Pat Rin . . ."

"We will begin by annexing Boss Deacon's territory."

Natesa shook her head, torn between impatience and pity. "Pat Rin, Boss Deacon is well protected. More, his territory lies in the opposite direction of our goals."

"You have not attended," he chided her gently. "I will unite the territories. Thus, we will take first he who has dared to deal death to one of mine. It shall serve as a lesson, and bring us to the attention of those others with whom we will need to treat."

"And, having done so," she said with asperity, "you will receive even more assassins into your presence, until one of them succeeds."

"Inas, we can prevail—not without blood, no. And perhaps we shall entertain more assassins before we win through. But it can be done. I see it. I know how to proceed."

Pity overruled impatience. His mind had broken beneath the burden of his griefs. Had she been other than a Sector Judge, she might well have cast herself to her knees and sent up a wail to the heedless gods, which was how one grieved for the dead and the demented on the distant, unlamented world of her birth.

Instead, she extended a hand and touched his shoulder, lightly, companionably.

"It is good that you have a plan. Mr. McFarland is below stairs. Let us go to him and discuss procedures over tea and cheese."

She had not expected to so easily persuade him, but he rose at her word, slipping the blanket from his shoulders and folding it neatly over his arm.

"Let us do that," he said, still in that soft, oh-so-sane voice. "Silk—we descend." He inclined his head, courtesy itself. "Inas, after you."

DAY 50
STANDARD YEAR 1393

LYTAXIN
EROB'S CLANHOUSE AND GARDENS

Despite his lack of haste, Shan reached the proper suite rather sooner than he would have liked, and, stifling a sigh, put his palm against the plate.

A chime sounded, faint on the far side of the door. The last note had not quite faded from the ear when the door whipped open, revealing a Liaden woman of exceptional beauty, golden hair sweeping her stiff shoulders, violet eyes wide in a face so rigidly calm, it seemed a sculpture, audaciously formed from pure, pale gold, rather than living flesh. Shan's ravaged Healer senses perceived the expected anger, twined with equal parts terror and relief—a volatile combination which did not bode well for calm discourse between siblings.

Well, nothing for it but to begin, he thought, and swept an elder brother's affectionate bow.

"Good evening, sister," he said, choosing the Low Tongue, which was Nova's preferred language, rather than Terran, which was his. "How delightful to find you here! I trust you had a pleasant journey?"

Nova's mouth tightened. "A pleasant journey," she repeated, so flatly as to be entirely modeless. She took a breath and stepped back, moving her hand in the gesture of welcome. "Pray enter, brother."

Perforce, he entered and wandered down the room to the wine table. He picked up a glass and poured a portion of Erob's agreeable, everyday red into it, which really was too bad of him. The Code dictated that he wait until he was offered refreshment, but, then, the Code also taught that informality among kin was acceptable. In any case, it offered Nova opportunity to be irritated in a minor chord, and perhaps would leach off a measure of that explosive mix of emotion.

"Wine, sister?" he inquired over his shoulder. "Erob's red is quite passable. The canary is a touch sweet and I found the jade musty the other day—though perhaps that was merely a bad bottle."

"The red, of your kindness," Nova said, calmly, beside him. Shan sighed inwardly. Well, he had survived the full lash of Nova's temper more times than he could count; he could doubtless survive it now. He poured a second glass of red, and handed it to his sister, who inclined her head and took one small sip.

Shan sipped his wine and counted, slowly, toward twelve.

He had reached *nine* when Nova abruptly put her glass on the table and brought her eyes up to meet his.

"I had occasion to trade news with Priscilla Mendoza just recently," she said, conversationally. "She tells me that our brother and Miri Robertson rejoice in a true lifemating."

"Oh, it's a wizard's match, plain enough," Shan said with false good cheer. "I can see the linkage clearly—any Healer may, who cares to risk having their Sight dazzled for hours."

"I see." She paused, tension screaming in every line of her. Still, her voice was calm and even when she spoke again.

"Priscilla now calls herself captain of *Dutiful Passage* and allows me to know that she is come into yos'Galan as a thodelm's lifemate."

Shan grinned. "Never have I held Priscilla's courage in higher esteem!"

Nova sighed. "Another true lifemating, brother? One would . . . dislike to believe that you set aside your first speaker's word from mere willfulness."

"*Mere* willfulness?" He raised his eyebrows. "Are we or are we not of Korval? We are never *merely* willful. Surely your study of the Diaries has revealed that to you!"

"Shan."

He sighed and rubbed the tip of his nose. "I cannot judge. The only measures I have are what I see between Val Con and Miri—and what I saw between our parents. I—we—are something—other. Though what manner of other, I am at a loss to know." Another sigh, sharper. "I need to see Priscilla." And that, he thought, was a piece of understatement worthy of Val Con himself.

"She expressed a similar need." Nova picked up her glass and drank off some wine as if it were a not-very-tasty tonic. "So, I find

both of my brothers lifemated with recourse to neither Code nor
first speaker. We will inaugurate a vogue, and bring runaway mat-
ings into fashion."

She finished the wine in a snap and put the glass back on the
table.

"Priscilla's other news concerned Val Con's health," she said,
calm, so calm, while the flames of her dismay and fury suddenly
leaped, fairly scorching him. "I am to know that he is desperately
wounded, barely escaping his death, and that he may arise from
the catastrophe unit unable to fly."

Oh, Shan thought. *Oh, damn.*

"The med techs have," he said carefully, "expressed differing
opinions. Some believe that Val Con will at first be all but entirely
disabled, but that he will, over time, improve, even learning to
walk again. That is the extreme view." He paused.

Nova's face had paled considerably, but she waved at him to
continue.

"The less extreme view is that Val Con will emerge able in almost every way, except in his possession of the reaction times
necessary to a master pilot, much less a scout pilot. These also believe that his health will remain fragile for some years, if not for
the remainder of his life."

Nova was now pale to the lips, but she watched his face un-
waveringly, and for a second time waved at him to go on. "The
most optimistic," he said, neglecting to add that this group was
comprised entirely of himself, two Clutch turtles, now soundly
asleep in Erob's atrium, and Miri Robertson Tiazan. "The most
optimistic believe that our brother will awaken to himself complete and unimpaired."

Nova blinked.

"How can opinions diverge by so much?" she demanded. "The
first and the second are consistent in effect, merely different in degree. But—that he awaken completely healed? How—"

Shan sipped his wine, deliberately buying time. Nova was
going to like the risk they had taken with Val Con's life even less
than the med techs had. And yet, to deny her hope, when he felt
her terror for Val Con almost as his own . . .

"You must understand that there are . . . variables," he said
slowly. "Did Priscilla tell you anything of the nature of Val Con's
injuries?"

Nova blinked. "She had said he was grievously wounded. I had assumed—piloting injuries . . ."

"There were some of those," Shan allowed. "Acceleration injuries, broken bones gotten by bouncing around in a cockpit built for someone twice his size—in every direction . . ." He sighed and rubbed his forehead; a headache was building, blast it. "You understand, there were no ships, so it fell to Val Con and myself and—another pilot—to take them from the Yxtrang. In the process of acquiring his ship, Val Con was nicked by an Yxtrang pellet carrying a load of nerve poison. A full hit would have killed him more or less instantly, as I understand it. The effects of the smaller dose over a longer time are . . . not well documented. Additionally, there are . . . variant methodologies . . ." He eyed her, wondering if she was swaying or if his vision was wavering. "Sister?"

"You—and Val Con," Nova repeated, voice shaking, "*stole* ships from the Yxtrang?"

"Well, they had so many, you see," he said apologetically. "It was necessary to mount an air strike, so naturally—"

"You could have been killed!" Nova interrupted.

Shan sipped wine. "It was war," he said, striving for patience. "I *would* have been killed had I huddled in House with the infirm and the children. And if you think me capable of turning Val Con from necessary action by an appeal to common sense, you vastly overrate my powers of persuasion!"

She stared at him for another heartbeat, then inclined her head, allowing him the point. "Just so. Now—'variant methodologies'?"

Here it came. He finished his wine and set the glass aside.

"In consultation with Clutch turtles Edger and Sheather, Val Con's lifemate became convinced that there was more effective healing available—a Clutch healing. I offered myself up as a test subject and found the healing . . . remarkably efficacious. Miri then decided—as Val Con's lifemate and for Korval—that he and she would undergo this healing. Edger and I labored some hours over Val Con, and left him sleeping easily, his condition much improved from when we had him out of the 'doc—"

"Out of the 'doc?" Nova demanded. Shan sighed. Well, and he had known she wouldn't like it.

"You dared to dice with the life of Korval Himself? When the medics—when you yourself!—admit that the long term effects of the poison are unknown, that—"

"Nadelmae Korval decided," Shan interrupted, somewhat louder than he had meant to do, "for herself, for her lifemate, and for Korval entire."

"Nadelmae Korval," Nova spat, "is a Terran-raised mercenary, ignorant of clan and of Code—"

"No, she's not."

Nova stared. "Explain."

He rubbed his forehead. Gods, he was *tired*. Quickly, he accessed a Healer's energizing routine. The expected jolt of vigor was more like a faint tremble of nervousness, but it would suffice. For a while.

"Miri and Val Con rejoice in a true lifemating—recall it? I'll wager cantra to kittens that you'll find her just as Code-wise as— why, as Val Con! And I'll further wager that she's found to fly like a scout. She knew very well what her decision might mean, and she did not make it lightly."

There was a long silence, while terror, fury, hope, and exasperation warred behind Nova's eyes. Finally, she sighed.

"I will see our brother."

Shan shook his head. "That would not be wise. We left him sleeping, in a state . . . somewhat akin to trance. He will wake himself, when he is ready."

"I will *see* him," she repeated, with barely leashed violence. "If he is entranced, he will not heed me, and I will have had some ease of heart." Her eyes glinted. "Surely, I am allowed kin-right?"

Surely, she was allowed kin-right, Shan thought, and truth told, it would ease his own heart to know that Val Con still slept sweetly, Healed and removed from all danger.

"Very well," he said. "But a glance, only, and then I will need to seek my own bed."

Nova inclined her head and turned toward the door.

"**Lady** yos'Phelium?" The med tech scrambled to her feet. She was showing a little white around the eye, for which Miri blamed her not at all, and doing pretty good—after the first, incredulous gape—about not staring at the patients. Miri inclined her head, trying for a sort of matter-of-fact haughtiness.

"These, my oathsworn," she said, choosing the High Liaden mode of employer to employee—which was close enough to true, considering that she was blood-and-genes of Erob, "require optimization. They have been underfed of late, and are doubtless in need of supplements. Also, the tattoo work will be removed. The med techs attached to the mercenary unit have an erasure program. Pray contact them and request its transmittal, in the name of Captain Robertson."

The tech swallowed, hard, and managed a fairly credible bow of acquiescence.

"It shall be done." She looked up—at Nelirikk, at Hazenthull, at Diglon—and down—at Shadia, and back to Miri. "Forgive me, but one is not able in the language of the—of the subjects. One would forestall an . . . unfortunate situation, my lady."

"I understand," Miri assured her, and moved a hand, bringing both Nelirikk and Shadia to the tech's attention. "Scout Lieutenant Shadia Ne'Zame, and my aide, Lieutenant Nelirikk Explorer, will stay here to assist you in any way required."

The tech actually looked relieved to hear it, which probably showed how little experience she had with scouts, bowed again and moved over to the first 'doc of the three in the infirmary.

"If the . . . elder soldier . . . will come forward?"

Nelirikk translated it in terms of an order and Diglon Rifle stepped smartly forward.

Miri exchanged a look with Shadia, who grinned and gave her a Terran thumbs-up. "We have everything under control, Captain Redhead."

"Why don't that make me feel better?" Miri asked, rhetorically, and went away to find Emrith Tiazan, to tell her what was going on in her medical center.

MIRI had gone to the med center to attend the needs of yos'Phelium's newest dependents, leaving Val Con alone with his father.

When he was a boy, he had used to dream of this meeting: his father would arrive unannounced, and swing him up into strong arms; his father would be sitting at his bedside one morning when he woke; he would be called from his studies to attend Uncle Er Thom in his office, and his father would be waiting for him there . . .

Child-dreams, which had nothing to do with this moment, in which he, grown and lifemated, stood in a garden far away from home, in the presence of a stranger, who smiled at him faintly and said, "Well."

In appearance, Val Con thought, one's father was the antithesis of one's foster-father. Nor had the holos of Daav in his youth prepared one, entirely, for the elder scout standing, serene and patient, before him in the pre-dawn garden. The holos had been of a man at the height of his powers, whip-thin and sharp-featured; his plentiful dark hair confined into a tail; black eyes looking boldly out of the image.

This man had thickened a little beyond slenderness; his hair more gray than brown, cut close to the head in a manner subtly Terran. His face, never beautiful, even in youth, had yet a certain austere charm, startlingly like Uncle Er Thom; and the black eyes assessed one with all of a scout's directness.

And, Val Con thought suddenly, *he has deliberately engineered this pause to allow me time to study him.* Almost, he grinned in welcome of this oldest of scout tricks.

Daav raised an eyebrow. "You had some pointed questions to ask me, I believe?"

"The most pointed I had asked: what have you been about all these years?" *While I waited for you, and Uncle Er Thom did . . .*

Daav's eyebrows lifted slightly. "Surely I made an entry in the Diaries? Yes, I'm certain of it. I distinctly recall your presence at the event—there's a blot on the page, where you jostled the pen."

And the other blots, thought Val Con, who knew the page well, *are tearstains.*

"However," said Daav, "since the substance of the entry appears to have slipped your mind—I was about the Balancing of my lifemate's death."

"But," Val Con heard himself, with no little astonishment, state, "your lifemate is not dead."

Daav appeared to experience no corresponding astonishment upon hearing this assertion. He merely raised a hand; the old silver puzzle-ring flashing like a zag of lightning 'round his finger.

"It was some time before that became clear to me," he said. "Our arrangement had been . . . flawed. And—forgive me—I had *seen* her die. It was far more reasonable to think I had gone mad from grief than to believe I was truly hearing her voice." He lowered his hand.

"In any case, since the assassin—say, rather, the one who had employed the assassin—so earnestly wished me to look to Terra for my villain, I could scarcely do less than accommodate him."

"Though perhaps," Val Con murmured, "not in quite the way he had wished."

"Well, what would you? Aelliana would never have wanted me to start a war in her name—even had it been absolutely certain that her death was called by Terra. Which it was by no means. The Code quite clearly states that, in matters of life-Balance, the wishes of the Balancer are secondary to the wishes honorably imputed to his dead." He lifted his shoulders in a common Terran shrug.

"My lady would have said that Terra struck because it was afraid, and that fear arises from ignorance. So, I have been teaching cultural genetics. To Terrans."

"Ah," Val Con said softly.

"Ah, indeed," his father returned. He tipped his head. "Your lady captain speaks common Yxtrang very like a scout—or perhaps she speaks it like *the* scout."

"I really ought to teach Nelirikk my personal name," Val Con said, musingly. He moved his shoulders, *not* a shrug. "I concede that the Common Troop had not been among Miri's languages before—recent events."

"Ah, yes! The heroic flight of captured Yxtrang fighters against the over-advantaged foe, in which action you were wounded unto death! Pray, do not be coy, sir—tales of your prowess precede you. Commander Carmody holds you as an object of awe, and appears to consider you thoroughly deranged."

Val Con laughed.

"Yes, well." Daav shifted a step or two aside and stretched, carefully, Val Con thought, as would a man who was concerned that his back muscles might protest.

"Tell me, if you would," he said, settling back from his stretch, "who is this puissant enemy with which Captain Robertson has beguiled my poor Yxtrang?"

Val Con lifted a brow. "I thought they were yos'Phelium's Yxtrang?"

"One feels a lingering tenderness," Daav told him earnestly. "They are such good children."

"You relieve me," he said. "As for the enemy—" He paused, head cocked; saw his father stiffen, and turn his head. The gate at the end of the garden swung on its hinges; and very shortly the shadows relinquished Clonak ter'Meulen.

"Half-an-hour and then some," he said, smoothing his mustache with loving fingertips. "Morning, Shadow."

"Good morning, Clonak," Val Con replied, considering the pudgy scout. Something was . . . shifting . . . at the edge of his mind, as if the pieces to an old, old puzzle were snapping, at last and inevitably, into their proper places.

"Clonak," he said again, hating what he was seeing, knowing that it must be true, "my father wishes to know the name of Korval's great enemy, that murdered his brother and his brother's lifemate. You can tell him that, can't you?"

The older scout tipped his head. "Already did, but I don't mind repeating it: Department of the Interior. You remember that, don't you, Daav? Though I'm not certain I'd write Er Thom against their account; what I heard from Shan was that he had died of his lifemate's dying."

"Which he would not have done," Daav pointed out quietly, "had Anne remained among us."

"True . . ."

Val Con took a step forward, drawing the eyes of both men. "You fed me to them," he said, and his voice was, perhaps, not quite steady. "The scouts *gave* me to the Department."

Clonak stared at him as if he'd taken leave of his wits. "Well, of *course* we gave you to them, Shadow! Who else did we have more likely to trump them than a first-in, pure-blood yos'Phelium scout *commander*? Concentrated random action. Would we waste such a weapon? Would you? I didn't think so. Besides," he finished, crossing his arms over his chest, "It's the duty of the Captain to protect the passengers. Er Thom *can't* have missed telling you that!"

"As close-kin, I ask that you not kill him," Daav said into the silence that followed this. "I allow him to be twelve times an idiot. But he is also my oldest friend, and I value him."

Val Con closed his eyes, ran the rainbow, sighed—and opened his eyes.

"Very well," he said, imposing neutrality, if not calm, on his voice. "It was my duty and I was suited to the need. But the plan has gone awry. The Department continues."

"Yes, it does," Clonak said, as if to a half-wit, "but you are no longer its creature, eh? I see our weapon returned to us, increased three-fold; a Captain with an intimate understanding of the danger from which the passengers stand at peril." He flung a hand out, palm up. "And scarcely a heartbeat too soon, all doom having broken loose. The scouts hold themselves ready to receive your orders, Commander."

Val Con shook his head. "Amuse yourself elsewhere. I've no patience for it."

"Now, Shadow," the pudgy scout said sternly, "do not, I beg you, come the kitten. I took losses at Nev'Lorn—and so did you."

Val Con blinked. "Nev'Lorn?"

"Clonak, the lad's been ill and away from the news." Daav's deep voice was perfectly serious. "He hasn't heard that the Department of the Interior mounted an armed attack against a scout base and that dozens of his comrades are dead of it."

The Department had openly attacked scouts? Val Con blinked again. The thing made no sense. The Department flourished precisely because it operated along hidden avenues, far removed from the ken of honest folk, and made no large, overt moves.

"Why?" he asked Clonak.

"Why? Why else but out of concern for yourself!" He sighed, suddenly and sharply. "Shadia found the mark of a scout in a derelict orbiting an interdicted world, and filed the report, all according to regs. She didn't make the connection between yourself and the mystery scout, though others of us did. The Department caught the report off our bands and moved in, apparently having performed the same leap of logic." He shrugged. "They were that desperate to have you back, Shadow. Or, at least, they were desperate lest someone *else* have you."

"You rate me high," Val Con said drily. "Certainly, the Commander would wish to recover—or neutralize—me before I became a threat to the Department. But to risk everything in an open strike against the scouts—" He shook his head. "That is not how the Commander does his math."

"Might have gotten a new tutor," Clonak offered. "Or perhaps he finds himself strong enough to commence upon a second phase, and begins to be bold."

Cold feet ran down Val Con's spine. *That*, now, was all too likely. The Department's Plan called for expansion, after all, and it might well seem the time to move, with Korval scattered to its various safeplaces. He was about to say as much to Clonak when a soft sound caught his ear, anomalous in the stillness of the predawn garden. He cocked an ear, waiting for a repetition, and raised his left hand in the scout's sign for *wait*.

•   •   •

Nova set them a brisk pace down the quiet pre-dawn halls of Erob's clanhouse. Indeed, they were moving so swiftly as they rounded the corner into the main hallway that they very nearly knocked over the red-haired woman in working leathers who was striding in the opposite direction.

Shan checked, boot heel skidding on the waxed wooden floor. "Miri—"

She grinned. "Hey, Shan. Worked a treat!"

He eyed her, astonished; Healer senses brought him a second astonishment in the luminosity of her pattern, by which time Nova had recovered both her balance and her glare.

"I'm speechless," he told Miri, "which my sister will tell you is no common occurrence. Nova, here is Miri Robertson Tiazan, Lady yos'Phelium."

Nova's glare solidified into disbelief. "*You* are Miri Robertson?"

"'fraid so," Miri said, not without a measure of sympathy. She nodded, easily. "Pleased to meet you."

"I—" Nova began. Shan, deciding that bad manners were the lesser part of disaster, interrupted her ruthlessly.

"We're on our way to see how Val Con does," he said to Miri's amused gray eyes. "Would you like to accompany us?"

"Can't—gotta find Aunt Emrith and give her some good news. Tell you what, though, if you're looking for Val Con, you'll find him in the garden at the end of the wing. He's having a talk with his father."

"His father?" Shan blinked. "Miri—"

"Daav yos'Phelium is dead," Nova, not to be outdone in any mode, including rudeness, interrupted.

"No, he ain't. We just did the whole welcome-back-to-the-Line thing an'—" Her eyes lost focus somewhat, and then widened.

"Something's wrong," she said, and was gone, running back the way she had come.

Shan was after her in the next heartbeat, Nova at his side.

Wrong wasn't the beginning of it.

Miri ran, her head full of gunfire, deadly shadows in the garden and Daav was down, Clonak beside him, and Val Con—Val Con . . .

She slapped the doorplate and dove through the opening, hitting the ground and rolling for the cover of the hedge to the right. Gun ready, she surveyed the enclosure.

Three dark, utterly still lumps in three widely spaced locations 'round the garden were deaders. A single huddle near the ornamental boulder in the center was the scout named Clonak ter'Meulen, working with rapid ferocity over another leather-clad form. At the opposite end of the garden, the gate swung open on its hinges. Heart in her mouth, she walked over to the busy scout.

"How bad?" she asked, as the door cycled behind her. She spun in time to see Shan and Nova whipping through, neck and neck, for all the worlds like they were running a race.

"Nothing a 'doc won't put right," Clonak said, sitting back on his heels, and sighing in plain relief.

"Right. Shan'll help you get him down to the med center." Spinning on her heel, she checked her inner sense of Val Con, locating him some distance from where she stood, his pattern a muddle of horror, stubbornness and sheer crazed adrenaline.

"The Department of the Interior," Clonak said, and she didn't stop to hear anything else, but ran, ran as she had never run, not even when Klamath was coming apart around her, out the gate and after him.

DAY 345
STANDARD YEAR 1392

HAMILTON STREET
SUREBLEAK

"Boss Conrad's here to see you, Penn."

Penn—Boss Penn Kalhoon, actually—frowned down at the balance sheet he'd been working on, and waited for the roaring in his ears to subside.

Boss Conrad was here. He'd hoped—never mind now what he'd hoped; it was too late for hope. Reality was that the man who'd come blazing out of Moran's territory less than a Standard

Month ago—the man the streeters called Boss Killer—was in his territory—in his *house*—and suddenly Penn Kalhoon was looking at ending the day early.

Thera . . . Thera'd be OK, he told himself. Conrad targeted bosses; streeters and staff attached to a particular boss' household were, by report, safe as anybody ever was, so long as they had the good sense not to draw on Conrad or one of his 'hands.

The exception to that'd been Deacon. Conrad blew the house, there, boss and crew—but did it so neither of the houses next to it blew, or took fire. They'd shimmied a little, maybe, when Deacon's crumbled down into its own cellar-hole.

And, according to Penn's sources, Deacon had bought that special bit of attention fair and square by doing something stupid even by his standards, and sending a team onto Conrad's turf to take him out. The team never made it back to Deacon's territory, but they managed to screw up good before they all got shot dead: they killed Conrad's kid.

After consideration, Penn had finally allowed that Conrad'd done just what he needed to do to Deacon, and not one bit less than Penn might've done himself, if it'd been *his* kid killed.

He just wished the guy hadn't gone off his head and decided to wipe out every other boss on the planet, too.

"Penn?" That was Marj, his second, still standing by the door and not exactly sounding calm. He sighed, capped his pen, closed the notebook, settled his glasses on his nose, and looked up.

"OK," he said, voice steady. "Please show Boss Conrad in, and have Dani bring us some hot tea—I hear he likes tea."

Marj was looking distinctly white around the mouth. "Penn, this is the guy who—"

"Yeah, I know who he is." He cut her off. "And what I want you to do—no matter what happens—is cooperate with Boss Conrad. Got that? You level with him—explain how you're my second and you'll be glad to show him whatever he needs to see. Be *smart*, OK? You seen the reports—the only one he wants is me. He'll be good for the streets—you seen those reports, too. Be smart, Marj. Tell me."

She swallowed, eyes wet. "I'll be smart, Penn."

"Great." He nodded. "Now go get him. It ain't polite to keep a guest waitin'."

• • • •

The reports all had Boss Conrad peaking at the lower end of average tall, with brown hair and brown eyes, a blue earring, a glittery hand-ring, and a liking for pretty clothes. All that was true, but Penn was still unprepared for the slim and elegant person who followed Marj into the office, his 'hand walking quiet and solemn at his back.

The 'hand—it was the woman. Natesa. Penn felt one of the knots in his gut loosen. Natesa was a pro; he didn't have to worry about a botched job. She'd be quick and she'd be clean. Not that the big guy's hand-cannons wouldn't't've done the needful, but there'd been an awful mess left to add to Thera's upset.

Much relieved, he stood up from behind his desk, keeping his hands in plain sight, and nodded politely.

"'afternoon, sir. I'm Penn Kalhoon."

Dark brown eyes considered him gravely from an ageless golden face. The reports put him in his thirties, which he probably wasn't any younger than. But he could've just as easy been ten, fifteen, even twenty years older. He inclined his head, more formal, somehow, than a standard nod of greeting.

"Good afternoon, Penn Kalhoon. I am called Conrad. Please forgive me for disturbing you at your work." His voice was soft and pitched in the mid-range, real easy on the ear.

"That's OK, sir. I've sorta been expecting you."

The well-marked dark brows pulled slightly together. "Ah, have you? I wonder why."

Penn shrugged. "My sources said you was tending in this direction." That was the truth—wasn't no use lying to the man. He was gonna need to know the state of things, and best he had it straight from the one who knew it best. Penn pointed.

"I'd be pleased if you'd sit. Dani'll be up real soon with some tea."

The eyebrows moved again, upward this time. "Tea would be most welcome," he murmured and did sit, graceful as a girl. His 'hand took up her post behind him.

Penn sank down into his own chair, wondering what to say now, and was saved from making an immediate decision by the arrival of Dani with a tray full of cups, pot, and cookies. She got everything down on the desk with no spills, which was pretty good, considering how bad her hands were shaking, and shot him a look from wide, scared eyes.

"Thanks, Dani," he said easily, like he was having lunch with Thera. "We'll take it from here."

"Yessir, Boss," she whispered, and fled, closing the door a little too hard behind her.

Carefully, Penn poured tea into one of the cups, sipped it, and bit into a cookie.

Having demonstrated his good will, he filled another cup and passed it across the desk.

"I thank you," Boss Conrad murmured and took a sip, then favored Penn with a straight look. "I hope that you will forgive me if I come quickly to the purpose of my call," he said.

Penn swallowed the rest of his cookie.

"Sure," he said, and his voice sounded a little edgy to himself. "You're a busy man."

"As you are," Conrad said. "So, then—quickly: I am here to offer you an opportunity to enter into a partnership with me."

Penn blinked, thinking he'd heard it wrong, and dared a quick look up at the pro. She smiled slightly, and inclined her head. "Um," Penn said, and had another swallow of tea to clear the sawdust out of his mouth. "What kind of partnership?"

"A perfectly unexceptional sort of partnership—or so I persist in believing, despite those who have felt they would rather die than accept it." Conrad sipped his tea. "I envision free passage and trade between my territories and your own, and a pooling of our various resources, for the betterment of all. You will continue to administer your streets, as you have been doing so ably for these last ten Standards. I will administer my streets, and hope to do as well."

Penn blinked again, then shook his head with a half-laugh. "I'm sorry. See, when you walked in here, I knew my day was done. Gonna take me a sec to focus." Something struck him and he looked into Conrad's smooth, calm face.

"You didn't offer this deal to all the—all the other bosses, did you?"

"In fact, I did not. The late Boss Deacon did not impress me as someone with whom it would be advantageous to associate. The rest, however—yes. I offered them this precise deal."

"And they turned you down?" Penn rubbed his nose. "How dumb are these guys?" He waved a hand. "I know, I know. Dumb enough." He closed his eyes, turning the deal around in his head, looking at it from this angle and that, seeing profit, growth, and— a snag.

"I worked hard to make my streets safe," he said carefully. "Some of those turfs you picked up are pretty rugged, according to my sources. The tollbooths don't keep all the trouble out, but they keep it down."

"True enough. We are in the process of developing a street patrol, which will eventually work to keep trouble to a minimum. In the meanwhile, we may leave the tollbooths in place, as check points only. Travelers would be required to stop and submit to a search, as they are now, but no cash would change hands."

"OK, that's a workaround—we can do that."

"Good. I wonder how you feel about trading people as well?"

Penn froze. "Trading *people*?"

Boss Conrad moved his hand, his big ring sparkling. "Gently. I only meant that it might profit you if—for an instance—I were to ask a master brewer who lives inside my territory to come to you for a time, to teach the craft to one of yours. Likewise, I am in need of assistance in the matter of inaugurating schools, such as you maintain. Now, we have a system of . . . itinerant teachers, who wander from street to street, teaching those who would learn how to read. I wish to do better than this, but I must be taught how."

"I get it," Penn grinned, excited now. "An' if your master brewer, say, didn't want to leave home, maybe I could send my student over to him for a while."

Conrad smiled, faintly. "Precisely."

"OK, so far this is easy." Penn looked at the other man seriously. "What's the catch?"

Another smile, slightly less faint than the first. "The catch is that I wish to secure the entire length of the Port Road, and I will require you to guarantee safe passage for all along that portion which runs through your territory. I will undertake likewise."

The Port Road ran more or less through the middle of Penn's turf, and it was as safe as the rest of his streets. But . . .

"We're cut off by Ivernet to the north, and Whitman, on the east. I can hold my piece of road, OK, but there ain't nobody gonna come walkin' out of Ivernet's turf. Whitman—I can talk to Whitman, if you want. She's not somebody who snubs a profit, if you know what I mean. But Ivernet—sleet, Ivernet's crazy."

"Ah. Nonetheless, I will be calling upon Boss Ivernet and offering him the deal. If the deal is not acceptable, then measures will be taken."

Penn shook his head. "You're a braver man than I am," he said.

"Merely foolhardy, I believe." Conrad leaned forward to put his cup on the desk, and came to his feet, smooth and graceful. Penn stood, too, feeling like his whole body was grinning.

"It seems we agree in principle," Conrad said, inclining his head. "Natesa."

The woman moved. Penn had time for one sharp spike of terror before he saw that it wasn't a gun in her hand at all, but a portable radio.

Shakily, he took it.

"If you need to speak with me—a consultation, an emergency—simply push the 'four' key. If I need to speak with you for similar reasons, I will use my radio and yours will emit three tones, from low to high. Is this acceptable?"

"Acceptable," Penn croaked.

"That is good. And now, I will take my leave and allow you to return to your work. Good-day, Penn Kalhoon. It is . . . a pleasure to do business with you."

"Good day, sir. Ma'am." He raised his voice. "Marj!"

The door popped open so fast he knew she'd been listening at the knob. Her face was white all the way to the hairline, but she was grinning fit to beat all.

"Marj, Boss Conrad and his 'hand are leavin' now. Please take them down to the door."

"Yessir!" she said snappily, and turned her grin on the man and the woman. "Right this way, Mr. Conrad."

They followed her without a backward look between them and Penn sank back into his chair, taking pleasure in the simple act of breathing.

After a while, though, his brain started in, like it always did, and he shook his head. Going to call on Ivernet, was he? That Natesa'd better be a *damn* good shot.

DAY 345
STANDARD YEAR 1392

JOLIE'S HOUSE OF JOY
SUREBLEAK

"Houses on Ivernet's turf?" Wyn, their host for the evening, shook his head regretfully. "There ain't no houses on Ivernet's turf, Mr. Conrad. We hear there ain't much on Ivernet's turf—least ways, not much anybody else'd want. Now, if you was going over to Whitman's territory, we'd be right pleased to direct you to Mirabell's House."

"Alas," Pat Rin murmured. "My fancy is quite set upon visiting Boss Ivernet."

Wyn looked over to his partner, the Jolie from whom the House took its name. She sighed.

"Mr. Conrad, Wyn's right—there ain't anything on Ivernet's turf you'd want. We had—when was it, Wyn? Two years ago? Three? When them kids come through?"

His broad forehead rumpled in thought. "Oh, hell, yeah, I remember them. Three years, it musta been—in the flat middle of winter."

Jolie nodded, leaned forward and touched Pat Rin's sleeve lightly with pale fingers.

"Two kids, it was. They made it outta Ivernet's territory just like Wyn says, in the middle of winter, their feet wrapped in rags and not a whole piece of clothing between 'em. How they got past the tollbooths, we never did find out. Lost one right off—she wasn't nothin' but skin over bone, an' so cold—we couldn't get her warm, and I'll tell you, we covered her over with every blanket in the house, with Nuce and Silbey one to a side. Nothin' we did was any good—she was that worn out with the drugs and bad food and then running through the snow to get away. To get safe." She turned her face aside, for all the worlds like a proper Liaden lady attempting to recover from a too-intimate display of emotion.

"So," she said after a moment, looking back to him, her blue eyes damp. "The second one hung on awhile longer—long enough that we thought she'd make it. Long enough to tell us how it is over there." She pressed her fingers more firmly onto his sleeve, and withdrew.

"Mr. Conrad, it's a hell-hole over there. Saying Ivernet's crazy don't begin to cover it. There's drugs—something they call 'nirf'—and most take it because it cuts down on the empty feelin' of not havin' no food. There ain't no houses, just like Wyn told you. Some work for whatever they can get—an' mostly what they get is nirf. Nor ain't there much in the way of business, like we got here in Boss Penn's territory—or like you got yourself, sir, in your turfs!—cause nobody knows when Ivernet'll blow a gasket and him and his 'hands'll come out on the streets, lookin' to go huntin', like they call it, and burn themselves down a buncha houses so they got enough light to see by."

It seemed an apt description of a hell-hole, Pat Rin allowed, grateful for the patient presence of Natesa, silently supping at his right hand. Apt enough that, had it been possible, he would have allowed himself to be persuaded to visit Boss Whitman instead.

Necessity, however, existed.

"I am forewarned," he murmured. "But, as it happens, there is one thing that Boss Ivernet holds that is of interest to me. The Port Road runs through his territory."

"Yeah, it does," Wyn said, sitting up a bit straighter, eyes bright with interest. "You after securin' the Road?"

"I am," Pat Rin said, well pleased with him. "I intend to have it open from the center-land to the spaceport, safeheld, with free passage to all."

Wyn whistled. "You talk to Penn about this?"

"Indeed, it was the purpose of my visit. Mr. Kalhoon and I discussed the matter this afternoon, and were able to reach a mutually advantageous agreement," Pat Rin said, and felt Natesa shift beside him. "Please do speak with him yourselves and ask what questions you may have. I am certain that a boss who administers as well as does Mr. Kalhoon must speak often with his people."

"Penn's the best boss in nine territories," Wyn assured him warmly, and shook his head. "Audrey told us you was a change-maker," he continued, glancing over to his partner. "We tried, Jolie. Audrey said he was stubborn, too."

"Yeah. Yeah, she did. *And* she said he was good for business, which he won't be, if he gets killed on Ivernet's turf." She glanced at him, a blush mantling her cheeks. "Not that it's my decision, really, or to say that Ms. Natesa ain't a pro . . ."

"I thank you for your care," Pat Rin said, sincerely, "but my plans are firm."

"And that's why he's a boss," Wyn finished, slapping the table, and grinning, wide and pleased. "Tell you what, stop over with us again on your way back out. We'll be happy to see the both of you."

Warmed, Pat Rin inclined his head. Audrey, of course, had provided the introduction to the house of Jolie and Wyn, as she had provided introductions to the other six whorehouses in the six territories that were now either his or allied to his. All the heads of household had been cordial, but none save Audrey—and now these—had shown any personal concern in himself. Indeed, why should they? Bosses came and bosses went, and even a boss who was good for business was bound to be murdered one day.

"I thank you," he said again, inclining his head. "It will be a pleasure to renew our acquaintance on my return."

"That's fine, then," said Wyn, coming to his feet, with Jolie at his side. Pat Rin stood, in respect of the host, and Natesa did, as well. "It's time for us to go on the floor and make sure everybody stays calm," Jolie said. "If you want company, just choose who you like—on the house. There's a morning buffet laid out for the early guests and the one's who're late going home—you're welcome to that, too."

"You are gracious," Pat Rin murmured. "I do not myself desire a companion this evening, though perhaps Natesa might wish to avail herself."

"Whatever suits," Wyn said. "I'll take you on up to your room and make sure the doormen know who you are. Staff quarters, up the back of the house. We don't get much trouble here, but sometimes a customer'll take a shine to one of the staff and make a little bit o' noise." He waved a hand, indicating that Pat Rin should walk with him.

He complied, being very careful not to look back at Natesa, who after all deserved what joy she might take, here in a place which was as safe as Surebleak came, on the eve of an enterprise of surpassing danger, if not outright stupidity.

Which is how he happened to miss the subtle gleam in the night black eyes thoughtfully considering him as he quit the room.

• • •

She came to him naked, which she had not done in his several dreams upon the subject, bearing a bottle of wine and two glasses.

Pat Rin, roused from his labors with the log book, himself divested of jacket and most of his weapons, opened the door to her knock and stood, quite plainly staring.

"Is something amiss?" Natesa's rich voice held an unsubtle note of laughter.

"Not in the least," he assured her, recovering his address with a quick mental shake. "I was merely trying to recall if I have ever before seen you stand weaponless."

"Ah." She smiled this time, and showed him the glasses. "May I come in? Jolie believes this to be quite drinkable."

"Does she?" He stepped back, allowing her to pass, and watched her walk to the table, marveling at the subtle beauty of her, slim and far too alluring in her creamy, soft shirt and form-fitting black trousers. Forcefully, he moved his eyes, and closed the door.

When he joined her at the table, she had already closed the log book and put it to one side, making room for the glasses and the wine.

"But I am not entirely unarmed," she murmured as he came to her side, "as you are not entirely unarmed." She slanted an amused glance into his face. "Even in the presence of friends, we are vigilant. Certainly, we are deplorable."

"And very likely deplored," he agreed, as she produced a wine knife from her waistband and addressed the cork.

"I wonder why you are here," he said then, watching her long, clever fingers ply the knife. "Do not mistake me—I am pleased to share wine with you! It is only that I had thought you destined this evening for the pleasures of the house."

"Ah, yes." A sparkling glance from black eyes as she extracted the cork and set the wine to breathe. "That was not well done of you."

"Was it not?" he asked, which was simple idiocy. Better to have denied having taken any action. *Much* better to have failed to understand her.

"No," she asserted. "It was not." She reached for a glass; her sleeve brushing his—the veriest whisper of cloth against cloth, and nothing to answer for the bright flicker along his nerves.

The wine was poured, neatly and without fuss. Natesa handed

him a glass. She held the other, but did not yet drink, only stood there looking at him, her face serious.

"You deny yourself the pleasures of the house, do you not?"

He inclined his head, allowing amusement to show. "Certainly. I am the boss and there is ever work awaiting me."

"Yes, of course." She raised her glass—a Terran toast—and he followed suit.

"To our success upon the morrow."

"To our success upon the morrow," he repeated, and they drank.

"Do you have concerns of tomorrow's outcome?" he asked her, after they had sipped again, savoring the vintage, for true wine it surely was, and nothing like the misnamed if pleasant Autumn Wine.

She laughed lightly, and sat, all grace and elegance, in the room's only chair. Pat Rin leaned a hip against the table, and looked down into her face. His fingers itched with the desire to stroke her soft cheek—which was beyond idiocy and well into madness. He had another small sip of wine, recruiting what sanity remained to him.

"Success is never assured," Natesa said, speaking seriously, for all her seeming gaiety "And tomorrow we go against an opponent who is neither predictable nor trained, which mixes in additional danger."

"We have known these things," he pointed out, "and made plans accordingly. We do not go to Boss Ivernet naked; and there will be back-up within reach."

"All true—and yet we are well-advised to go lightly. Indeed, was I not already certain of your answer, I would ask you to reconsider and remain at holiday here while Mr. McFarland and I, with a small team, go in to smooth the way."

He did not immediately reply, being engaged in a thoughtful study of her face. She returned his regard, widening her eyes a little, her lips curving into a slight and unmistakably seductive smile.

He understood then that she meant to punish him for his temerity in leaving her to the pleasures of the house. He breathed in, deep and careful, deliberately cooling the growing warmth of his blood. Balance was her right, as it seemed she considered that he had transgressed. But Balance did not require him to act the fool.

So, business: "We had gone over this. It is my intention to offer to deal with every boss; extreme force being reserved for those who violently refuse. We cannot simply murder a man on his reputation. It may be that he is . . . misunderstood—although I grant that seems unlikely. However, we cannot discount that it *may* be possible. Shall we try to number between us those who now believe that Jonni was my true-son, his dead mother my wife, from whom I was long separated by malicious circumstance?"

She inclined her head. "True. Yet I would not see you put yourself in unnecessary danger. If Boss Ivernet is harmless and maligned, then no harm is done to him by sending an emissary first. If he is as has been reported, sending a forward team means that your life is preserved."

She finished her wine and stood. Gently, she set the glass on the table, and turned to face him, resolution in her eyes.

Pat Rin put his glass down, straightening away from the table—too late, she had swayed one step and was close, her hip grazing his side, her hand rising, slowly and stringently in sight, toward his cheek.

So much for Balance, he thought. So much for honor and right action. Desire electrified his blood. He looked up into her eyes, and knew he was lost—knew that he *must not* lose.

"Inas," he whispered. "Inas, do not."

Her hand paused. "Why?"

"Because—because I hold your oath," he managed, though his voice shook shamefully. "I would not dishonor you."

Something moved in her face; in his distress, he could not have said what.

"Ah," she said, softly, her breath warm against his cheek. "I see." Her hand moved; a light finger touched the gemstone in his ear, then she stepped back, bowing in the Terran mode, innocent of nuance.

"Pat Rin, good night. Sleep deeply. Dream well."

"Sleep well, Inas," he returned, and watched her go lightly away from him, and let herself out of his room.

DAY 346
STANDARD YEAR 1392

INDUSTRY STREET
SUREBLEAK

Gwince guided the car to what passed for a curb, set the brake and looked up. Pat Rin could see her worried frown reflected in the rear view mirror.

"Boss, I ain't likin' this street too much."

Which only proved her a woman of superior sense, Pat Rin thought. In his recent travels, he had seen bad streets—even very bad streets.

This street was—an affront to the honorable, a blight upon the eye; a dismay upon the soul.

Burned out buildings lined both sides of the pitted road, broken windows gaping like fanged entrances to black and bottomless gullets. There were no trees, nor flowers, as there had been seen on some of the streets under Penn Kalhoon's care; there were no *people*; no vehicles on the street, saving their own.

One house stood, unburned and unbroken, along the whole doleful thoroughfare: a glowering gray pile, protected by a rusty fence which had been draped with a glittering net of metallic spikes.

"Very well," he said, steeling himself, and turned to meet Natesa's eye. She inclined her head, novice to master, with no discernible irony.

"Gwince, please contact Mr. McFarland and have him bring his team in close. Natesa and I will see if Boss Ivernet is at home."

Gwince bit her lip. "Boss, it might be a good idea to wait 'til Mr. McFarland gets here."

"Call now," he said, patient in the face of her concern. "Surely, they will not open fire without first discovering who we are."

He was wrong.

He had taken precisely fifteen steps up the shattered walkway toward the house, Natesa at his back, when the first pellet snarled past his ear. He found his target, fired and leapt in the same instant, coming down heavily on his shoulder behind a pile of broken concrete that might once have been part of a wall.

The air was full of pellets, snarling and whining, pinging off his scant cover. Pat Rin leaned out, found a target, fired and ducked back, face dusted with concrete. He leaned out again—and froze.

Natesa lay, exposed and unmoving, on the walkway leading to the house. Even as he stared, disbelieving, a pellet chipped the stone by her head. He could not tell if she were alive—no, her hand! Surely, her fingers had twitched toward her fallen weapon?

More pellets stormed and he ducked again, measuring the distance with his eyes, ignoring the old, self-taunting voice telling him he was too slow, far too slow He would not fail in this. He would not leave her out there to die.

Carefully, he holstered his gun. Carefully, he got his feet under him. The storm of pellet fire lessened; he focused on the still figure lying on the broken pavement, took a breath—and ran.

Fleet and desperate, he reached her side, lifted her in his arms and hurtled back toward the dubious shelter of broken concrete.

He almost made it.

DAY 51
STANDARD YEAR 1393

LYTAXIN
EROB'S GROUNDS

He was too late.

Swearing, Val Con went to his knees beside the still form huddled beneath the curtain edge of the forest. Carefully, he turned her over, wincing as he uncovered the contorted face. Beldyn chel'Mara. She had been a scout, once.

The wound she had taken in the firefight was serious enough, though not by any means a death-wound. No, the agony recorded in the dead face told the tale: Agent chel'Mara had understood that she was being followed—and by whom. Her Loop would have presented the calculation demonstrating that he would catch her before ever she reached her ship; and would further have elucidated her odds of winning an encounter with him, depleted and panicked as she was.

So she had obeyed the implanted orders, and accepted the Loop's Final Routine, suiciding to avoid capture.

Damning the Commander to the torments of twelve dozen hells was futile from this distance—and he had no spare seconds to waste.

Quickly, fingers swift and steady, he went through the dead Agent's pockets, belt and hidden pouches, stripping out everything, even the coins and her licenses. Cramming his harvest helter-skelter into the pocket of his vest, he rose and backed away. Any moment now . . .

"Who is it?" Miri's voice was breathless. He held up a hand, warning her away, counting: *one, two, three, four, five*—

Beldyn chel'Mara's body blazed into white radiance. Val Con threw an arm over his eyes, felt the heat and the stench of burning flesh wash his face, heard the roar of incineration, and—nothing.

Cautiously, he lowered his arm.

The thin grass upon which the Agent's body had lain was lightly scorched. Nothing else remained.

"Who," Miri repeated, from the approximate vicinity of his elbow, "was that?"

He looked down into frowning gray eyes. "Agent of Change Beldyn chel'Mara."

"Suicide?"

He nodded, and hesitated before he asked his own question, seeing once more in his mind's eye the gate slamming open, hearing the first shots snarl over his head as he hit the ground, rolling, the long body crumpling . . .

"My father?"

"Clonak's got him in a 'doc by this time. Didn't seem too worried. My turn to worry, I guess." She used her sleeve to mop her damp face.

"If we're gonna have this lifemate link—and I ain't saying it's a bad thing, necessarily—then we need to fine tune some stuff. All I knew is you was scared, you was mad, and you was gone.

Clonak said it was the Department, and I lit out, thinking they'd managed to snatch you."

"That argues for fine-tuning, indeed. We have a project to embark upon during our unencumbered hours."

"Of which it don't look like we're gonna have that many for a while. These people ain't gonna give up, are they?"

"No," he said, slipping his arm around her waist in a brief, absurdly comforting hug. "In fact, Clonak's news indicates that, far from giving up, the Department is moving into Phase Two of the Plan."

"Phase Two? What's that?"

"They move more openly, dispose of their enemies, disband the Council of Clans, and establish themselves as a government."

Miri's eyes widened. "Are they serious?"

"Very serious," Val Con assured her. "And—much worse—the odds are good that they will succeed." He stepped back and pulled the assorted jumble of Beldyn chel'Mara's belongings from his pocket. "And somewhere in this is . . . ah." He held it up; Miri squinted, and sighed.

"Ship key. Great. Now all we gotta do is find the ship."

"That is not a difficulty," he said, depressing the appropriate button. The device came alive in his hand, quivering with the desire to be re-united with its ship. Val Con closed his fingers loosely around it, and spun, very slowly, on one heel. Three-quarters of the way through his revolution, the key lunged against the prison of his fingers.

"This way," he said softly, and moved off, the key bouncing in his hand, Miri walking silent at his side.

"**No,**" Shan said firmly. "We are not going after them."

"Shan, the nadelm and nadelmae of Korval are—"

"What you don't seem to grasp," he said, raising his voice to interrupt his sister and his First Speaker for the second time in an hour, "is that the nadelm and nadelmae of Korval are *extremely fierce individuals*. Miri Robertson is a captain of mercenary soldiers. She has within recent memory led soldiers into war, survived several battles, retaken an airfield held by a hostile force—oh, and attached an Yxtrang explorer to her command.

"You will recall that Nadelm Korval holds rank as a scout commander. While this is not of itself a guarantee of ferocity, I will tell you that I have it on his authority and on the authority of that same Yxtrang explorer that Val Con yos'Phelium bested a soldier twice his size, and desperate besides, in single combat, each of them armed with a knife."

"Shan—"

"All of which means," he swept on, making his third interruption on the night, "that the universe is more in peril from them than they are from the universe; and that the enemies they cannot vanquish with a glare and a wave of the hand are no one that we want to meet, out strolling in the dawning forest. Furthermore, Erob has dispatched actual soldiers in pursuit of the remainder of this enemy—who and how many they might be. *And* I will remind you that you are Korval-pernard'i. As your subject thodelm, referencing Chapter Eight, Paragraph 15 of the *Code of Proper Conduct*, I *forbid you* to risk yourself while the nadelm is unavailable to us."

He took a deep breath, in preparation of even more forceful arguments, if need be, but she stood silent, staring at him out of a face rather paler than usual.

However, if Nova was speechless, there were others present who were not.

"Bravo!" Clonak ter'Meulen brought his palms together in appreciative applause. "Well acted, sir! Yes! *Well* acted! I'll have the tape, by the gods!"

"Clonak," Shan said, warningly. "I am—"

"No, no, darling, don't speak! You have delivered yourself of a masterful performance. Recruit your strength. Allow me to carry on in your stead." He came forward and bowed, all correct and very High House: honor to a delm not one's own.

"Lady Nova, how delightful to see you again! Did you enjoy the war?"

She glared, which deflated Clonak not one bit. "Alas, that I missed the more robust episodes. I arrived only hours ago."

"Is that so? Then you will not have met dear Lieutenant Nelirikk! A jewel of the first water, is Lieutenant Nelirikk. I am persuaded that you will like him extremely. As you have heard, he was defeated by your foster brother, the inestimable Shadow, in hand-to-hand combat, winning, thereby, a place of service to your House. A man of many excellencies—and so fortunate that he was with us, when we picked up the others yesternoon. It is of course too soon to predict their own worth to the House of Korval, but I feel certain that they will strive to give good service."

"Others?" Shan repeated, stomach suddenly cold. "What *others*?"

Clonak turned a beatific smile upon him. "Why Hazenthull Explorer and Diglon Rifle, none other, who have only an hour ago given their oaths of service to Lord and Lady yos'Phelium."

Shan closed his eyes.

"Tired, darling?"

"Exhausted, if you will have it," he said, and sighed. "Line yos'Phelium holds service oaths of *three* Yxtrang?"

"I don't doubt but they'll be found useful to have about the house. Indeed, Captain Robertson waxed eloquent upon the point." He paused to smooth his mustache. "I doubt it's occurred to Shadow as yet, though it will—awake upon suits as yet undiscovered, your foster brother!—but I'm certain Daav had the possibility of a breeding pair in his eye." He moved his shoulders. "Well, he would, you know. We are all but products of our training."

"A breeding pair," Shan repeated faintly, but Nova was after other game.

"If you believe for one moment that I will accept that man as Daav yos'Phelium, no matter what sort of hoax you and he have been able to foist upon my brother—"

"Ah!" Clonak cried, slapping his hand to his forehead. "Forgive me! You put me in mind of why I had come to seek you out. Wait, I know I have it here . . ." He made a show of searching his pockets, and eventually produced, with a flourish, a much folded sheet of printout.

"While they had him in the 'doc, I asked the techs to do a gene match. I knew you would care, dear Lady Nova, and sought only to put your mind at rest."

Frowning, Nova all but snatched the proffered paper, unfolded it—

"Korval," she read. "Out of Line yos'Phelium."

"Which is precisely as it ought to be," Clonak said, and turned toward the door. "It has been delightful chatting with you, children, but I must be off now, to find how Shadia goes on. Ta!"

The door slid closed behind him.

"**Just** a little arrogant, ain't they?' Miri asked, settling on her belly under the bush they'd chosen for cover. "No guards, no whistles, no man-traps. Just . . ." She waved a hand at the ship nestled against the wooded hillside, in full sight of anybody who cared to look for it, now that Val Con had puzzled out the key combo and turned off the invisibility routine.

" 'They' depended upon the cloaking device to hide it," he murmured. "And there are no guarantees that the ship itself is free of traps."

"Huh." She glanced at him. "It's probably set up to report back to base, ain't it?"

"There will certainly be a trans-light locator, as had been hidden on Agent sig'Alda's ship," he said, brows pulled together in a frown. "Also, it will be programmed to dispatch a distress call, if it is left too long alone. The Commander is not a fool. He will doubtless have discovered by now that Agent sig'Alda's ship never was in orbit about Waymart. It may be expected that he has caused this ship to carry . . . upgraded security."

"Terrific." Miri glared at the ship, but it refused to dissolve like a bad dream in the brightening sunlight. "We can't just let the damn thing sit there—it's a bomb waiting to go off."

"Agreed." He nestled his chin onto his folded arms, eyes on the ship. "It might be possible to disarm it," he said eventually. "I have Beldyn's license. Using it, I should easily be able to access maincomp and initiate a complete systems shutdown."

"The word 'easily' is bothering me, here."

He turned his head to smile at her. "Of course it is. However, I cannot *easily* envision another course of action, given that the ship is here, four of its Agents are dead, and it is almost certainly going to apply to the Department for assistance when its countdown is done and no one has reported in." He looked back to the ship.

"I suggest that you await me here, with most of Beldyn's belongings. I will use her license to access maincomp. If I cannot trigger a systems shutdown—if maincomp requires two or more licenses to validate the order—perhaps I can at least reset the timer."

"And give us time to get the other licenses and come back to try again," Miri said. Silently, she went over the plan. It was a nice, simple plan; it had some play in it, and a built-in contingency scheme, which the gods knew wasn't standard for either of them. Still, she didn't like it much and said so.

"Alternatives?" Val Con asked, which she might've known he would. She sighed and shook her head.

"I can't even think of a good argument to support us going in together, instead of splitting up," she said. "Must be getting old."

He smiled. "We are decided, then." He looked at her, green eyes serious. "I will be very careful, cha'trez."

"You always say that," she complained, and sat up, wary of tangling her hair in the near branches. "Guess we better move on it, then."

"Indeed. The best path to finish is through begun."

He came to his knees, fishing in his vest for the stuff he had taken off the dead Agent. Most of it, he handed to her, reserving for himself the ship key, a metal card that was the late Beldyn's piloting license, and a flatish, notched piece of long metal.

"Interior key," he murmured. "For unlocking chests and inner hatches in times of disrupted power."

"Right," she said, and pocketed the jumble as Val Con ghosted out from under their bush and moved toward the Agents' ship.

The hatch rose in response to the key's command, and Val Con entered the ship of the Department.

The cabin lights came up as he proceeded, alert for traps and trip-beams. He achieved the center of the piloting chamber without mishap, and paused there to look about himself.

The board was locked down, screens blanked; the status lights showed all systems at first level standby—primed to leap into complete wakefulness at the touch of a pilot's hand. A prudent measure, Val Con thought, for a pilot who had chosen not to land at a port, where he might command the luxury of a hotpad, and who could not know if he would depart hotly pursued by enemies, or at leisure and in his own good time.

Well. Quick and silent, he went through the rest of the ship, satisfying himself that he was alone, then returned to the piloting chamber, pulling Beldyn chel'Mara's piloting license out of his pocket.

Miri shifted under the bush, her eyes on the ship. The hatch had come up without any fireworks going off and Val Con had walked on in. Inside her head, she saw the particular pattern that meant he was being careful, and thinking in small, tight steps. There was no sense that he saw anything that struck him as odd, or dangerous, or—

Silhouetted against the wooded hill, the ship's hatch descended, inevitably and with dignity. Miri flung herself to her feet, heedless of the scratches inflicted by her passage through the bush, her shout swallowed by the accelerating whine of engaged gyros.

The Agents' ship hurtled into the sky.

His hands flashed across the board, calling for an abort. The ship ignored him.

He slapped up navcomp, which obligingly displayed the laid-in and locked course, the coords of which were all too familiar.

The Department's ship was taking him to Headquarters.

Val Con bit his lip, letting the force of the ship's rising press him into the pilot's chair. His hands on the board—the very keys had recognized his fingerprints, he thought, and gave a wry mental bow to the Commander, who was, after all, no fool.

The ship hurtled upward. Maincomp allowed him to activate the screens, so that he could see the ground falling away beneath him, the bush where he had left Miri already indistinguishable in the blur of green.

Headquarters, he thought, and then thought of the Commander, and of the likely fate of one who had broken training, to the several-times loss of the Department.

Returning to Headquarters was not an option.

Val Con reached to the board and opened a comm line.

A chime sounded. Priscilla, more than half of her attention on the systems report cluttering her main screen, reached absently across the board to hit the toggle.

"Mendoza."

"Priscilla, this is Val Con." His voice came out of the speaker, calm and clear, immediately recognizable, though she had not heard it for more than three Standards. She sat up, staring.

"Already?" she demanded. "Shan said it would be days yet—"

"Shan was mistaken," he interrupted. "Attend me now. There is a ship rising from Lytaxin at longitude 76.51.33 west, 39.24.17 north, at an acceleration of 7.8 local gravities. Acquire it, please."

Her fingers danced over the board. "I have it."

"Good. Destroy it."

She blinked; checked her instruments. "Val Con, you're on that ship."

"Indeed I am. Fire at will."

"No."

"Priscilla, if you refuse, you will destroy the clan. The ship will not obey me and the course laid in will deliver me into the hands of our enemy." Calm, so calm, his voice. It was his very calmness that convinced her that his order was right and necessary, though, Goddess, what she would say to Shan . . .

"It would be best," he said, "if you fire while we are in atmosphere."

She smiled. "Yes, of course it would." Her fingers moved on the board again, unhesitant and certain. "Beam up," she murmured. "Target locked."

Miri craned up into the brightening sky, watching the ship that was taking him away from her. It was at the edge of her vision, now, a speck against the white clouds of morning. Soon—

Slashing through the white clouds came a slender radiant beam. It touched the speck, surrounded it, pulsed.

The ship blew up.

Miri screamed.

Ren Zel woke, suddenly and entirely.

A glance across the dark room at the glowing ice-blue digits of the clock proved that he had been asleep just over an hour. Despite this, he felt extraordinarily alert, even a bit restless. A walk, he thought, would be just the thing to put him restful once more.

So thinking, he arose from his bed and dressed rapidly in the near darkness. Stamping into his boots, he reached out and plucked his pilot's jacket from its hook. His fingers caressed the worn, scarred leather, running over the tiny seams that each marked a place where the leather had been torn and, later, mended.

He smiled, there in the darkness, and swung the jacket up and on. The next instant, he stepped into the hallway beyond his door and strode off toward the right.

The hall bent sharply to the left, then to the right. Ren Zel moved out with a will, senses wide open, more energetic with every step.

The hall bent again to the right. He rounded the corner and walked into a garden, stepping from carpet to grass and pausing at last, his face turned up to a sky silvered with starlight. He took a deep breath of fragrant air—and felt something bump against his shin.

Carefully, he looked down, his vision tainted with silver, so that the large gray cat making a second, even more robust, pass at his leg seemed for a moment to be outlined in light.

"Gently," Ren Zel murmured, bending down to offer a forefinger in greeting. "That leg has already been broken once—and very thoroughly, too."

The cat blinked up at him and touched its nose, dainty, and slightly damp, to the offered finger. The demands of courtesy having thus been satisfied, it pushed its head hard against Ren Zel's hand, startling the man into a soft laugh, as he obligingly rubbed the sturdy gray ears.

A small wind moved among the leafy things, bearing sweet, unaccustomed scents. Ren Zel drew another deep breath, and straightened with a final chuck of the cat's chin.

"Come now, let me walk through this garden. I have been— long away—from gardens."

He strolled forward, boots whispering across the grass, smiling as his sleeve brushed the leaf of a misty night bloomer and released a scent as sharp and as satisfying as cinnamon. Precisely such a small treasure might have been found in the garden maintained by the House into which he had been born, years and worlds away.

Directly ahead, the grassy route he followed dead ended in an opulent sweep of greenery, but before one reached that, one came across the roots, and then the trunk, of a monumental tree.

Ren Zel picked his way across the surface roots. Glancing down to be certain of his footing, he saw that the cat companioned him still, gliding silently over the irregular ground.

Arriving at the tree itself, Ren Zel steadied himself with one hand flat against remarkably warm wood, and craned upward.

Above him, he saw shadow, sketching, perhaps, the shapes of leaf and branch. The stars were quite obscured, and the brilliant, silvery sky. He squinted into the vastness of the shadow in vain; details eluded him, though he gained a vivid impression of strength, of . . . age . . . and . . . warm regard.

From the high branches came a sound, as of something come loose and falling swiftly groundward. Pilot reactions flung Ren Zel back half a dozen paces, which was well, else the small plummeting object would have struck him squarely on the head.

Instead, it smacked into the dark grass and was immediately leapt upon by the cat, who planted both white front feet firmly on its prize and looked up at Ren Zel with unmistakable challenge, as if to say, *Well? I've caught it for you, Master Timid. Are you too fainthearted even to look at what it is?*

Ren Zel stepped forward and bent down, not without a certain amount of wariness, recalling the antics of tree-toads in the garden of his youth. The cat stepped back, tail high, and flicked out a negligent paw, moving the object sufficiently for his eye to find it.

No tree-toad here. Frowning slightly, Ren Zel bent and picked up what proved to be a seedpod—*two* seedpods, connected by a thin branchlet. He looked at the cat, sitting primly, tail around toes, its gaze very much on Ren Zel's face.

"Your tree is throwing things at me, eh? Am I to infer that I am unwelcome?"

One quicksilver paw came out, passing lightly over the whiskers, then the cat was walking away, tail high. Ren Zel moved his shoulders, thought to drop the seedpods, and then did not: they felt warm and comfortable in his hand and it came to him that he would have need of them, later.

Halfway across the glade, the cat paused in its purposeful perambulation and looked over its shoulder. Again, Ren Zel had the distinct impression that, if the animal could speak, it would this moment be saying something rather sharp to one Master Timid Sandfeet and urging him to come along quickly, now

Thus gently persuaded, Ren Zel stepped forward. The cat watched him for a moment, then, apparently satisfied that he would do as he was bid, took up the lead.

Pieces of what had once been a ship fell, tumbling, out of the sky.

Miri, stirring beneath the shelter she did not remember taking, watched them fall, and gingerly, ready to snatch back at the first cold shock of emptiness, extended her thought to the place where his pattern should have been.

It was—there. Pre-occupied right this second, but displaying no signs of attenuation like she'd seen when he'd been dying on the Yxtrang fighter. In fact, he seemed quite amazingly busy for a man who ought to have been vaporized when the beam pierced his ship.

Carefully, not wanting to disturb his concentration, she pushed her thought a little deeper into his pattern. Her vision side-slipped crazily, and she was seeing the ground from high above, turning gently and rising slowly beneath her as—as?

Escape kite, Val Con murmured in her ear. *The manual key opened the emergency drawer, and triggered the escape hatch.*

She closed her eyes, which didn't quite get rid of the disorienting far-view of the ground. Even more carefully, she withdrew her thought from his pattern, and opened her eyes to the sky.

High up against the clouds, she saw a long, black wing, spiraling lazily downward.

The path culminated in a door. The cat stopped and looked at him over its shoulder.

Ren Zel surveyed the situation. The door was set into a section of wall. The section of wall was part of a greater wall, which formed, so he was persuaded, part of the first story of a clanhouse. He glanced down at the cat.

"I am afraid I'm no use to you. My print will not open this."

The cat yawned, sauntered over to the door, stood on its back feet, braced itself with one paw against the lower door and stretched toward the latch with the other. Ren Zel sighed sharply.

"Understand me, it's useless! This is a clanhouse—I am clanless. There is no door on all the worlds of Liad which will open to my hand."

The cat stretched higher, its paw questing well below the latch.

"Merely disobliging, am I? Well, the proof is easy enough." He went forward two steps and snatched at the knob, already hearing in his mind's ear the blare of bells as the house took alarm from the touch of an intruder.

The knob turned easily in his hand. The door swung wide, silent on well-oiled hinges. The cat strolled inside, then stopped and looked over its shoulder in a way grown far too familiar.

"No." Ren Zel stared down into glowing eyes. "I cannot."

The cat came back, stropped itself one way and the other, soft and caressing, against his legs, then moved on again, down the dim hallway.

It was risky—even given the malfunction which had allowed him to open a coded door. He did know the risk. Yet the house lured him, with its promised glimpses of the life he had been denied. Surely, he thought, just a short stroll down the hall, a glance into a room or two—surely there was no harm in that?

Knowing his peril, Ren Zel stepped inside, closing the door carefully behind him, and being quite certain that the lock had caught before he followed the cat into the deeps of the house.

Time and route blurred. He thought they might have crossed a dark, deserted kitchen, he and the cat, and gone up a thin flight of stairs insufficiently illuminated by night-dims, and down another hall, or possibly two . . .

Time righted itself. They stood before another door. The cat stroked, long and sensuous, across Ren Zel's legs, then stretched high on back feet, reaching for the palmplate set far above its head.

"This is the private apartment of someone who belongs to this house," Ren Zel said, his voice barely a whisper. "*Surely*, my hands are useless to you here."

The cat did not even deign to turn its head. Ren Zel sighed, stepped forward and put his hand with absolute certainty against the coded plate. His palm tingled as the house scanned him. His shoulders stiffened beneath his many-times mended jacket, as if tensed against the grip of a hostile hand.

Silent and stately, the door slid back on its groove. The cat made a pleased burble and all but leapt within, tail held tall, fairly quivering with joy.

Ren Zel took a step back. That is, he *meant* to take a step back, to retrace the half-remembered path through private, richly carpeted corridors, to descend the back stairway, cross the kitchen, and gain, first, the starlit garden, and shortly thereafter the familiar, beloved halls of *Dutiful Passage*.

He went forward another step, clearing the beam, and heard the door slide shut behind him.

It occurred to him, somewhat belatedly, that he had lost his mind.

Mad or sane, his traitor feet kept on, walking him softly and without haste through a pleasantly cluttered parlor, 'til he crossed yet another forbidden threshold, into the very sleeping room of one who was clanheld, alive, and joyous.

The inner room was spacious, the center held by a bed of noble proportion, set directly beneath a skylight, from which silver beams illuminated the rumpled coverlet, and wove stars into the long, dark hair of the woman asleep against the pillows, one rounded arm flung high over her head, a frown disturbing the smooth expanse of her brow.

Sanity returned, quick and cold, freezing his feet to the carpet. They would kill him, the people who belonged to this house. Truly, they would kill him—and justly so—a stranger who had forced himself, alone and uninvited, into the very sleeping room of one of the clan's precious children.

Biting his lip, he half turned to go—which was the moment the cat chose to leap upward from the floor, landing solidly on the stomach of the sleeping woman.

"Ooof!" The lady jack-knifed into a sitting position, snatching the cat into her arms. "Horrid creature! First, you refuse to share my sleep and now you refuse me solitary slumber! Unhandsome, Lord Merlin! I had thought you for the garden all the night—" She stopped, hearing her own words, so Ren Zel thought, and put the cat gently to one side, staring across the rumpled blankets to—himself.

"Oh," she said, and tipped her head to a side, as one puzzled, but in no wise terrified to find a stranger standing at the very foot of her bed. "Good evening, Pilot." Her voice was slow, the tone oddly reverberant. She spoke in the mode between equals.

By the Code, he should throw himself on his face and despoil her no further while she got on with the business of screaming for her agemates, or her elders, or her delm to come quickly and dispose of him.

Ren Zel inclined his head, matching her grave, unfluttered attitude. "Good evening, Lady."

In the starlight, she smiled, and tossed the coverlet aside, sliding out of bed and coming toward him on silent, naked feet, her bed shirt floating 'round her knees.

"Now, *you*," she said. "I confess I had not expected you. May I know your name?"

He did bow then, very gently, in the mode of introduction. "Ren Zel."

She smiled again, and shook her hair back. He thought it threw off sparks in the starlight.

"A brief name, but well enough." She paused, standing so close that he could see the color of her eyes beneath the winsome dark brows—silver, like the starlight.

"My name," she said, "is Anthora." She held out a hand, the lace of her sleeve falling gracefully back along her arm. "May I hang your jacket away? We are all pilots here."

"I—" His throat closed. He took a breath. "I should not stay."

"What—when you have come so far? At least take your ease for an hour before the exertions of the journey back."

She swayed forward another half-step, the silver eyes wide in a face not precisely beautiful, with its sharp cheekbones and pointed chin. It came to him, as if from a distance, that he had seen a like face—then lost the thought in horror as he found his hand rising, drawn as if by a magnet toward her silken cheek.

Her eyes flickered, following the motion, and he used the moment to go back a step and to lift his hand higher, displaying the twin seedpods, still attached by their branchlet.

"A gift," he managed, his voice sounding unsteady in his own ears. "If the lady pleases."

"A gift?" For an instant she merely stared, then threw back her head and laughed, fully and without artifice. Ren Zel felt his mouth curving into a smile, his eyes following the perfect curve of her throat down to the rounded thrust of her breasts against the thin stuff of her shirt—his breath caught, blood heating; and in that moment she met his eye, still grinning, and reached out to pluck up the pods.

"A handsome gift, I own, and perfectly suited to the occasion! Come, let us share."

He blinked at her, tongue-tangled with mingled desire and dismay. "Lady, I do not—"

"No, have a care!" She raised an admonishing finger. "You have brought the gift; our duty is plain. So!" She broke one of the pods from the branchlet. It lay for a moment on her open palm, then neatly halved itself, showing a plump, sweet-smelling kernel.

"Thus, for the guest." She extended her palm, and perforce he took up the offered nut. "And now for me." Again, the pod lay quiet for an instant before falling apart in perfect halves. Daintily, she plucked the kernel from its nest, raised it to her lips, and paused. Silver eyes slanted up at him, mischievous and gentle, as if she perfectly comprehended his dismay—and his desire. "Eat, denubia. I swear that you will find it good."

Denubia. She should not call him so, he thought, plucking the kernel free of its nut-half. He was no proper recipient of a Liaden lady's endearments. Carefully, he slipped the kernel into his mouth—and gasped as a riot of taste exploded along his tongue, and exploded a second time—and yet again, so that his eyes perceived strange patterns in the aether and his ears heard music behind the silence, and his treacherous, traitor body cried out against its incompleteness.

He gasped again as the sensations faded, though they did not dissipate entirely. It seemed to him that he could still see lines of power and probability intersecting in the air all about, and that the low hum of music trembled just inside his ears.

"Gently . . ." Her voice was—and her hand was on his arm, which should *not* be.

"Lady, cry you mercy . . ." He could not allow this, whatever *this* was, to go on. If he was a-dreaming, he would wake. Now. Closing his eyes, he drew on—why, in some way on the lines he perceived about him, pulling this one *thus*, and this other one *so* . . .

"Sit the board serene, Pilot. Sometimes, it is wisdom to do nothing." She stroked his arm, tracing lines of fire on his skin through the much-mended leather. He made the error of opening his eyes and beheld her face before him, silver eyes worried and teasing at once. The threads he had gathered slipped from his grasp; the building surge of music settled back to a sweet hum. Anthora smiled.

"It is well," she said and stepped back, holding out both hands. "Your jacket, Pilot. You do not need it here."

True enough, he thought, and had it off, placing it in her hands with a lingering touch.

She held it for a moment, as if considering the weight of the leather, then looked back to him, her brow knit in puzzlement. "This jacket carries many wounds."

"Healed," he told her, striving for some measure of lightness. "Both of us healed, well enough. That jacket saved my life, Lady."

"All honor to it," she said, silver eyes solemn, and shook it sharply, as if she snapped a rug free of dust, and moved away to drape it over the edge of a chair.

She was back in the next instant, and it came to him that the room was growing lighter, for he could see the full curves of her body plainly through the pale shirt.

"Time grows short," she said, moving close and smiling into his eyes. "May I have your kiss, Ren Zel?"

He had been born for no other purpose than to give her his kiss. And he came to her too late: dead and beyond them both to heal it. He shook his head, realized that she might not understand the Terran gesture, and murmured.

"No. Lady—I am clanless. You are—I should not be here . . ." he finished, helplessly.

"Poppycock," she said in plain Terran and grinned, lopsided and adorable. "Well. Let us try another face of the fortress. You will see that I am quite without shame—so: since I am a lady and may mind my own melant'i—would you spurn *my* kiss?"

He looked into silver eyes and knew that he should lie.

"Never."

Her grin softened as she closed the final distance between them, setting her naked feet carefully beside his boots. They were much of a height, and she easily lay her arms about his shoulders. Her breath was warm against his cheek and he held her waist between his two hands, cradling her closer still as their lips touched—

And the universe took fire.

DAY 349
STANDARD YEAR 1392

HAMILTON STREET
SUREBLEAK

He woke with the echo of gunfire in his ears, and a searing sense of loss.

"Natesa!"

Someone nearby whispered her name, the voice unfamiliar—thin and ragged—and yet if there were a friend of hers nearby . . .

"Dammit, don't you start that again!" *That* voice was immediately identifiable: Cheever McFarland, and in something of a pet, to judge by the volume.

Pat Rin opened his eyes, gaining an immediate view up into the big Terran's face, which showed more worry than temper, despite the volume—and, just now, a profound and dawning relief.

"Now, why didn't I think of doin' that before?"

"Doing what?" Pat Rin asked, and heard the unfamiliar ragged whisper emerge from his own mouth. Other details of his condition were beginning to emerge: he hurt, comprehensively; and his left arm was immobilized.

"Never occurred to me to just tell you to shut up," Cheever

was continuing. "Well, o'course, it wouldn't—when in your life have you ever done what you were told?" He frowned, trying for ferocious.

"You been layin' here for the better part of two days, out cold, and feverish—which would've been worrisome enough—*and* you been talkin' Liaden non-stop, except for the occasional hour when you'd yell for Natesa. Which is what happened to your voice. What happened to the rest of you is you took a pellet in the arm and another one in the thigh, and you're in Penn Kalhoon's personal house, being taken care of by his personal staff, none of who speak Liaden, by the way, which is probably a good thing, considering the little bit of it I could scan."

He did have some memories of . . . conversations; long, intimate talks with his dead kin, of the sort they had rarely engaged in. There had been those things that he had wished to say—most especially to his son; and also to Shan, with whom he had so often been out of charity, so often for such little cause . . .

"It was not my intention to disturb the staff," he managed now, his ragged voice waking the discomfort of a raw throat. He drew a breath, which also was painful, but not beyond his ability to endure.

"Natesa."

Cheever grimaced and Pat Rin felt again the fiery pain of loss, as the pilot's face dissolved in a shameful wash of tears.

"Naw, now, don't go jumping to endings." The other man's voice was unexpectedly gentle. Pat Rin closed his eyes; the tears leaked beneath his lashes and left cold, wet trails down his cheeks.

"Listen, Boss, she's gonna be fine. Caught a pellet in the shoulder—the jacket took most of it. If it hadn't been a custom load, it wouldn't've stopped her at all. As it is, she's gonna be outta bed and raisin' hell before what passes for the doctor 'round here lets you eat better'n oatmeal."

He paused, then added, thoughtfully, "Thing is, Natesa's some peeved about you putting yourself on the line like that—I ain't exactly happy about it, myself. We're your security—I'm sure we told you this, couple dozen times, maybe. We take the chances while you get under cover—which this time, you did, according to Gwince, but then what'd you have to do but *leave* cover and set yourself up as a target nobody who wasn't drugged outta their brains—which Ivernet's were, your luck—coulda missed."

"My oathsworn," Pat Rin whispered, eyes closed against the slow leak of tears, "are not expendable."

"*Yes, we are*," Cheever said, plainly exasperated. "That's the point—ahh, never mind. I'll let Natesa pound it into your head. Maybe she'll have better luck."

He lay there, letting the sense of it sink into his bones. Natesa was alive. She would be fine. Life went on.

"And Boss Ivernet?" he asked, recalling at last the why of placing himself and his—gods pity him—his beloved, into such danger.

"Wasn't enough of Boss Ivernet left to take to the crematory after the mob got through with him." There was a certain grim satisfaction in the Terran pilot's voice. Pat Rin opened his eyes and stared up into his face.

"Mob?"

"Right. See, after you went in and practically got yourself killed over this, wasn't much Penn Kalhoon could do but back you, not to mention Ivernet's own streeters suddenly understanding that there might be a way out and joining in . . ." He shook his head. "Wasn't pretty. Quick, though—it was that. Especially with the bosses on the other side of Ivernet comin' in to lend a hand. Turns out everybody wanted him outta there, but none of 'em could figure out how to go about it 'til you come along." He shrugged.

"So, you got the turf. Penn's second—Marj Fender—she's sittin' in the Boss Chair, temporary-like, tryin' to get everything sorted out and stable. Penn wanted me to make sure you knew they was just holding it temp, and not making a turf-grab. You bled for it—it's yours. That's his words."

"All honor to him," Pat Rin whispered, closing his eyes again. He was, ridiculously, exhausted, his face wet with more than the unabated run of tears.

"We will need to send word to our other territories and—"

"Done," Cheever interrupted. "*Some* of us been workin'."

And all honor to Cheever McFarland, who held the course, as a pilot should, despite near catastrophe.

His ears registered a sudden bustle across the room, and a brisk female voice, borne closer on the clatter of heels against tile.

"Mr. McFarland! You promised!"

"Sorry, ma'am. Got to talkin'."

"Well, you can get to talkin' with Chim, downstairs," the unknown woman scolded, "and leave Mr. Conrad to rest up. Even bosses get timeout for gunshots and fever!" A sharp sound, as if she had brought her palms forcefully together. "Go on, now—out! That's enough damage for one day!"

"Yes'm. Boss, I'm within range if you want me, got it?"

"Yes." His voice was barely audible, even to himself. "Thank you, Mr. McFarland."

The bed shook slightly, echoing Cheever's path across the tiles. Pat Rin opened his eyes by a raw application of will, and found himself looking up into the round face of a smiling woman of about his own age.

"I'm Kazi," she said. "Mr. McFarland says, 'the doctor, so-called.'" She lay one cool, plump hand against his forehead, *tsk'd* and brushed his hair back, as if he were a fractious child.

"Wore you right down to nerves, didn't he? I don't know why, but people think bosses ain't human, somehow. Well. Let's wash your face, then I'll check your progress. You were lucky, if Mr. McFarland didn't tell you—the thigh shot missed the artery and the bone; it's a nice, clean wound. No problems there. The arm's a little trickier, but I think you're gonna be just fine, so long as you're sensible. Can you be sensible?"

She had produced a bowl and a cloth from somewhere. He watched her through slitted eyes as she dipped the cloth in the bowl and wrung it out.

"Perhaps . . . I . . . can," he whispered. "I have . . . not attempted . . . recently."

Kazi smiled, leaned forward and used the cool cloth to wipe his face. "There, that feels better, doesn't it?" She dropped the cloth into the bowl and put it aside.

"OK, now I'll check the wounds. You can have a nap after—or if you fall asleep while I'm poking you, I won't be offended. I do want you to have some broth a little later, but the nap comes first." She folded the coverlet back from his left side and reached forward. "This might hurt you some. Feel free to yell and swear."

Indeed, it hurt amazingly, though her hands were light and certain. Pat Rin closed his eyes and gave his attention wholly to recalling the order in which the books were shelved in his mother's study, starting from the topmost of the floor-to-ceiling shelves. He was just starting on the second shelf when Kazi spoke again.

"They both look good." He opened his eyes to her face. She smiled and nodded. "Whyn't you go to sleep now? I'll be back in a while with something like dinner."

Sleep. His weighty eyelids closed. "Thank you," he said—meant to say—and let the black velvet tide of sleep bear him away.

DAY 355
STANDARD YEAR 1392

HAMILTON STREET
SUREBLEAK

"Boss?" Gwince paused in the threshold of the parlor Penn Kalhoon had set aside for Pat Rin's use. "Boss Melina Sherton's here to see you."

He looked up from the book he had been reading—a bow to Kazi's insistence that he "rest" between entertaining callers. Melina Sherton held a large territory considerably out from his present location; bordering on the almost-mythic "country", with its fresh vegetables, fields and wineries.

"Pray show Ms. Sherton in," he said, putting his book aside, "and ask Dani to bring refreshments."

"Yessir."

Pat Rin straightened in his chair, careful of the arm in its awkward rigid bindings. A cane leaned against the table at his side, another concession to the doctor's list of instructions.

He had not, of course, been able to acquiesce to all of her demands, though he did make a push to be *sensible*. Behold him, for an instance, guesting yet in Penn Kalhoon's household, rather than returning to his home turf, or going on tour with Cheever McFarland.

Light footsteps sounded in the hall. Pat Rin turned his face toward the doorway, and inclined his head as his guest came through the door.

"I hope that you will forgive me if I remain seated," he murmured. "I mean no disrespect to yourself."

Thin reddish eyebrows arched above tan eyes.

"I think a man who went down with a couple pellets in him six days ago has a right to stay seated for as long as he wants," she said.

Her voice was strong and emphatic; her person thin of flesh; her face long and bony. She nodded.

"Melina Sherton. I hold the territory behind Ira Gabriel."

Boss Gabriel had called on Pat Rin yesterday afternoon, one of three on the day, as opposed to two, the day before. He had proven himself to be a sensible man, and willing to deal. They had parted amicably, Ira clenching his portacomm in one outsized fist.

"I have met Boss Gabriel," he said to Melina Sherton. "An excellent individual."

"He knows what's good for business," she allowed, moving forward and seating herself in the chair facing him. "I've been dealing with Ira for almost eight years; he's a man believes in that Road, same like you do. I guess you talked about that."

"Indeed, we did. And yourself?"

She blinked. "Me?"

"Yes. Do you believe in the Road? I anticipate that holding it open might cause difficulties for you, with your territory situated as it is."

"Because a road goes both ways, you mean." She tipped her head to a side, considering him. "I thought about that—thought about it a lot, if you want to know, because I got an interest in the border farms, and some trade further in. And what I decided . . ."

Here, Dani appeared with the tray, which she disposed quickly and quietly on the table. Hands steady and sure, she poured—for Pat Rin, who took a sip to demonstrate that the beverage was undrugged—and for the guest. She departed, also quickly, but without seeming in haste, leaving the door slightly ajar behind her, as per his standing instructions.

Pat Rin sipped again and put his cup on the table. "Forgive me," he said to the other boss, "we had been discussing your decision regarding the freedom of the Port Road through your territories."

"Right." She held her cup against her knee, and leaned forward, tan eyes intense. "I decided that it's OK for the Road to go to the Port and to the country. Sleet, I started in trying to figure out how we could have more of them—a safe-road out to the coast and back! Another one up into the hills and back!" She laughed.

"Same sorta thinking that got me in trouble eight years ago, when I decided the only way to protect our farms was to set up as boss of the turf next in—act as a kinda buffer zone. That's what it was gonna be, a safety zone between the rest of the city and the holdings. Then I got to looking around my streets, seeing what was needed and who was where. Got in touch with Ira and found him to be of the same general tendencies . . ." She shook her head. "Ancient history. What I'm trying to tell you is, if you're still offering that deal like you got with Penn, I'll be pleased to sign on and hold the Road clear, share out info and help settin' up schools and clinics. Might be some of mine could teach some of yours to grow eatables in little land-patches, or up on the roofs."

Memory's eye provided a vivid picture of a garden shrouded on a rooftop, awaiting the touch of the gardener who would never come again . . .

Carefully, he took a breath; another—and met Melina Sherton's eyes.

"That is precisely the sort of partnership we wish to form—a cooperative of skill and knowledge, which will benefit everyone."

She nodded. "Sure would. And if anybody can hold that kind of cooperative open, it's you. A boss who ain't afraid to put his life down on what he believes to be best? I'll team with him."

"Thank you," Pat Rin murmured, reaching for his tea cup. He sipped at leisure, and turned the conversation to the particulars of her turf. Sometime later, they found themselves in agreement, with a date set on which Pat Rin would call on her at home. She received her portacomm gravely, and Gwince showed her out, closing the door gently behind her.

Pat Rin wilted against the back of his chair, and closed his eyes. He could feel the trembling in his legs and in his unbound arm. Though he was much improved in health, yet even seated negotiation had the ability to exhaust him, and Melina Sherton had been his fourth interview on *this* day.

Seated thus, he might have dozed. In fact, given his weakened condition, it was inevitable that he doze. The next thing he was aware of was the light *snick* of the door being pushed to.

He opened his eyes and beheld Natesa.

Their paths had crossed but seldom in past days. As Cheever had predicted, she had risen from her sickbed while he was yet confined by weakness, and set herself to whatever tasks had need of her skill. It did occur to him that it was anger which kept her from his side, a notion he had tried—without much success—to put down to the morbid effect of ill-health.

And now, she was here, having sought him out of her own desire, whether to throttle him or to mock him remained to be discovered.

"Master." She bowed, elegance itself, and straightened, her black eyes and grave, sweet face unreadable.

He inclined his head, approximating the bow between equals as best he might, seated and awkward as he was.

"Natesa. I am pleased to see you, well and dancing."

"I am pleased to see you, also, Master, though it must on the mend, with the dance yet before you."

He smiled, rueful. "Both Mr. McFarland and Doctor Kazi allow me to know that I am fortunate to be able to hear the music."

Natesa inclined her head. "You did a very foolish thing; that is so. Very brave and very foolish. I have often marked how frequently courage and foolhardiness make partners. I am persuaded that you have made this same observation."

"Alas, mine has not been an existence where courage is commonly found, although certainly I have seen fools. The most recent, in my mirror."

A frown disturbed the serenity of her brow "No," she said eventually, as one who had given the matter due consideration. "No, I would not have it so, though you must, of course, please yourself." She paused, then bowed once more—oathsworn to oathholder—and Pat Rin felt his blood chill.

"Master, I have come to ask you for a thing. I hope that you will be able to accommodate me."

He inclined his head. "I would not be so churlish as to refuse you anything," he said softly, while he felt his chest muscles tighten, as if in anticipation of a blow.

"Ah." Another grave inclination of the head, before she looked directly into his eyes.

"I would have my oath returned to me."

The familiar flames of loss blew high, taking his breath, and his voice, incinerating what was left of his heart.

He bought time with a stately, seated bow, straightened and raised his one good hand, palm up, in the gesture of release.

"Your oath is returned to you, honored and unsullied," he said, and it was the High Tongue that came off of his lips, though he had not willed it so. "Pray accept my gratitude, for service given well and without stint."

Deeply, she bowed. "I receive my oath with joy," she said, which was the proper beginning of the ritual phrase, properly spoken in the High Tongue. She straightened, and finished, in Terran: "I do not want your gratitude, Pat Rin yos'Phelium."

He had thought himself beyond any further hurt—thrice a fool! Gasping, he averted his face, his cheeks stinging as if she had struck him—and felt her fingers in truth against his cheeks, cool and soft and soothing.

"Gently," she murmured. "Pat Rin, hear the rest."

He allowed her strong, cool fingers to turn his face, so he looked into her eyes, inches away from his own.

"I do not want your gratitude," she repeated, the vicious words transformed by her voice into a caress. "I want your love."

Shivering, he raised his hand and touched her satin cheek. "You have it, always."

She laughed, softly. "And he asks for nothing in return! Very well, sir, I will give you a gift."

She bent closer, her breath warm and sweet against his face.

"I love you, Pat Rin," she said, in the mode between intimates. And kissed him on the lips.

DAY 51
STANDARD YEAR 1393

LYTAXIN
EROB'S CLANHOUSE

Shan sat on a chair in the hallway outside the room where his long-absent uncle Daav was reported to be in the care of the autodoc. Nova had gone to Erob, in order to offer what assistance an allied clan might in the aftermath of the discovery of murderous intruders in a protected garden.

Having begged off this duty, Shan closed his eyes and meticulously went through several levels of exercise designed to raise his energy levels, clear his thinking, and sharpen his flagging Healer senses. He would of course pay for this indulgence later, and he would be well-served indeed if he fell flat on his nose just when he was needed most.

And whether that would be when he was called to identify the dead, broken bodies of his brother and his brother's lifemate, the gods alone knew.

Really, Shan, have some sense, he told himself, opening his eyes with a sigh. *Didn't you just explain to Nova that they are very fierce individuals?*

Which in no way meant they were invincible.

Beside him, the door swished open. He turned in his seat and found himself doubly netted by a straight black glance and the heart-stoppingly familiar glitter of a pattern that he had last seen in his childhood.

"Shannie?" The deep, grainy voice was precisely the same. He came to his feet, feeling his mouth stretch into an idiot smile.

"Uncle Daav. Where have you been?"

He held up a hand on which a ring flickered silver lightnings. "Now, do not, I beg you, begin! I have done quite enough explaining to your cha'leket. Apply to him for details."

"If he shows himself, I will," Shan said, suddenly somber. "He and Miri are missing in the aftermath of your little fracas in Erob's garden." He tipped his head, Healer senses tracing an anomaly. "Will my brother also explain the very odd . . . resonance that I find in your pattern?"

"Ah, you did become a Healer! Excellent." Daav smiled. "He might very well explain it, as he deduced both its presence and its cause with what I would have said was extremely scanty evidence. However, as you *are* a Healer, a practical demonstration might be of benefit to you . . ." He closed his eyes, and said, quite distinctly, in the mode between lovers, "Aelliana, here is Shan, wishing to make his bow to you."

There was a pause; a sense of something shifting. Healer sense processed the change as a fading and a solidifying; not at all the expected manifestation of a completely new pattern.

The person before him opened black eyes and smiled—a sweet and somewhat tentative smile, entirely different from the lightly edged expression he had been offered moments before. The muscles of the face were used differently; the shoulders less square, and more rounded. Healer though he was, Shan felt the fine hairs lift along the back of his neck. Manifestly, absolutely, evidentially, the person before him was *not* Daav yos'Phelium.

He was seeing a ghost.

The soft black eyes widened, and the smile did, too. "Shannie!" The deep voice was lighter, the graininess softened by the burr of a Chonselta accent. "Now, shall I come the flutterhead and exclaim over your gains in height?"

"Aunt Aelli." He smiled at her, as gently as he knew how. "You were never a flutterhead. Even I knew that."

She gave a peal of appreciative laughter. "Well done! But if you wish to make a bow, you know, you must do so quickly. It would be too bad of me to give Daav a headache, which he will have, if I linger overlong."

"I see." He bowed, affectionately. "Aunt Aelliana, it is good to see you again."

She extended a hand to touch his cheek. "Thank you, Shannie. I am glad to see you, too. Take good care, now." She closed her eyes.

"Well." The voice had returned to its proper depth, the accent of Solcintra highlighting the grain, rather than softening it. The eyes opened, black and incisive. "That was a quick chat, for kin so long apart."

"She wished not to be the cause of a headache."

The smile was soft, but not in the least tentative. "She guards my health closely." He paused, as one considering the issue from all sides. "Someone should, I suppose." He moved his shoulders, something of experiment, or so Shan thought, and nodded, Terran fashion.

"Well enough, for an old scout," he said. "Now, what news? Your brother and his formidable lady have not yet returned from their pursuit of our enemy, you said. Have they been long away?"

"A few hours. What's worrisome is that the soldiers dispatched by Erob have not as yet picked them up in their sweep."

"Which only means they've gone beyond, or gone aside, or stayed within," Uncle Daav pointed out. "A scout commander, as I hardly need to tell you, is no inconsiderable force in his own right. A scout commander seconded by Miri Robertson Tiazan . . ." He shook his head. "My imagination trembles."

Shan grinned. "Would you like some tales from the late war?"

"I have had tales from Jason Carmody, and from Nelirikk Ex-

plorer, enough to fray the nerves of even an old scout who is well
accustomed to Clonak ter'Meulen." He lifted an eyebrow "I suppose that Clonak is with Line yos'Phelium's newest dependents?"

Shan shook his head. "Last seen, he was off to confer with the
techs who had charge of the dead, leaving Scout Ne'Zame and
Nelirikk to wait for the others to emerge from the 'docs. When I
looked in, the scout was coaching the explorer on the finer points
of Terran poker. The tech let me know that the two in the 'docs
had fallen on poor times of late and were in need of supplements,
in addition to the cancellation of their *vingtai*." He paused. "In all
fairness, you should also know that my sister Nova is to house.
Just now, she's with Erob—"

"Which is where we should be," Val Con said.

Shan spun, gasping. "How many times did father ask you *not*
to do that?"

His brother grinned, and shook the renegade lock of hair back
from his face. "My deplorable manners."

"He forgot," his lifemate said earnestly from his side. "He's
never at his best right after he's blown up a ship."

"I'll remember that." He blinked. "Blew up what ship?"

"Surely, the Department's ship?" Daav murmured.

Val Con nodded, and looked seriously to Shan. "Brother, will
you bear us company? Father?"

"Certainly," Daav said, quietly.

Shan sighed. "I've been doing my utmost to stay out of Erob's
path—and you'd be wise to do the same. The moment you meet
her, she'll be demanding that you remove the Clutch turtles from
her garden."

"Yes? Could she not simply ask them to go? Edger is a courteous man, and Sheather only one step from timid."

"They're asleep."

"Ah. That does put another face on it." He looked at Miri.

She grinned and shrugged. "Have to risk it, I guess."

"Indeed." He tipped his head. "Hazenthull and Diglon?"

"Still in the 'doc. Now that she has them, the tech refuses to let
them go until they have reached perfection."

"An artist. That is good. Now, which way to Erob?"

"I am to understand that these outlaws, then, were in pursuit of
Nadelm Korval?"

Nova inclined her head. "Erob, it is so. Scout ter'Meulen had performed a preliminary identification of the three who were . . . dispatched on-site. Nadelm Korval and his lady are thought to be in pursuit of the fourth."

"Scarcely healed and already in turmoil." The old woman sighed. "If it were not unworthy of an ally, I should insist that you depart, Korval-pernard'i. This planet has lately endured two military actions. We need no more peril, just now."

A rebuke, Nova thought, and a just one. She inclined her head. "Indeed, it was not our intention to burden Erob with our unseemly disputations."

"However, the dispute in question is not merely Korval's, but of all Liadens."

Heart in mouth, Nova turned in her chair.

There were four walking into the conference room, but she had eyes only for one.

Dark hair overlong and a little mussed, as if he had been out in the wind, the errant forelock falling, as it always had, across the smooth forehead and almost into the brilliant green eyes, her brother Val Con stood tall on his own two legs, one hand hooked in his belt, the other finger-woven with the red-haired woman at his side.

He might have been a shade too thin for a sister's comfort; the high curve of his cheekbones a thought too sharp, but he was Val Con, alive, walking—and even now one well-marked eyebrow was rising, as it certainly should, with her gawking at him like a half-wit.

"Sister ain't talking to you?" Miri Robertson asked him, while Shan and a grizzled man in scout leathers paused behind them.

"Alas," he said softly. "I fear I am in disgrace." The eyebrow was well up, now, the green eyes quizzical. "Come, Nova, cry friends."

"Frien—" The word died in her throat. She took a deliberate breath, and made another attempt.

"Friends," she said, and then, more sharply than she had intended—*much* more sharply, gods, but it was such a relief just to behold him—"Where the devil have you been?"

Val Con laughed, and bowed, jauntily, still holding hands with the red-haired woman. "A theme, in fact! I fear that a complete answer will need to wait upon current business." He looked to the woman at his side.

"Cha'trez, have you met my sister Nova?"

"Real quick, in the hall, right before the little dust-up in the garden," she said. She produced a nod and a grin. "Hi, Nova."

"Good morning," Nova told her, quellingly, and was not at all comforted to see Miri's grin grow wider.

"Good." Val Con moved a hand and the elder scout stepped forward. "And here is my father, Daav yos'Phelium, joyously returned to us, and accepted of his thodelm."

Thus introduced, Daav yos'Phelium inclined his head and smiled. "Good morning, child," he said, gravely. "You resemble your father extremely."

"So do you," she said, which was true, in some way that she could not quite quantify.

"Hah. An artifact of our upbringing, perhaps." The black eyes moved. "Good morning, Emrith," he said to Delm Erob.

"Daav yos'Phelium." She sighed and leaned back in her chair. "It needed only you."

His eyes gleamed. "I hold neither Ring nor rank. What possible harm can I do?"

"Do you know," she said dryly, "I was only just asking myself that same question."

He laughed. She did not.

"Win Den will want to see you. He owes you a cantra, I believe."

"So much? I will be certain to look him up immediately."

"Yes, do that." She looked to Val Con. "So, Korval, what is this danger which threatens all Liadens?"

"It is called the Department of the Interior," he said, softly. "Four of its Agents came into your garden last night."

Erob moved a hand. "Korval-pernard'i allows me to know that those persons were in pursuit of yourself."

He inclined his head. "On this occasion, they were. However, the Department has taken from every clan. Pilots, scouts, accountants, scholars—if the Department has a use for someone of talent, it matters not to which clan that one belongs. The Department subverts and makes them their own." He paused, green eyes thoughtful.

"The odds that the Department of the Interior was instrumental in engineering the domestic dispute which preceded the Yxtrang invasion borders on certainty. Erob became a target because of its ties with Korval. I do not hide that from you. They will try again to cripple you—I do not hide that, either."

She considered him, silently, for some few moments. "You can, of course," she said eventually, "provide proofs for these assertions."

He bowed. "Proofs may be obtained, yes."

"So. And what is the great House of Korval doing to stop this terrible enemy of all Liadens? I believe protection of all Liadens falls within your contract of hire?"

"Indeed it does." Once more he bowed—employee to employer, as Miri read it, with a movement of the hand indicating both irony and dedication to duty.

"Korval plans a return to Liad," he said, straightening and looking directly into her eyes. "We shall take the war to our enemy in his home."

"We certainly shall not!" Nova surged to her feet, staring at him in horror. "Have you taken leave of your senses? Plan B is in effect—do you know it? I refuse to sanction any such madness." She raised her hand, showing him Korval's Ring. "As Korval pernard'i—I forbid it."

"Oops," Miri Robertson said, into the absolute silence that followed this.

"Precisely," Val Con agreed. Hand-linked, they walked forward, until they were two paces from where Nova stood, rigid and outraged.

Together, they bowed honor to the trust-holder. Together, they straightened. It was Val Con who said the words—his right and his duty as delm genetic.

"The Ring passes."

What Nova should have done next, according to the Code Miri had sleep-learned, was bow in exactly the same mode, repeat "The Ring passes," and hand the thing over, no muss, no fuss.

Nova shook her head, bright hair swinging around her shoulders.

"The Ring does not pass merely because you have taken a pet," she said, scolding, in the mode between kin.

Shan moved forward a step. "Nova . . ." he began—and stopped when Val Con raised a hand.

"Sister," he said, very softly, "we are facing an enemy that I know all too well. I *am* the Captain Genetic, truly lifemated. We have made promises and taken oaths, on behalf of Korval and of the passengers. The Ring passes now because it must. I will tell you plainly that I wish it fell into any hands but ours."

Nova hesitated for a heartbeat longer while she searched first Val Con's face, then Miri's. Finally, she bowed as the Code set forth. Straightening, she announced, "The Ring passes," removed it from the second finger of her left hand, and held it out in her palm. It was a massive thing, heavy with enamel-work, taking fire from the room's dim lighting.

Solemnly, Val Con received it, turned and held it out. "Cha'trez, please familiarize yourself with this object."

Blinking, Miri took the Ring, and stood frowning down at it.

Brilliant it might be, but up close, it showed its age. There was a runkle on top of the band, as if somebody had used the edge to strip wire, or maybe to scratch a message into hull plate. And while the intarsia work depicting Korval's Tree-and-Dragon was intact, one of the two emeralds framing the carved *Flaran Cha'menthi* showed a dark crack at its heart, and the other, whole, held more than a tinge of yellow.

"Emerald's bust, boss," she said, turning the Ring around and peering inside the band for an engraving.

"It has been so for . . . quite some time," Val Con said.

The inside of the band was smooth; any engraving that might have been there had probably been worn away by generations of Korval fingers.

She gave it one more hard stare, then handed it back to Val Con.

"Got it."

"Good." He stood for a moment, his eyes on the thing cupped in his palm. Then, with an air of decision, he slid it onto the third finger of his left hand. In her head, Miri heard a *snap*, as if a something had been locked tight into place.

There was a funny couple seconds, then, as if nobody was sure of what to do next.

It was Daav who finally moved, stepping forward and sweeping a profound bow to the delm's honor, beautifully timed and directed precisely between the two of them.

"*Korval.*"

They bowed together, delm to clanmember.

"Korval Sees Daav yos'Phelium," Val Con murmured, which was what the Code stipulated he had to say.

Shan was next, face stern and silver eyes austere. His bow, deliberate and eloquent of more than mere duty, was in the mode of thodelm to delm.

"Korval. yos'Galan is yours."

Beside her, she felt Val Con sigh, and then they both bowed, as they had to, from delm to thodelm.

"Korval Sees Shan yos'Galan, thodelm," Val Con said.

Shan went back a step and it was Nova's turn, bowing simply as clanmember to delm.

"Korval," she said, softly.

For a third time, they bowed together, delm to clanmember. Miri caught the shoulder twitch on the way up, and took her turn.

"Korval Sees Nova yos'Galan," she said, with a seriousness that went clean through to her soul. Nova had just given them life-and-death over her and hers—and they had just accepted. Miri didn't know how Nova felt about it—the other woman's face was a cool, golden mask—but she felt like bawling.

Nova stepped to Shan's side, and Daav stepped forward once more, bowing honor to the delm.

It was, Miri thought, a much different bow than his first—plainer by several degrees of flamboyance, and considerably less bold. When he straightened, she saw that his face was also considerably less bold, the eyes wide and soft.

"Korval," he stated, and his accent was different, too.

Biting her lip, she bowed with Val Con, caught the signal again as they came up and hoped she was right.

"Korval Sees Aelliana Caylon," she said, and Daav went back to his place beside Nova.

Emrith Tiazan rose from her chair at the table, and bowed the bow between equals.

"Finally," she said.

DUTIFUL PASSAGE
LYTAXIN ORBIT

In receipt of his delm's order, Shan lost no time in repairing to the spaceport and hiring a lift to *Dutiful Passage*. Ostensibly, he was dispatched to insure that all was in readiness for departure, a detail that could have been retired by a short comm call to the captain of the vessel. However, his delm had most particularly desired him to attend to this task personally.

His brother had asked that his affection be conveyed to Priscilla, which Shan certainly intended to do—directly after he had assured the lady of his own passionate regard.

In the passenger section of the hired ship, Shan reclined his chair. He was well asleep before they cleared atmosphere; and woke, as he had primed himself to do, when they docked.

He sat up, eyes on the amber caution light over the hatch. The instant it turned green, he was on his feet.

"My thanks," he called to the pilot, and hit the bar, passing from the shuttle into the blessed familiarity of Docking Bay Six.

Three long strides and he was through the second door and into the alcove beyond, where she waited for him: tall, beautiful and stern—a goddess. Almost, he fell to his knees before her.

Even as his stride faltered, the goddess vanished, and it was a woman before him, her black eyes overflowing with tears given the lie by her smile, and by the arrow of joy that blazed from her heart to his.

She came into his arms—or he into hers. What did it matter? They embraced, neither speaking, allowing the tides of emotion to sweep between them, open as they were Healer to Healer—and, somehow, more.

And when the emotion had found its level and the joyful tears had stopped, Priscilla stirred in his arms, and lifted her hands to cup his face, her eyes searching his, puzzled, and perhaps a little afraid.

"Shan?" she said, in her deep, thrilling voice. "What have you done to yourself?"

Miri and her lifemate were on their way to the atrium, along with Daav and his. Daav claimed never to have seen a Clutch turtle before, a confidence Miri took with a cellar of salt.

"OK," she said. "Turtles out of the garden, then what? Jase?"

"Clonak," Val Con murmured. "Since he is to house. Also, we should find how Hazenthull and Diglon go on—for that matter, we should find how Nelirikk goes on. Then, certainly, Jason." He pushed his hair out of his eyes. "Haste is necessary. The ship—were I the Commander, I would have arranged for a direct beam to headquarters the instant the ship recognized me. We must assume that they know the trap was sprung—and that the ship has died. They will assume four Agents dead or out of commission."

"And they'll send an army right here to Lytaxin," Miri finished, because they'd hammered all this out 'round the conference table. "Which is why we gotta grab their interest and keep them busy. I got all that. What about Edger?"

"An excellent question," Val Con allowed. "I wonder if our father might be willing to undertake an ambassadorial mission on behalf of his clan?"

Daav glanced at him, one eyebrow up. "I will of course undertake any task my delm requires of me. Am I allowed to know what it is that the Clutch might bring to the effort, in light of the need for haste?"

"You are sent at a tangent, if you will, on behalf of an ally which may require . . . alternative quarters."

There was a slight silence. "You speak of Jelaza Kazone."

"I do. You know our case is desperate—not only does the Department target Korval, it targets all of Korval's works. If we lose this throw—which is all too possible—the Department will not rest until we are eradicated. Even should some of us survive, it would be chancy in the extreme to attempt to remove the Tree."

"I would call an attempt to remove the Tree from Liad in times of peace and placid harmony chancy in the extreme," Daav commented drily.

Val Con smiled. "Which is why you go as our emissary to the Clutch. I believe that the Elders will find the project appeals—and falls within their ability to accomplish." He paused, one eyebrow up. "There must be a scout in it, you know."

"And so there must be," Daav agreed. Silence, and a sense, Miri'd swear, of him consulting with an advisor. Or a lifemate.

"We are able to negotiate on behalf of the clan's ancient ally, Jelaza Kazone, with the Elders of the Clutch," Daav said eventually. "My lifemate wishes it known as her heart-wish that any arrangements for the removal of the Tree from Liad will be found—unnecessary."

"Yah, we do, too," Miri said, as they passed through the door into Erob's inner garden. "But hope don't win the war."

"Soldier Lore."

They were in the captain's office, wine to hand and a ravished tray of eatables on the side table. Shan had told the story of Weapon Hall, and his meeting there with his other self.

"The most dangerous thing in the Hall," Priscilla said now. "What possessed you to take it?"

"Lute gave it me—he said I'd need it, and that it wouldn't weigh very much." He sipped wine. "I believe my reasoning may have run along the lines of, 'Well, am I likely to lie to myself except for a *very* good reason?'"

Priscilla closed her eyes, and it *was* fear he saw, in her face and in her pattern—fear of the man he had allowed himself to become.

"I can put it back," he said, tentatively.

She shook her head. "No," she said, her sorrow tugging at his own heart. "You can't—"

It was rare you saw two creatures so completely asleep, Miri thought, considering the somnolent bulk of them, tucked all tidy and peaceful into a pretty little cave that was 'way too small for them.

"They can sleep for months," she said, as if Val Con maybe didn't know that.

"Yes."

"Do you know how to wake them up?"

"No."

"Great," she said, and stared at them some more, a certifiably dumb idea tickling at the back of her brain.

Well, she thought, *can't hurt anything. And then it'll be outta your system.*

So thinking, she took one step forward, cleared her throat and said, clear, but not particularly loud, "Edger, wake up. We need you."

Nothing happened. *Of course nothing happened, Robertson,* she scolded herself. *You didn't think anything would happen, remember?*

She was just turning to Val Con to let him know that she'd taken her shot and it was his turn now, when a shudder rippled Edger's skin—and then another one, more pronounced.

The green eyelids flickered—and drew back, disclosing eyes as round and as yellow as moons.

"Sister," Edger said, at about a quarter of his usual boom. "How may I serve you?"

LIAD
JELAZA KAZONE

The kitchen was awash with morning sun before the cat and the robot detected, each in its own manner, the sound of light, quick footsteps upon the back stair.

The robot slid the waiting muffin into the heating unit, and was pouring tea into a pale porcelain cup when the lady herself danced into the room, silver eyes sparkling, her hair a-crackle with power.

"Good morning, Jeeves!" she greeted the robot, her usually slow voice nearly brisk with merriness. She paused at the stool by the window and bent down to offer her finger to the cat sitting there. "Lord Merlin. You're looking very pleased with yourself this morning, sirrah."

The cat touched her finger with his nose and turned his head to gaze out the window. Anthora laughed and danced over to the counter, where her place was laid: teacup gently steaming, a single crimson flower in a tall, simple vase, napkin and jampot to hand. She slid lightly onto the tall chair, shook out the napkin—and gave a crow of laughter.

"Oh, no! Jeeves, where did you find this?"

"In the linen press, with twenty-three others exactly like it," the robot replied, slipping the muffin from the heating unit onto a plate and rolling across the floor to her side. "I thought it appropriate to your station."

"Good gods." She blinked, first at the robot, and once more at the napkin and its intricately embroidered tree-and-dragon, which she yet held at arm's length before her. "Two dozen of them, you say? It must have been done as a joke." She tipped her head, considering. "Or perhaps Cousin Kareen had them made. *She* would think them no less than needful."

The robot placed the plate before her and she dropped the napkin to her knee.

"Thank you," she said, and reached for the teacup.

"You're welcome," said Jeeves, rolling back a respectful distance. The orange sphere at his apex—his "head," as Val Con would have it, though it was no such thing; Jeeves' computational unit was enclosed by his stainless steel mid-part—the orange sphere flicked gently.

"Did you sleep well, Ms. Anthora?"

"Do you know," she said, setting the cup down and neatly breaking the muffin, "I do believe I slept most profoundly during the first half of the night, which, as it transpired, was a good thing, eh, Lord Merlin?"

The cat flicked an ear, but did not deign to turn from his study of the birds in the bush outside his window. Anthora smiled and bit into the muffin. There was silence for a time then—an easy silence, they three being well accustomed to each other's oddities.

The cat watched out the window; the woman ate and drank; the robot cast his awareness wide, downloading data from the perimeter points and initiating a security check of the house computer.

"Did you know," Anthora said at last, leaning back and pushing the plate away, "that, on Casiaport, there is a teashop on the same street as the Pilots Guildhall, where one might find the best winter soup on all the world?"

The robot's orange head flickered. "No, Miss Anthora, I did not know that. Shall I archive the information?"

She shook her hair back. "I don't think that will be necessary. Though perhaps you should find their recipe for winter soup. We will wish to feed Ren Zel what he likes best."

"This would be Ren Zel dea'Judan, first class piloting license re-issued out of the Terran Guild, countersigned by Shan yos'Galan and Seth Johnson; five hours certified test flight short of master class?"

Anthora straightened on the stool and looked thoughtfully at the flickering orange ball. "It sounds very like him. Has he been here before?"

"I have no record of the pilot before last evening," Jeeves said. "His palm-print is on-file in the house computer. He has access on all levels."

"Perfectly correct," she said, and looked over her shoulder toward the window "*Really*, Lord Merlin."

The very tip of the cat's tail twitched; stilled.

Anthora shook her head. "Record Ren Zel dea'Judan as my lifemate, please, Jeeves." She paused, frowning lightly, then nodded. "Send the announcement to the *Gazette*. List his rank in place of clan—First Mate, *Dutiful Passage*."

The light in Jeeves' headball steadied. "Yes, Miss Anthora."

"Good," she said, slipping off the stool and moving purposefully down the room. "I will call Mr. dea'Gauss."

LYTAXIN
EROB'S CLANHOUSE

Orders were to await the captain's word. The captain's word being some time in coming, Nelirikk and Shadia set about exposing the Troop's newest recruits to the intricacies of poker.

Diglon Rifle grasped the rules of play with a speed that would have been notable in an explorer, and was presiding over a solid wall of money-chips when Nelirikk heard the cadence of a familiar voice in the hall.

"Attention!" He slapped his cards face down onto the table and surged to his feet, Hazenthull and Diglon scarcely a breath behind him. Shadia turned in her chair, the better to see the door.

Came the captain and the scout—well enough. And behind them . . . Nelirikk swallowed, heart slamming into overdrive.

Behind his captain walked one of *them*—a Clutch turtle, slayer of soldiers, destroyer of fleets, despoiler of worlds.

Beside him, Nelirikk heard a small, breathless sound, and dared to move his head the fraction necessary for him to see the recruits.

Hazenthull's naked brown face was stiff, her eyes wide, her lips compressed into a thin pale line. Diglon Rifle had the appearance of a foot soldier ordered to hold the rear against the approaching line of enemy war-wagons.

Scout Shadia, seated and at her ease, inclined her head. "Commander Shadow, Captain Redhead. Your Wisdom. Be welcome."

"Gently said," the slayer boomed in a voice that rattled the brain inside the skull. "May I know your name?"

The scout inclined her head once more. "Scout Lieutenant First-In Shadia Ne'Zame—in the short form. In the shortest available form, I am called Shadia."

"Yet another scout!" the creature exclaimed. "One's elder brother is even now conferring with the scout who is the direct ancestor of our own brother—he whom you this instant greeted as Shadow, which I had not known was a part of his name."

"Only," the scout murmured, "when Scout ter'Meulen is onworld."

Shadia grinned. "That's so, Clonak being an inspiration to us all. I should mind my manners more closely—but truly, sir, it's so *apt* a naming!"

"Others have remarked upon it as well," the scout said, not without a sigh, and glanced up into Nelirikk's face.

He expected something, then—an explanation, a raised eyebrow, the offer of the scout's own crystal grace blade with which he might honorably cut his throat before the shelled one bit his legs off and left him to die in agony.

It was not, however, the scout who spoke, but the captain. She came forward some few paces, hands behind her back.

"Beautiful. What's wrong with you and the recruits?"

"Captain." He hesitated, his eyes drawn irresistibly to the Clutch turtle. The old battle reports had not overstated the enemy: the horny and impervious hide, the shell that covered the back and the soft, vulnerable belly, the pitiless and unblinking yellow eyes.

"If the captain pleases," he managed, and was ashamed to hear

that his voice was not . . . completely . . . soldierly. "Many, many
years ago, Clutch turtles handed overwhelming losses across several battle zones to the Troop. The conditions of defeat state that
the Troop will, from that time on, be considered the fair and just
prey of the victors."

"That so?"

Nelirikk met her eyes. "Yes, Captain. It is so."

"OK. You wanna explain what that has to do with you?"

He stared at her, then looked to the scout, who returned him a
glance that was blandness itself.

"Captain, it has to do with me and with these recruits that—"
He stopped, inwardly cursing himself for an unblooded crechling.
Carefully, he saluted.

"Captain. The treaties between Yxtrang and Clutch have nothing to do with those who serve as soldiers in Jela's line."

She nodded. "That's what I thought, too." She pointed, over
her shoulder and up, and continued in the tongue of the Common
Troop.

"Soldiers, attend me! This is Seventh Shell Third Hatched
Knife Clan of Middle River's Spring Spawn of Farmer Greentrees
of the Spearmakers Den: The Sheather; field name Sheather. He
is the brother-by-oath of myself and the scout. You will serve him
and also his brother, who you will meet, as members of Line
yos'Phelium. Am I understood?"

They all three saluted. "Yes, Captain!" rang in unison.

"Good. We will shortly be moving on the enemy of our Line."
She looked at Nelirikk, and spoke next in Liaden, oathholder to
oathbound. "Prepare them as befit, those in the service of yos'Phelium," she said and dropped into Terran. "Draw leathers and arms
outta the Gyrfalks stores. Give Diglon a short sleep-learn in Trade,
and lay a base in Terran, if there's time. Drill 'em both in the signs
and calls. You'll be called when it's time to board ship."

Once more, Nelirikk saluted. "Captain," he said, and then, "If
the captain pleases."

"Now what?"

"What is our destination, Captain?"

"Had to ask it, didn't you?" She glanced at the scout, who inclined his head, ironically.

"Liad is our destination, Explorer."

Nelirikk allowed himself a grin before he again saluted his
captain and turned to give orders to the recruits.

DAY 376
STANDARD YEAR 1392

SPACEPORT
SUREBLEAK

Etienne Borden, Surebleak nightside portmaster, leaned back in the duty chair and grinned up at dayside 'master Claren Liu.

"Another exciting shift at Surebleak Port," he said, stretching the kinks out of his long arms. "Read all about it in the night log!"

Claren snorted. "If you've written 'Nothing happened during night shift. Nothing ever happens during night shift. Why is there a nightside portmaster here? Why is there a port here?' again," she said, crossing the room to the dispensing unit and punching up coffee and a bun, "you're going to call yourself to the attention of the guild, which just might pull you and send you someplace worse."

"Produce this someplace worse!" he challenged.

She paused in the act of removing her cup from the dispenser, and looked at him. "There must be someplace worse," she said eventually.

"Hah! I say hah! If there is any other world in the galaxy more backward or barbaric than Surebleak—notice the use of the word *if*—it cannot possibly support a spaceport. By this logic—*therefore*, Madam Dayside—Surebleak is on the last rung of the great ladder of worlds, poised to topple into the roiling pit of chaos below—and *any* other world in the galaxy—*any other world*—must, by an extension of pure, emotionless logic, be a better, cleaner, saner world."

"Or maybe not," said Claren, and took a bite of her pastry. "Mithlyn was pretty bad."

"Mithlyn is a paradise," Etienne proclaimed. "I woo it! I embrace it! I make love to it!"

"Try, and you'll find you've lost some equipment in the process," she returned. "They're pretty strict about that kind of thing on Mithlyn." She sipped coffee and pointed at the master board with her bun.

"You signing out, or what? I want my dose of excitement."

"Excitement!" He spun in the chair, signed out with a flourish and surged to his feet. "The chair is yours, Madam Dayside!"

"Great." She approached it, unhurried, leaned over the board to put her coffee cup in the slot and her thumb on the scan-plate, glanced at the main screen—and stared.

"What the—" She brought the image up, diddled with the resolution—and stared some more. "There's a line of cars," she said over her shoulder to Etienne, "seven, nine—twelve cars coming in through the main gate."

"What?" He was next to her, blinking at the screen like an idiot. "We are invaded, Madam Dayside. The natives have come to claim the spaceport, that they may profit by selling the tugs for scrap."

"Could be, I guess," Claren said absently, watching the long, stately, *well-behaved* progress of the caravan, as it passed along the row of empty storefronts and vacant repair shops. "Anything strike you as funny about this?" she asked.

"Funny?" he repeated. "You mean, besides the fact that we are about to die in a farce engineered—no, I see. They came through the main gate. They came in by the Road."

"They did. And look at the cars—those aren't jalopies. Those are—" She stopped.

"What?" he demanded. "Those are *what*?"

"Fatcat cars," she said, having recognized the one belonging to Boss Vine, who held the territory outside the main gate. "Etienne, we've got twelve different bosses coming in here."

He gaped at her. "But—why?"

She sighed, straightened and crossed the room to take her jacket down from its peg. "Guess I'd better go find out," she said, looking at him over her shoulder. "You up for some overtime?"

By the time she reached the yard, the cars were parked in neat lines of three under the shadow of the tower, their noses pointed at the main gate.

Claren stopped a couple strides out from the door, firmly squelching the urge to walk up to one of the men or women disembarking from their vehicles and ask them what the hell they were doing. She was Dayside Portmaster, after all; a post of some dignity, even on Surebleak. She straightened her jacket, so the portmaster beacon stitched onto the breast could be seen.

The crowd had sorted itself out and was moving toward her as a unit, headed up by a man in a blue jacket, leaning lightly on a cane, his left arm in a sling, the empty sleeve neatly pinned up.

He halted a comfortable four paces out, the rest ranging 'round him. All of them, Claren saw now, carried something—one woman held a basket filled with shiny green fruits; the man next to the leader held a bouquet of red, gold and white flowers in his arms; another, very large man, held what appeared to be a roll of multicolored fabric on one broad shoulder.

The leader inclined his head—something more formal than the local nod and less formal than a full-mode Liaden bow.

"I am called Conrad," he said, his voice melodious and cultured. "And these are my associates. We have come to inform you that the Port Road stands open from the main gate to the inland farms, and to solicit the assistance of the portmaster in matters of off-world trade."

"Off-world trade?" She stared at him, and was returned a bland and velvet brown glance. "This is Surebleak," she said, sternly. "Just because the Road's open today doesn't mean it'll be open tomorrow. If one boss in line gets assassinated, the Road goes down again."

"Not necessarily," he replied, softly. "We are crafting ways in which chaos may be avoided in the future." He once again inclined his head in that curiously formal gesture. "Please, allow us to name ourselves to you, and to give the gifts we have brought."

There wasn't much use in telling him no, Claren thought, looking at the crowd of faces. Some looked cocky and tough; most were poised, with a touch of tentativeness, as if they weren't quite sure what she'd do. It was the realization that they were as nervous of her as she was of them that led her to bend her head, trying to match Conrad's style.

"I'd be pleased to learn the names of your associates, Mr. Conrad," she said, and was rewarded with a slight, charming smile.

"Very good," he said and used his chin to point at the man holding the flowers. "This is Penn Kalhoon, of Hamilton Street."

He came forward a step—a thin, bookish looking man, wearing a pair of steel eyeglasses, his pale yellow hair brushed painfully flat—and offered the bouquet. She took it, trying not to think how hard it was going to be now to get at the pistol under her arm, and nodded.

"A pleasure, Penn Kalhoon. I'm Claren Liu, Dayside Port."

He smiled, which did nice things to his face. "A pleasure, Portmaster," he said and stepped back, making room for the next one in line.

It went pretty quickly, and much smoother than she would have thought possible, and then there was only the tall man with the fabric over his shoulder left to be introduced.

"This," Conrad said, in his soft, cultured voice, "is Mr. McFarland, who is in my employ. Recent injuries make it . . . difficult . . . for me to carry my own gift. I hope you will receive it with pleasure."

McFarland stepped forward, shrugging the roll off his shoulder, catching it in deft hands and unrolling it on the tarmac at her feet: a simple and cheery little rug, made out of tied and woven scraps of cloth. Claren smiled—it was that kind of rug.

"So." Another faint smile. "We are delighted that you were able to speak with us this morning. We do not wish to keep you longer from the duties of your day. May we set a time when three of our number may come to you for a discussion of opening trade—and also, perhaps, to offer some franchise business in port."

This was a man who knew what a port should look like, Claren thought, and made a mental note to ask him, sometime, where he was from.

For now, she had another try at that formal nod of the head, and offered a time six days in the future as well-suited for a meeting between herself and the representatives of Conrad's "association." That should give her enough time to get some background and guidance from the guild.

"Excellent," he said, softly. "Our representatives will be with you upon that day and hour." One last inclination of the head, with the rest of the bunch giving the standard nod, and they were moving away, back toward their cars, leaving their rug, baskets, and bottles on the tarmac at her feet, and Conrad's 'hand, McFarland, rising up like a mountain in front of her, holding one hand out and empty, reaching into his pocket with the other.

"Thought you'd like to see today's newspaper, ma'am," he said easily, and displayed it—a single broadsheet, folded in quarters. He bent and put it on the rug, gave her a nod, and moved off after his boss.

Claren stood there, holding the flowers, and watched them get into their cars and pull out. When the last had disappeared down to the main gate, she turned around and gave Etienne the all-clear.

DAY 376
STANDARD YEAR 1392

BLAIR ROAD
SUREBLEAK

In his former life, Pat Rin had often given parties.

Indeed, he had enjoyed a small reputation as a superlative host, whose most casual morning-gather was a jewel of charming companionship and graceful conversation. Despite the considerable effort he put forth to ensure the worthiness of these affairs, he had never experienced the slightest tremor of nerves regarding their outcomes, and had observed with puzzlement the agonies of uncertainty borne by other, very gifted, hosts prior to the brilliant success of their latest soiree.

He had always supposed this lack of delicate feeling to be further testimony of the general impairment of his warmer emotions. Certainly, a man who, upon searching his heart, had once declared that he truly loved but two creatures in all the universe could hardly be expected to lavish a great deal of passion upon a ball.

Well, and the universe had changed, and he with it.

There was to be a gathering this evening in his own house, where he would host not only those associated bosses who felt comfortable leaving their turfs in the hands of their seconds for one more day, but several as yet unassociated bosses of territories removed from the Road.

He expected perhaps fifteen guests on the evening—certainly not a party of any size, though at that more bosses than had been together in one room on Surebleak in many a long year. He had satisfied himself that his cook was up to the challenge of providing a buffet meal and desserts for the expected few, and decreed that neither beer nor whiskey would be among the beverages. They would offer instead an array of fruit juices provided by Melina Sherton, tea, and coffeetoot. He might have gone a bit further and advised upon the particulars of the sweets being baked, but saw that his presence was hindering progress in the kitchen, rather than helping, and had retreated, nerves a-jangle, to his private parlor.

This chamber was adjacent to his newly painted and appointed office, and was, in truth, a wonder and a marvel.

A former storage room, it had been cleared of rubbish, the walls painted a soft and restful green, the scrubbed floor treasuring one of Ajay's large oval rugs. A shelf had been hung on the right wall, and held six bound books, none new, or familiar. He had not given them more than a perfunctory examination, merely running his hand down the spines and opening one or two at their beginning, but he found their presence soothing in some small way, much as the few modest flowers in the vase upon the lamp table.

This afternoon, he found the room occupied before him; Silk the cat was asleep on the astonishment of a genuine wooden rocking chair—a gift from Audrey, or so he was given to understand. He rather thought that the chair, like the parlor itself, was a gift from his lady; certainly, her hand was obvious, and because that was so, he smiled.

Bending, he picked Silk up, awkwardly one-handed, and sat in the rocker, draping the cat across his knee. Surprisingly, the creature stayed where he was placed, sputtering a few sleepy purrs. Pat Rin sighed, put his hand on the soft flank, and leaned back in the chair.

His leg ached, a little; his wounded arm, rather more. Perhaps, once trade was established, they might acquire an autodoc. He sighed. First, they needed to rejoin the Health Net. He would make a point of introducing the subject during his conversations with his guests this evening—planting the seed, Uncle Daav would have said. And something very much needed to be done about that ghastly and moribund port. A gaming house, perhaps. Certainly, a greengrocer, a trade store . . .

A light step interrupted these ruminations.

"Pat Rin," a soft voice murmured in his ear. Strong hands

came down on his shoulders, kneading. "You promised that you would rest this afternoon, denubia."

He smiled and leaned back into her hands.

"I am resting," he murmured. "I am sitting in a comfortable chair, with my cat on my lap, and my beloved by me. Were I any more restful, I would be asleep."

"Ah. But there remain some hours until the first guests arrive. Perhaps a nap would not be entirely out of order." He felt her fingers against his hair. "Not entirely out of order," she repeated, her fingers moving in long, soothing strokes.

He felt his eyelids growing heavy, and the cat curled on his lap began to purr in earnest.

"I am surrounded and overpowered," he complained, forcing his eyes open—just. "Wretch—you have attached a potent ally."

She laughed low, and came 'round to offer him her hand. "Come, upstairs with you! Silk and I will engage to sit on you, if that is necessary to making you rest."

"I scarcely think I *would* rest under such conditions," he commented, shifting his knees. Silk woke with a long, sensuous stretch, leapt to the floor and strolled off. Pat Rin put his hand into the hand of his love and allowed her to help him to his feet.

"We shall mount an investigation," she said, slipping his arm through hers. "And then, perhaps, both of us will rest."

They received twenty, in the final count, with rather more of the associated bosses in attendance than Pat Rin had anticipated. It seemed that, despite the commonly held goals, there remained some, certainly understandable, rivalry between the allies, and none wished to quit the floor to the potential advantage of another.

He mentioned this to Penn Kalhoon when his hostly duties brought him at last to that gentleman's side; the other man nodded, unsurprised.

"We gotta expect that. I mean, most of the long-holders—Ira, Whit, Melina, me—we shot for boss because we thought we could do it better'n it was being done. And mostly, we were right. Not to say we didn't make mistakes." He sipped his juice and sighed. "That's good. I need to talk to Melina about getting some of this into my turf, now the Road's open." He grinned suddenly.

"See? Boss-think. You got it yourself, only bigger, better, flashier. None of *us* figured out how to open the Road, and I gotta tell you I been kicking myself about it daily since the day you come into my office and offered to deal." He had another sip of juice, and glanced up, light shining off the lenses of his spectacles. "That newspaper of yours—you know it's feeding the jealousy, don't you?"

Pat Rin frowned. "Is it? I had no notion. My thought had been to . . . inform . . . the residents of my own streets on subjects of interest to themselves. It was a severe shock, if you will have the truth, when Ira showed me the copy that had been brought into his territory. It was long out of date, but . . ." He hesitated on the edge of a possible indiscretion.

"But he was all warm to know that Deacon'd had a waterfiltering plant in his turf, and that you was sponsoring free reading lessons to all comers. Now the Road's open, and news is easier to spread, we're all gonna find out pretty quick that Melina has a winery, and Ira's got six clinics, and Penn's got a school system—and everyone of us is gonna want what we're short of."

"Well, then." Pat Rin had recourse to his own glass—grape cider, according to Melina, and very pleasant, indeed. "If that is the case, then we must discover how to bring improvements to all territories, each according to their needs."

Penn laughed.

"Bigger, better, flashier. Count me in, whatever you come up with. Meantime, this is a—a *triumph*, in case you don't know it. Twenty bosses in the same room—bosses *only*, no 'hands to cover 'em, and their personal guns on file downstairs with your people?" He shook his head. "Never thought I'd see it. Sleet, never even thought of the idea. Something else to kick myself for."

"Surely," Pat Rin murmured, "you have had enough to occupy you in keeping your territory stable for ten years?"

"Yeah, but see, I *knew* keeping my streets clean wasn't enough. What I didn't know was how to expand without—well, without starting a war. Now I seen it, and I learned something."

"Ah," Pat Rin said, and turned the conversation, gracefully, to Penn's wife and children, whom he had met during his convalescence.

Later, moving among his guests, he was stopped by a young person scarcely beyond halfling, her dark eyes darting nervously from side to side.

"Boss Conrad?" Her voice was high and louder than necessary.

He admitted it and she nodded, jerkily. "Voral Jene. Gough Street turf."

"Ah, yes." One of the unallied bosses. He inclined his head, remembering to smile. "I am pleased that you were able to come this evening."

"No problem," she said. "I wanted to talk to you about—I mean, couple the other bosses here say the Road's really open, that I can walk end to end, from the port to the farms, an' nobody'll stop me or make me pay a toll."

"That is correct."

Her busy eyes searched his face. "Why?" she asked, voice keying higher. "Why'd you do that?"

Something was wrong, here, Pat Rin thought, considering the frantic young face. Perhaps she had partaken of one of the all-too-common street drugs, which had now turned on her. He glanced casually to one side, saw Melina Sherton over by the buffet table, talking to Ira Gabriel.

"Why?" Voral Jene demanded.

Pat Rin frowned. "Because the trade is important," he said, keeping his voice soft and reasonable. "Both between territories and between the world and the greater galaxy. The trade will—"

"The plague come from the spaceport," she interrupted, very loudly, now. "You know that, don't you? It come outta the spaceport and damn near killed everybody! I was just a kid, but I remember it! And you went and opened up the Road again! You're trying to kill us!"

The room was alerted now. From the edge of his eye, he saw Melina moving in, and Penn Kalhoon, too. Many of the other bosses were staring at them, their conversations interrupted by Voral Jene's shouted accusations.

Something else moved—out of place and stealthy—behind Melina. Pat Rin turned his head at the motion and the girl grabbed his wounded arm, shouting now. "You're going to kill us! We're all going to die!"

Gasping, he shook her loose and saw the man behind the buffet pull an outsized gun from beneath his jacket.

"'Ware!" Pat Rin shouted, and Melina spun.

Her first kick destroyed the gunman's aim, sending the pellet into the blameless ceiling; her second knocked his legs out from under him. Ira Gabriel was there in a rush, first kicking the weapon out of the man's hand, then kicking him in the ribs. The gun skittered a few paces across the floor before being snatched up by Penn Kalhoon.

Two other bosses were holding Voral Jene by her arms, despite her cries and struggles. The door burst open, admitting Natesa, Cheever, Gwince and Filmin.

Cheever was at the buffet in two strides, and had the downed gunman by the collar. Scarcely less quick, Natesa gained Pat Rin's side, her eyes cold, and her mouth tight.

"Search her," she directed Gwince, and the two bosses obligingly escorted Voral Jene to the nearer wall.

A few steps away, Penn reversed the gun he had captured and handed it peaceably to Filmin.

Cries of "Kill him!" "Kill them both!" were rising as Cheever hauled the erstwhile gunman to his feet. The man moaned and shook his head, and Pat Rin recognized him as Victor Armhaut, of Conklin turf.

Pat Rin took a breath. "Silence!" he snapped, the Command mode ringing against the shattered ceiling.

Silence there was.

"Is anyone hurt?"

Against the wall, Voral Jene was sobbing, while Victor Armhaut reeled in Cheever McFarland's grasp, shivering and panting for breath.

Save for the ceiling, there were no injuries.

"What do we do now, Boss?" Cheever asked, shaking his captive a little.

Pat Rin raised a hand, drawing all eyes to himself. "An excellent question. We have gathered for a party, not an execution." He eyed the assembled multitude. His associates, all of whom had been in danger of the gunman; all of whom had some right to Balance.

"It is in my mind to fling these two into the street so that we might continue our evening," he said to his associates, acutely aware of Natesa's presence at his side. "What to you think?"

The room filled immediately with voices, and opinions.

"Can't just let them get away with . . ."

"Ought to shoot 'em both . . ."

"Kick 'em in the head . . ."

"No, wait! Conrad—I know!"

"Josh Cruthers," Pat Rin said, raising his voice to be heard above the din. "What is your solution?"

The angry shouts died back to a bass rumble, then fell into silence as a thin bald man scarcely taller than Pat Rin himself stepped into the center of the room.

"Josh Cruthers, boss of Arcadja Alleys," he said, looking around at the assembled bosses. "Look, Conrad's right—we come here to get to know each other, not for a killin' . . ."

"They drew on the man in his own house!" somebody shouted from the back of the room.

Josh Cruthers held up a hand. "Hear me out. Just hear me out, and if it don't make sense, well, then we ain't no worse off, right?"

There was a mutter of approval, and he continued.

"So, what I'm thinkin' is, I'll have my car drive these two back to Gough Street and let 'em out so we ain't gotta see 'em. Then, tomorrow, the gab-rag puts out the news on 'em. Let everybody know Boss Jene and Boss Armhaut ain't gonna be allowed to join the Affiliation 'cause they pulled a gun on Conrad in his house, while we was all here on his invite. Ain't none of us wants to deal with 'em—so Gough and Conklin turfs won't get no help with clinics, or school tutors, or gardens, or nothin'—not till they got themselves bosses willin' to see there's a better way to get stuff done . . ."

Pat Rin heard Penn Kalhoon's "They won't last a week!" amid a chorus of agreement.

Privately, he thought that the two renegade bosses would do well to last a week, but the Balance was no more than precise. Pat Rin inclined his head.

"With Boss Cruthers' loan of a car and Mr. McFarland's assistance as an escort, I believe that our party may continue. Please—take them away."

He looked 'round the room, remembering to smile, and set about putting his guests at ease, which was the duty of a host.

"My apologies for the disturbance," he said to the room at large. "I direct everyone's attention to the buffet, where we still have many delights to share! Please, friends, party on!"

DAY 51
STANDARD YEAR 1393

DEPARTING LYTAXIN

Daav had been taught patience, years and worlds away, at the tent of an expert, but he had never learned to delight in its practice.

Therefore, he waited, patiently, at the airfield with a small kit-bag composed mostly of necessities others thought he needed. Before he had departed Erob's house, young Alys Tiazan had come to him with a tin of tea, as well as a surprise: a flatpic of Val Con and Miri, captured, so Alys said, on the night Miri was acknowledged kin to Erob. Miri's expression was grave to the point of grimness, as she stood very close to full attention, as if her dinner dress were a particularly uncomfortable uniform. Val Con stood easier, as a scout would, bland-faced and non-committal.

Daav had thanked the child for her gifts, and was rewarded with a beguiling smile and a bow so accurate in its complexity that he thought she must have practiced for hours—a bow to the parents of one's most admired mentor.

Now, rather than pace—which would not have been patient—or taking the offered observer's seat at the temporary control tower, where he might have been diverted by this or that happenstance, Daav lounged on a small hummock, with the airfield, the Truax Liftmaster Plus, which was the Clutch turtle's idea of a world-to-space shuttle, and his kit-bag all in view

The kit was, as he well knew, inadequate. Even dangerously inadequate. Beyond the gifts, and a few odds and ends of toiletries, he had packed several changes of clothes, a pocket recorder, extra ammunition . . .

"Daav, don't fret so," her voice murmured in his ear.

"Well enough for you to say it," he responded, glaring at the kit as if he might transmute its contents by will alone into the appropriate and needful equipment—aye, and a working team of scout specialists, too. "I'm merely waiting for the Honorable to arrive—and doing quite a creditable job of it, too."

Aelliana's voice carried an undercurrent of amusement. "Ah, yes. I see you being patient, patient, patient. Truly, van'chela, if you become any more patient you will kick your poor bag down the hill and—"

He laughed, half-hearted, for all that she was right, and ran a quick rainbow to center himself—and perhaps to buy some real patience.

"I am concerned of this mission, too," Aelliana continued. "But I cannot see how we might have altered events in order to accompany those returning to Liad—not when Korval Themselves gave us the task."

"Light-witted, ill-conceived . . ." Daav began and heard his lifemate chuckle.

"Yes, as much you like," she said, soothingly. "Of course we cannot create from thin air a proper scout diplomatic mission, outfitted with experts of protocol, biology, language, and geology. Nor could our delm. We are the cards they had to hand—and so they play us. You know very well that you had done just the same, when you stood Korval! And while we are *not* a scout team, we are certainly better than thin air. Besides, the Tree of Erob has gifted us at our new daughter's bidding, and so we are doubly fortified!"

"That," Daav admitted, "was unexpected. For her to calmly hold out her hand and expect to catch such gifts as if she had been born beneath a Tree and spent her childhood at home in its branches—and for the Tree to so willingly comply . . ."

"Here," Miri had said, handing the two seedpods to Daav. "One for each of you. Eat 'em when Edger shows you to your cave."

"See," Aelliana murmured, at the near edge of memory, "she too masters thin air!"

Daav laughed again, more fully this time.

"How not? Our son and our daughter expect that all of us are the masters of thin air—and we cannot disappoint."

"Just so," she agreed. "And, now, you have been patient long enough—the Honorable approaches his ship."

Startled, he looked down to the field, saw the large, green shape, striding ponderously toward the Truax, and swept forward to pick up his kit.

"Do you think we will truly have a cave to call our own?" he asked as he walked down the hill, but Aelliana was elsewhere, and did not answer.

Braced in a custom-built gel-stand, Edger flew the Liftmaster like a scout. Designed to take compact, heavy objects into orbit, it was a most perfect ship for its purpose, a Clutch turtle being no one's light packet. Daav noted the ship's near-new condition with nothing more than the twitch of an eyebrow, yet Edger made answer, as if he had expressed his surprise aloud.

"When my brother, your egg-son, required the use of the clan's vessel in an earlier phrase of this artwork, I perceived that I was challenged to provide proper access to all human ports. Many of the smaller ports-in-space cannot receive the clan's vessel, for its mass is much greater than theirs; likewise, our vessel cannot access planetary ports without risking grievous damage to the facilities. In the past, we had merely by-passed those ports and dockings which could not accommodate us, reasoning that we could not trade with those who could not receive our ships. However, the possibility that my brother the dragonslayer might require the services of the vessel of the clan and be unable to board—this is not how kin care for kin. And so we have acquired a solution."

Aelliana remained quiescent, gone to wherever it was she went when she was absent from his awareness. Daav, strapped in to what would have been the observer's seat in a normally configured Truax piloting chamber, found the pattern of the lift so reassuring that he very nearly fell asleep during the zero-g phase.

"I would be honored," Edger boomed, breaking him out of his doze, "if you will scan the frequencies of which I might not be aware, or which those who have aligned themselves with scouts might find informative. We will dock very soon, now."

You should have thought of that, Daav scolded himself silently.

"Of course," he said, reaching for the board. "The honor is mine."

While there was some chatter on bands Edger was not otherwise listening to, neither its quantity nor its quality was worthy of note, excepting that it was so very earnestly normal. An uninformed listener might well suppose that all was well; the Clutch transport rising from the surface the merest commonplace; the mop-up phase of Erob's little difficulty stabilized; and that nothing was in the least out of order.

In the interests of thoroughness, Daav assayed an excursion through the side bands, which were also achingly normal. His explorations had brought him fully awake and he watched with interest as "the clan's vessel" made its debut on the screen, looking like nothing so much as an asteroid, sitting tamely in orbit about Lytaxin. Of course it was, as near as Daav understood the matter, precisely an asteroid, from which the Clutch had carved a space-going vessel adequate to their standards and needs, filled with whatever strange machinery was necessary to make a ship work the way Clutch vessels worked.

Daav had read technical analyses of the Clutch's so-called Electron Substitution Drive. Human research into the drive had been given up hundreds of years gone-by as its peculiarities resisted control and its necessities warred with common sense.

In short form, the ESD took advantage of the amusing tendency of electrons to show up in orbit elsewhere before they quite leave the orbit they are departing. Left to behave naturally during alterations in energy levels, this eccentricity goes unremarked by the larger universe, the trick being omni-directional.

However, it had been found that motion could be induced in certain plasmas and fields—and, by extension, to entire macroscopic bodies—simply by imposing *direction* upon the electron's absurd little dance.

Terran and Liaden researchers had struggled mightily, and had at last managed, by dint of applying outrageous amounts of energy to a test object about the size of a human head, to propel said object for very short distances. Having achieved this double-edged success, they had then thrown up their hands and conceded that the drive was less than cost-effective. For humans.

In the meanwhile, the Clutch had solved the scale problem, and effortlessly moved worldlets through space, one electron at a time.

The Clutch ship filled the viewscreen, now. Daav held his breath as Edger brought the Truax in at a speed nothing less than breakneck, plying the board nimbly with his three-fingered hands. Daav scarcely had time to note the new metal mated to native rock, and the lock hubs braced against pitted stone, before the shuttle latched solidly home.

As familiar as he was with spacecraft, stations, and even moon-based research colonies, yet Daav was unprepared for the scale of things inside the asteroid ship. The piloting chamber could easily accommodate the expansive main control room of *Dutiful Passage*; the primary corridors wide enough for twelve battle-ready Terran mercs to march abreast; high enough that they might each stand upon the shoulders of a comrade and never scrape helmet along ceiling rock.

Even the "guesting room" where he and Edger carried the various boxes of supplies hastily culled from a stone-clad storeroom, might easily sleep a squad of soldiers.

Trotting along at the turtle's heels, feeling positively buoyant in the slightly-lighter-than-Lytaxin gravity, Daav idly did the math. Estimating the size of the "ship," he assumed that only an inner core approximately forty percent in diameter of the whole was habitable. Of that forty percent, non-trivial portions must house power sources, machinery, shielding . . . All of which meant that—conservatively speaking and with no real number in sight—that "the vessel of the clan" encompassed a living space roughly equivalent to the entire inside area of the twenty-nine story building where he had taught on Delgado.

"If you will attend me now," Edger said, as the last carton was stowed. "We shall walk through those areas of the vessel that are most likely to be of need or interest to you. I fear that we are but an eyeblink away from commission of a grand and hasty side work. In celebration of the haste that will soon come upon us, then, I would ask that we address each other in the shortest form possible. As you are aware, the short-form of my name is Edger."

Daav had inclined his head, wondering what sort of haste might be coaxed from such a vessel.

"I am honored if you will use my personal name," he murmured, gravely.

"I thank you, Daav," Edger rumbled and fell silent, huge, cat-slit eyes looking down upon him.

The silence stretched, becoming uncomfortable even for one who had prospered as a scout. Daav was beginning to wonder if he had perhaps missed a cue, when Edger said, as delicately as his big voice would allow . . .

"Might I ask the short form best used for the other pilot?"

Daav felt the familiar stirring. His vision faded somewhat, as he heard his voice—though not *quite* his voice, really—reply, with suitable gravity, "Forgive me, Edger; I was reposing at a distance. My favorite sister had sometimes called me Aelli, and so does my nephew, Shan. It would please me if you would use it."

The turtle sighed, great eyes blinking once, twice. "Aelli is a name rich in vibrations. I shall speak it with great pleasure."

It was a quick tour, then, with Daav aware of his lifemate, awake and receptive just behind his eyes. It seemed to him as though she walked at his right hand, though he was well aware that she did not. Following Edger, they passed several garden rooms—one remarkably similar to Erob's inner garden—and an area for swimming and taking one's ease beneath sun-bright lamps. Edger displayed a rather startling book room, several large empty spaces, the purpose of which he apparently assumed was self-evident, by-passed yet another pool-room, cut through the cathedral-like piloting chamber, and returned by a secondary corridor to the "guesting room," with the supply boxes and his kit bag stacked neatly along the far wall, and the lighting which was adjusted for human eyes.

"I leave you now to nourish and rest yourselves," Edger said. "We will become underway as closely as I am able to approximate 'immediately,' and will be utilizing our vessel in the upper ranges of its capacity. A gong will sound to warn you of impending motion. If you are standing or walking, it would be wise to immediately sit upon the floor with your back against the wall. A second, lesser, gong will signal when it has become possible to perambulate. Should you elect to rest, please engage the webbing over the bed." There was a pause, not nearly so long as the previous pause.

"We three here—we understand that haste is of the essence. Therefore, it will be necessary that the journey be taken in several episodes. These are not the Jumps of which your ships partake with such elegance, and it is possible that you will experience altered conditions—even discomfort. It is my understanding that any feelings of disorientation are but passing, neither harmful to the body nor the song. However, if you experience difficulties, merely speak my name in the direction of this object—" He put a three-fingered hand against what appeared to be a sculpture of red stone—"and I shall hear you."

He bowed then, surprising, and very nearly nuance-perfect: "From one who is honored to be permitted to act for a master of the art," Aelliana read—and left them, moving with quite fearful haste down the stone corridor, toward the piloting room.

Daav shook his head and turned on a heel to survey their quarters once more.

"It seems we should have invited a dozen of our closest friends!" Aelliana commented, as their eye fell upon the Clutch-sized bed.

He grinned and flung them onto the thing, laughing aloud when the low gravity rewarded them with a high, gentle bounce.

The quilt, when they were on it again, proved to be handmade, of a material Daav thought might be real cotton, and showing the precious irregularities of hand-sewing.

Acceleration webbing hung at the foot of the bed, to prevent rest-period lifts to the high ceiling, and a pair of what proved, upon experimentation, to be nothing more exotic than light plates were set into the rocky headboard.

Daav climbed out of the bed—no easy task, lacking a piton and ropes—and gazed meditatively at the carefully stowed supplies.

"Do you suppose we have been hoodwinked, Aelliana? That our delm has sent us off on this quiet, safe little mission to keep us out of harm's way? I begin to think that we might have remained on Delgado, oblivious and content, and left the proper ordering of the universe to our children."

"Had you not become just a trifle bored," she asked, "since Theo left us?"

He snorted. "That was not boredom, my lady. That was relaxation. Doubtless you misunderstood the state, having seen it so seldom these last twenty years."

Aelliana laughed.

"My own beloved lady mocks me," Daav said mournfully, crossing the room to the sculpture of red rock which their host had indicated was a communication device.

The structure proved to be an amazement, for it was not, as he had first thought, bonded to the stone floor, but grew out of it, as if some natural vein of rock had been purposefully and carefully mined out from the more common rock of the walls, then faceted and polished into a pleasant work of art. Daav ran his fingers along each of the seven faceted sides, marveling at the texture of the stone . . .

"I believe we have the cave we were promised," Aelliana said. "It pleases, odd though it is. Shall we honor our daughter's wishes?"

"Why not?" Daav returned, abandoning his contemplation of the red rock. "Though I warn you, she will never believe us so obedient."

The seedpods became dessert to a snack foraged from the assembled supplies. Aelliana concurred in the wine, and in the crackers-with-cheese-spread from a commercial camping pack. Daav opened the bottle with his utility tool, and sipped slowly.

It was his belief that Aelliana and he tasted different essences; that when she wished to put herself forward wines were slightly more complex. This hour she was alert—even playful—and he found the wine very good, indeed. The crackers were amusing, like a return to some childhood picnic, a theme that the seed pods continued, for how long had it been?

Daav sighed. Why, only since he had fled Liad, seeking Balance, sanity, and heart's ease.

In the dark days just after her death, he had been concerned—overly concerned—for his sanity in everything he did, for Aelliana had yet to find a way to let him know she was truly with him. Well he knew the power of habit and wishful thinking; and the willingness of the heart to cling to hope, despite whatever brutal facts the mind might wearily recite down the endless hours of grief-filled nights.

He refused to believe that he heard her voice. He *knew better* than to believe. Had not Master Healer Kestra herself assured him that theirs was a lifemating of uncertain prognosis? Was it not true, and despite all their efforts and wishes to make it otherwise, that Daav had never once rejoiced at the touch of his lifemate's thought against his own? Aelliana—she had some small bit of that: touching him, she could read him. He had never envied her the gift—gods knew, she had few enough joys in her life—but the gift had been *hers*, not his. And she was dead.

He would never hear her voice again.

Desolate, he perversely attempted to embrace yet more desolation—deliberately refusing the Tree's urge that he take seedpods with him; refusing to tell Er Thom his plan; refusing to contemplate a return. Refusing to believe with every bit of his will that he heard his beloved's voice, until desolation itself betrayed him, and Aelliana caught him nodding in exhaustion before a computer screen . . .

"Daav? Shall we share?"

He smiled. "Indeed we shall." Taking a pod in each hand, he offered—and Aelliana accepted—the first bite.

Their snack finished, Aelliana was pleased to accompany him on another tour of the strange vessel on which they found themselves. Daav wandered them leisurely back along the path of the tour Edger had given them, the tantalizingly glimpsed library the first goal.

Path was a more accurate description than corridor, Daav thought. There were irregularities in the stone beneath his feet, and apparently random turnings in the way, which put one in mind of a forest walk, rather than a tame hallway. Strolling along, he indulged himself in a scout-like amusement: in his mind's eye, he attempted to connect several of the rooms in a straight line. Perhaps it could have been done, but there seemed a certain shape for doorways, and an alignment—or perhaps lack of alignment—in a pattern he could not quite understand.

Aelliana offered the opinion that the water rooms—which she counted as rooms containing open pools or flowing water—of which they had passed at least four, appeared to be situated at a mathematically constant distance from the ship's core.

"I suspect we have a combination of the technical and the aesthetic at work, Daav," she said, excitedly, as such discoveries invariably excited her. "Closer to center there would be no whirlpool pattern to the drains—water would flow directly in from all sides. Situated as they are, the pools and brooklets follow a rhythm and flow more natural to a spinning world."

Very likely, she was right, Daav thought. Gods knew, he was no authority on Clutch aesthetics.

Ambling, they passed periodic gaps in the stone walls, and the gleam of fittings for a metal door. Otherwise, the ship was very much the cavern Miri had promised them—a cavern shaped by an intelligence far from human.

Daav ran his fingers along the wall as they walked, discovering patterns—or perhaps merely the marks of ancient chisels—and sighed. At every turn, he was reminded of the difficulty of the task his delm had set him. Negotiate with the Elders, forsooth! Convince a council of beings unimaginably old to offer refuge to a sentient tree as old, or even older, than they.

If the Clutch Elders are wise, he thought sourly, *they will decline the honor, with speed and force.*

"Daav." Aelliana's voice was urgent in his ear. "The ship . . ."

He paused. Indeed, he did feel something change in the rock beneath his feet—the briefest vibration, as if someone had slammed a door on the far side of a large building.

"Perhaps Edger is adjusting our orbit—" he began—and his voice was overwhelmed by the voice of the gong.

The entire ship rang with the sound, disorienting him for a fragment of a second. He made a pilot's quick recover and dropped to the stone floor, sitting with his back pressed against the rock wall, distantly amused at the new vogue in acceleration couches.

He leaned his head against the wall, closed his eyes and waited for transition.

Another vibration, so low he felt the long waves of it sweep up his legs and body, through his chin, and over his head.

He opened his eyes.

The walls were full of color; shot with veins of gold and silver, coruscating, so that he felt that he—that they!—were deep inside a quartz meteor revolving around a star of lambent blue.

He realized almost immediately that he should not have opened his eyes, for the busyness of the light disturbed his sense of direction. He looked down, bracing a hand against a floor streaming with pearl pink and aqua. His hand sank into the stone—he *felt* it; felt the textures of the colors—and now his equilibrium was disturbed, the stone hallway stretching up into the filaments of the blue-toned quartz . . .

The ship—or the universe—lurched; his inner ear protested; and he was seeing *through* dozens of layers of rock, threatening to reveal cold space . . .

Aelliana was with him, he could feel her presence, as if she too were amazed and appalled at the spectacle before them.

He twisted against the wall, trying to recover his shattered balance, but his body did not properly obey him. It was as if he were twinned, with two right arms to move, using two sets of muscles, superimposed . . .

"Daav!" Aelliana mirrored his panic, her voice echoing sweetly off the stone corridors.

"Aelliana!"

Briefly, disorientingly, he *did* see two right arms, braced by two ghostly right hands leaning on and into the flowing colors.

There was fog boiling out of the rock floor, the air thick with motes of light . . .

He winced, lost that vision—lost everything but the confusion of trying to move an arm following someone else's orders—and her voice.

"Daav! Daav, I am—*here!*"

He took a breath, imposing discipline. "Aelliana, *where* are you?"

Somewhere beyond the chaos of color, a gong sounded, vibrating into his very soul. His vision cleared, and there again was the rock wall, bleeding color into the foggy floor, and the whole corridor was vibrating, as if the rocks themselves were singing, and the light-thickened air was as lascivious as silk and Aelliana was beside him, her hand was on his shoulder, and he turned his face into her kiss—

No. She was not there. Rather—she was everywhere. He could feel the flow of her thoughts, feel her deciding where to look, feel her adjusting her balance against the wall she braced against—

His eyes—her eyes—focused on the wall opposite, shimmering with bolts of gold and green, but more solid, now, no longer threatening to fade into transparency.

"Daav," his beloved said in his ear. "I can see that this will need work!"

He half-gasped a laugh, as she lifted his right hand and caressed his face.

"I think the worst is over," she murmured. "Let us return to our cave."

"An excellent idea," he said. "A glass of wine would be most welcome. And a nap, if you will have it. Edger should be more considerate of an old man's frailties."

"To Edger, you are the veriest babe," Aelliana retorted. "But, yes, a nap—and then we must talk."

Edger stood with his intricately shelled back to them, engaged in a close study of the control board built into a rock buttress. He was also, Daav realized, humming, or possibly singing, as he touched first this, then that, on the board—

The tune altered, and though he did not turn to look at them he raised a bit from the board as he spoke.

"Please, Aelli and Daav, if you will but tarry for five or six more moments I will join you. I have news of interest to you both."

So saying, Edger returned to his hum, leaving Daav and Aelliana to continue exploring this new, higher-level melding.

It was, of course, the lifemate-bond, but somehow expanded, broadened, deepened beyond anything they had thought possible. Daav, wary of joy unleavened, proposed it to be an effect of the drive, which would fade upon the return to normal space. Aelliana considered that the drive was a factor in the . . . speed . . . of their joining, but offered the possibility that the seeds they had eaten were the motivating force.

The exchange was far faster and far fuller than their usual, even the pleasant after-effect of the wine had not dulled the transfers. Occasionally, one or the other might be distracted by this memory or that sudden bit of information . . .

Aelliana had sensed the change coming first, for the images and information she had been receiving through Daav had sharpened all at once—as if she were seeing with her own eyes—and she was able to conceive of moving an arm. Later, she proved herself capable of walking, without Daav's active assistance.

The nap had been not quite that—instead they had relaxed with eyes closed and shared: thoughts, emotions, *essence* . . .

There were some few of Daav's memories which Aelliana could not properly access, nor could he grasp all of hers—but in every case, those tended to be memories each had done the most to forget. And there were certainly enough tantalizing—and sometimes dismaying—glimpses to beguile them both. For Daav, of her brother Ran Eld and his friend; of a marriage full of taunts and pain; of his own young and subtle face. For Aelliana, of planets she had never seen; and the tender tuitions in patience . . .

New to Daav was his ability to access a larger part of Aelliana's intuitive understandings of mathematics; new to her was sharing Daav's immediate and nuanced interpretations of the motivations of people. New, too, for her, was the surprising overlay of the Diaries, richly illustrating and informing her altered realization of her beloved, of Korval, and of Liaden history.

It had taken effort—a willful exchange of thoughts rather than the subconscious communication they had allowed themselves to be enveloped by—to go to Edger.

"Aelliana, my love, we cannot stare into this mirror until the stars cool. I do believe that this will, as you say, take some work. And perhaps the assistance of a master."

So, they had gone to find Edger, with Daav, like a youngster learning to trust the way a simple lean could take advantage of a duocycle's momentum, accepting Aelliana's direction of their hike.

"I will miss this," she said, "if you are right, and it is solely an artifact of the drive."

"I know," he whispered, and felt her feeling his regret—and his fear.

The gong sounded once more. Here in the control room it rang through them foot to head . . .

Edger turned, sweeping into a full bow and speaking in a booming, formal voice.

"True elders of your clan! I am humbled to be the first to see you thus."

He straightened, and continued in what passed for a more conversational tone. "The art of your children, my kin, has strong roots; stronger than I knew. Already their names are spoken among the Elders—and your names, as well. My request was that the Elders act in unprecedented haste and see you immediately, in the human sense.

"I am informed that the outer chamber will be open when we arrive, and that I might bring you directly there. The Elders make haste—surely, this is a work of art like none before! They will see you, I think, very quickly."

There was a pause, which Daav allowed to stretch.

"The Elders will see us," Aelliana breathed, for him alone. "Van'chela, can you imagine it?"

"I can," he answered, in the same way, "and it concerns me greatly. Recall that I know the Tree very well indeed, and I know what Jela's bargain has cost us . . ."

Before them, Edger bowed slightly, as if rousing from some deep process of thought.

"It would be pleasant if you would walk with me to the waterfall park. There, we may enjoy a small repast, and an hour of talk."

"It sounds a good plan," Daav admitted. "Might I know the ship's schedule—and your own? If we are to travel the next weeks with you . . ."

Edger blinked his huge yellow eyes, one, then the other.

"I see that you have studied the effect of our ships at low drive," he said. "For a task of such moment and urgency, I have utilized the higher drives." He turned, widely, motioning them to follow.

"We will enter my home atmosphere shortly after your next sleep period. You will be in the outer chamber, awaiting permission of the Elders to enter, in sixteen Standard Hours."

LYTAXIN
EROB'S HOUSE

"What else?" Miri asked Val Con, after the last late meeting was done and they were alone in the sitting room of their suite.

He turned from the wine table, bottle and glass in hand, eyebrow well up. "We have put such things into motion as may be put into motion. All that remains us is to defeat the Department, vanquish the Commander, and reclaim the Agents."

"Piece of cake." She moved across the rug toward him. "Can the Agents be reclaimed?"

"The Healers will know," he said softly, pouring. "If I was able to break training, perhaps others may do so, as well."

"Or maybe not." She took the glass he handed her, and stood sipping, staring at nothing in particular, going over the plans they had laid. It was, she thought, going to be dicey.

To say the least.

"The kids?" she asked, that being a detail left in flux.

Val Con raised his glass. Korval's Ring gleamed on his finger, big and flashy and flawed.

"Do you think we should dispatch the *Passage* to the children? Shan and Priscilla are able, and the ship now runs as a battlewagon."

She frowned, weighing it.

"It'd draw attention—"

The comm buzzed. Shaking her head, she crossed to it and pushed the button.

"Robertson."

"Cousin, it is Kol Vus. A person has called for yourself and for your lifemate. He awaits your pleasure in the public parlor."

Miri's brows drew together in a small frown. "I thank you, cousin," she said, dropping effortlessly into the High Tongue. "Has our guest a name?"

"He produces Greenshaw Porter. He says it with remarkable ease."

Her frown deepened slightly. "I see. Pray allow Mr. Porter to know that we are on our way to him."

"Very good." The line went dead. Miri glanced up.

"Odds that Greenshaw Porter's another one of ours? Who ain't here yet?"

"Of the adult males? Luken bel'Tarda—and Pat Rin. Luken's duty under Plan B lies with the children, and I cannot this moment conceive of a circumstance that would cause him to abandon it. Pat Rin . . ." He moved his shoulders, abruptly aware of an uncomfortable home truth. "I cannot predict what Pat Rin might do, though I would not *expect* him to adopt a Terran persona. Certainly, not on a Liaden-held world."

"Well, something's got Kol Vus' hair up." She shook her head, and regretfully put her wine aside. "Guess we'd better find out what."

Greenshaw Porter was on his feet in the public parlor, which was only reasonable, the available chairs being much too short to accommodate his lanky frame. The House had provided him with neither tea nor wine.

He was a long-faced man, unmistakably Terran, his tan-colored hair short and bristling, his eyes gray and alert, and Val Con felt a curious sense of relief that, after all, it was *not* Pat Rin, come to add yet another Korval life to the tale of those present upon Lytaxin.

Their visitor bowed as they entered the room, entirely in the Terran mode, then straightened and stated, in the staccato accents of Standard Terran, "Greenshaw Porter, Juntavas courier. Miri Robertson and Val Con yos'Phelium?"

"That's right," Miri said easily.

"Yes," Val Con assured him, noting the position of at least two guns and a blade distributed about the courier's person.

The man nodded, apparently unsurprised. "The Juntavas has been looking for you. The offer is aid and comfort. We cooperate with Clutch turtles Edger and Sheather. I have verification."

"Ah, do you?" Val Con murmured.

The Juntava cocked a sapient eye. "Turtles thought you'd want it." He raised his hands, fingers spread wide. "I saw the rock in orbit. I heard there are turtles on planet. Order from Headquarters is proceed according to plan. Verification in my right outside pocket. You can take it, or I can give it "

Inside his head, Val Con heard Miri's song, alert and watchful. Deliberately, not really certain that it would work, he looked at the places where the Juntava carried his concealed weapons—one, two, three—and heard her song shift. Almost, he thought he heard her murmur "gotcha."

He raised his hands, fingers spread, returning the offered gesture of peace.

"Please," he murmured, "feel free to display your verification."

"Right." Slowly, fingers still held wide, he slipped his right hand into the outside pocket of his long jacket and withdrew something so sharply luminous it seemed that he held a star between his thumb and first finger.

Still moving deliberately, he extended the brilliant token. Val Con held his hand out, fingers cupped. The crystal hit his palm, unexpectedly heavy, warm, its edges sharp, but not sharpened. He glanced down, eyes narrowed against the whiteness of it, saw without surprise that it was luminous at its core.

"Flashlight?" Miri asked from beside him.

"Exactly," he murmured, and handed it to her, returning his attention to Greenshaw Porter.

"We have received verification," he said, carefully. "More, we have only lately seen Clutch turtles Edger and Sheather, who know us to be well and at liberty. Please inform Headquarters that the Juntavas is quit in this matter."

"Not exactly," the Juntava said, and Val Con raised an eyebrow, feeling Miri come to full alert beside him.

"Explain."

"The Juntavas is missing a Sector Judge."

"Ah. I commiserate with the Juntavas upon its loss."

Greenshaw Porter grimaced. "Supplemental data. I'm attached to the Justice Department. High Judge himself petitions Korval for info. The missing Judge put herself on detached duty. Last known to be in company with Pat Rin yos'Phelium." His forehead wrinkled slightly. "Your brother, maybe?"

"Cousin," Val Con said absently, trying to reconcile Pat Rin with a Juntavas Sector Judge. And, yet, how *could* he predict what Pat Rin might do? He and his cousin were scarcely intimate. Indeed, Val Con had gathered that Pat Rin had few intimates. His foster-father, perhaps. And surely Luken bel'Tarda had taught his fosterling to give the Juntavas wide clearance.

"Cousin," the Juntava repeated and nodded. "Questions from the High Judge: does Korval know the location of Sector Judge Natesa? If yes, as a personal favor to the High Judge, who values his judges as a delm values his kin, will Korval divulge her location? Follow-up: if something happened to her, the High Judge asks for that info, too. No rage, no Balance. But he would like to recover the body." He hesitated before adding: "Myself, I know that Judge. She'd be hard to kill."

"I am desolate to disappoint the High Judge," Val Con murmured, "but his inquiry marks the first time I have heard of Sector Judge Natesa."

"You said she's on detached duty," Miri broke in. "Maybe she decided to quit the judging business?"

Greenshaw Porter shook his head. "No'm. Judges put themselves on detached duty at will. They have discretion. Only Judges tell another Judge what to do. Or how to do it."

She threw a glance at Val Con. "Sounds a lot like being a scout."

"Perhaps," he returned, and looked to the Juntava. "Has my cousin been seen since Judge Natesa exercised her discretion?"

"Nossir. Both were in a dust-up—gunplay, unidentified deaders—then went off-grid simultaneous. Neither one resurfaced."

Gods, if it didn't scan like a Departmental "dust up," Val Con thought. *And never think that an Agent was less than the match of a Sector Judge, no matter how hard she was to kill.*

As for Pat Rin . . . Let it be known that Pat Rin was not an idiot. Let it further be known that he was a wizard with his pistols, and that he had once killed a man. And against whatever the Department might wish to inflict upon him—from mere death to menticide—he would hold no defenses whatsoever.

He looked up at the Juntavas courier.

"I am hardly in a position to trade fairly with the High Judge," he said carefully, feeling Miri drawing closer to his side. "However, I would be honored, were the Juntavas to allow me to know the time and the place where my cousin and Sector Judge Natesa were last seen."

Greenshaw Porter nodded. "I'm cleared for that. I have the report from Housekeeping. I'm cleared to share that, too."

"Thank you. That would be most helpful."

"I'll transfer it from my ship. Need a comm address."

Val Con recited the code for the unit in their upstairs rooms.

The courier repeated the address, nodded and bowed once more in the Terran mode.

"I'll asap that. I'm on-planet until tomorrow mid-day. Aid-and-comfort is in force until I lift."

"Thank you," Val Con said again. "I do not believe it will be needed."

Ren Zel stirred, stretched, smiled, opened his eyes—and stifled a curse. The clock across the room was adamant: three minutes until the start of his shift on the bridge. He rolled out of bed, realized abruptly that he was fully clothed and not a little rumpled; his boots showing smudges of what might have been grass stains. To appear on-shift so . . . He looked again at the clock. *Two* minutes until he was wanted on the bridge—and far worse to be late than untidy.

Ren Zel ran.

They read the reports from the Juntavas together, Miri sitting on the arm of the chair, her hip against his shoulder.

There was a short bio of Sector Judge Natesa, accompanied by an image of a slender lady of good countenance, dark-skinned and sloe-eyed, her hair a silky black cap 'round her neat head.

Miri gave a low whistle, and leaned forward to tap the screen over the bio. "This girl can cook, boss. No wonder they miss her."

"She appears competent in the extreme," he agreed, scrolling down through a surprising number of missions completed on behalf of the Juntavas, most at the upper echelons of power.

Sector Judges might well be able to declare themselves on detached duty at will, but it appeared that Judge Natesa had been happy in her work, and had only thrice previously removed herself from duty—twice on recuperative vacations and one comprehensive disappearance, from which she reappeared within a relumma.

"First class pilot," he murmured, going through the remainder of her accomplishments, "master shooter; explosives expert. Yes—a lady of many competencies."

Who had very competently disappeared, so the next, extremely brief report stated, on Day 289, Standard Year 1392, from a Juntavas maintained yard, after filing the appropriate intention with her office.

Gods, so long ago? Val Con shivered and hit the key for the next file. The report from Housekeeping, prepared by order of Sector Judge Natesa, was admirably detailed, listing descriptions of the dead, contents of pockets, wallets, pouches; types and numbers of weapons. A blue evening jacket, well-splattered with blood, but whole, was noted, and a square of cleansilk, its virtue destroyed by the blood.

"Note the guns," he murmured. "Note the other items inventoried . . ."

"Picks, garrotes, pipettes of acid, poison." She sighed. "You're thinking the Department."

"I am. The jacket is . . . distressing. Pat Rin often wears blue."

"Yeah, but there's no pellet holes in this one. Whoever was wearing it probably ditched it on account of it ain't polite to wear bloodstains on the street," Miri said sensibly. "Unless you got a match further up?"

He shook his head, unrelieved. Death was certainly preferable to the living agonies the Department was capable of inflicting. Kin might wish a clean death for kin, against so terrible an alternative.

"No," he said, aloud. "No, he is not listed among the dead."

"But that ain't making you feel any better." She frowned down at him. "In fact, it's making you feel worse."

He met her eyes. "I would not willingly remand my direst enemy to the Department's care, much less kin." He sighed. "Even kin scarcely known."

She blinked, then turned back to the screen, leaning forward to manipulate the keys, scrolling back up through Natesa's last filed contact with her office.

"She don't say anything about him being with her," she muttered. "Shit, she don't even say why she was in it in the first place."

"Aid and comfort," Val Con said, staring over the screen, seeing Pat Rin as he had last seen him, years ago: a creature of grace and poise, assuredly, with a needling wit and a languorous manner which could be put on and dispensed with in the flicker of an eyelash.

Vulnerable; so very vulnerable, did he fall into the hands of the

Department. Which would, almost certainly, remake him into a bomb.

"What?" Miri turned to stare at him, her eyes wide with alarm. "What's wrong?"

He took a breath, trying to think it through, to get past the horror, to put himself in the place of the Commander, sworn to bring the Department's Plan to fruition. Which Plan included Korval's annihilation.

"Miri . . ."

"Don't say it—I think I just got the download." She closed her eyes, and in his mind's eye Val Con saw a blurring spin of color—redyelloworangegreenblueviolet—followed by a warming sense of calm.

"OK. So the Department might've got Pat Rin, either at this massacre, here, or sometime real soon after, and the Judge might be on the lam to save her skin, she being no dummy in a big way. And if the Department's got Pat Rin, they're gonna rework him." She bit her lip.

"How long's it take?"

He moved his shoulders, snapped to his feet and stalked down the room. "Eternity." He came to the window and stopped, staring out over Erob's nighttime gardens. The silence at his back was tangible. He sighed.

"Forgive me, cha'trez. The length of the process depends in large part upon the reserves of the candidate. Certainly, if the Department has had Pat Rin in their care for nearly two relumma, they will have completed their work long since. Especially as they will not be constructing an Agent of Change, but something far simpler."

"Q-ship. Got it. But we're forewarned."

"Not all of us," he said, turning from the window. "Pat Rin's foster-father and true-mother have the duty of protecting the clan's children. I do not believe either would deny him entrance to their safeplace." He reached up and pushed his hair out of his eyes. "Jelaza Kazone would admit him. Anthora would perhaps understand that there was something amiss—but she might not understand it in time to prevent him killing her."

"OK." Miri stood up, showing him palms in the gesture of peace. "OK. This is all might-have. We don't know where Pat Rin is. He might be holed up cozy on an outworld, waiting for the allclear."

"True. Though that might-have does not tell us why the Sector Judge has run away."

"Might've taken a lover. Might've needed time out. Might've got drunk, fell down and broke her neck. We don't know she's hiding because of the business in the warehouse. We don't even *know* that she's hiding."

"And we do not know that she isn't."

Silence.

"Another might-have," Val Con said, slowly, hating it, and gods, if it were true . . .

"Go."

"The Department has acquired *both* Korval's child Pat Rin and Juntavas Sector Judge Natesa."

She blinked at him. "She's Agent material."

"Indeed she is. More, she has access to the highest levels within the Juntavas. The Commander might put such a tool to very good use."

"I bet he could." She shook her head. "We still got no proof."

"We have no proof," he repeated, looking not at her, so much as through her. "We do, however, owe the High Judge some *info*."

He came back to himself with a visible start and moved across the room to the comm unit. Miri sighed and went over to pour them each a glass of wine.

DAY 52
STANDARD YEAR 1393

DEPARTMENT OF INTERIOR HEADQUARTERS
LIAD

Commander of Agents was not one to allow the natural losses of warfare to overly dismay him. It was understood that there would be casualties—even, many casualties—as the Plan unfolded and the Department met with the resistance of small minds and imbedded interests. Thus, while he did not view his losses lightly, the Commander was able to maintain the dispassion necessary to ultimate success in those instances when the Department was momentarily thwarted.

The loss of a ship of the Department and four full Agents of Change on the planet Lytaxin—that was a different matter entirely. Very nearly, in fact, could the Commander be said to be— angry.

The ship had reported Val Con yos'Phelium on-board some time after the fourth Agent's implanted monitor went off-line. The ship itself had exploded some few minutes after lift-off. Commander of Agents was not so naive as to believe that Val Con yos'Phelium had died with the vessel.

So: four Agents, lost on Lytaxin. One Agent, lost on Interdicted World I-2796-893-44, his ship captured and then destroyed. Three more Agents lost to the bitch half-breed . . .

Lost thus far: eight Agents and two ships. And what profit did the Department show from so great and widespread an expenditure?

Sand and ashes. Val Con yos'Phelium remained at liberty; Anthora yos'Galan slept secure behind the formidable walls of Jelaza Kazone.

Commander of Agents rose from behind his desk. He paced his office from end to end and side to side. At the beginning of his fourth pass, he checked, and deliberately called to mind the calming exercise he had first been taught as an Agent-in-Training, many years ago.

Slowly, he brought his heartbeat down, normalized his breathing, bled off the unneeded adrenaline. When he had done, he stood yet another few heartbeats, eyes closed; meditative.

Eventually, he opened his eyes and returned to his desk, ordered the hardcopy which he had in his agitation flung down, and set it to one side while he accessed his screen.

Alas, that ill news stalked the hour, the latest in the form of a memorandum from the financial department chair. Another of the Department's bleed-off funds had been uncovered, the program destroyed by the Masters of the Accountants Guild.

Commander of Agents flicked through the report, until he found the name of the Master in charge of the investigation.

dea'Gauss.

Very softly, Commander of Agents sighed.

dea'Gauss. Korval's man of business.

Commander of Agents extended an arm and touched the switch on his console.

"Commander?" His second's voice betrayed an edge of startlement.

"That matter we wished to place before the Council of Clans."

"Yes, Commander. We have been awaiting the most appropriate moment."

"So we had. I advise you that the moment has arrived."

"Yes, Commander."

"On another matter—I will wish to meet with a squad leader in . . ." He glanced over at the chronometered wall. "In fifteen Standard minutes, in the Level A meeting room. That is all."

"Yes, Commander." The connection light went out.

DAY 31
STANDARD YEAR 1393

SUREBLEAK SPACEPORT

Villy bent over the table, black pick held delicately, hook properly extended, between thumb and forefinger, eyes narrowed in concentration.

The pick hovered over the jumbled pile of brightly colored sticks, flicked out and deftly flipped a silver from the tangle onto the counting cloth. The boy took a careful breath, and the pick stabbed out again, three times, placing a red, an orange and a blue stick next to the silver on the cloth.

Pat Rin, viewing the performance with an expert's eye, saw the tell-tale quiver of a purple stick three layers down in the tangle, but Villy, in pursuit of the gold, either ignored the tremor or had determined that boldness would win the day.

He extended the pick, delicate—so delicate—touched the gold stick . . . lifted it . . .

"Oh, *sleet!*" he exclaimed as the sticks broke from their self-described formation and went rolling and tumbling every-which-way. He looked up, shamefaced.

"Sorry, sir."

Pat Rin raised an eyebrow "Not entirely. Indeed, I see that you have been working. Your touch is much improved. Now, you must sharpen your eye. Attend me."

He swept the twenty-four brightly colored sticks up in a practiced motion, tamped them, placed them on end in the yellow-tiled circle which had been set into the table-top for just this purpose—and let go.

Obedient to gravity, the sticks fell, creating a satisfyingly complex multi-colored tangle.

"So," he said, receiving the black pick from Villy. "We have a dreadful mess, here, do we not? I will wager you twenty cash that all of those sticks may be extracted and placed on the cloth while disturbing no other in the formation. Have we a bet?"

Villy shook his head. "I know better than to bet against you."

"Youth today," Pat Rin mused aloud, while his eyes traced the intricate pattern created by the sticks, "lack the adventurous spirit." It was, he decided, a difficult fall. He could easily see his way clear to acquiring sixteen, even eighteen, of the twenty-four. The rest . . . well.

"Only twenty cash?" a rich voice asked from near at hand. "Why not a wager worthy of your skill?"

Calmly, he looked up and met Natesa's amused black eyes.

"What would you wager, my lady?"

"Let us consider." She tipped her head to one side, a finger over her lips as she ostentatiously considered the matter.

"I know," she said at last. "If you miss the twenty-four, I will have the Sinner's Carpet out of Ms. Audrey's house."

"Ah, will you?" He looked at her appreciatively. "And what is my prize, should I succeed?"

She smiled at him, slow and seductive. "Why, something very nice."

He laughed.

"Done," he said, fingering the pick into the proper hold. "Attend now, child," he said to Villy. "This may be the last time you see me play."

He looked down to the bright jumble, and let the room fade out of his consciousness, until it was only himself, the sticks, and the necessity to win.

The pick flashed out.

The first eight were simple liberations, after which the challenge began in earnest.

Quickly, he proceeded, dexterously avoiding anchor-sticks and rolling traps, while with every cunning infiltration of the pick another stick fell to the counting cloth.

It came at last to three, lying one against the other.

Pat Rin reversed the pick, inserted the flat tail in the whisker-wide space between the yellow stick and the blue, rolled the yellow, reversed the pick, and caught the stick in the hook to flip it, with a showy snap of the wrist, to the cloth.

The blue stick was likewise appropriated, and then the final orange, delivered to the cloth in a toss that sent it spinning high, turning over three times on its descent to the cloth.

Pat Rin placed the pick on the cloth next to the sticks, and smiled at Villy.

"That is how it is done, do you see?"

The boy shook his head. "I see that I'm gonna hafta practice a *lot* more."

"I did not say it would be easy, working in the casino," Pat Rin reminded him. "Perhaps, you would rather Sheyn took the sticks table?"

Sheyn was Villy's chief rival in popularity at Audrey's house, and though the rivalry was mostly friendly, still Villy would not easily bear having a task taken from him and given to the other boy.

"Nossir, Mr. Conrad! I'll practice."

"Good," said Pat Rin, stepping back from the table. "I will return later today."

He walked away, Natesa at his side.

"So," he said to her softly. "When may I collect my winnings?"

"Youth today," she said, calmly, "lack patience."

"Ah, but I am far beyond my youth. What you choose to see as impatience is merely the necessity of a man with too few hours left him."

She looked at him gravely. "Yes, exactly so."

"I was certain that you must see it eventually," he murmured, allowing her to precede him through the door and into the port proper.

The day was cool and bright—Surebleak high summer—and the port itself displayed a gratifying amount of activity. Work was going forth on several collaborative efforts, notably the duty-free shop—boldly named The Planetary Cooperative—and situated in the space formerly occupied, according to the ancient signage, by a Learning Shop, a fresh fruit, vegetable, and flower stall, and no less than two repair stations. Individual efforts included a beverage bar, featuring local fruit ciders, and a pastry shop. And, of course, the casino.

Pat Rin had hopes of a restaurant in the future, as well as a gemstone and spice exchange. But, for the moment, progress was made. And it was good.

Side by side, they proceeded, slowed considerably by the numerous, "Morning, Boss." "Mr. Conrad, sir. Ms. Natesa. Good to see you both." One of the mechanics called out that the concordance books had arrived; and plastic cups of cider were pressed into their hands, with a smiling, "Just in from the farms this morning. Boss Sherton's compliments, Mr. Conrad."

"You are well loved," Natesa remarked as they went on.

"So well loved that you yet insist upon tasting my drink ahead of me," he said ironically. "When shall you give over security, Inas?"

Black eyebrows arched. "Why, I have done so. If my care now seems more particular, it is because I have a personal stake in your continued good health."

He looked at her consideringly. "I see that I have done ill, then, in returning you your oath."

"Not at all. I asked for its return because my interest had grown beyond mere business. You complied because the request was reasonable." She inclined her head, formally. "Thus, we comported ourselves with honor. What lies before us is a different game entirely."

"Which cannot be won," he said, soberly. "Attend me, my lady. This is Surebleak; I may be murdered in the next hour—and you, at my side. And if that fails, there are always those other enemies of my clan, who may discover me at any moment, and likewise slay us both."

"That is," she said in her calm way, "acceptable." She sipped from her own cup. "But not likely. The cider is good."

"You amaze me," he said, and sipped, finding it very good, indeed. So good, in fact, that it was quite gone by the time they reached the portmaster's office, a scant stroll from the new juice stand.

"Good morning, Mr. Conrad—Ms. Natesa." Claren Liu nodded easily as they entered.

"Portmaster. A pleasant day to you."

"It has been so far." She waved a hand at the main screen. "Never thought I'd see Surebleak Port so busy. If it keeps up like this, we'll be in competition with Terraport!"

"Never so large as Terraport," Pat Rin said softly. "Will you settle, I wonder, for a small, rustic jewel of a port?"

Portmaster Liu laughed. "Sure, I'll take that." She pushed out of her chair and went to her desk, pulling some few sheets of hardcopy from a file.

"'beam came through for you last night. I knew you were gonna be here today, or I'd've sent it in to you."

"Thank you." He glanced at the papers, saw the Health Net logo, and folded them into his pocket for later perusal.

"Other thing we're gonna want," she said abruptly, "is traffic. Fine as it is to have a small rustic gem of a port, if nobody lands, what we got is no better'n what we had."

"True enough. My associates and I have been considering that. There are trade bands, are there not? And pilot frequencies, where the goods and services of this or that port may be advertised?"

She blinked. "Well . . . sure. You're thinking about *advertising* Surebleak?"

"What harm can it do?" Pat Rin asked reasonably, feeling Natesa's presence at his shoulder as a comfort. "A few small advertisements only—perhaps in praise of our ciders and—our handmade rugs. We are not so out of the way that ships *may not* stop, if given good cause. That they *have not* been stopping has been due to our . . . reputation as a dangerous and backward world, served by—forgive me—a port of the lower tier."

"Nothing to forgive in the truth," Claren Liu said, brusquely, and stared off over his head for a long moment, before coming to herself with a nod.

"Tell you what. The port'll go in half with whatever the association comes up with for advertisement. We got a promo budget. Up 'til this second, I didn't have the barest idea of what to do with it." She grinned, self-mocking. "Add Surebleak to your payroute! It's cold and they'll break your neck, too!"

At his shoulder, Natesa laughed.

"And now we may say—Stop at Surebleak, and enjoy the play."

"Not bad," Claren Liu told her, the grin somewhat less mock-ing. "Hold on a sec—I've got the rate book here." She bent again to the desk, rummaged briefly and emerged triumphant, waving a tattered brown booklet.

"Here you are," she said, handing it to Pat Rin. He glanced at the cover, found the rates in force until Day 96, Standard Year 1393, and slipped it away, too, for later study.

"Thank you," he said, inclining his head. "As always, it has been a fruitful visit. One of my house will be on the port in two days' time. If you have need of me before—"

"I'll call," she said, interrupting good-naturedly. "Those talkies were a good idea. Yeah, like you've had a bad one." She attempted the formal nod—at which she was slowly gaining pro-ficiency, Pat Rin allowed—and straightened.

"Good to see you, then, sir—ma'am. Hope to see you again soon."

"Good day, Portmaster," Pat Rin murmured.

"Good day," Natesa echoed and the two of them departed, heading for the casino, a second training session, and an afternoon meeting in Elva Whitmore's territory.

"**Still** awake, Boss?" Cheever McFarland's big voice preceded him into the room.

Pat Rin glanced up from a frowning study of the Health Net papers.

"As you see, Mr. McFarland, I am not only awake, but irritable."

"Long hours'll do that," Cheever said cheerfully. "I've got a report, if you want it."

Pat Rin pushed the papers aside. "Indeed, I do." He considered the man, noting the subtle signs of weariness. "However, I would not keep you from your bed. Tomorrow is soon enough, if you are in need of rest."

Cheever shook his head. "Too wound up to sleep. What I'm after right now is a sandwich and a beer. What say we compro-mise and hit the kitchen?"

"Very well." He rose, leaving the papers on his desk.

"It's comin' along fine," Cheever said some minutes later, around a truly formidable sandwich constructed of cheese, greens, and onion between thick slices of the cook's homemade bread. "Got the rubbish cleared out. Got a couple of the local techs through the sleep-learner and put 'em to work fabricating the equipment. Got a couple building squads throwing us up some bays and dorms. Talked to somebody just 'fore I left this morning—sharp one, name of Perl—anyhow, she's been studying on the schematics for the cradle and thinks she's got a line on the how-to. Ain't gonna be pretty, right at first, but we'll have us a working yard that ain't dependent on the port."

He took a bite of sandwich and washed it down with a mighty swallow of beer. Pat Rin sipped his fruit cider. The warehouse district they had taken over for Korval's first ship yard on Surebleak had been burned out in some long-forgotten riot, and remained unclaimed by any current boss. Pat Rin had annexed it by the simple expedient of sending Cheever McFarland and a work crew to the area with the goal of cleaning it up.

"Where we're gonna get in trouble—soon—is cash," Cheever was saying. "Labor's cheap enough, but materials is high—and a lot of the equipment's just gotta be made, ground up." Another bite, another swallow

"Where we're gonna get in trouble later—assuming we can get the rest of the job funded and online—is pilots, supplies and derelicts."

"The derelicts," Pat Rin murmured, "are, as we discussed, possible."

"Yah, OK, you got a line on the spaceship graveyard," Cheever said, grudgingly. "If it ain't watched. If it's still there. If the codes're still good. If, if, if."

"There is a risk, but not, I think, a major one."

"So you said. All right, we assume you can deliver the ships," he grinned, wolfish. "Next problem's pilots."

"We are at work on that problem," Pat Rin told him. "Only today have we received from the hand of Surebleak Portmaster the book listing all public piloting and trade frequencies. Our plan is to advertise Surebleak's charms, and thus beguile pilots to us."

"Yeah?" Cheever said interestedly. "That's an assist. But, then you're gonna need a hiring hall on the port."

Pat Rin inclined his head. "I thank you—I had not thought of that."

"Would've, though. Think too damn much, if you want my opinion—which you don't." He finished his sandwich and leaned back, nursing what was left of his beer.

"Keep in mind you'll have to pay risk money, for anybody bringing in a ship from the graveyard."

"Well." Pat Rin finished his cider, set the mug down, and sat gazing into its empty depths.

"Well," he said again. "It appears we are at a stand, Mr. Mc-Farland. In addition to the necessity of . . . Korval's yard, there is upstairs a notice from the Health Net, informing me of the current membership rates and citing a substantial sum due in penalties, as Surebleak's previous departure from the 'Net was in violation of several conditions of contract."

"The other bosses are s'posed to give us a percentage," Cheever commented after a few moments had passed in silence.

Pat Rin looked up. "So they are. And the funds thus far received have immediately gone into increasing the numbers of clinics and schools, and training for the medical personnel."

"So called." Cheever sighed gustily before quaffing the dregs of his beer.

"We're gonna need cash, or the gold-plated promise of cash within the next—fifteen, twenty days, or it's gonna get ugly. An' if we lose 'em because we ain't paid 'em, they'll never come back, if we was paying hard cantra. Better to shut down now, while we can settle everybody and tell 'em we'll do a recall in a month or so."

Pat Rin frowned. Of course, one did not solicit labor and then fail to pay. But it was hard, very hard, to contemplate halting the project so recently and so well begun . . .

"Let us delay decision until tomorrow," he said to Cheever. "Will you be with us, or must you return at once?"

"Figured on going back tomorrow afternoon. Wanted to check in with you. Should oughta talk to Natesa and Gwince; maybe do an inspect of house security, just to throw the fear of cold space into 'em and make sure they stay honest."

"Ah." He smiled. "Your vigilance is appreciated."

"Sure it is." Cheever thumped the empty mug to the table and stood. "I'm for a nap. You look like you could use the same, if you don't mind my saying so. Or even if you do."

"Yes." Weariness suddenly weighed upon him, waking the ghost of an ache in the arm that had been wounded. He rose, and put his mug in the sink to be washed. "Good night, Mr. McFarland. We will talk tomorrow"

"We sure will. 'Night, sir."

Pat Rin climbed the stairs, and slipped as silently as he was able into the bedroom.

"Good morning, denubia." Her voice was soft, barely blurred with sleep.

"There, I had not meant to wake you," he murmured. "I shall need to learn to walk like a scout."

"Only like Silk—who has appropriated your pillow."

He smiled in the dark, and undressed quickly, slipping into the bed beside her. Silk put up a brief defense of the pillow—for honor's sake—before stomping down to the foot of the bed.

"Victory is yours," she whispered, and moved near, entwining him in warm silken limbs, and nestling her head on his shoulder.

"Only until the morrow," he said, feeling muzzier by the moment, the ill news of the evening fading into a warm glow of contentment.

Sighing gently, he lay his cheek against her hair and slid, seamlessly, into sleep.

DAY 32
STANDARD YEAR 1393

BLAIR ROAD
SUREBLEAK

Natesa lay the Health Net report on the desk and picked up her teacup.

"Three cantra in penalties. Three cantra earnest money, based on previous violations. Two cantra to rejoin." She sipped and shook her head. "The penalties are two cantra too high, and we can certainly force the earnest money down by a cantra. Yet, in our current state of budget, five cantra is as difficult as eight."

"Add Mr. McFarland's little matter," Pat Rin murmured, from his perch on the corner of the desk, "and we discover ourselves run entirely off our legs, with no hope of a quick recover." He moved his shoulders, irritated.

"And all the while, there are more than enough cantra to do the work, if I could but dare access them!"

Natesa stared at him, teacup arrested. "Is that so?"

Pat Rin met her eyes, frowning at her astonishment. "Is what so? That there are cantra sufficient to the task—and more—held on my accounts? Did you think you had joined with a pauper, lady?"

"It was not a consideration," she said composedly. "But, Pat Rin, this other—why do you not dare access your funds?"

He bit back a sharp retort. It was rare enough, after all, to find Natesa at half wit.

"You will see that I am not clever," he said mildly. "When I was about arranging the details of my former life, it never occurred to me that, some day in my future, I might very much wish for hidden funds. All of my accounts are woefully in sight, and the Department of the Interior will be watching every one. They will trace any transfer immediately, and follow it to us."

She sipped her tea, then put the cup down on the desk.

"Here is where the Juntavas is uniquely placed to serve you," she said. "Merely hire a courier."

"Yes, certainly!" he cried, descending into sarcasm. "Tell someone else where we are, so that they may sell the information to the Department!"

"Not so," she contradicted. "If we broke our contracts, who would deal with us?"

He sighed. "In fact, breaking contracts is bad for business."

"Precisely." She frowned, staring off into the middle air. Pat Rin reached for his cup and sipped, awaiting the outcome of her thought.

"It will be," she said eventually, "expensive. More so, for I cannot waive my fee in the matter. You will, however, retain between seventy and seventy-five percent of the total deliverable funds."

"The Juntavas takes one-quarter?" He raised a hand, signifying peace. "I make no quibble, if we have guarantee of anonymity."

"The fees cover several things—anonymity of the client is one. Discretion, timely delivery, real costs. My fee—is insurance. The Juntavas guarantees delivery, from our own accounts. Once the money is identified, and the transfer made to our various accounts, why, we do nothing but deliver the funds from our own nearest bank. No need to have couriers bounding to and fro like grasshoppers. If our courier is robbed of your funds, still we will deliver to you the agreed amount upon the specified date. So, you see why my fee must be taken."

"I do." He took his own turn at thought, weighing danger against necessity.

"Guaranteed anonymity," he said again. "The Department of the Interior, if we are to believe its agents—and I have predicated the subjugation of an entire world upon that belief—is no dismissible opponent."

"Allow us to know our business," Natesa murmured, retrieving her teacup. She sipped, black eyes considering him over the rim.

"There is no guaranteed safety," she said eventually. "However—if you will accept my advice—I think this course offers us more safety than any other; and gains us access to needed funding."

"My funds are in cantra," he said. "No more than twelve per cent of the delivery should be in cantra—the rest must be in Terran bits or regional currencies."

She shrugged. "A detail only. For such affairs, where the client pays a percentage, we calculate the conversion using the daily exchange tables published by the Bank of Solcintra." She inclined her head, ironic. "Unless the client requires another source be used."

"The Bank of Solcintra conversions are adequate, I thank you."

"Ah. You should also know that the flex in the fee structure has to do with the degree of difficulty in accessing the funds."

"I can provide pass-codes and ID numbers," he said.

"Good. Assume the deliverable will be closer to seventy-five percent; though there may be a hazard surcharge." A subtle smile. "Thus, the Department of the Interior is accorded the respect that it deserves."

"That is well." He finished his tea while considering other details. "So. I will take delivery at the Port . . ."

"I beg to disagree. Mr. McFarland will take delivery at the Port, with Gwince and myself as his backup. You, my love, will remain well-guarded in your house, or perhaps you will visit Melina Sherton."

"Surely you and Mr. McFarland are of more value—" he began and stopped when she held up her hand.

"There will be no contract," she said, with an austerity one rarely had from Natesa, "unless this is done as I say."

He looked at her. "What shall I do if you are slain?"

"Avenge me." She lowered her hand. "Will it be as I have said?"

He slid to his feet. "Since the plan now involves Mr. McFarland risking his life, we will ask for his assessment. If he agrees, then we go forward."

Natesa smiled. "That is acceptable."

DAY 38
STANDARD YEAR 1393

LIAD
DEPARTMENT OF INTERIOR COMMAND HEADQUARTERS

The radio muttered in the background, whispering of ships, of trade goods, and of scheduling changes. Commander of Agents paid it no heed, his attention squarely on the file before him.

The campaign against the Juntavas, which had unwisely involved itself in Departmental business, was well under way. Given the opportunity to choose his battle, the Commander would not have attempted the Juntavas. Not yet. Alas, the Juntavas itself had forced the matter by interfering with the Department's attempt to attach Pat Rin yos'Phelium.

That Pat Rin yos'Phelium had grasped the opportunity created by confusion to slip through the Department's net—that he remained unrecovered to this day—was both unfortunate and unexpected.

The search continued, of course. Pat Rin yos'Phelium—a creature of self-indulgence, a slave to play and pleasure—was certain to err, soon or late. And when he did, the Department would move.

In the meanwhile, the Juntavas was being dealt—

". . . Surebleak Port!" The radio chirped.

Commander of Agents froze, and turned to stare at the tiny device. "Our duty free shop boasts a variety of local fresh fruit ciders and jams; made-by-hand rugs; pigup sticks made from local woods, and much more! And while you're on port, don't for-

get to visit the Emerald Casino. It's all here at pilot-friendly Surebleak Port!"

Surebleak, the supposed homeward of Tiazan's so-called Miri
Robertson. *Pilot-friendly* Surebleak Port.

Commander of Agents allowed himself a smile.

DAY 53
STANDARD YEAR 1393

DUTIFUL PASSAGE
LYTAXIN ORBIT

Running, he cut the corner into the main hall close,
skidded and threw himself into a somersault in order to avoid the
collision.

He landed on his feet by the opposite wall, and only then saw
who he had very nearly run down.

"Captain." He bowed deeply, feeling his face heat.

"Alas, no longer," Shan yos'Galan said calmly. "But don't, I
beg you, be cast into despondency on my account! The truth is
that I am perfectly well-satisfied to retire to the rank of master
trader and laze through every shift while Priscilla and yourself accomplish the hard work between you."

This was a pleasantry, as Ren Zel well knew, and felt relief,
that the cap—that Master Trader yos'Galan's experience of war
had not altered him out of recognition.

"But tell me, do! Wherever were you rushing off to at such a
pace?"

He bit his lip. "I am late to my shift on the bridge."

"A grievous thing, I agree." The silver eyes considered him,
and there was something—someone . . .

"I wonder," Shan said, interrupting his line of thought, "not
that it's any business of mine, of course! But, still, I do wonder
what has happened to your jacket?"

"My—" He looked down at his arm, blinking. Why in the

names of the gods had he been sleeping in his jacket? "I—" he began again and tentatively, unbelievingly, ran his hand down the unmarred leather sleeve. Memory stirred and he saw her again in the starlight, taking his jacket—*All honor to it*—and shaking it, shaking it *out* . . .

He looked up and met Shan yos'Galan's silver eyes and it came to him all at once where he had seen the like.

Ren Zel took a deep breath. "I had—a dream," he said, knowing that it explained nothing.

"I would say that you had quite a marvelous dream," Shan said, straightening from his lean against the wall. He beckoned, the master trader's ring blazing purple fires.

"Come along, child. We'd best sort this out."

"**Will** you have wine, friend?" Shan yos'Galan asked, some few moments later in the captain's private office.

Ren Zel hesitated, thinking of wine on an empty stomach after an evening, or so his memory insisted, rich in exercise.

"I think," he said carefully, "that I would rather—tea."

"And something with which to break your fast," Shan said, leaning to the comm unit. Priscilla was standing near the sofa, Ren Zel's mysteriously healed jacket held in her two hands, her eyes intent and her face peculiarly unfocused.

"Thank you, BillyJo," Shan said into the comm. "It's good to hear your voice again, too."

Priscilla blinked, and sighed, as if the jacket were too heavy for her. Ren Zel stepped forward to take it out of her hands, his fingers delighting in the supple new feel of the leather.

"Well?" Shan asked, leaning a hip against the desk.

"Anthora," she said, "definitely Anthora. She's the only wizard I know who might have done something like this so seamlessly." She sighed once more. "Breakfast?"

"On the way."

"Good." She looked to Ren Zel and moved a hand, inviting him to take one of the two easy chairs as she sank down onto the sofa. "I think you had better tell us about this—dream."

Breakfast arrived as he was describing the garden with its massive tree and welcoming cat. He made a detour there, to summarize the previous dream and the impossible whisker caught in his coverlet. Shan put a plate in his hand, and he ate, not really attending, his mind on the memory of the dream, straining for every nuance, every description.

They listened silently, captain and master trader. At some point in the narration the comm buzzed, and by silent agreement it was the master trader who rose to answer.

Finally, he reached an end, and looked down into a teacup he did not recall emptying, and back to Priscilla's brilliant, dramliza eyes.

"It was a dream," he said, for perhaps the dozenth time.

"I don't believe that it was just a dream," Priscilla said gently.

"Other parties are likewise unconvinced," Shan added, lounging beside her on the couch. "That comm call was an encoded pinbeam from Jelaza Kazone." He looked at Ren Zel, slanting brows high, silver eyes—amused?

"My sister Anthora wishes to advise her elder and her thodelm of the fact of her lifemating with Ren Zel dea'Judan, first mate of *Dutiful Passage*. Very proper of her, don't you agree?"

EROB'S CLANHOUSE
LYTAXIN

"**Have I heard from Pat Rin?**" Nova's golden brows pulled together, and she shook her head. "But I have been off-grid, you know, brother, and involved in other matters. It is true that I have not heard from Pat Rin, but it is equally true that I have not heard from Anthora."

They'd invited Nova to a dawn breakfast, after which they would escort her to the spaceport and the shuttle that would take her up to the *Passage*. For now, they sat on the balcony of their guesting suite, eating warm rolls, soft cheese and fresh fruit, beneath an orange-and-silver sky.

"Well enough," Val Con murmured, breaking open a roll. "But am I correct in recalling that there is a check-in protocol? For instance, had we been less engaged elsewhere, we might have accessed the pirate's band and sent an all's well."

"Pirate band?" Miri asked, spreading cheese on her roll.

"It is not really a pirate band," Nova said. "Shan began calling it that to irritate our father, and I believe—although I am certain he will correct me if I am in error—that Val Con began using it to irritate Cousin Kareen." She moved her shoulders. "In any case, it's simply a private clan-held frequency."

"As if I would ever *wish* to irritate my Aunt Kareen," Val Con said softly, and glanced over, green eyes warm. "We must get thee to a library, my lady. You have quite a lot of reading to do."

"Suits. Call me when the war's over."

Nova frowned, which she seemed to do a lot. "We are not going to war!"

Miri blinked at her, looked to Val Con. "We ain't?"

"It is like the pirate's band," he explained kindly. "If we call it a war, we will annoy Nova."

She grinned. "Got it."

"Val Con—"

"Is there a way to access the log," he interrupted, softly. "To see who has and has not checked in?"

"Yes, certainly. I can do so from Erob's comm room, if you wish. Indeed, you should have the new codes. Sit with me and I will give them you." She hesitated, and the frown this time seemed more worried than irritated, to Miri's sharpening eye.

"I wonder, brother—have you had ill news of Pat Rin?"

"Ill news—no," he said slowly, and Miri felt him picking his words with careful precision. "Say rather that we have . . . inconclusive news, and wish to assure ourselves that he is well." He extended a hand and lay it briefly over Nova's where it lay fisted beside her plate.

"I do not wish to distress you—I know that you and he are friends."

"Insofar as Pat Rin allows himself to be anyone's friend," she said, sharply.

"But truly," she said, after a long moment, probably to reassure herself, "he should be well. Pat Rin is very far from a fool—and Shan had hired him an extremely portwise pilot."

"*Shan* hired Pat Rin's pilot?" Val Con said, incredulously. "Matters must be very changed between them."

"Say rather that it was Shan's idea to place Mr. McFarland as Pat Rin's pilot, when he came to us with the message from Edger. It was in the clan's interest that Mr. McFarland not return . . . immediately to his usual rounds, and Pat Rin was preparing for one of his tours. Mr. McFarland was willing to be hired, and Pat Rin was willing—after I spoke to him, for I will not hide from you, brother, that *of course* Shan put his back up—to hire. So it was done. I checked Mr. McFarland's credentials myself—and Anthora pronounced him an honorable man."

"Well, then, it sounds as if our cousin is both well-served and well-protected," Val Con said, after a moment, being so careful Miri felt an ache starting between her eyebrows. "Doubtless our check of the roll will establish him in comfortable safety, and only a little bored."

"As to that," Nova murmured, "he had used to say that he would welcome being marooned on a backward world for a relumma or two, so that he might catch up on his reading."

There didn't seem much to say to that, Miri thought, polishing off the last bit of roll with mingled relish and regret.

Apparently Val Con thought the same.

"Tell me," he said, reaching for his teacup. "Have you found all the citations you require to make our case before Council?"

"Not all, certainly, but a good start has been made," Nova answered, pushing her plate aside. "The *Passage* carries the full text of the Diaries, as well as the Council book. I will be able to conclude my research en route and be ready to stand before Council the day we raise Liad."

Val Con looked at her, one eyebrow up. "But you will not do so," he suggested. "Until you have had word from your delm."

She sighed. "I will, of course, await the delm's word."

"Good." Val Con smiled, though to Miri he felt more wary than approving, and drank his tea.

Anthora leaned back in her chair, silver eyes focused on a point just above and light years beyond the top of the comm unit.

Mr. dea'Gauss had her instructions regarding the settlements, which he was to send to Ren Zel, for approval or adjustment. She had herself 'beamed the *Passage* with the proper announcement to her thodelm, which might very well amuse Shan, but for Ren Zel one *would* behave well and do everything that was proper. He should not suffer wounds on her account—he had wounds enough.

That she knew his wounds as her own was—piquant. That he would have acquired a similarly intimate knowledge of herself was—not harrowing; not quite that. She was, after all, of the dramliz, and accustomed to interfacing with her fellows and with some of the stronger Healers. Those interfacings were of necessity less absolute than the immediate and complete merging which had joined her to Ren Zel last evening; and while there was no help for it now—and while she would not trade this morning for last—she did rather wish that she had been . . . more decorous at some times in the past.

That Ren Zel would forgive her transgressions, she knew. Had he lived other than an exemplary and blameless life, she would have freely forgiven him all his sins. They could neither do otherwise, as closely as they were joined—in all but body.

Anthora sighed. She had felt his absence keenly this morning, when she had woken from her second sleep to find herself solitary in the tumbled bed. More than that, she had felt some alarm. Surely, he had expended enormous amounts of energy in his walk from the *Passage* to her bedroom. To make a like expenditure so soon after the first, and, moreover, a half-night of enthusiastic lovemaking, was foolhardy in the extreme. She would not have wished to undertake such a course, and she knew herself for a wizard of stamina, and will.

In fact, she thought, how *had* he managed that walk? She could quite understand the process—it was, after all, very similar to a piloting problem—but she was not persuaded that she could reproduce the effect . . .

She straightened in her chair, frowning as she tried to reconcile the equation.

The comm unit chimed.

Anthora jumped, blinked, and leaned forward to accept the call.

She blinked again as the screen coalesced into an image of a dark-haired woman in the uniform of a Clerk of the Council of Clans. The woman bowed, from greater to lesser, by which Anthora understood that the Clerk was speaking on behalf of the entire Council of Clans, by order of the Speaker.

"Do I address Anthora yos'Galan Clan Korval?"

Anthora inclined her head a fraction, striving for Nova's air of cool competence.

"You do."

"Speaker for Council requires Korval's presence at a full meeting of the clans scheduled tomorrow for the hour after midday. Korval has been called upon to answer certain very serious charges."

"What charges?" Anthora demanded. "And who accuses us?"

"I am not authorized to divulge that information. Because of the seriousness of the charges, Speaker for Council will assess Korval one Class A Jump ship for every day it fails to send a representative to answer."

Anthora glared at her, which the Clerk bore with patience. Behind the glare, her mind raced.

The Council was empowered to levy penalties for a failure to comply with its rule. The weight of this threatened levy argued the presence of serious charges indeed, though what they might be—

Really, she thought, there was no choice. She could hardly explain that with Plan B in effect there was quite simply no way that she could authorize turning a ship—any ship, down to the meanest two-place shuttle—over to the Council. dea'Gauss himself could not order it done. She considered quickly. The Council knew Korval would not relish the loss of a ship, so she must let them believe that their threat was potent. To tell them that Korval would resist any such attempt was folly . . .

And, surely, she thought, she would be safe in the very Council hall.

Once again, she inclined her head that austere and irritating inch.

"I thank Speaker for Council, but there is no need to descend to threats. I will attend the meeting scheduled for the hour after midday tomorrow and will answer all charges then."

Ren Zel had been excused from his shift on the bridge; another pilot set, by the captain's word, to cover his board. Truly, he would have rather been allowed to escape back into routine, to explore the strange dream that was not a dream in his own way and come to terms with his . . . with his lifemating.

For it seemed he was no longer clanless, outcast—dead. Abruptly, he had kin to care for—Shan yos'Galan was his brother, Priscilla Mendoza, his sister. He found another sister in Nova yos'Galan—she who was no longer Korval pernard'i, for the news from the planet was that Val Con yos'Phelium had taken up the Ring and his rightful melant'i as Korval. Which was well for the clan, Ren Zel thought, distractedly—clans should be properly led by the delm, rather than held in trust, year upon long year . . .

In a daze, he had received the kiss of his thodelm and thodelmae; immediately thereafter, Priscilla had accessed the ship's roll and amended his file. *Dutiful Passage* had previously known him as a pilot; now it knew him as a *pilot of Korval*.

"You look shell-shocked, child," Shan said to him, sometime after the second pinbeam arrived from Liad, this from a certain dea'Gauss, directed to Ren Zel dea'Judan Clan Korval.

Printed, this document occupied several sheets and proved, to his horrified eyes, to be a list of the properties, funds, and quartershare settled upon him.

"I—it is too much," he had managed, not quite certain himself if he was referring to the settlements—offered his choice of no less than *three* Class A Jumps!—or the abrupt and . . . irregular . . . alteration in his melant'i.

"Yes, I can understand how it might be. Anthora's a minx, and never fear that I will tell her so at my earliest opportunity."

Memory showed him the lady in question, her breasts heavy in his hands as she poised teasingly above him, her hair woven with starlight . . .

Face hot, he looked down at the printout.

"Perhaps," he whispered, "not entirely a minx."

There was a small pause. "Well, I am glad to hear you say so. For I will not scruple to tell *you* that—as much as I enter into your entirely reasonable dismay of the process—I wish you will accommodate yourself to these new arrangements, and allow us to embrace you fully. The clan can only be richer by your lifemating. Certainly, yos'Galan *does* rejoice in receiving you, and I am delighted in my new brother."

The printout smeared out of sense, as tears rose, and—shame to him—spilled over. In the act of throwing his arm up to shield his face, he recalled that it was no shame at all to share one's joy with . . . kin.

Nor was it useful to water the printout beyond readability. He made some shift to bring himself under control, and looked up to meet Shan's serious silver eyes.

"I wonder if I might have some time to . . . myself," he said tentatively. "I wish to relocate center, so that I may accommodate myself—and serve the clan usefully."

Shan grinned. "As to that, I have no fear at all. But, go, rest yourself, settle your mind. Come to us for prime, eh? And after that, I swear we will allow you to return to the comforts of your schedule."

And so Ren Zel had escaped, at least to the familiarity of his own cabin. Now, showered, and fulfilled by one of BillyJo's sandwiches, he lay himself down to sleep—and, in sleeping, dreamed.

He dreamed a starmap—*the* starmap: *Balent'i tru'vad*, the

starweb of all creation. Vast, awesome in its balances and harmony, it lay revealed before him: suns, stars, worlds, lives, glittering, busy and inevitable. And throughout it all, woven into the very fabric of the universe, golden lines of power, such as he had first beheld in Anthora yos'Galan's chamber.

He bent his attention to those lines, apprehending the ebb and flow of their substance, the tectonic intricacies, the cohesion of their purpose. As he had in Anthora's chamber, he extended his hand and very carefully gathered two glowing lines to himself.

Far off in the starweb, a cluster of lines constricted about a lesser sun. Ren Zel released his hold; the lines relaxed, the flow of power resumed.

So. Once again, he extended his attention, this time in an attitude of seeking, rather than command.

He heard a tone, as if a council-bell had been lightly struck, and in the next heartbeat, *Balent'i tru'vad* was lost, and his sight filled entirely with pulsing golden light.

It had been Chi yos'Phelium who had insisted, upon his succession to his mother's position as qe'andra to Korval, that the office defenses be upgraded to a standard she referred to as "adequate," and which Mr. dea'Gauss, in those younger days, had privately considered to be . . . draconian.

Today, reading the message in the lights of the "control board" she had caused to be installed in his office, he very much wished that he could return to those forever vanished days of his youth and most humbly beg her pardon. For it was truly said that delm's eyes see far—and the eyes of Korval see farthest of all.

Time-travel not being an option, the best way to atone for his doubts was to ensure that her care had not been in vain.

Carefully, adhering to a protocol altered and memorized every Quarterday, Mr. dea'Gauss pushed three buttons in sequence, alerting his staff and apprentices to the approach of danger. They would now, according to drill—for Chi had also insisted that there be drills, and routine practice of drills—close their work, touch the key sequence that would simultaneously download the information in their computers to the house computer at Jelaza Kazone, and scrub their own systems. That done, they would exit the building using one of the three "escape routes."

They had twelve minutes to accomplish these things.

At twelve-minutes-point-one, the building would seal itself.

Since the walls and windows had years ago been reinforced with hullplate and blast-glass, Mr. dea'Gauss was comfortable in his belief that it would take both effort and time for the approaching enemy to gain entry.

His own task required some time—a little. Merely the retrieval of two letters, written long ago at the outrageous suggestion of that same Chi yos'Phelium; a moment to copy and address them as appropriate; the touch of a key to send. That done, he typed in the sequence that would initiate the download and wipe of his own records, and bent to retrieve the gun from the right-hand drawer of his desk.

They'd thrown the Erob comm tech out for a tea break she was more than willing to have, once it was explained to her that the pinbeam was needed for private Korval business.

Now, Val Con was seated beside Nova at a console in the inner bridge, Miri on his knee, both watching her fingers move, and taking note of the new access codes.

"Your codes would have worked, of course," Nova told Val Con, "but as a bounce to Jeeves. I set it up that way when you had been gone so long and had not . . ." Her voice faded, then strengthened. "Of course, I could not compromise our integrity, but Jeeves has your voice-map on file and he is very discreet."

"In fact," Val Con said, for Miri's benefit, "he has the ability to spread himself over eight different frequencies, re-routing on the fly, which makes him remarkably difficult to trace."

"Just so," Nova said coolly, and fed in the last string of code. "There, that should . . . yes."

A datalog shimmered into being on the center screen, displaying the call-ins for Day 52, Standard Year 1393. Nova scrolled upward.

"Luken, Padi, Shindi . . ."

"Shindi?"

Nova glanced at him. "Did not Shan—well." She caught herself with a shrug. "You would have been otherwise occupied, I suppose. The clan rejoices in fraternal twins, heirs to Anthora yos'Galan. Their names are Shindi and Mik."

"Ah." He smiled, and put his hand on Miri's knee. "The clan increases, cha'trez. We are doubly fortunate in twins."

She looked down at him. "Twice as much trouble, you mean?"

He laughed, and had the pleasure of seeing a cool smile pass over Nova's features before she turned back to the screen, scrolling ever upward through the long list of dates and names.

She reached an end, and waved her hand wordlessly. Foreknowing, Miri sitting tense on his knee, still he took a turn, scrolling downward through the names of his kin.

Excepting only one.

DAY 54
STANDARD YEAR 1393

THE CLUTCH HOMEWORLD

They had been made known to Handler, of Edger's clan, who sat with them quietly through the hours of waiting. Occasionally he would speak; if asked a question, he would answer, most courteously; but in general he worked silently, alternating between the handles of several knives.

The food they had packed in was adequate, and Daav was permitted a few moments outside every few hours, which he used to circumnavigate the asteroid they'd come in on. Otherwise, he—and Aelliana—awaited their summons.

Also in the chamber was a vast and silent member of the Clutch, lightly shelled, withal, and holding a naked crystal blade reminiscent of spear or sword. Daav had first thought the creature a statue, until Handler, upon hearing a gong from within the chamber, addressed a quick word to it. The guard-Clutch had answered with a brief whistle and a slight bow, thence returning to silence.

The waiting room was carved from rock, with three visible tunnels running off, and, as far as Daav was able to deduce, down. Edger had gone into the middle tunnel, to the meeting room of the Elders, many hours ago.

So they whiled the hours. Daav talked with himself, or wrote in his notepad, while inwardly he and Aelliana played games of discovery, sharing memories of kin, and of friends.

Too often Daav found himself projecting comfort, or worse,

disdain—and once heard himself say, "For that, yes, we may have some Balance, for I am sure we still own some stock there, and I never liked the fellow . . ."

"Daav, so long ago, and so—"

"Knowing what I know, I can do nothing but this—would you have our children's children exposed to a clan permitting this?"

At other times, Aelliana showed Daav what it looked like, what it felt like, to explore the beauty of numbers; to see something as simple as a ship's course, or as complex as a star system, object by object . . .

And then Edger was returned to them.

"Come," he said, and his big voice reverberated with weariness. "They will listen. You must tell them of the Tree and the necessities of my brother and sister. You will need to speak, each of you, father and mother, and you will needs speak as elders. You must hold nothing aside, for the truth of things invests the walls of this place. What questions you may be asked I cannot say, nor may I offer comfort, for within are those who watched the stars and slew dragons and ruled clans before my first shell was dry."

**DAY 44
STANDARD YEAR 1393**

SUREBLEAK

The portacom on his belt beeped for attention—an increasingly ordinary, not to say annoying, event. Pat Rin frowned. He had rather been enjoying the ride back from Melina Sherton's country territory, sharing the large back seat of his car with half-a-dozen bottles of Upcountry Canary, watching the peaceful streets of the Affiliation roll by his window. The pace Gwince set was rapid enough to make progress, yet slow enough that he could be seen, and have an opportunity to return the waves of those he passed.

The comm's beep changed from the single "attention" beep to the three-toned phrase belonging to calls from Security—Natesa or Cheever McFarland, that would be. Both of whom were at Surebleak Port, awaiting the contracted delivery from the Juntavas. He snatched the unit free.

"Conrad," he said, terse, no longer hesitating over the assumed name.

"Our shipment has arrived in good order," came Natesa's musical voice, unstrained and unsurprised. "Transhipping is well under way. I must admit to an error, however, in scheduling your visit to the country. It appears that certain matters have run ahead of us and your countenance is required at port, rather sooner than later. The portmasters themselves make the request."

Pat Rin sighed—for both portmasters to be on duty together was not a good sign.

"No news without complexity, eh, Natesa? Shall I rush?"

"Yes, denubia. It would be best."

Silently, Pat Rin damned the device for its lack of visual screen—or even a speaker capable of transmitting nuance.

"Soonest, then," he said, briefly, discreetly. "I will be there."

He thumbed the comm off, leaned forward and spoke to the driver.

"Gwince, if you please, we are in need of the banshee. Take me to the portmaster's office quickly."

She nodded. "Right, Boss. To the port!"

The siren wailed into life, startling the peaceful street outside his window into chaos. Lesser vehicles pulled quickly aside. Pedestrians, reflexes honed by years of violence, jumped for the meager protection of doors and alleyways. Some few, bolder, stood their ground, staring wide-eyed as the big car surged forward, pressing Pat Rin deep into the comfort of the big back seat.

"**What** we have here is a conundrum," Dayside Portmaster Claren Liu said, from the head of the hastily cleared conference table. "The port has taken the report of First Class Pilot Bhupendra Darteshek—" This was, Pat Rin had learned, the name of the very tall, very thin, very dark-skinned Juntavas pilot—"and the corroborating report of First Class Pilot Vilma Karapov—" Pilot Darteshek's co-pilot, a well-muscled blonde with skin so pale it seemed tinged with blue—"that we've got what might be pirates in the system. They say that they were shadowed into Port—and they've provided instrument verification."

As the ability to come and go like shadows themselves was the claim the Juntavas—through Natesa—had made for their couriers, this hardly seemed auspicious. Pat Rin spoke across the table to Pilot Darteshek.

"How is it that you allowed yourselves to be followed?"

White teeth gleamed in a thin, feral grin. "We don't be followed. They was here when we Jump in."

Pat Rin felt a chill run his spine, and inclined his head courteously. "That does put a different face on the matter. Thank you, Pilot."

"Right," said Portmaster Liu, and looked 'round the table to be sure she had everyone's attention—everyone being the two courier pilots, Pat Rin, Natesa, Cheever McFarland, and nightside portmaster Etienne Borden—before proceeding.

"We all know that Surebleak is a low tier port. We do have two guild portmasters; we've got a few hands and two back-up volunteer portmasters who're on call in case of an emergency. We have two weather satellites to back up comm traffic and a comm satellite that backs up the weather satellites. We've got one spacegoing tug. What we don't have is defense." She shook her head.

"Why this is so . . ." She made a wry mouth and sipped from a dispenser cup of coffee.

"History lesson," she said apologetically. "See, Surebleak is a corporate world. It belongs—belonged—to something called the Gilmour Agency, which was set up to develop the planetary timonium deposits. They were pretty good-sized deposits, and the planet itself was near enough to habitable that they had some big plans for it—the designs for the orbiting mirrors they were going to use to eventually bring the temperature up a few degrees are on file in the port 'base." She shrugged. "The assumption was that there'd be a real economy here. Timonium and by-products going out, with maybe some specialty ores, gemstones, local lumber, and such to sweeten the load. Incoming would be supplies for the mines and the miners. In addition to development rights, Gilmour Agency was empowered to establish a local government corporation, which would have the responsibility of upgrading and maintaining the port." She had another sip of coffee and continued.

"Gilmour had barely gotten started here when their competitors located Tanzir's System two light years to galactic west. Three big airless rocks of not much else but high-grade timonium left over from the same event that helped make Surebleak the garden spot of the galaxy that it is. Gilmour Agency folded—de-

faulted on everything—and the local government never did get
established—" She looked sharply down-table.

"I hope I'm not boring you, Boss Conrad."

Pat Rin bowed slightly in his seat. "Not at all. In fact, I expect
that I will be needing as much of the formal history of Surebleak
as you have . . ."

"Right," she interrupted. "You will. Because all this comes
down to the reason why we don't have weapons or defense. It's
because the local planetary government has to approve, authorize,
certify, and assist in providing all planetary or system defenses.
And until just lately, Surebleak hasn't had a planetary government."

Pat Rin stared at her, deliberately haughty while his mind
raced. He was, by a vote of the Affiliated Bosses, Head Boss, empowered to speak for all if the need arose. His proposed structure
had been somewhat different, modeled, as it had been, on the
Council of Clans. His fellow bosses, however, had insisted that
there must be one Head Boss—"Boss Boss," Penn Kalhoon had
joked—and he had bowed to that, seeing that this was the model
they understood. He had then appointed Penn Kalhoon Second
Boss, and between them they had begun to match the tasks that
needed to be done with those who had the talents to accomplish
them. Which in effect meant . . .

He looked up to find Claren Liu looking at him with grim
amusement.

"Boss Conrad," she said, with a formal nod of the head. "As
Surebleak portmaster, I request your approval to begin planetary
defense planning, your permission to act in the name of Surebleak
in the case of incident, and your agreement to assist in developing
an on-going security net." She paused. "Without your OK, all I
can do is pass a note to the guild, saying I've got possible pirates
in-system."

Pat Rin glanced out the window. The second level port office
was bathed in sunlight, and overlooked the tarmac to the east, and
with a portion of a road that connected to the Port Road. On the
tarmac sat two ships—the port's tug and the courier's surprisingly
large vessel.

"I assume that I must regard this as an official request?" he finally asked, facing the portmaster once more.

"That's right. It has to be witnessed by two master pilots or a master pilot and three first class." She offered him a sympathetic grin.

"We can't have ships running around shadowing our incoming now that we have an ad out," she said. "It'd be—"

"Bad for business," Pat Rin finished gently along with her.

He rose, and inclined his head.

"I acknowledge your proposal, Portmaster, and I hereby approve your request to begin planetary defense planning. I give you permission to act for Surebleak in case of incident. As for a planetary security net—" he glanced aside, catching Cheever McFarland's eye. "I may be able to provide assistance, especially if there are pilots to hand."

Cheever's eyes widened, then closed. Pat Rin suppressed a smile and sat down.

"I will sign documents, if that is required," he told the portmaster. "Mr. McFarland, if you would do me the favor of going to the car and bringing up the contents of the back seat. Portmaster, I propose a working lunch."

She grinned at him merrily. "Right you are. I'll send for food—and there's a couple others we'll want here, if you'll let me call them in?"

He inclined his head. "Certainly."

DAY 45
STANDARD YEAR 1393

SHERZER SYSTEM

"Told you there was something spooky about them 'quations, Shugg. I must know something deep down . . ." that was Andy Mack—the Colonel, so-called—idly stropping a credit chit along the flowing silver hair falling across the front of his leather jacket as he leaned against the back of second board's acceleration couch.

"Well, the screwy thing is it ain't exactly obvious, no matter how much you think about it . . ." Shugg agreed.

The grizzled and short-haired Shugg—Flyer Shugg to his Surebleak acquaintances—sat second board at the moment, with Cheever McFarland at first. Crowding behind them were the other seven members of the expedition: Boss Conrad, Natesa, Etienne Borden, Juntavas pilots Darteshek and Karapov, Andy Mack, and "call me Dostie," the taciturn pilot of the port's official tug, whose hair—today at least—matched the electric pink tunic she wore beneath her jump jacket.

They had all sat second at one point or another during the trip. Pat Rin's glare had been ignored by the master pilot when his name came around on the roster; perforce, he had taken the seat warmed by Dostie, who had had it after the Colonel, who had it after Natesa, and had run his board with a cool aplomb he was very far from feeling. Now Shugg sat second, his grin slow and easy as he played with the screens.

"Lookit. We got a brown dwarf as primary and one-two-three neat as a pin stepping stone blue-and-green gas cousins with halos and then little Miss Blue running a bit askew in an outside orbit. Me, I'd like to know what happened to the missing planet!"

"Oh, hain't *missing*, Shugg!" Andy Mack scolded him genially. "You always want to find something *missing*. Check the resonance and you'll see . . ."

Natesa smiled and raised her eyes; Pat Rin smiled in answer. He had, quite unexpectedly, *enjoyed* the trip, despite the crowding and the lack of opportunity to be private with his lady. But truly, he had not found a group this convivial since . . . well . . . ever.

"Might be some rocks out beyond," Dostie offered. "But the Colonel's right, anything bigger than grains will get swept out of that gap because the mass ratio's almost a perfect 9, 5, 4, 3 . . . and with orbital periods being what they are—might be your Miss Blue *is* what's missing!"

"Now," Cheever said, raising his voice to be heard over the chatter, "we get to the fun part. If you were looking for a shipstack out in the middle of this nowhere, where would you look?"

It was, of course, a joke, and Pat Rin was relieved to hear Pilot McFarland refer to their destination as other than a "ship grave-yard"—an image not conducive to hope, which had so delighted the pilot that he had used it in every other sentence. Likewise, he had dropped the word "derelicts," which the ships they sought assuredly would *not* be, from his vocabulary.

"Shall we ask them where they are, Mr. McFarland?" Pat Rin murmured.

Cheever, careful of watchful eyes, keyed in the call phrase, shrank the info screen to thumbnail on the second's board, and said, "I'll take bets. Who'd care to name time—minutes and seconds—before we get an answer from the beacon? Boss, you sit out, OK?"

The assembled pilots laughed, placed their bets, and settled into an animated exploration of the Sherzer system by instrument.

The universe was not something Pat Rin yos'Phelium contemplated often, he being too much in it to feel apart from it. Now, however, he sat at the second board of *Fortune's Reward*, listening to its systems chuckling wistfully against the sudden silence of a ship with no one else in it, and shivered.

He had been to the brown drawf's system only once before. Cousin Er Thom had brought him—as surly and as graceless a halfling as one might ever wish to drown—insisting first that he memorize the coords, the call phrase, and the gate codes.

He had not, of course, wasted his time with Er Thom contemplating the universe. Instead, he had with cold dignity refused the shuttle's controls when they were offered, having already failed his piloting test for the fourth time. The terms of his refusal must have distressed his cousin, but Er Thom had merely nodded and changed the subject, filling the hours of the trip with stories of Clanmother Cantra, tales of Uncle Daav, arcane bits of ship lore; and, as they approached their goal more nearly, he had told of the strange mechanism which kept this collection of ships and ship parts together, for the use of Korval—and those whom Korval allowed.

Unwillingly, Pat Rin had listened, and despite his firm intention, found himself charmed out of surliness, so that he actually enjoyed sharing the picnic lunch Er Thom had brought along. After, and in closer accord, they crossed to the automated office, where he was shown the keys and the folders, and had his palmprint filed with the guardian computers.

That done, Er Thom had taken him on a tour of the stacks, showing him the controls and several ancient ships—one of which was still spaceworthy some six centuries after it was built!

Eventually, they had returned to the shuttle. As the ship-stack dwindled behind them, Cousin Er Thom had spoken to him seriously of his future, offering several alternative courses of education—all of them based away from the homeworld—borne his clumsy, halfling scorn with patience, and taken him back to the *Passage* as if all were well.

Now Pat Rin—perhaps the last of his clan; perhaps Korval-in-Truth—had returned to mine the ship-stack, for the defense and preservation of the clan. He had been astonished that the access numbers he had memorized so long ago still worked; that the robot guardian recalled his palmprint; that the system of key and folder was precisely as the ill-tempered halfling had recalled it . . .

Around him, the ship burbled, and the familiar cycling of the air system failed to disturb his patient consideration of the past.

It was, truth told, the first time Pat Rin had ever been quite so alone. He had never—as his younger cousins had—done a solo run; and, though he not infrequently traveled alone, there had never been a time in his life when he had been more than a moment or two away from another human; even in space he had always had a pilot of superb skill to depend upon.

Now, the person nearest him was a pilot he'd barely met—Dostie. She, too, sat alone in a ship, more than two dozen Standard Minutes away from him. Natesa—alone in her vessel—was approximately three dozen Standard Minutes away, while Cheever McFarland, Flyer Shugg, and the nightside portmaster oversaw the checking and selection of the last of their potential fleet, lashed neatly together nearly four dozen minutes away.

To beguile himself, Pat Rin sat at second board, and began to tentatively explore the Sherzer system with instruments and screens. Sherzer II loomed in front of him; one long range screen showed the remaining cluster of ships to be explored, as well as the seventeen other "ship-stacks"—some no more than a collection of parts—with the limb of the planet and a distant view of the multi-hued planetary ring beyond. *Fortune's Reward* was in effect orbiting in formation with all of these ships, in the trailing LaGrange point of Sherzer II.

It was a lovely place for a junkyard, and Pat Rin found himself absorbed in the shimmer of the innermost ring; the colors of the storms swirling across the planet's surface; and the beautiful tracery of the lightning flashes—

"Boss?"

Cheever McFarland's voice boomed into the quiet ship, star-
ling Pat Rin out of his reverie.

"Yes?" he snapped. There was a delay, longer than could be ac-
ounted for by the relative nearness of their ships.

"Um, yeah," Pilot McFarland said. "Sorry to bother you. But
anyhow, we might have ourselves a problem, a kind of decision
problem, if you know what I mean?"

Pat Rin shook his head, a habit which his mother had deplored
n his cousins, and to which he had finally succumbed on Sure-
leak.

"Pilot, I am destined for *problems of decision* on this project,"
he said, making a conscious effort to lighten his tone. "If you can
explain the situation in non-technical terms I will hear it and con-
tribute what I may to the solving."

Again, he shook his head. The decisions. First had been the decision of which cluster of ships was most promising; then, after
nearly two days, the decision to abandon them in favor of a potentially more . . . useful . . . solution.

The first cluster chosen had been a mixed collection of ships,
all operable, but with visible problems ranging from missing
spacesuits to thruster fuel supplies too ancient to be reliable. A no-
tation in the folder indicated that they had been for sale and were
awaiting inspection of a potential buyer—fifteen Standards before. Apparently they had been passed over, and for good cause.

The possibly more useful solution came in the form of a pod of
vessels of strange design and even stranger decor. Passed over in
the first glance because they were parked among what looked to be
random parts of two or three space stations, they proved on second
glance to be asteroid miners. One side of each ship was painted flat
black, and the other a white so bright that it was nearly silver. And
gaudily adorning each side—in white on the black side, in green
on the white side—was the tree-and-dragon shield in so large a
size that it could easily be seen before the true shape of the ships.

There was no way, of course, to quickly alter the look of the fleet,
and because they were non-standard ships, checking them for utility
was more difficult. Moreover, their keys had been filed in a folder
marked "reserved," though for whom Pat Rin had been unable to
discover. Thus, each vessel was serially inspected and tested, and
proved to be in remarkably good repair for ships left on their own in
deep space. So far of the dozen, five had been found unfit.

Cheever McFarland cleared his throat. "Boss, this boat here is the queen. Call it a command ship. We got the complete package running and everything looks to be in great shape. Got a test program right here on the board that lets me check out the other ships remotely."

Pat Rin considered. This hardly seemed to be a problem ... but the other man was continuing without waiting for an answer.

"Thing is, we got eight ships here that are in great shape. Got a lot of power, a lot of shields—these things are set for heavy duty asteroid belt mining!—Shugg says we can modify some of the rock drills and blasting charges—set 'em up as weapons."

Again, thought Pat Rin, this was good news, and not a problem at all. Eight ships and eight pilots was perfect.

"So, I'm thinking that the best thing is for us to bring these back and for you to fly that one home," Cheever McFarland finished.

Pat Rin froze; the words "I cannot!" stuck edgewise in his throat, caught up somehow with the lightnings across Sherzer II. With memory's ear, he heard Cousin Er Thom's soft, sweet voice, explaining why it was that Korval bought used ships, out-of-date ships, ships that had been foreclosed on—and why it was that they invested in repair yards, gave scholarships to pilots, and paid a good percentage of the Scout's maintenance bills.

"Your mother—she lives for the Code. Its study has become her life, and she excels at it. But, Korval—Korval is not the Code. Korval is *ships*. Always remember: Korval is ships."

He was brought to himself by Cheever McFarland's voice. "Boss? Other thing we could do is leave that one here and come back for it later."

Pat Rin blinked. Leave his ship? "No," he snapped, and took a deep breath.

"I will bring *Fortune's Reward* home, Mr. McFarland," he said, deliberately calm.

There was a slight pause, then, "Right. That's settled, then."

"**Welcome,** pilot." The words were warm amber against a dark screen. "Please log in."

Taking a deep breath, Pat Rin leaned forward, gingerly set his fingers against First Board's keypad and typed *Pat Rin yos'Phelium Clan Korval*.

"Please insert license."

Pat Rin glanced at the place in the board where a true pilot would slot his license for the ship's perusal, then back to the screen.

As he watched, the amber letters faded; reformed into another query.

"License available?"

Lower lip caught between his teeth, he typed *No*.

Astonishingly, the ship remained undismayed. "Palmscan, please," the next screen directed.

He placed his left hand on the pad, felt the tingle of the scan . . .

"Confirmed. Full access available."

Something *clicked* nearly beneath his fingers, loud in the silence of the piloting chamber. Pat Rin snatched his hand back as a section of the control board to his left parted neatly at the seam and an auxiliary panel rose, locking into place with a snap.

For a long moment, he stared at it. Full access, indeed, now that the weapons were available to him.

"Autodefense?" his ship inquired. "Autoshield?"

What did he know of such things? He touched a key, accepting both.

That quickly the board came fully back to life, with lights blinking and switches setting or resetting themselves. The screen layout went from Cheever McFarland's idiosyncratic groupings to default—and stabilized into a pattern familiar to him from childhood: this was the layout Uncle Daav and Cousin Er Thom had preferred; he himself had drilled on a dummy board set up just this way . . .

Low on the screen to the right was radar and sensor scan forward; low on the left was radar and sensor aft; low in the center was Jump status, and what—according to Cousin Er Thom—Uncle Daav had called the go-dial, a graph showing the balanced Jump potentials of the three strongest nearby gravity wells.

Above—and largest—was the "forward" visible view, with the aft view smaller to the left; ship status reports sat to the right, all cheerfully green: air supply, backup air supply, sensor power checks, weapons functions (green for the particle beam, green for the missiles: eight marked *short*, eight marked *mid*, four marked *long*, and one green for something marked chaff-bomb), and multi-channel receiver and back-up.

"Boss?" Cheever McFarland's voice came, quietly, over tight band. "Problems?"

Pat Rin sighed, gently. "I am acclimating myself, Pilot. The view from first board is somewhat larger than that from second."

There was a brief delay. "That's all adjustable—" the pilot began, and broke off. "Yeah, OK," he said after a moment, and somewhat sheepishly. "I think I know what you mean. But really, Boss, there ain't gonna be any problems. All you gotta do is tell the ship where you're going—check it against the book, you got plenty of time. Hell, after you put in the coords, set the auto-count, and sit back and snooze 'til it's time to punch the 'fresh scan' button for the sensors when you pop out."

"Which is why most pilots rejoice in having someone of wide experience sitting second for their first few dozen hours of flight, if I recall correctly." Pat Rin could hear himself getting testy with his absent stalwart, and authorized a complete systems check to take his mind off his tension.

After a moment, Cheever McFarland's voice re-emerged from the speaker, sounding suspiciously as if the pilot were suppressing a sneeze, or perhaps a chuckle.

"Right. On the other hand, you done right well for yourself with the jump in and kick butt approach—and we both know you got the math cold. But listen, while you been sitting there talking to yourself, we've been getting ourselves together out here. We're all sitting within sight of each other, and we're setting up a Jump plan. I'm figurin' we can take this whole shebang outta here in about three hours. As it comes to happen, Natesa don't have a whole lot to do—won't for another hour or two. You want I should have her walk you through the check-out procedures a couple times?"

Pat Rin looked down, saw the ring on his hand, the tree-and-dragon bold and new—and bowed slightly toward the unseen speaker.

"Indeed, Pilot, that sounds like an excellent idea. I will await her signals with anticipation."

DAY 47
STANDARD YEAR 1393

SUREBLEAK SPACE

Jump had consumed seventeen Standard hours, forty-four minutes, twenty-seven and numerous odd-bits of seconds, during which time Pat Rin did what he always did in Jump: he read and studied.

This time, however, he read not of the whimsical philosophy of Harshaw, nor the patient rhymes of yos'Sandow, nor even from the Code—which, until lately, he had studied several hours a week.

No, during this historic and unlikely Jump he had studied tactical manuals and piloting theory, and technical manuals, as he had not since he was a halfling. He studied the dozen pre-logged destinations in the ship's computer, laughing at the ironies of Liad and Lytaxin; puzzling over the one marked with a symbol from a Terran card deck, until he suddenly understood what the venerable *ace of spades* had to do with a Liaden pleasure-yacht.

The pre-logged Jumps were all what Cousin Er Thom would have called "dirty Jumps," calculated for broad energy levels and without updating for current mass or velocity. Emergency runs, all of them, for use in times of dire trouble, pilot injury, or the tragedy that put the ship into the hands of one who was no proper pilot at all . . .

He checked weapons—both the ship's armament and his various pistols. Gods, he was bringing a small fleet into Surebleak, each double marked visually as belonging to Korval. Yet, what choice had he?

And so with an hour to go he brought himself again to the pilot's seat and molded it and the board to him as best he might. He had become accustomed to seeing the transmission recordings, and added them above the main forward view. Pulling the chair up to the second stop, he locked it at an angle slightly less rakish than that required by Cheever McFarland's frame; raised it, turned the seat temperature down several degrees, then set it to automatic. The board he moved down, then brought it back to its original position. He engaged the shock webbing and sat back, eyes on the Jump grayed screens.

Carefully, deliberately, he reviewed those things Inas-called-Natesa had told him, both the quiet love-talk—which had been a comfort and a distraction in his isolation—and the practical matters that pilots share between themselves.

"Let the ship tell you if there is a problem," she had murmured, for his ears alone. "Your eyes will be quicker than your fingers in the first seconds of breakout. Place defense on automatic, and bring up your shields. Be in the seat well ahead of time, and always strap in when you sit first board, even in quiet orbit about a friendly world. Test the alarm levels because alarms should warn, not frighten or distract. Be certain that you can easily reach the controls and be certain that your ring will not hamper you nor catch on a toggle. I love you . . .

"You will Jump first, denubia; and we will come in around you. We will be no more than a minute or two behind, and within a tenth-sec or closer on radio. I expect you to pilot like you shoot . . ."

Breakout.

Fortune's Reward announced itself around its Jump glare as *Bitty Kitty*, out of Fron Du Lac; the ship's air system purred, and his hand moved as if of its own accord, slapping "refresh scan." A glance at his screens oriented him wonderfully: Surebleak's port beacon was located and centered. There was no sign yet of his fleet, the Jump gauge was moving toward ready, and the gravity well indicator showed he was in tight. A good Jump, in fact. Pat Rin smiled.

"Pilot Cheever McFarland and Owner Pat Rin yos'Phelium," the voice snarled in Trade over the broadband. "You will maintain course and prepare to match locks in three Standard minutes. This is the Department of the Interior. Repeat: Maintain course and prepare to match locks. Disobey at your peril."

Pat Rin jerked forward, brought up short by the webbing. The scans showed nothing, and then several small bursts of energy— a ship maneuvering, perhaps. Or two—

An alarm warbled to life, and the aft radar scan showed him the signature of a ship, closing rapidly.

"*Fortune's Reward*, you are in our sights. The Department of the Interior is authorized to fire on you if you fail to comply. Your reply is mandatory."

Warning lights were flashing now, rippling across the board in waves of yellow. The scans showed him a second ship, starboard—and a third, hanging back, to port.

Natesa had walked him through the firing procedure, accepting the fact that his ship was now armed with her usual serenity.

Now, as she had taught him, he sighted on a ship, touched the acquire key, waited for the flash; moved to the next. And again. *Fortune's Reward* recorded its enemies, and he glanced to the status bar. The coils were recharged. Good.

Quickly, quickly, he brought the coils up, armed his weapons with a snap of a toggle, and pulled up the screen of dirty Jumps. He snatched the local coords with a slap of his hand, and took a deep breath.

Then he played the ace of spades, the gambler's best friend.

Reality shifted.

Jump glare. *Bitty Kitty* automatically declared itself to the universe. The snatched coords of his departure point were locked in, and the ship's Jump gauge showed a slow-building energy. Surebleak was a cloudy, distant disk.

There was an eternity to wait, then, knowing that any second Natesa would be Jumping in, all of his would be Jumping in—vulnerable and unwarned . . .

His hand moved, slapping up the hailing frequency.

"Intruder alert! Port Surebleak, beware! Boss Conrad declares the highest alert!"

And, finally, coils were ready. He held his breath, touched the button—

Reality shifted.

He broke in just a few minutes from his departure location, the Jump glare of four other incoming ships blossoming at the corners of a great square before him. Also before him, on courses at tangent to his—the ships of his enemy.

"In the name of Port Surebleak," he broadcast on the hailing band, his hands busy on their own errands across the board. "I demand your immediate surrender!"

He glanced down to see what his fingers had wrought; saw an interception course charted and locked; and a digit poised above the acceleration stud. He pressed it. *Fortune's Reward* answered, pushing him into the cocoon of the pilot's chair.

Across the open bands, Korval ship *Patience of Stone* announced itself. Korval ship *Handtruck II* announced itself. Korval ships *Timonium Core* and *Survey Nine* announced themselves.

The screens flared as three more ships broke Jump in a tight, triangular formation, directly into the path of the closing enemy.

"Boss Conrad requires an answer!" It took him a heartbeat to recognize the voice that lashed across the frequencies. Natesa. Chest tight, he looked to his scans; found her ship—as surely the ships of the Department would find it . . .

Korval ships *Diamond Duty*, *Crystalia*, and *Pebble Probe* announced themselves.

Natesa repeated her demand, and the three enemy ships were rotating, as if seeking targets . . .

Glare and noise. A single ship broke Jump dead ahead of Pat Rin, turning the four, three, one configuration into a cone-shaped gauntlet for the enemy ships.

Korval ship *Survey One* announced itself.

The enemy ship closest to Pat Rin increased its rotation; and a voice blared across all possible bands: "Pat Rin yos'Phelium, you are declared outlaw by Liad. Surrender or we fire!"

Surrender. Yes, certainly. He bit his lip, fingers sure and quick as he pressed acceleration, engaged the weapons comp and brought up the stored configurations.

"Flaran cha'menthi," he said quietly to the open band, and pressed the launch button.

Fortune's Reward's first missiles spread out toward the enemy. The ships of the Department, neatly contained by the oncoming Tree-and-Dragon ships, returned fire in all directions at once.

The whir and thump of the missile launch unnerved him—he knew his ship's sounds and this was new to him. Then a whir again and the ship sounded normal.

He realized that he should have been in his spacesuit *before* engaging the enemy when his shields took a hit from an energy weapon. Fortunately, the shields—like the missiles his enemy may have been surprised to find launched from a supposedly unarmed ship—were late model, of a type most usually carried by those accustomed to going into harm's way, and easily up to the task of fending off a glancing shot.

His screens had multiplied, showing him missile tracks and beam markers, energy levels and a variety of ranges. A light came up on the board and abruptly there was chatter—his small fleet talking among themselves—

"Way to go, Boss! We're on 'em now. Just let me—" Shugg.

"I'm warmed and ready on the main cutter, Cheever."—Dostie.

"I'm closing on the lead . . ."—Natesa!

He wanted to shout, to warn her off, but his throat was too tight to admit the words and his quarry had fired again and the screens showed him things he had never needed to know before and he loosed two more missiles at the computer's prompting.

"It's the perfect globe—we'll get them all!" shouted the Colonel.

"Fire on the shields," Bhupendra Darteshek said quietly. "Going to yellow."

On screen, Pat Rin saw the first of his missiles disappear—intercepted. The tracking computer reported the second and third still on course, and—

Cheever McFarland's voice came across the tight band, as easy and calm as if he were suggesting wine before dinner:

"Let's break the middle rock. If you're not engaged, hit button number four on your red board. If you can't mesh, tell me."

The range guide was fluctuating rapidly as he closed on his enemy. *Fortune's Reward* prompted him to fire two more missiles. The circle over the enemy ship was a bright, blinking green—not ready, not ready.

The ship in the forward screen changed abruptly, as if sections were peeling away . . .

It took him too long to understand what had happened, but *Fortune's Reward* was quicker. Yet another screen flashed "evasive action" and he felt the ship take itself out of his hands, and he was pressed back into the chair, while numbers began to decrease on the weapons board. The newest of his screens flashed "autodefense."

Fortune's Reward showed him the path of the nine missiles his quarry had launched, and then beeped at him.

The blinking green circle was now a dull red, firmly centered on the ship he was pursuing. He depressed the stud. The red circle changed to blinking yellow briefly, then back to ready. He fired again, eyes as much on the incoming missiles as anything else.

The ship's shield gauge went red; around him strange blos-

soms on the screens, around him silent explosions, around him
missile tracks skating away—and then sound on the hull, as if rats
ran across it, and more dull bangs and clinks—missile debris.

The board beeped. He blinked the screen into focus, saw the
question: "Acquire new target?"

The radio was filled with static and the forward screen showed
empty. His enemy must have Jumped, he thought dazedly—but
no, not that.

He had killed a ship.

A cheer arose from the radio.

"Boss got 'em!" yelled the Colonel. "Let's go to town!"

Pat Rin shook his head and leaned to his scans, searching out
the signature of Natesa's ship, heart in mouth and fingers shaking . . .

Another cheer erupted; Pat Rin saw the second enemy ship
evaporate on his aft screen, but Natesa—

Her ship sat quietly in orbit, with none to oppose her, and her
voice came wearily into the midst of yet a third round of cheer-
ing.

"I could not close quickly enough. They Jumped out."

DAY 54
STANDARD YEAR 1393

SOLCINTRA
LIAD

She went as quickly and as safely as she knew how.
She carried a hidden pellet gun, because Nova would have wished
her to, and, in truth, she was a fair shot—even Pat Rin said so.

That her sister—and quite possibly her brothers—would not
have wished her to leave the safety of Jelaza Kazone for any reason whatsoever, she did not allow to weigh with her. Even in
childhood games, her elder siblings had always desired her to
stand behind them in moments of danger, or to run away and hide

herself from whichever pursuing monster might have walked out of the pages of novel or log-book, as if she were not capable of dealing with such apparitions, as well as the realities that spawned them.

And, truly, her melant'i was clear, as she had explained to Jeeves. She was Korval's representative on planet, and it fell to her to protect the material resources of the clan, as well as its melant'i, insofar as she could.

Certainly, she had pointed out, she could not in conscience allow the Council of Clans to attempt to strip Korval of its Jumpships, one by one, in accumulated "penalties." Whether the Council's goal was to strip Korval of its ships, she could not have said. But any attempt to attach a ship would be resisted by Korval's employees and allies, with violence, if required. Thus, it was safer for all that the Council not be given any reason to make the attempt.

In keeping with her resolution to be just as prudent as Nova would wish, Anthora bowed to Jeeves in the matter of transportation, and thus found herself arriving at Solcintra in a ground car chauffeured, long-distance, by himself. She did not discover the second passenger until the car pulled to the busy sidewalk in front of the Council building.

"Really, Lord Merlin, this is the outside of enough!" she said in half-amused exasperation. "I should think *you* at least would understand my competencies."

Merlin flicked an ear and jumped out of the car with her when the door opened. Anthora paused, disconcerted for the first time since taking the decision to obey the summons of the Council.

"I believe it would be best for all if you remained with the car," she said to the cat, heedless of the people who were forced to detour around her.

Tail up, Merlin went down the walk, across a lush strip of lawn and vanished into a bank of ornamental shrubs.

"Merlin!" Anthora cried, opening her Inner Eyes, which was of course useless. If Merlin did not want her to See him, she might search fruitlessly until Liad's star cooled. Behind her, she heard the purr of an engine and turned around in time to see her car pulling into traffic. Too late, now, to return Merlin to the robot's care, even if she could find him.

"Well, then," she told the shrubbery, with a good attempt at nonchalance. "I hope you know the way home."

She waited a heartbeat or two, in case Merlin chose of his own will to reappear. He did not so choose, however. Anthora bit her lip, then moved her shoulders in an attempt to cast off concern. Merlin had his own resources, gods knew. Doubtless she would find him asleep in the middle of her bed when she returned from her imminent adventure.

Squaring her shoulders under the stiff silk of the formal Council jacket, she went up the walk and through the ornamental wooden doors, and then the security doors, made of hullplate. She crossed the common room, with its domed ceiling painted with galaxies, suns and ships, and its stone floor, worn treacherously smooth by the traffic of centuries.

At the reception desk, set before the carved metal door to the Council Chamber itself, she bowed.

"Anthora yos'Galan Clan Korval," she said. "Korval's name has been called."

She straightened, looked defiantly into the retinal scanner, and moved forward. The door swung open, slowly, before her.

The Chamber was already full; the delms of Liad in their tiered seats, some silently doing paperwork, others talking between themselves. There were no dark screens, no flags of absence. Every seat was occupied, saving only one, which indicated a concerted effort by *someone* to fill the hall.

Unusually, there were a pair of guards flanking the door, another pair on the next tier down, and two more pairs along the stone side-walls.

At the bottom of the Chamber, Speaker for Council sat behind her high desk. She looked up as the door opened and leaned slightly forward, her amplified voice colder, even, than the High Tongue could account for.

"Anthora yos'Galan Clan Korval, stand forward and face this Council."

Slowly, with what she hoped was dignity, Anthora walked down the long aisle to the floor. Around her, she felt the sharpening of attention; conversations died as she passed; her inner senses processed the climate of the room as frigid, with a stiff, damp wind a-building.

Head up, shoulders square, unhurried and deliberate, she walked down the aisle that had grown miles since the last time she had accompanied Nova to Council. Finally, she passed Korval's empty station. Twelve more steps along a blessedly flat surface brought her into proper proximity of the high desk.

Anthora stopped, bowed gently into the bitter gale of the Speaker's contempt, and turned to face the Council.

Row after row of faces, many of them people she had known all her life; cool, formal faces, looking down upon her. Deliberately, she sought out Korval's known allies and friends: Justus, Guayar, Ixin, Reptor, Mizel . . . No smiles, no bows of welcome, no gestures of support. Waiting, all of them, waiting for her to answer a question she had yet to hear.

From the nearest row, where sat the delms of the High Houses, one arose and bowed. Anthora's heart sank. Aragon was not a friend of Korval.

"Aragon calls upon Korval to answer charges of kin-stealing, and of murder. How does Korval make answer?"

It was on the end of her tongue to make answer by telling him he had taken leave of his sanity, but she could See that he had not. Aragon did not pose this question lightly; and he believed in his heart that Korval had committed these crimes. The taste of *proof* slid across her senses, which was . . . terrifying.

She bowed, with courtesy, allowing the puzzlement she felt to be seen.

"Honored Aragon has the advantage of me. Who has Korval stolen? Who has Korval slain?"

His mouth thinned. "Aragon calls upon Korval to provide the location of—"

The door at the pinnacle of the Chamber swung open and a man descended the long aisle, running, though he was far from young, making no bid for dignity at all.

"Precedence!" he shouted, breathless and out of mode. "I claim precedence!"

"You are out of order!" Speaker roared, her amplified voice a thunderclap. "The Council sits in Judgment, which is of the highest precedence!"

"I claim precedence," the man repeated, arriving on the floor. Thus close, Anthora could see that he was sweating, and trembling, with the effects of exertion, yes, but also with fear.

"Who are you?" Speaker demanded.

He bowed, in the mode of introduction merely. "Har Par dea'Liss Clan Tuxent. I sit as one of seven equal Masters of the Accountant's Guild. I claim precedence, based on planetary security."

There was a short silence. Anthora, staring up at the wall of faces, saw frowns, and puzzled glances, saw delms leaning to their nearer neighbors, heard the swelling wave of whispering.

"Explain," Speaker ordered Har Par dea'Liss.

"Yes. I and five of my colleagues have received from the seventh of our colleagues—Mr. dea'Gauss—a communication indicating that his office was under attack by enemies of Liad. He informs us that he has taken certain measures, on behalf of the planet. These include having the dies for our currency removed from the treasury to a place of safety."

The whispering delms stopped whispering, and sat staring, shock making an electric tingle in the air. The Chamber was silent.

Speaker for Council cleared her throat. "This is, of course, fabrication. The honored dea'Gauss has fallen ill and is suffering delusions. Come, Master dea'Liss, call the treasury and assure yourself that—"

"I have called the treasury," he interrupted. "Two of my colleagues have gone to the treasury. The dies are no longer there. They were removed some hours ago, by unknown persons, who showed an order from Mr. dea'Gauss." He took a hard breath. "Two more of my colleagues went immediately to the offices of dea'Gauss in the city. It is abandoned and ransacked. There are dead men in the upper halls, near what had been the private offices of the dea'Gauss. They have been shot. None carry identification. Of dea'Gauss, there is no sign." He bowed.

"I repeat: I have precedence, based upon planetary security."

Mr. dea'Gauss had been attacked in his office? Anthora shivered, and threw forth her thought. It was difficult, with so many other signatures nearby, many of them noisy with growing agitation . . .

"Aragon demands to know Korval's place in this outrage!"

She turned and looked at him, read his loathing and loaded her words with absolute certainty.

"Korval knows nothing, and demands that the Council bend all efforts to recover Mr. dea'Gauss, who has obviously fallen into the hands of brigands."

Aragon blinked, and bowed, very slightly.

"By what right does dea'Gauss remove the dies from the treasury?" someone in the mid-tier called. "Those dies belong to Liad."

Master dea'Liss turned. "The dies belong to Korval," he said flatly. "They are leased to Liad, now as from the first striking. As Korval's qe'andra, dea'Gauss has every right—indeed, it is no less than his duty—to remove the dies to safety, if he has cause to believe they are at risk. His letter makes clear that he had ample cause. The dead men in his office underscore his point."

There was an outbreak of talk at that. Behind Anthora, Speaker for Council touched her chime. The talk quieted.

Anthora saw the Speaker glance in several directions, felt the multi-leveled tension as the glance turned into a survey of the room, and then the snap of a decision taken, as if from someone in the back of the room.

"Master dea'Liss rightly claims precedence. As Anthora yos'-Galan is not empowered as a member of Council she will await the Council's attention in the Clerk's Retiring Room." She touched the chime.

As if the sound had conjured her, a Clerk appeared at Anthora's elbow

"If Lady Anthora will accompany me?" she murmured, and led the way across the front of the room, to the discreet doorway. Anthora felt the weight of eyes on her back, and felt, too, the movement of several of those guards . . . The Clerk pressed her palm against the plate and stepped back as the door swung open.

"Please await the Speaker's word here. There are refreshments, and a screen."

In the chamber behind them, several voices vied at once for the chance to be heard.

The Retiring Room was pleasant enough, with an open window overlooking the famous sunken formal Council gardens.

Anthora glanced over her shoulder as she stepped through the doorway, seeing Aragon still on his feet, with Bindan and also Etgora—and two guards falling in directly behind her, no doubt to flank the door. The Clerk pushed gently on her shoulder, hurrying her, guiding—and Anthora felt a quick, sharp prick as of a needle—

Anger flared, even as she felt the drug begin its work, seeking to slow her, to dull her senses—Idiots! Didn't they know she could turn any drug in a matter of seconds if she could but . . .

The two guards entered the room, crowding her, distracting her, as she tried to locate the mental template to match the drug and a hard hand slammed between her shoulder blades sending her reeling into a tiny chamber, seemingly filled with fog. She bumped her head, staggered, and went to her knees, gagging, continuity shattering. Fiercely, she re-established center, while the drug set up a high buzzing in her ears—and she had it! Bellaquesa and cytaline: someone had wanted her very docile, indeed.

In a heartbeat, she had neutralized the drugs; though she felt a residual queasiness. She forced her eyes open.

The door was sliding closed. She lurched to her feet and threw herself forward, hitting it full-force, bouncing backward. She twisted in mid-air, meeting the floor with hands and knees, four-square and ready, rather than flat on her back and stunned.

She had landed on a curious, sooty stain. She blinked as the information leached into her consciousness. Zena tel'Woda had died here, by her own will, rather than allow the ones who had built this device to make her into their creature.

Her inner eyes were useless; all she saw was silver, cold and reflective; her other senses were fogged in, obliterated, useless. Worse, she felt ill, weak, her thoughts fragmenting. It was not the drug at work now, but some fey power the like of which she had never imagined. It felt—it felt as if her very blood was draining into the floor she knelt upon.

Anthora screamed.

DAY 47
STANDARD YEAR 1393

SUREBLEAK PORT

Fortune's Reward landed itself neatly and with no unseemly assistance from its pilot, who then busied himself with end-of-run checks and the orderly shutdown of systems with one eye on the hull light.

Mercifully, the routines were new to him and eventually engaged his full attention. When everything was locked down to his own and his ship's satisfaction, the hull was cool enough to allow egress.

He stepped out onto the field, shivering in the ice-toothed wind, and looked about him.

Eight mining ships were grounded nearby, their tree-and-dragon emblems a-glow in the wavering dawnlight. Gravely, he bowed to them—gratitude for service well given.

"They are warriors," she murmured from just behind his right shoulder. "All honor to them."

Turning, he saw her eyes widen, though he had no time to wonder at it. "Inas." He lifted a hand, fingers silking along her dusky cheek. She smiled, extended one finger to touch his earring, and leaned forward. He caught her mouth on his.

"You terrify me," he whispered into her hair, some time later.

"We are in balance," she replied, her arms tightening about his waist. "Whatever possessed you to engage that ship?"

He stirred. "It was the ship of our enemy and it lay within my means to stop it."

"Ah." Her arms tightened painfully, then she released him and stood away, smiling ruefully.

"Come, denubia, I have turned you from the course of duty. Did the portmaster not wish you to come to her immediately?"

"So she did," he said, and offered her his arm. "Best she know me for a rag-mannered dog at once."

Natesa laughed and slid her arm through his. "Yes, I am certain she will know just that."

"I confess that I am comforted by one thing," he commented, as they strolled arm in arm toward the tower.

"What is that?"

"Why, despite having broken what I am certain are many dozens of regulations, I need not suffer the indignity of having my license pulled."

"You." Portmaster Liu sat in official state behind her desk, a professional frown on her face. Pat Rin, seated across from her in a plastic chair with one short leg, steeled himself for the impending scold.

They were alone, Natesa having been waved into the conference room, where the rest of the pilots were talking at volume, replaying the recent battle. Pat Rin folded his hands on his knee, and gazed down at the counterfeit ring, reminding himself once more that the worst the portmaster might do was read him the long form of what Anne Davis would have termed "the riot act".

"You," Claren Liu repeated. "Deploying weapons within planetary space. Firing upon and destroying a ship within planetary space. Employing non-standard Jump technique. Failure to clear Jump with this station—*twice*. Violating established space lanes. Inappropriate acceleration within planetary space. Flying without a license."

Pat Rin looked up.

The portmaster shook her head. "Why in the hell don't you have a license? Sir."

He raised an eyebrow. "Because I am not a pilot. Ma'am."

She snorted. "Best imitation I've seen in a while, then. Defend your actions—it's required for the incident report."

Pat Rin glared at her. She glared back. He shifted in his chair, which rocked unpleasantly off its short leg, and sighed.

"The ship on which I had fired was intent on performing an act of piracy. I fired to protect my ship, myself, and this port. Certainly, I would not broadcast my piloting decisions under such circumstances."

The portmaster nodded. "OK. We got the tape—that'll go with the report." She cocked an eyebrow at him. "There's names on the tape—nothing I can do about it. Just like I can't help but notice how that ring of yours has the same design as those mining ships. Should've seen it before, I guess. I've worked on bigger ports. I've seen Tree-and-Dragon tradeships."

He inclined his head, and after a moment she sighed.

"Flyer Shugg tells me he can convert those things to defense units."

"He has said the same to me," Pat Rin acknowledged, "and I fear he will need to work quickly. For you also know that one of the three pirates escaped." He met her eyes squarely. "We must assume that they will return, with reinforcements. Of the eight mining ships, four will remain here as planetary defense."

Claren Liu frowned at him. "Where are the other four going?"

"The other four—and my private vessel," Pat Rin said, softly, "are going to take the quarrel home."

The conversation snapped off as Pat Rin followed the portmaster into the conference room, and eight pairs of pilot eyes pinned him.

"Well, here's the man hisself," Andy Mack said from his lean against the far wall. "Dressed up in his nice blue jacket, just like he ain't nothin' but a dirt-hog." He looked pointedly at Claren Liu. "Thought you was gonna take care of that."

"By the book, Colonel," she said, with edged patience. "We're doing it by the book." She looked around. "Master Pilot McFarland."

The big Terran stepped forward. "Yes, ma'am."

She pointed at Pat Rin, who mustered a glare for his pilot. Cheever smiled and nodded. "Morning, Boss."

"Mr. McFarland," the portmaster insisted. "You've said that this man sat second for you, and that you'll vouch for his board skill and his knowledge of the basic piloting equations. Is that correct?"

"Basic piloting 'quations?" howled Flyer Shugg. "Portmaster, that boy pulled a smuggler's ace outta his sleeve just as pretty as any of us ever seen and you're askin' does he know his *math*?"

"Quiet!" the portmaster snapped. "Mr. McFarland?"

"Yes, ma'am, I vouch for him. He knows his math and he knows his board. Bit thin on flight time, but there ain't no doubt he's a Jump pilot." His smile grew to a grin. "I'll be pleased to sign his card."

She nodded. "I'll countersign," she said, and turned to Pat Rin. "What name do you want on your license, pilot?"

Pat Rin took a breath, sought out Natesa's face in the crowd.

"This is a farce," he said.

She shook her head. "Indeed, it is in verymost earnest." She moved a hand, showing him the portable viewer on the table. "If you wish, you may review the tape, as we have done. It plainly shows that your ship was under the hand of a pilot of skill and daring."

"Son," Andy Mack added, "ever' single one of us here saw you in action and ever' single one of us watched the tape, too. No use sayin' you ain't a pilot—we know better. Now, tell the portmaster what you want your card to call you and let Cheever here sign you up. This port needs all the pilots it can fly." He shook his head, long silver hair moving over his shoulders like fog, disreputable face unwontedly serious. "Or don't you think that feller bolted right back home, yellin' for help all the way?"

Pat Rin moved his shoulders, throwing off tension, and met the Colonel's eyes. "I think he did exactly that," he said, and looked to the portmaster.

"The name on the license should be Conrad," he said steadily. "Jonni Conrad."

Across the room, Natesa smiled. Closer to hand, Cheever McFarland nodded.

"Jonni Conrad," the portmaster repeated, and it seemed to Pat Rin that she was trying to suppress a smile of her own. "OK. It'll take a couple minutes—and I want you to know that I'm putting a limit on you. First Class, grade S—that's "small ship." The S'll drop off as soon as you complete the required flight time across all classes of Jump ship. Understood?"

Yes, as if he would live long enough to master the intricacies of moving a passenger liner—or a tradeship—through Jump. Pat Rin inclined his head. "I understand."

"Good." She pointed at Dostie, who stood up from her place at the table, cradling something supple and dark in her arms. Cheever took it from her, shook it, and held it out.

Pat Rin swallowed hard in a throat gone dry. The license—it was true that he had been sitting first board, though he had only used the ship's programs, punching buttons at the computer's prompting. Still, he could allow the license, technically. But this—no. He had no right to a Jump pilot's jacket.

"Natesa," Cheever McFarland called over his shoulder. "Boss here needs some help with his jacket."

"Certainly," she said, and stepped forward.

"Natesa . . ." he breathed, as she came to his side. "It was the ship, not me."

"Very well," she said, in her calm, soothing voice. "When we have done with the present emergency, we will lift, you and I— and you will show me. In the meanwhile, we here are all, as the Colonel has said, seasoned pilots, and we must accept the evidence of our eyes and our experience." She took hold of his jacket and perforce he slipped out of it, remembering too late the gun in its hidden pocket.

"OK," Cheever said. "Now the new one."

He held it out—a jacket in black spaceleather, of a style perhaps not recent, lined in satiny black wickaway. Hesitantly, Pat Rin slid his arms into the sleeves, felt the weight of the thing settle across his shoulders . . .

"*Yes!*" Dostie yelled.

Shugg and the Colonel howled and stamped their feet. Juntavas courier Karparov clapped politely; Pilot Darteshek bared his teeth and shook a fist in the air. Etienne Borden shouted, "A brother! We increase!" Cheever McFarland winked and gave him a broad thumbs up while Claren Liu nodded, no longer trying to hide her grin.

Natesa hugged him and kissed his cheek, which set up another round of hooting and stamping from Shugg and Mack, and gently slipped his pistol into the new jacket's inside pocket.

DAY 54
STANDARD YEAR 1393

DUTIFUL PASSAGE
JUMP

Ren Zel awoke in good time to ready himself to take prime meal with his sister and brother. As he dressed, he considered his new estate with a good deal more calm than he had been able to bring previously. Certainly, it was no ill thing to be en-clanned. Lifemated into Korval—that was . . . peculiar, certainly, and nothing that the son of an outworld mid-House might ever have aspired to, even had he not been made outcast. He wished, rather, that he might speak to the lady with whom he had shared so very much pleasure, to find what she thought of their mating, and to plan with her the best structure for their lives. Would it suit her if he remained a-ship, returning to her one relumma out of six? Was she perhaps a shipmaster in her own name, and—

He paused in the act of sealing his sleeves, blinking thoughtfully at nothing, as he recalled that Anthora taught at the College of the Dramliz in Solcintra. She held a first class license, and had completed some hours toward her master's. However, she had allowed her piloting to languish while she pursued the wizardly studies.

That there should be aught for so powerful a wizard to study at such length and depth astonished him, but there was no doubt that his recollection was correct.

And what might he bring, he thought, shaking himself free of recollection and finishing with his sleeves, to a lifemating with one of the dramliz? Shan seemed to believe that his sister had chosen him as her mate, but Ren Zel doubted that. She had not been expecting him—and she had not known his name. Therefore, some other agency was at work in the matter—the cat, perhaps; or its enormous ally, the Tree?

Well. Soon enough to ask these things when he might have actual speech with his lifemate. He only hoped that she would not repent the choice, no matter how it had been made.

He glanced at his reflection—brown hair, brown eyes, symmetrical, unexceptional face—and then at the clock. Time to make his way to the captain's office, to partake of prime with his . . . family.

The hatch came up, silent and slow, revealing the lean length of the Juntavas courier. He nodded and stepped back, waving them inside.

"We're set to lift as soon as you're strapped in."

Val Con went first, Miri at his back, her song edged with wariness. The entry corridor was thin and short, blossoming into a piloting chamber of less than spacious proportion. The board was, unusually, tiered, screens set close in a semi-circle at what would be eye-level for a pilot of Terran height. A Liaden-sized pilot would need to do something about lifting the chair, or put painful strain on her neck muscles.

"Like I said, we're cozy here," Greenshaw Porter said, leading them to the far side of the chamber. A door slid away at his touch, revealing two acceleration couches, one over the other, webbing retracted.

"This is it—first class accommodations."

Val Con inclined his head. "We thank you."

"My job," the Juntava told him, with a shrug. "I'm to say: the High Judge is grateful for the info."

"May he make good use of it."

The man grinned at that—amused savagery. "No doubt there." He slapped the upper couch, and turned away. "Make yourselves comfortable. I'll let the Tower know we're gone."

A passenger. Val Con looked at the couches, trying to remember the last time he had been *passenger* . . .

"Well," said Miri, from his shoulder. "Which do you want? Up or down?"

•   •   •

The door slid open to his palm; he stepped over the threshold and caught up short, face to face with she who had been Korval pernard'i—his sister, Nova.

It could not be said that she smiled, but at least she refrained from frowning, and inclined her head with calm cordiality.

"Pilot," she said—her usual greeting to him, but given now in the Low Tongue, in the mode between kin. "I hear I am to wish you happy."

"Pilot," he said, matching her mode with only a tiny flutter of panic. "I thank you for your good wishes."

A moment longer she stood, studying him, or so he thought, out of bland violet eyes. Almost, it seemed that she would speak again, but she lost the opportunity in the arrival of her—their—brother.

"There, now, that wasn't so bad, was it?" Shan asked brightly, though of whom he asked it was not entirely clear. "Sister, don't eat him! I swear he's better behaved than any of us here—including Priscilla—and will gain Korval entry to Houses long since closed to us by reason of our dreadful manners."

"I make no doubt," she murmured, and of a sudden *did* smile—faintly, but with real warmth. "I feel for you most strongly, new brother—joined to a clan as outlaw as it is odd!" She glanced aside. "Shan, surely he wants some wine."

"Surely he does, as he's hardly a lackwit," their brother replied, and put a big hand on Ren Zel's shoulder, urging him gently toward the bar. "Come along, child, let us fortify you. Red? White? Brandy?"

"Red, if I may."

Shan extended a long arm and held the decanter high, apparently considering its all-but-full state.

"This seems sufficient to fill your glass, and mine, too. Though I fear we're out if Priscilla is drinking red."

"White, please," her deep voice said.

Ren Zel turned in time to see the door to the innermost chamber—the quarters she shared with her lifemate—slide shut behind her. She smiled.

"Good shift, brother. Have you resigned yourself to your fate?"

He felt his mouth curve into an answering smile. "As fates go, it appears . . . less tiresome than some," he told her. "I do look forward to a conversation with my lady. There are those things that we must settle between us."

There was a sound to the right, as if Nova had sneezed, but Priscilla merely nodded gravely.

"You may then rejoice in the news that our sister brings us," Shan said, putting a glass of the red in his hand. "We are returning to Liad, immediately!"

"Do not allow Shan to persuade you that you will be with your lady *immediately*," Nova cautioned, stepping forward. "The delm's word is that we are to raise Liad, yes. But there we will hang in orbit until he releases us to the planet."

"Weeks, months, years!" Shan intoned, with mock dismay, handing Priscilla her glass.

"Very likely," his sister said gravely, though Ren Zel thought he saw the glimmer of her faint smile.

"Well, in that case, we do what we can to strengthen our spirits. I see a feast has been laid for us, and the only thing that keeps us from enjoying it is Gordy." Shan raised his glass, silver eyes quizzical over the rim. "Or, shall I say, lack of Gordy?"

Priscilla smiled. "He'll be here—soon."

The request for entry chime sounded.

"Or even at once," Shan said and called, "Come!"

The door slid away to admit Gordy Arbuthnot, foster-son of Shan and Priscilla, as well as Shan's true-cousin, on the Terran side.

"Cousin Nova." He bowed, correctly, as between kin, and then walked straight up to Ren Zel, face and eyes serious, shoulders just a little stiff.

"Hi, Ren Zel."

"Hello, Gordy," he said, gently, careful of the moods and manners of a halfling. It was not impossible, after all, that Gordy held his cousin Anthora in . . . esteem—and who was Ren Zel dea'Judan to call him a fool?

"Priscilla says you're lifemated—truly lifemated—to Anthora. Is that true?"

"Yes."

The young face relaxed into a smile. "That's great. I'm really glad." He bowed, jauntily. "Ge'shada, pilot. I wish you and yours a life of joy."

Ren Zel felt tears rise, hid them with his own bow. "My thanks."

"And now," said Shan, "we can eat."

• • •

The meal was rather less boisterous than the informal reception, for Nova bore news of yet another kinsman. It seemed that Pat Rin yos'Phelium had not followed protocol in terms of reporting in. Nova was inclined to find this disturbing, and solicited the advice of kin. The conversation turning on where Cousin Pat Rin might most reasonably be supposed to have taken himself, and strategies for finding him, Ren Zel was left to listen, and watch, and grow acquainted with these who were now his family.

Listening, he reached for his glass—and froze as his ears became filled with a roaring, not unlike wind, and a voice edged with panic rang inside his skull.

"Ren Zel! I need you!"

There was a moment of heart-numbing cold, and a sensation not unlike passing through a bank of particularly tenacious fog. Ren Zel shook his head, banishing the mist, and discovered himself kneeling on an icy metal floor. Beside him was Anthora, on hands and knees above a char mark.

"Ren Zel?" she whispered.

"Here." He stood—say, he tried to stand, but the ceiling was too low to allow him to do so in comfort; he must need round his shoulders and duck his head. Uncomfortably bent, he looked around him, taking in the hard silver walls, seeing the bright lines of fire bent and twisted back upon themselves, warped and pale, excepting only the conflagration that streamed from the kneeling woman down into the cold floor, for all the worlds like blood rushing from a wound.

"Anthora!" He dared to use the mode of Command. "You must stand."

"Yes." Clumsily, she gained her feet, to stand bent as he was, her hair draggled and limp around a face that was shockingly pale.

"What place is this?" he demanded, moving to her side, crabwise, and slipping an arm around her waist.

"I don't know. I—it is drinking me. The walls—they reflect any ripple of power back, at double—quadruple!—strength. I dare not force the door . . ." She made a breathless sound he scarcely recognized as a laugh. "If I could." She swallowed and pushed her head against his hunched shoulder. She was trembling. He raised a hand and stroked her cold hair.

"Then we open it another way. There must be a control box . . ."

He frowned at the featureless walls, the bitter floor, but all was—

"There!"

Anthora stirred, lifted her head a fraction and shook her hair away from her eyes. "Where?"

"Below the decking, there, do you see?" He released her and hunkered down, studying the various relays and switches in the box below the floor. He felt her hand on his shoulder as she lowered herself beside him, peering.

"Yes, I see it," she breathed. "But, beloved, it's on the other side of the floor."

"Hmm," he said, tracing wires with his eyes. "I believe . . ." He pointed. "Do you see that connection? If that were bent aside, the door would open and we could walk away."

"Ren Zel, I cannot reach those elements, and neither can you." Her voice caught. "We're going to die."

"No." He spun on a heel, nearly bowling her over. "We are *not* going to die. Believe it and you do their work for them!"

For one heartbeat—two—she stared at him, eyes wide. Then, she extended a hand to touch his cheek. "I see. Forgive me, denubia. I'll not be so fainthearted again." Her eyes dropped and there was the control box, plainly visible to Ren Zel, and through him, to her. The connection he had pointed out was a fragile thing; why, a cat might bend it aside . . .

"Yes!" Ren Zel whispered. He bent forward and she lost contact. The floor solidified; her inner vision fogged. She grabbed his shoulder.

There, beneath the floor plate, the connection. Hooked around the connection were four pearlescent claws adorning a large and rather furry white foot. The foot pulled, down and sideways. The connection bent, twisted—broke.

Across the tiny silvered room, the door slid open.

Anthora half-rose, staggered, vision whiting, and felt strong arms around her waist, sweeping her off her feet . . .

"Run!" Ren Zel shouted, his voice already shredded by distance.

She tucked, and hit the floor of the antechamber rolling. She heard a shout; felt hands on her shoulders and wrenched out of the guard's grip, slamming into the legs of a chair, the hidden pistol falling into her hand. The guard lunged, trying to grab her; trying to throw her back into the box.

She fell sideways, and fired point-blank into his face.

The room was quiet, bird song wafting in the open window. Anthora lay on the floor, her back against the chair legs, retching, unable to escape the sight of the guard's head exploding, though her eyes were closed.

Something furry slapped her cheek. She opened her eyes to slits and encountered a familiar furry face very close to her own.

"Merlin." Clumsily, she disentangled herself from the chair and clawed her way to her feet. The door leading to the Council Chamber had an ancient mechanical lock on it, which she snapped into place, singing the praises of whichever god or goddess held soundproofing among their honors.

Door locked, she leaned her back against it, feeling Merlin pressed against her leg. A pleasant breeze informed the room, spiced with the scent of the tripina tree shading the open window. After the draining silver horror of the box, she felt entirely safe and secure here.

And that, she told herself sternly, *is illusion. Look to reality, dramliza!*

Unwillingly she moved from the door; forced herself to approach her former cell, and look within. Empty. That was good. Ren Zel had indeed escaped to safety.

Which she should do—and that quickly. For surely whoever had set the trap would return to remove it. She attempted a scan, wincing as the din from the Chamber slammed into her abused senses.

"We must leave," she whispered. "Merlin . . ."

But the cat was already moving, purposefully, away from the door to the Council Chambers and the misshapen black box, its door gaping open on horror. Anthora turned her face away and followed, averting her eyes as she edged past the body of the guard.

Merlin set a brutal pace through the service corridors. She was soaked with sweat and shaking badly by the time they gained the door that opened to the outside. At that, the luck had held; they'd met no one else on their escape route.

The luck changed when they hit the sidewalk.

"Wait!" she heard a man's voice shout, quite close at hand. "That's her!"

Anthora ran, the sound of pursuit too close behind; caught a glimpse of gray to her right and slightly ahead.

Dodging respectable pedestrians, she turned a corner, and heard the roar of a familiar motor.

"Jeeves!"

The car accelerated, door rising.

"There she is!" came the shout from behind. Involuntarily, Anthora glanced over her shoulder, saw her two pursuers round the corner, saw the guns in their hands—and the streak of gray, which was Merlin, launching himself, claws extended into the face of the lead gunman.

Roaring, Jeeves arrived. Anthora threw herself into the open hatchway. "Merlin! Come quickly!"

The cat leapt—not for the safe haven, but for the second gunman. He hit the man's shoulder, claws sunk deep.

"Merlin!" Anthora screamed, acceleration pressing her into the seat. The door began to drop. "No! Jeeves, we cannot leave Merlin!"

Implacably, the door fell, locked; the car surged forward, braked, back end swinging 'round and they were hurtling forward into the everyday traffic of a Solcintran afternoon, considerably exceeding the public safety speed, leaving her pursuers, and a large gray cat, behind.

Anthora began to cry.

"Run!" he shouted. "The door is open!"

Gasping, he fell, his shoulder slamming against the hard floor, his vision a chaos of images, overlain by fiery threads. He concentrated, saw her hit the floor rolling, as a pilot would, gun in hand as she fired and—and lost that image entirely, replaced by a bright-lit room and the unmistakable taste of ship's air. An arm came 'round his shoulders, easing him up; a squeeze bottle was forced into his hand.

"Drink," said Priscilla Mendoza. "Electrolytes."

He managed to get the bottle to his lips, squeezed a healthy mouthful and swallowed with a shudder. He felt the vile stuff hit his stomach, mixing uneasily with dinner and terror.

"Easy." Priscilla's hand was firm and sisterly on his shoulder; squinting through the haze of golden lines, he made out Nova standing above him, purple eyes holding an emotion he identified as astonishment.

"Drink again," Priscilla told him. "Then food."

"And at some point, when you feel it proper," said Nova, "you will tell us what just happened to you."

"Nova, let be," Shan said sternly, from beyond Ren Zel's vision.

"Let be? Did he or did he not sit there—frozen and scarcely breathing—for the best part of half-an-hour? Does he have these fits often? I wonder what will go forth, should he have one at the board."

"Nova . . ." A clear warning note, there.

Ren Zel finished the stuff in the squeeze bottle, concentrated and set it carefully on the floor. He looked up into Priscilla's face, squinting a little to bring her into focus among all the pulsating golden threads . . .

"Better?" she asked.

"There is a device," he said, "that eats dramliz."

Her face hardened. "There have been several such, throughout history."

"This one is new," he told her. "It—they caught Anthora."

"What?" Nova drew nearer. "Anthora is at Jelaza Kazone. Not even she would be so shattered-brained as to—"

"Wait." He held up a hand, agitated. "Wait, I . . ." He closed his eyes, and memory flowed.

"The Council—Korval is called to answer—to answer for kin-stealing, for murder—and dea'Gauss—dea'Gauss is missing, and he has hidden the dies. They asked her to wait in a Clerk's room and the trap—the trap was there."

"In a room off the Council Chamber?" That was Shan again, his voice as serious as Ren Zel had ever heard it. "Sister, if the Council itself is hunting us, I doubt the delm's wisdom in returning to Liad."

"We must," Nova said, but she hardly sounded certain. "At least to orbit—but Anthora is a prisoner!"

"No, she's not," Priscilla said coolly. "The door was open—you heard him say so."

"The door opened," he agreed. "But I could not stay with her. I do not know . . ." It came to him that he might use those glowing lines of power to his own ends. He might, in fact, go back to her, stand at her side and work with her to the destruction of their enemies. He—

"Gently, friend," Shan said, dropping into his range of vision in a veritable burst of gold. "You have done much this hour. Eat first." He held out a sandwich. Ren Zel took it, suddenly ravenous, despite the food he had already eaten, and wolfed it in three bites. A second sandwich appeared and he accorded it the same treatment, then drained the glass of tea that came after.

He sighed. "I am glad," he murmured, "to find the gridwork so strong here. Inside the box, one could hardly see the threads, and those that could be seen were pale and fragmented."

There was a pause.

"You of course," Nova said to Priscilla—or possibly to Shan, "know what he is talking about."

"Not . . . entirely." Priscilla cleared her throat. "Ren Zel, what threads are these?"

He blinked up at her, seeing the lines so crowded about her that she fairly shone.

"Why, the lines," he said, somewhat baffled, for surely *she* could see them, dramliza that she was? "The lines that tie everything together."

"Oh," she said softly. "Those lines." She exchanged a glance with her lifemate.

"Can you see these . . . lines?" demanded Nova.

"No," Priscilla said, still soft. "No, I can't. But I have it on the authority of those who can that they do indeed exist and perform exactly the function Ren Zel describes."

"The only difficulty," he said, in an effort to be as clear as possible, and not in any way to complain, "is that they are so plentiful and vibrant here that it is difficult to see beyond them to—to everyday things. I fear that I might put my teacup down on a line and have it smash against the floor . . ."

"Now that," said Shan, "I can help with." He leaned forward and held up a broad brown finger. "Focus on my finger, if you please—no, *not* that way—use your outer eyes! Look as nearly as you like, but only at my finger."

After a brief struggle, he was able to manage it—and felt something click, as if a relay had snapped into place. The lines of power vanished from his awareness and the totality of the captain's office snapped into being.

He sighed, as did Nova yos'Galan.

"Dramliza?" she said.

"There was never any doubt," Shan said, rising and reaching a hand down to Ren Zel. "Up you go, Pilot."

• • •

The car fishtailed 'round a corner and fled down an alleyway at a speed that was far from considerate of human sensibilities—even when the human in question was a pilot.

Anthora had long since stopped crying, and now sat, tense, her hands fisted on her lap. Four times had Jeeves struck out for Jelaza Kazone. Four times, they had been blocked, and nearly surrounded, hounded back into the city.

"Go to the port," she said quietly.

"Ms. Anthora, you are Korval's presence on Liad." The robot's voice was shockingly calm as the car careered madly down an alleyway, and swung into another, more narrow, speed, if anything, increasing.

"If you leave Liad, Korval's claim to its material goods and properties is forfeit."

"Go to the port," she repeated. "*I* abandon nothing."

There was a pause—short for her, long for Jeeves—then a respectful, "Yes, I see. The port."

Even traveling at speed and with stealth, they arrived at Binjali's barely ahead of their pursuers.

Anthora had dared one call, and Master Trilla was expecting them. The gate began to open as they came into the approach, and closed after them with a clang. Jeeves gunned the motor, fair flying down the yard to the singleship on its hotpad and the woman in working leathers standing by.

The door rose, and Anthora leaned forward.

"Go," she told the robot. "Leave the car."

"Yes," said Jeeves.

The control panel went dark as the car rolled to a serene stop. Anthora stepped out onto the tarmac and inclined her head.

"Master Trilla."

"Anthora," Binjali's owner said, in her outworld accent. "Ship's ready when you are."

"Thank you," she said. "Be warned. They are directly behind us.

Trilla grinned, feral. "We've some surprises, never fear it. Go on, now. Good lift."

"Safe landing," Anthora returned properly, and entered the ship.

• • •

The ship rose swiftly, breaking a dozen regs in the first six seconds of flight. Grimly, Anthora flew on, ignoring the outraged demands of the Tower, flying by hand, so there was nothing to spill
and be captured by Korval's enemy.

Up, up, very nearly straight up, then a sharp roll, and down, as
swiftly as she dared, not quite a scout descent, not quite—but
swift enough, as the luck willed it.

In her screens was the Tree, rapidly growing to enormity. The
house screens were active, a blue crackle along the edge of her
inner vision. She keyed the short sequence in, sent along the pirate band.

The blue crackle died, the ship fell through and she slammed
on the retros, fighting gravity now—and winning, as the singleship touched nicely down in the center of Jelaza Kazone's formal
public gardens.

It had been a grand and busy several days of transit; so busy that
Hazenthull Explorer had been able to immerse herself in the various learnings of language and custom—and forget for long hours
together that the senior was dead. And why.

But it came at last that Commander Angela-call-me-Liz
Lizardi, to whom the troop had been detached for this portion of
the venture, had ordered them to ready themselves for departure.
Reluctantly, Hazenthull folded away her studies, found Diglon
Rifle in the rec hall listening, with four tens other of the merc
common troop, to the turtle Sheather tell of his campaign against
the Juntavas upon the world called Shaltren.

Returned to the quarters they kept in common, Diglon set
about an efficient and orderly weapons check. Hazenthull undertook the same, and likewise made a review of the plan as they had
been allowed to know it.

It was a simple enough plan, on its surface, but Hazenthull believed that a man who had engineered the theft of three Yxtrang
fighter craft from the very fields of the Fourteenth, envisioned a
more complex undertaking than she, in her youth and ignorance,
could apprehend. Still, it would be a welcome thing to close with
an enemy—and the scout's plan, simple or complex, promised action.

Weapons checked and plan reviewed, Hazenthull hesitated on
the edge of her next duty—but it was a duty, and one she had
shirked, for reasons she did not care to study too closely.

Squaring her shoulders, she walked across the room, to where Nelirikk Explorer, Hero and aide to Captain Miri Robertson, sworn to the descendants of Jela's blood, sat over a piece of fancy work.

He looked up as she came forward, his eyes blue and non-committal, as befit a Hero. Hazenthull hesitated—which was her weakness—steeled herself and spoke in the explorer's dialect.

"You asked a question, before, and I gave you no answer. We are on the edge of action and I may find glory upon the morrow. I would tell you, now, between ourselves, why explorers marched with the common troop."

He used his chin to point at the chair opposite him. "Sit and speak."

Sit she did. Speak—that was more difficult.

She mustered discipline, aimed her eyes forward and just over Nelirikk Explorer's right shoulder.

"We—Gernchik Explorer and Hazenthull Explorer—were assigned to march with the common troop in a disciplinary action following Hazenthull Explorer's field report in which Major Shevnir Quartermaster was named as keeping slack discipline, which had lost for us several interesting and irreplaceable specimens. Gernchik—would have written a different report. I believed that an explorer's duty outranked a major's pride."

She stopped, then finished it, though the section of wall she had been staring at was starting to blur.

"The senior died because I am a fool, and not worthy—never worthy—of his teaching."

Silence followed this, which was oddly comforting, though she would not have hesitated if Nelirikk had ordered her to draw her sidearm and shoot herself through the ear.

"Your answer is heard," he said, which was the old, familiar explorer's acknowledgment. "Now that your senior has gone to glory's reward, it comes to you, as his junior, to perform your duty as he would have performed it. It is no light charge, for Gernchik was an explorer of the first rank."

Hazenthull blinked. "He was that," she said hoarsely.

"Go now," Nelirikk Explorer told her. "There is an hour for rest before Commander Lizardi calls us."

She did not feel like resting, but Gernchik would not have argued the point. Hazenthull stood, saluted and went over to her bunk, where she stretched out beside her weapons and her pack, and closed her eyes to think.

"**You** left him!" Anthora shouted.

On days other than this one, her emotion was such that teacups would have trembled against their saucers and wine glasses chimed their cheeks against each other. It was not entirely impossible that a stool might have become spontaneously airborne.

Today was a day like no other. Anthora stood in the middle of Jelaza Kazone's back kitchen, dirty and draggled, tears of anguish and of fury cutting rivulets of cleanliness down her grimy cheeks, and was reduced to stamping a foot for emphasis.

"You left Merlin among our enemies and I ordered you to stop!"

Jeeves' head-ball flickered soft orange lightnings; his wheels rumbled against the floor as he rolled over to put a kettle on for tea.

"Miss Anthora, you are aware that I have priorities. The highest of those is the protection of the human lives of Clan Korval. I must insure your safety at any cost, no matter how high."

Anthora scrubbed at her face, widening the muddy streaks. "But you and Merlin are—friends."

"Old friends," Jeeves agreed. "Merlin was among the first to make me welcome when I came to be yos'Galan's butler." There was a pause; the flickerings in his head-ball increased in rapidity—and all at once ceased.

"Perhaps it will ease you to learn," the robot said slowly, "that Merlin has undertaken a task in coordination with Jelaza Kazone. In essence it is a guerilla action, which carries a high factor of risk. But Merlin is old and skillful. I have confidence that he will succeed in taking the war to the enemy."

Anthora closed her eyes. "You say that Merlin goes ahead, to pinpoint our enemy's location so that more . . . concerted action may be brought against them."

"That is the core of our strategy, yes."

"We have no army to call upon, Jeeves. Only yourself, and me—and the Tree."

"Well," said Jeeves, lifting the kettle from its ring and pouring tea into a tall, workmanlike mug, "that's a start—and you must not discount your lifemate, who seems, if you will allow me to say so, a wizard to reckon with."

She blinked, and fell suddenly still, the way of Ren Zel's walking through hyperspace suddenly and most shockingly clear.

"Yes," she said, softly. "He is a wizard to reckon with. And so, of course, is the Tree."

Alone in his cabin, Ren Zel staggered and grabbed the wall.

It came again—a cool, green rippling across his vision, longer this time, deeper, almost displacing the reality of the walls around him. He closed his eyes, and the green resolved into an image of the vast Tree in Korval's garden, seen as if he were looking up into the branches from below.

Good evening, elder, he heard her voice in his mind's ear. *I wish to undertake a journey.*

"Anthora," he whispered, and had the sense that she heard him—though it was impossible that she could, with the *Passage* in hyperspace and her standing in the free air of her garden. "Anthora, what are you doing?"

Beloved. Jeeves tells me that Merlin has been sent ahead into the heart of our enemy's territory, to act as our scout and our trojan. I go to his side, to rescue our servant, and to confound our enemy.

"Our enemy? Who is—" Memory rose and spilled over, flooding him for a moment or a lifetime, and when he at last shook his head free and gasped a deep lungful of air, he knew everything that she knew of the Department of the Interior, of Merlin's probable whereabouts—and dea'Gauss', too.

Yes, he heard her in his mind's ear, *now.*

"No!" Ren Zel yelled, waking echoes from the metal walls, but he was too late.

The image of the garden and the Tree faded, leaving only gray.

CLUTCH HOMEWORLD

Aelliana walked the circumference of the ship in company with Handler as Daav searched his memories of Diary and scout lore and went over, again and again, what they had said to the Elders. She admired the home star on the horizon and calculated orbits and probabilities, considered the carefully placed moons, and considered, too, the new crystal knife worn at their hip . . .

"Go." The voice had come up from the depths of that strange room buried six thousand paces deep in the hillside. The room's shape was such that whispers could be heard, one end to the other, and half-a-dozen flickering flames enough to give each of the dozens of Elders substance as they . . . sat . . . motionless the while. How long that while had been . . . was difficult to fathom.

They had asked. They had asked of clan, they had asked of the nature of lifemates, they had asked of the Tree, and of Jela, and of the Tree and Jela, from the Diaries, about Daav's suppositions regarding Jela, about Val Con and Miri, about the Tree, about the seed pods and, once again, the Tree and how it shared—and then they asked about Aelliana and Daav.

Finally, they had asked about seed pod distributions and the known locations of the children of the Tree . . .

And then, they had said, "Go. Thank you for the gift of your time, Elders of Korval. Go."

"Daav, one comes—"

It was Edger, moving quickly.

"Aelli and Daav, you must come with me," he said. "The Elders have decided."

DAY 53
STANDARD YEAR 1393

SUREBLEAK

It was late. His household, saving the night guards, slumbered about him. He had risen from his own bed some hours ago, taking great care not to awaken his lady. Now, he sat behind his desk, Silk the cat a coiled, heavy warmth against his belly, writing in the log book.

He had long since given over trying to reproduce the original Diaries—his memory was too desperately incomplete. Rather, he had summarized what he knew of the crisis which had brought Korval-pernard'i to invoke Plan B; related his encounter with the agents of the Department of the Interior; and then meticulously noted down the minutia of Boss Conrad's days, taking great care to show how these actions had bearing upon the finality of the clan's Balance. He was disciplined, and wrote every day, so the book was fully caught up to event.

Indeed, it was somewhat in advance of event, as he had already written of the departure of four mining ships and a pleasure yacht for the homeworld, there to exact Balance from the enemy.

He had recorded the names of the pilots who were sworn to fly in this mad venture: Master Pilot Cheever McFarland, First Class Pilot Bhupendra Darteshek, First Class Pilot Andrew Mack, First Class Pilot Dostie Welsin, First Class Pilot Jonni Conrad. He also listed the names of their ships: *Diamond Duty*, *Timonium Core*, *Crystalia*, *Survey Nine*, *Fortune's Reward*. He had paused a moment, then, listening to the cat purring sleepily on his lap, and meditating over the list of stalwarts.

Pilot Darteshek had been a surprise enlistee; Pat Rin had expected him to return to the Juntavas, now that he had delivered his package and satisfied his curiosity. But, no. He had stayed behind while Vilma Karparov returned to their employer, and Pat Rin's inquiry into the matter had won him the pilot's thin smile—and nothing else.

He had no doubt it was Natesa who had arranged for the courier pilot's presence among what Cheever McFarland had dubbed, with no apparent irony, the "strike team." He had not found it necessary to ask. If it comforted her to know that there would be a Juntavas pilot by him during the upcoming affair, then surely it was no more than simple kindness to accept both her talisman and her hope.

For himself, he saw . . . some hope. That his hand had been forced and his timing thrown askew—well, what choice had he? The Department of the Interior had located him easily. He did not do them the disservice of believing that they would hesitate for an instant to hold Surebleak at hostage. He preferred to go to them on his own terms, using what advantage might come from consternation.

He closed his eyes, going over his arrangements once more.

"Pat Rin?"

He opened his eyes and turned his head, finding her, a shadow in the shadowed doorway.

"Inas," he said, feeling Silk shift against him in protest. "You should be asleep."

"And you should not?" She came forward, shadow taking substance, the flame-stitched gauze robe blazing as she crossed into the light. "*I* do not lift in six hours. Indeed, should it suit me, I may sleep the day away."

"Indeed you might," he said cordially. "And did you say that you would do so, I should certainly put off my lift in order to observe this miracle for myself."

She laughed, low and musical, and leaned against the desk at his side. The gaudy robe illuminated her dark beauty, and flowed tantalizingly along her slender shape. The sash was done but loosely at her waist, and her dainty feet were bare.

"You will freeze," he told her, but she shook her head lightly.

"Not if you come back to bed and warm me."

He raised an eyebrow "Underdealt, my lady."

"Do you think so? I merely wish to bid you a proper farewell. How am I in error?"

It was the word 'farewell' that caught his ear and sent his glance to the log book, sitting open in its pool of light, pen ready to hand beside it.

"No error at all," he said slowly, and lifted his eyes to hers. "Inas . . ."

She returned his gaze calmly. "Yes, beloved. What has gone amiss?"

"Amiss . . ." He looked away, and bent forward to lay his hand on the book. The movement disturbed Silk, who leapt to the floor with a sleepy protest.

"This becomes yours—as my—as my lifemate and—my heir. If I do not return . . ." He shook his head. "In the back of the book, I have written . . . somewhat . . . of our kin. If any should come here, calling for aid, they must be cared for . . ."

She placed her hand over his on the book. "As your lifemate—and your heir—I will honor the book and study it. I will write in it every day, as you do, for the instruction of those to come. And in the meanwhile, should any of our kin find their way here, I will care for them as best I am able, until your return."

Pat Rin cleared his throat. "The dice may fall with whimsy," he said softly. "I may not return."

"That is not acceptable," she replied, and lifted her hand from his, sliding her fingers caressingly under his chin and turning his face up to hers.

"You will return," she said. "Swear it."

Tears filled his eyes. He blinked them away and smiled for her.

"You hold my heart," he said. "If I am able, I will return to you. I swear it."

She smiled then, knowingly. "Liaden," she murmured, and kissed him, not at all gently.

DAY 54
STANDARD YEAR 1393

SOLCINTRA
LIAD

The distress signal blasted through the Tower, bringing the technical crew scrambling back from its tea-break, slapping up emergency screens, pulling in satellite feeds—and swearing, softly, and in several different languages.

"*Kynak-on-the-Rocks*, we have you located," the traffic controller murmured, her hands busy across her keyboard. "State the nature of the problem, and whether you are able to assume orbit."

"Shit no, we can't assume orbit!" Irascible Terran erupted out of the speakers. "We're holed, damn you! Nothing other than plain and fancy piracy. I call upon the Department of the Interior to Balance the damage it has deliberately dealt to Mercenary Unit Higdon's Howlers. I want a representative of that Department to meet me when we land—and we *are* landing, Tower! Give us an approach!"

There was a hurried consultation between the scan tech and the assistant Port Master on Duty—

"We've got leakage," he muttered, upping the magnification of his scans so the rest of the crew could see it.

"We've got a ship approaching Port on a dangerous course, claiming damage and an oxygen emergency," the traffic controller snarled, fingers flying over her board. "They're coming in, no matter what. I'm giving them to Mid-Port general yard. Comm-tech, call the proctors and get a squad over there! Who knows what this Department of the Interior is? Call them, too!" She subsided into silence then, excepting the occasional mutter featuring mercenary ships landing in Solcintra Mid-Port and that had better be two squads of proctors . . .

The comm-tech swung 'round to her board, alerted the proctors, then accessed the planetary directory. Department of the Interior was not listed. The tech bit her lip, and shot a query to the incoming Terran.

"How the bloody hell do *I* know how to get hold of them?" the same hugely annoyed voice snarled. "All I know is that they claim to be in charge of Liad and that they've holed my ship, damn their eyes, and they *will* pay for it—and pay handsome well!"

Proper enough, thought the comm-tech, if the Department—whatever it was—had damaged the Terran's ship, as he seemed certain. And the Department claimed to be "in charge" of Liad? The comm-tech was Liaden, and knew of only one entity that could remotely be supposed to be "in charge" of Liad.

She punched in the code for the Speaker of the Council of Clans.

"The Department of the Interior is not represented by this Council," Speaker for Council told the port comm-tech testily.

"Request assistance in locating this Department, Speaker," the tech sent back, one eye on her screen, where the Terran transport was growing larger and more dismaying by the moment. "Incoming ship cites a matter of Balance with the Department of the Interior. I allow it to be Terran, ma'am, but the captain further informs us that the Department of the Interior is "in charge" of Liad."

"That is absurd," Speaker stated. "Its wits are wandering."

"Yes, ma'am, possibly so. However, it is crying Balance. Someone must answer, else they may sit here for as long as they like, using port resources and paying nothing, contingent upon receiving an answer."

There was a pause, long enough for the comm-tech to reconsider the wisdom of teaching law to Speaker for Council.

"Very well," Speaker said. "Please convey to the captain of the Terran vessel the compliments of the Council and inform him that, in order to pursue his claim of Balance we must know the name of an individual representing the Department of the Interior."

"Yes, Speaker," said the comm-tech, with no small amount of relief. "I will pass that message."

"They want a name, do they?" the Terran demanded of the comm-tech. "Fine, here's a name you can give them: Bar Vad yo'Tornier. He calls himself Commander of Agents."

SOLCINTRA
LIAD

The prisoner was not young. He was not Scout-trained. He was—no longer—armed. He inspired neither fear nor the premonition that he was both a danger and a threat to the organization—and to the completion of the Plan.

In fact, the prisoner was old. He sat quietly in the tiny holding cell, the dim blue light casting strange shadows along his face. From time to time, he spoke—numbers, most often. Sums. Account identifiers. Dates. Followed by such elucidations as, "account confiscated," "permissions rescinded," "account inactive." There were few surprises, there.

Prompted, he made other statements, not entirely understood by his auditors: "Phase Two begins when the fourth roll-call is missed."

"Phase Three begins when the fifth roll-call is missed."

"The Exchange declares a trading holiday when the sixth roll-call is missed."

Commander of Agents allowed himself a sigh. This was the second set of drugs. Neither it nor the first had elicited information regarding Korval's effective and surprising defense of the planet Surebleak. The prisoner was likewise ignorant of the locations of Korval's hidey-holes and safeplaces; and resistive of the suggestion that Surebleak might be such a place.

The Commander moved a hand, calling for the third and most potent drug.

The technician hesitated.

The Commander turned his head to look at her.

"Forgive me," she bowed as one to the ultimate authority. "It merely occurs to me, Commander—if this man does indeed hold information vital to our success . . . He is an old man, in good general health, but lately subjected to several severe systemic shocks. There is the possibility of an overload, should we introduce the next drug before this dose has run the system."

"Understood."

The Commander considered the prisoner. Did he hold information vital to the Plan? Surely, he did. And, just as surely, he would be made to give that information into the Department's keeping. The third drug—the third drug was ruthless. Possibly, it should have been administered at once, despite the unfortunate side-effects. The Commander had reasoned that the lesser drugs would leave the prisoner largely intact, and that there might well be need for him sooner than an . . . amended . . . personality could be stabilized.

The need for the information he held was greater than any nebulous future usefulness. After all, it was not unusual for old men to die.

He felt a vibration run up his right arm and glanced down at his wrist-comm, noting at once the "most urgent" tag, and the request that he return to his office.

"Call me before you administer the next drug," he told the tech, and moved toward the door.

"GR17-67. GR17-68," the prisoner said, tonelessly. "Drawing rights invalidated."

The Commander checked, dismayed—for, here, at last, was information, plain, unambiguous—and crippling. If the prisoner was to be believed, the Department had lost access to two of its most lucrative funding sources.

"Check that!" he snapped at the agent standing silently at the prisoner's back.

"Commander."

"GR 24-89," the prisoner said. "Drawing rights invalidated."

The Commander turned and stared at him, seeing an old man slumped in a chair, the dim blue light accentuating the weary lines of his face, eyes unfocused and dull.

"Check that," he directed the agent, and let himself out of the holding cell.

The loss of funding source GR 24-89 would be . . . catastrophic. The Commander held himself to a walk, allowing no taint of turmoil to touch his face. It would have to be checked. It would all have to be checked. Possibly the prisoner had lied—but when had the dea'Gauss ever lied?

• • • •

Funny, how familiar it was: the gravity, the taste of the air, the smell of the grass, the green-tinged sky, the warmth of the sunlight against her hair—all of it said, "Welcome home."

Of course, this wasn't her home—not even close. The feeling of welcoming familiarity came straight from Val Con, just like the "memory" of the path she was walking to Jelaza Kazone, and the access codes tingling in the tips of her fingers.

She paused on the top of the last hill sloping down into Dragon's Valley, and turned to look back. Squinting, she could make out the Tower at Solcintra Port, stretching tall and black into the greenish sky. Val Con'd be well out of the port by now, she reckoned, resisting the impulse to find out for sure.

Don't jog the man's elbow, Robertson, she told herself severely, and turned to look out over the valley.

There was the Tree, dark green, dark brown, and 'way too high, its branches tangling with clouds . . .

Welcome.

It was the same sense of warm green joy that had overwhelmed her in her dream—only days ago? She smiled, more wry than not, and nodded toward its mile-high form.

"Jelaza Kazone," she said. "The safest place in the galaxy."

Right.

She brought her sights down, and got her first look at the clan seat, Jelaza Kazone, the house. Distance and the looming Tree worked to make the building seem small—a scale model, maybe, or a toy. She knew better. She could've recited the number of rooms, drawn a map of the public halls—and the private ones—and a map of the inner garden, too.

All from Val Con's knowledge of the place.

"I grew up at Trealla Fantrol," he told her, softly, from memory, "but I was born to be Korval. Uncle Er Thom had been fostered at Jelaza Kazone. He made certain that I knew it as well as he did."

Miri sighed.

Standin' here, gawkin' like a tourist, she scolded herself. *Get a move on, Captain; you got work to do.*

Not to mention explaining herself to Val Con's sister Anthora. She took a breath, feeling Korval's Ring move between her breasts. The last thing Val Con had done was put the Ring on the cord from his shirt, and knot the cord 'round her neck—that, and kiss her—before he went his way and she went hers.

She understood the reasoning—he was going inside enemy lines—against her best, most vehement, objections. If he was taken—her blood started freezing up, just to think it—or if he was killed, the Ring would be free, and she would be Korval Herself.

Next target, please, she thought wryly, remembering Daav and Aelliana, likely tied up for months on the Clutch homeworld, like a trump held hidden in a sleeve. If everything bad went down, there were two more yos'Phelium pilots in reserve, to tend for what was left of the clan. Or carry Balance to its fullest.

She wondered if they'd figured out yet that they'd been had.

Get moving, Robertson.

She took one step down the hill, toward the house of the clan—and dropped flat.

The grass was high here, though not high enough to hide her from a determined look-see. Fortunately, the guy she'd spotted had his back to her, his attention on the house. The movement she'd caught had been him taking a pair of field glasses off his belt.

He put the glasses up and got still again. Real still. Scout still. *Agent* still.

Miri nestled her chin on her arm, watching him watch. Eventually, there was another flash as he snapped the glasses back onto their hook, then a smooth rustle of movement, as he came up into a crouch, and eased down the hill, toward the house.

Her house, currently occupied by a young woman acknowledged to be, by those who loved her best, more than a little feather-erbrained, an old war 'bot—and some cats.

Oh, and, yeah—the Tree.

Down the hill, the grass shivered as if a light wind had combed through it—the Agent, moving closer to the house.

Knowing it was stupid, Miri rose into a crouch and went after him.

His second bowed, and waited until he was seated.

"News from the port, Commander," he murmured and touched the appropriate button.

". . . a name, do they?" an uncouth Terran voice snarled out of the speaker. "Fine, here's a name you can give them: Bar Vad yo'Tornier. He calls himself Commander of Agents."

The Commander folded his hands deliberately atop his desk, closed his eyes and indulged himself in a breathing exercise.

When he opened his eyes again, a cup of his favorite blend sat, steaming, at his right hand, and his second was gone. A prudent man, his second.

Commander of Agents sipped his tea.

Bar Vad yo'Tornier. His name. His personal name, that he had taken care to hide and hide well, in the filthy mouth of a Terran—

A Terran what?

One-handed, he reached to the console, touched a series of keys and listened, impassive, from time to time sipping his tea, to the tale of the holed ship, the conversations between Solcintra Port and the Council, and once more to his name, shouted along the open bands by a heedless, idiot barbarian who—

Had no reason to know—or means to discover—such a thing.

Commander of Agents put aside the teacup, and brought his screen live. His second had, of course, compiled the necessary information, which the Commander read once, rapidly; then again, more slowly.

There was no doubt that the ship, Mercenary Transport *Kynak-on-the-Rocks*, wholly owned by Higdon's Howlers, Inc., displayed signs of damage on both the orbital scans and the schematic. That it was actually *holed*—well, perhaps it was, or perhaps it was not, and the portion of Solcintra Port was clear. The mercenaries had been cleared to land.

In the interests of thoroughness, Commander of Agents opened the file on the Surebleak incident. He had not expected *Kynak-on-the-Rocks* to match the specs for Surebleak's defenders, nor did it—still, it would have been tidy, and provided a link between Korval and this ship, this barbarian commander, who knew his name.

Mercenary Sergeant Miri Robertson . . .

The Commander blinked at the thought.

Could it be so simple? Val Con yos'Phelium—the Commander could believe that former Agent of Change yos'Phelium might ferret out even the most deeply buried secret, as nothing more than an exercise to pass a slow hour.

Both subtle and ambitious, Val Con yos'Phelium. And given to flights of unadulterated madness, before the training provided by the Department had normalized him.

yos'Phelium's last known location was Lytaxin, where mercenary units in the employ of Erob had recently turned back an Yxtrang invasion.

Methodical, Commander of Agents checked the lists of units known to have been on Lytaxin—and very nearly smiled.

Higdon's Howlers, commanded by one Octavius Higdon, had been on Lytaxin, one of several units hired by Erob to quell the war which the Department had nurtured.

The Commander's smile faded. Simple enough to suppose that Val Con yos'Phelium had hired Higdon's Howlers in turn, providing them with a drama, a name, and a port of call. Simple enough . . . And yet yos'Phelium was not a simple man, nor was he a fool. He would suppose that the Department would access just this information—and draw just this conclusion.

Commander of Agents flipped through the files open on his screen, glancing at the profiles of the odd vessels that had defended Surebleak. A positive identification of those vessels had not yet been made, though the tactical report on *Fortune's Reward* was thorough. To find a Korval fleet there, obviously in the midst of maneuvers—and now, here, this other ship, carrying mercenaries and cleared to land, crying Balance owed by the Department of the Interior, invoking his own personal name . . .

Commander of Agents felt a sudden light chill crawl down his arms.

Val Con yos'Phelium was on Liad. And he meant the Department to know it.

She'd lost the trail a dozen times, found it again in a bent stem, the outline of a boot-print in a patch of soft soil, a solitary scattering of unripened grass seeds.

On some level, she was aware that she, Miri Robertson, had never been trained to track like this, moving like a wisp among the high, rustling grass, in deadly pursuit of deadly prey.

The prey stopped some distance ahead. Miri crouched, consulted her—Val Con's—mental map of the territory, and sighed.

She was very near one of the perimeter access points—in fact, the gate she'd been making for herself before she took it into her head to stalk wild waterfowl.

Miri bit her lip. The perimeter was guarded and coded. The gate wouldn't open for a bogus code, though it would deliver a shock, progressively nastier, if anybody was stupid enough to keep trying in the hope of hitting the winning combination. Any attempt to force the gate—also won a shock. The beam was nice and wide, too, which made jumping the fence an equally bad idea.

Which fortifications and failsafes were all so much fairy dust, if the man she'd been tracking had good access codes—like Pat Rin's, for instance.

Miri swallowed around a cold surge of horror that felt more like Val Con's than hers, and made her decision.

Silently, she eased forward, pistol in hand, though she needn't have worried; her prey—sighted barely one hundred paces from her previous position—was completely intent on a project of his own.

She watched while he worked with a remote unit, apparently keying in pass-code after pass-code, with no success—and without receiving a tangible token of the gate's esteem, either. He'd managed to sync the remote to the gate's keypad, and was apparently committed to tapping in codes 'til the heat death of the universe.

Or the gate opened.

Miri closed her eyes briefly, ridiculously elated, as if the lack of access codes was an excuse for a party.

Can it, she snarled at herself. *His not having the codes don't prove Pat Rin's at liberty the same way his having them would prove the opposite. Loobelli.*

She opened her eyes, bringing the gun up, easing the safety off. She could hardly miss at this range; especially when she wasn't trying nothing fancy, only a simple kill.

She squeezed the trigger, the *snick* of the pellet simultaneous with the larger click of the gate opening.

Miri came up in a rush, running forward. The guy was down and he wasn't moving. She dropped to one knee beside him, confirming that her aim had been good, and reached for the fallen remote.

"Drop your gun and surrender!" a voice snarled.

Miri jerked around, saw the woman, the business-like set of her pistol. Behind her, she heard a click. The gate closing, that would be.

"Drop the gun," the woman repeated. "Or lose a hand."

"Wouldn't want that," Miri said, softly, feeling the weight of the weapon in her hand. She shifted into a crouch. The woman's finger tightened on the trigger of her gun.

Miri spun sideways, throwing her gun, punched a button on the remote, her finger guided by blind, stupid luck.

The gunwoman grunted, her shot in the air, and Miri was up

and through the gate, running low; there was a shout, a second shot, and the sound of the gate going home.

Miri staggered, feet tangling, stumbled and went down, rolling. She fetched up against something hard and gritty, and lay there, heart pounding.

Her right arm was on fire—she'd probably caught the second pellet. A quick inventory discovered nothing else worse than bruises.

She opened her eyes.

The hard, gritty thing was a goodish-sized rock. She used it to pull herself, swearing, to her feet, and looked around.

The good news was that she was now well inside Korval's perimeter. The bad news—that there was at least one enemy, probably more—and more remote lock-picks, too—around the perimeter, doing their all to get it. And the arm—that was bad; she didn't need the evidence of the blood-dyed sleeve to know she'd already lost too much.

Not in much shape to go hiking around the countryside, Robertson, she thought, snapping open her pouch and pulling out the first aid tape—and quietly crumbled to the ground.

Here at last was the place.

Val Con breathed a quiet sigh of relief. The distance from the rendezvous site had been somewhat longer than he had estimated—long enough that he had begun to doubt his memory. But, here it was, at last: overgrown, tumble-down, and, gods willing, forgotten . . .

He held up a hand, halting the rest of the small troop, and turned to catch Liz Lizardi's eye.

"We part company here, Commander."

"Here?" She glanced around at the vine-covered walls, scrub trees and broken blocks of stone.

"Here," he repeated, suppressing a smile. Miri's fostermother was not a woman to spend three words where a gesture would serve. "Have you questions regarding the part of yourself and your troops?"

"Nope, sounds like a paid vacation to me," Liz said. "'Bout a klick to the north, we'll find us a park and a street and a door. We guard the door. Anybody tries to go in, we stop them. Anybody tries to go out, we stop them, too." She shrugged. "Higdon sending backup—that a go?"

"Yes."

"Then we're set." She looked over her shoulder at her troop of two. "OK, let's take a walk."

"Commander." Diglon Rifle saluted with alacrity, his demeanor closely resembling that of a child given run of a sweet shop.

Hazenthull Explorer's salute was more sedate, her face properly devoid of expression, but Val Con could not help noticing the alert set of her shoulders. Nor did he miss the glance she sent to Nelirikk before following her commander down the path to the north—quite a speaking glance it was, too, for all it fell upon a face as giving as stone.

Ah, youth. Perhaps after . . .

If there was an after, which was by no means assured. Val Con closed his eyes briefly, thinking of Miri, going overland to Korval's Valley—to *home*—where she would be safe—or at least safer. This—it was mad, what he proposed to do. Capture the Commander in his own warren? Stop the unfolding of the Plan with a word? Rescue the passengers—oh, aye, just that. And who remembered the old contract—never canceled, never bought out, that tied Korval to Liad—and to honor—down the long years from Cantra to himself?

They have murdered us—us and ours. It ends, and ends now. No more of mine will be shot down in the streets.

"Scout?"

Val Con blinked and looked up into the stern brown face of Nelirikk Explorer.

"A quick nap," he said lightly. "Pay it no mind."

"A soldier fights best when he has rested well before battle," the big man agreed.

"Just so." He looked over to the third of their party, standing a little apart, gazing about himself with—perhaps it was wonder—the tile work of his shell showing pale ripples of purple in the shadowed light.

"Brother."

Sheather turned, his big eyes inward-lit.

"Brother," he said courteously. "Is the time of our departure upon us?"

Val Con walked forward, showing open palms. "Certainly, the time draws near. Forgive me that I come to you once more and say—it is not necessary that you accompany us after you have assisted in the opening of the door. Stay and watch, if you will. Return to the ship, by my preference. But, to come within—it is more than my heart can bear, brother, that you might be slain in the course of a hasty and ill-considered human quarrel."

"Your feelings do you great honor," Sheather said solemnly. "Certainly, kin wish to do all within their scope to preserve kin from harm. Just as certainly, we are bound to the word of the T'carais, who has bid me accompany you upon this vendetta, in which you will fully answer those who have slain others of your kin and keeping. This is your duty, as you have told us, and it is a duty the Clutch know as well. The T'carais sends me to his brother, the Delm of Korval, to fight, and to prevail."

He blinked, one eye after the other.

"The T'carais has done me the honor of adding to my name. As time is short, I will refrain from speaking it to you in fullness. However, I will tell you that my name now includes a phrase roughly equivalent to 'student of men'." He blinked again, both eyes in tandem.

"I am the first of our clan to undertake this scholarship. I began because my heart would know certain things. I continue because my T'carais would know in fullness—and my heart is not adverse."

Val Con bowed, deeply and with sincere respect. "Scholarship is a heady and dangerous undertaking," he murmured. "And of course the T'carais may not be gainsaid."

Which was true enough, he thought—no word of his would prevent Sheather from following, if the word of the T'carais sent him on.

He straightened.

"Attend me, then, brother, if you will. Explorer, guard us—and monitor the broadband. Our signal should find us soon."

The ancient and weary locking mechanism scarcely resisted Sheather's song: a note, another—and the thing was done. And done not a moment too soon.

"Scout," Nelirikk said quietly, "the signal arrives." He paused, head cocked, listening to the tiny comm-link behind his ear.

"Third repeat."

Val Con swallowed, thinking of Miri, safe at home.

Go on then, he told himself. *The time is come.*

Dutiful Passage was in orbit.

• • •

Miri woke with no memory of having fallen asleep, and blinked lazily up at the orange cat sitting on her chest, solemn green eyes fixed on her face as if it sat sentry to her awakening.

"Hey, cat," she said.

The animal blinked its eyes, and a voice spoke from across the room—a male voice, talking up-scale Terran.

"Good afternoon, Korval," he said, over a sound like wheels across planking. "Are you feeling well?"

She turned her head on the pillow, but there wasn't anybody there, unless he was hiding behind the heavy-looking metal cylinder, fully equipped with three articulated arms, topped by a lighted orange globe, which was itself weirdly familiar, in a nother-own-memory kind of way.

"Jeeves?" she asked, but it had to be it—him.

"Yes," he said, the orange ball flickering slightly.

"Great." She pushed herself up, forgetting the cat, which jumped sideways off her chest to the floor, venting a small, peevish hiss. "Plug into the perimeter's brains, there's people trying to get inside the valley."

The ball flickered—*he's thinking*, Miri caught from Val Con's memories, and swung her legs over the side of the cot she'd been lying on, unsurprised to find that it was part of a field 'doc.

"The interlopers have been dispatched, ma'am," the robot said. "Though I expect there will be more. Perimeter protections have been intensified.

"I must apologize for allowing you to be wounded. My attention was engaged by concerted assaults at the south and east gates. The lesser attempt at the north gate was hidden beneath the noise. I sent transport immediately after I had your direction from Jelaza Kazone, and brought you in to the 'doc."

She moved her right arm, experimentally. It hurt like hell.

"Again, I apologize if I misunderstood your necessities. Extrapolating from Plan B, however, I merely initiated a quick-heal."

"You did exactly right," Miri told him, standing up. "I'm Miri Robertson, by the way."

"I had surmised as much," Jeeves replied. "How shall I address you?"

"Miri's fine," she said, wincing as her first step jogged the half-healed arm. "Look, I need the control room, quicktime.

There's stuff I gotta be doing, especially if I shot the timing by being an hour in the 'doc."

"You were in the 'doc for no longer than a quarter hour," the war 'bot told her calmly. "You must try not to strain your wound." He rolled forward, wheels rumbling over the floorboards.

"Follow me, please, and I will take you to the control room."

"Right," she said, stretching her legs to keep up with the pace he set down the hallway. "Tell Anthora I'm here, and where she can find me, OK? I'll need her to fill me in on what's been going on here."

"Miss Anthora," said Jeeves, "is not to home."

"Not home?" She looked at him, but the orange ball gave her no clues. "Where is she?"

"I believe," he said, as they took a sharp turn into a narrow hallway, "she is at the headquarters of the Department of the Interior."

They had found out soon enough what the more cryptic of dea'Gauss' drugged mouthings had referred to. As payment accounts were shut down, so too were the services and supplies they purchased.

Commander of Agents sat in an office lit by emergency dims, and glared at his screen. Behind him, the radio mumbled along on back-up power, whispering the names and the business of ships.

The power problems had been resolved. For the moment. The facility was running—as could be told by the noise of the intermittent fans attempting to move sluggish air about, at considerably less than half-efficiency—on its own emergency generation system. This situation would change for the better once the prisoner was under control and functioning on behalf of the Department.

But the man would have to survive.

The prisoner's health was—not good. The third drug, rather than inducing the desired state of submissive obedience, had elicited a strong allergic reaction. On advice of the drug-tech, he had been removed to the infirmary, where he remained stable, but feeble, guarded by a full Agent of Change.

Perusing the roster in his dim-lit office, the Commander reconsidered that assignment: Agents were in short supply. Surely a lesser operative might be set to guard one ill old man?

But no. dea'Gauss had deprived the Department of three Agents, each dispatched with a precise shot to the head. Records belatedly obtained from Tey Dor's demonstrated that dea'Gauss had been a regular at the club for fifty years; that he maintained several weapons and match-pistols, list appended; that he often shot with other of Tey Dor's patrons, list appended. Indeed, Tey Dor's records held all that one would wish, save the man's marksman rating. They also failed to note—though this was scarcely an area where Tey Dor's could be expected to concern itself—that the old man in question had worn clothing made of anti-pulse and anti-pellet materials; and that he had turned his office into a fortress.

No, the Commander decided; the dea'Gauss had won the honor of having an Agent at his bedside.

Which left the diminished roster and the rather longer number of tasks to be done.

A team of Agents had been sent to the Council of Clans, with orders to arm the devices in place. Likewise at the Council of Clans, the Protocol Officer, long ago subverted by the Department, consulted with the Speaker on the precise placing of Balance against Anthora yos'Galan, who had casually and brutally murdered an unarmed Council Proctor.

A second team of Agents, augmented by Departmental sharpshooters, was en route to Low Port, explosives and coordinates to hand. Another full team of Agents was attempting to invest Korval's valley, while others undertook the infiltration of Higdon's Howlers.

The Commander blinked, bringing the screen before him into focus. Shipping stats. There were no Tree-and-Dragon ships currently orbiting Liad, which was odd. Scout ships were likewise in short supply—though that was less odd. One would expect Val Con yos'Phelium to have ships in support, whatever his plans. The absence of ships was . . . unnerving.

As yos'Phelium no doubt intended.

Commander of Agents extended a hand, calling up the list of secondary operatives. Surely some use might be made—

"*Dutiful Passage*," the radio blared so loudly the Commander missed his key.

"*Dutiful Passage*, Solcintra, Liad, Captain Priscilla Mendoza. Stand clear. Stand clear! We are on business of Korval and we are armed."

• • •

Silence was as important as haste, and haste they made: Scout, explorer and Clutch turtle. The pipe easily accommodated the larger members of the party, though boots and claws alike sometimes failed to find purchase on the water-smoothed surface.

Sheather, with his dark-seeing eyes, led the way, Val Con following, carrying a mini-torch to aid his poorer eyesight. Nelirikk brought up the rear, burdened with explosives, extra firearms and ammunition.

The *Passage* was in orbit, Val Con reminded himself. Soon, it would be joined by allies. Soon, they would know whether this bold strike at the heart of the enemy was lunacy or genius.

Speed-marching, they had covered distance, passing three gates at roughly equal intervals. When the aqueduct had been in use, the gates had functioned as flow control devices. They rested at each for five short minutes, then resumed the march.

"Ahead lies another gate, my brother," Sheather said in a remarkably quiet voice. "It appears to be both new and locked."

Val Con sighed. So quickly. He closed his eyes, allowing her song to fill his head, his heart, his soul. Deliberately, he extended his will, and sang a new phrase into the song. Then, he opened his eyes and stepped forward.

The warrens the Department had taken for their own had been carved out of sub-surface limestone to create tremendous storage bays for low-pressure gases. Portions of the original waterworks were marked out as points of historic interest, somewhere overhead. But down here, far beneath the planet surface, the aqueducts had also fed underground pressurizing reservoirs in off-peak moments. Eventually abandoned as Solcintra's needs grew beyond the water offered by the River Kainbek, and as the necessity for a safer location for storing volatile energy than beneath the city itself became understood, the underground maze was a natural place to house a secret headquarters.

This door, now. This was the airlock; the interface between the old pipes and the new facility. Val Con inspected the controls, understanding them with a sense of relief twined irrevocably with terror.

"I had intended to use my blade here," he said to Sheather, "and on the other side, speed. That is still an option. But I ask, is there a note or two known to you, which will unlock the way for us with less danger?"

Sheather blinked his enormous eyes. "My brother is wise, to

prefer a stealthy entrance to the cave of his enemy. I believe the key to this door may be discovered, if I am allowed a moment of study."

"Certainly," Val Con said, and fell back to Nelirikk's side. The explorer looked down at him with a grin and gave him a very Terran thumb's up.

Lit by emergency dims, only the most essential of machinery online, the infirmary was a place of shadows, enemies and storybook monsters on the lurk for the fanciful.

Agent ter'Fendil was neither fanciful nor inclined to simile. He kept guard over the old man, as ordered, equally alert for signs of treachery or waking. Neither manifested, as the weary hours crept along—nor did the old man die, and release Agent ter'Fendil to duties more worthy of him.

That there were such duties, Agent ter'Fendil knew, having been present when the full team was called to attend to the future needs of the Council hall. He had awaited his own orders with anticipation, for surely the Commander would not fail to recall those treasures which Agent ter'Fendil, extrapolating from studies he had made as a scout, had recovered and delivered to the Department. He dared hope that the Commander would place the controls in his hand, allowing him the honor of deploying those treasures against the enemies of the Department.

Yet, here he stood, on guard at the bedside of an accountant, while he might be—no. The Commander was not one to forget past service; nor to fail of using what weapons came to his hand. That he was assigned this minor duty, now, did not mean he was forgotten. The Department taught that all duties furthered the Plan, and Agent ter'Fendil had been well taught. Yet—

A shadow moved among the shadows, and vanished, into shadow.

Agent ter'Fendil frowned.

The shadows flickered again, fluid and quick.

Agent ter'Fendil blinked, and ran a quick diagnostic. Finding that he was slightly, though not by any means dangerously, low on energy, he accessed the Loop's energizing routine, feeling an immediate sharpening of his senses.

Straightening, he deliberately turned his gaze to the place he had last seen the shadows waver.

Something . . . moved.

Agent ter'Fendil walked forward.

The shadow solidified, taking shape as it strolled across a dim strip of illumination, gray tail held high and jaunty, white feet soundless on the noise-absorbing floor.

"Cat!" said Agent ter'Fendil, in disbelief.

The cat turned its head, blinked and continued on its way.

The Loop indicated that a cat in headquarters was an anomaly.

Agent ter'Fendil went after it.

M i r i hit the chair in the control center a little too hard, swore, and opened the board with a sweep of her good hand.

"Get me some painkillers," she said over her shoulder to the war 'bot. "And some stim."

"I regret," Jeeves said, his high-class voice sounding apologetic, "stim is known to cause fetal damage."

The screens were up, she fumbled, then found the general shipping band.

"What's that got to do with me?" she asked, her mind more than half occupied with locating the other, more tricksy band. This one, even Val Con was hazy on . . .

"The 'doc reports that you are pregnant," Jeeves said.

In the midst of making an adjustment, Miri froze, before spinning the chair around to face the 'bot.

"That's the craziest—" she began, and then clamped her mouth shut.

Oh, Robertson, you prize fool.

Because it wasn't crazy, was it? Not with her fresh outta the 'doc, and him, too, both returned to normal baseline functioning—read 'fertile'—and neither one of them remembering to ask for the shot.

Miri, let us make love . . . he murmured in memory, and if she found out he'd known—that he'd *planned* . . .

She'd kill him.

Uh-huh. First he's gotta get home alive.

She spun back to the control board, adjusting the volume on the ship band, which had been plenty loud enough, and had another go at the local band.

This time, her fingers were smarter—or the three-times-damned Korval luck was in it. Whichever, her inquiry elicited an answer.

"Binjali's," said a woman's matter-of-fact voice.

Miri took a breath. "This is the Captain," she said, in the mode of Ultimate Authority. "Situation Red."

"Dutiful Passage, seal your weapons," Solcintra Tower said—which it had to say, as Shan knew well. Had he been portmaster, faced with a sudden battleship in orbit around his peaceful and orderly world, he would have said precisely the same thing, most likely with a good deal more heat.

Priscilla touched the reply stud. "This is Captain Mendoza. We are on business of Clan Korval. Our weapons are live and under our control."

"That is in violation of regulations, Captain Mendoza. The guild has been notified."

Priscilla's mouth tightened. "Copy," she said, voice steady, and closed the connection.

"Never fear, Priscilla, there remains one license between us. And the Code tells us that what one lifemate owns, the other owns as well."

She looked at him, black eyes betraying her amusement. "Tell it to the Pilots Guild."

Shan snapped his fingers with a grin. "*That* for the Pilots Guild! We'll get you a Terran license under an assumed name, and no one will be the wiser."

"Now, why don't I think that will work?"

"Because you are an innocent and pure of heart." He turned back to his screens. "The portmaster will satisfy herself with the complaint to the guild," he murmured, pulling in the traffic reports. "She can fire on us, of course, but we've done nothing to merit that."

"Yet," Priscilla said, with a glance to Ren Zel, quiet and efficient at third board.

"Any sign of our friends, Pilot?"

"Not as yet, Captain," he answered, "but we are ahead of schedule."

"By three entire minutes," Shan said. "Trust a scout to—"

"Jump-flare," Ren Zel said sharply. "Close in."

His fingers moved, and Shan's did, too, locating the flare and the coords—*close*, gods. Which meant it must be the expected scouts, though there was no reason—

The comm crackled as the flares died and the ships announced themselves, one, two, three, four: *Diamond Duty*, *Timonium Core*,

Crystalia, Survey Nine. Tree-and-Dragon, Tree-and-Dragon. Tree-and-Dragon, Tree-and-Dragon.

"What the devil?" He isolated the four of them, Jumped as a unit, had they? Master pilots, then—or, yet, it could be scouts, though in such strange, unscout-like vessels . . .

"Jump-flare!" Ren Zel cried again—and so it was: a fifth ship Jumping into the hollow square formed by the first four, a maneuver so chancy that Shan half-averted his face from the expected collision.

But no. The comm crackled, and a fifth ID rang across the general band.

Fortune's Reward, Solcintra, Liad. Tree-and-Dragon. Tree-and-Dragon.

The transfer was complete. The last light on the status board was lit.

Miri wiped a sleeve across her damp forehead, leaned forward in the chair, bum arm braced against the board, and pushed the button that connected her to receivers located at the Council of Clans; Scout Headquarters; each of the major halls: accountants, pilots, trade, and Healer; the offices of Solcintra and Chonselta portmasters; the editorial offices of The Gazette; the general shipping band; and a number of strategically placed public speakers.

We cover the world, she thought, as the master light went to green. *You're on, Robertson. Don't forget your lines.*

Normal space. The screens reformed. The comm came live.

On the private band: "Boss is here, let's party!" "Well flown." "Make a master outta you yet, son!" "Good work, Boss."

He'd done it.

Pat Rin sagged back into the pilot's chair, shivering with relief.

He'd done it.

Now, to do the rest.

The voice that came out of the old, forgotten receiver was female. Her accent was Solcintran and her message, thought Speaker for Council, raising her head and staring, entirely absurd.

". . . Captain's Emergency. I say again: this is a Captain's Emergency. In accordance with the conditions put forward in paragraph 8, section 1 of the original contract of hire between the Houses of Solcintra and Captain Cantra yos'Phelium, which requires the captain, her heirs, or assigns to safeguard the welfare of the passengers, I, Miri Robertson Tiazan, Delm Korval, declare a Captain's Emergency. The Council of Clans will hold itself subservient to Captain's Law. Control of the planetary defense net rests with the Captain.

"Passengers are advised that the name of our enemy is the Department of the Interior. They have stolen and murdered members of every clan, High House and Low. They have subverted the cash flow of entire clans. They have pressed ships and pilots into service, to the detriment of Liad. They will be stopped. Now. Locations of known Departmental offices and safeplaces follows.

"Repeat, repeat: This is a Captain's Emergency."

It was the custom of Kilon pel'Meret to visit the old Waterway Park with her small son every day before Prime. This exercise gave double benefit, refreshing Kilon and allowing young Nev Art room to run off excess energy in a manner not likely to earn him a sharp rebuke from his grandmother.

The pattern of the walk was well known to both mother and child. Kilon would stroll along the old path from the park's entryway down to the silted-in pond, while Nev Art might run circles about her, or dart off in all directions at once, saving only that he did not disappear entirely from her sight. He would rejoin her at the pond and they would then both walk back along the path to the entrance, practicing seemliness; thence down the city sidewalks to home, and grandmother, and Prime.

Today, Nev Art darted up and grabbed her hand. "Thawla, look! Yxtrang!"

Kilon was a sensible woman. She was also familiar with her son's imaginative prowess. So, she did not scream, or gather him up in her arms and run. Rather, she allowed herself to be tugged 'round by the hand, fully expecting to see a tree wearing a uniform of shadow, or a stealthy weed peering over a crumbling section of ornamental stonework.

"Look!" Nev Art said again; and look Kilon did, breath caught in her throat.

For across the rumpled grass toward them came three tall persons—two much taller than the third—dressed in what was indisputably military style, packs on their backs and their belts hung about with all manner of objects.

"Yxtrang, Thawla," Nev Art insisted, pulling on her hand. "I want to see their guns!"

"No!" she said sharply, and tightened her hold on his hand. "They are only Terrans, my son." She hesitated. Terran soldiers, here, strolling through an abandoned and all-but-forgotten park in the Low House district of Solcintra? Abruptly, she turned, dragging Nev Art with her.

"Come along, child, it is time to go home."

"It's not!" he protested, but she was adamant.

Walking briskly, holding her son firmly by the hand, she went down the path. He stretched his short legs until he was all but running, and so they gained the entrance—and, a moment later, the street.

"Go after them, Commander?" Diglon asked hopefully.

Liz shook her head. "No. It ain't like they're the only ones gonna see us." She pointed. "Let's go."

"**Boss?**" Cheever McFarland's voice came low and easy across the tight band. "You ready to cook?"

Pat Rin took a deep breath, and another, deliberately calming. "A moment, Mr. McFarland. I am afraid that I found the Jump in . . . exhilarating."

"Was close, wasn't it?" the Terran said, cheerfully. "Just think what we could do with practice."

Alone in his ship, Pat Rin smiled. "Next, you will have us touring as a precision flying unit."

"Something to that. We're out here if you need us, Boss. All lines open."

Pat Rin inclined his head. "Thank you, Mr. McFarland."

"Right." The line closed.

Another deep breath and Pat Rin leaned to the board, his finger on the switch . . .

The main screen flared, awash with Jump-flares—one! three! eight! one dozen! Two!—Pat Rin snapped back, eyes narrowed, the bands fizzing with static; and then the IDs hit, one after another, gathering intensity, until they blurred and became a single shout; a challenge:

Scout.

Tree-and-Dragon.

The beast had vanished entirely.

Not a little disgruntled, Agent ter'Fendil returned to the accountant's bedside—and stared, heartbeat spiking, breath gasping—the Loop, barely submerged since his last check, kicked in, bringing both into normal range, but the bed—the bed remained empty; blankets rumpled, pillow showing an indentation.

dea'Gauss was gone.

The old man was recovered.

Ren Zel smiled at his screen, attention divided between the countdown in the lower corner and a wholly imaginary, but completely accurate, screen in his mind.

"Go home now, beloved," he sub-vocalized.

Soon, she answered. *We must wait for Merlin.*

The scout ships had settled into their orbits, and if Tower had a sharp word or two to say to them, it was on a private band and not for the entertainment of common ships.

Steeling himself, Pat Rin extended a hand to the board. The bogus Ring flashed and flared in the cabin's light. He touched the comm switch.

"This is Pat Rin yos'Phelium, speaking for Korval and for the Captain. I call on the Council of Clans to witness formal Balancing with the Department of the Interior."

"Speaking for Korval?" Shan repeated blankly, but Priscilla had touched a key on the captain's board, releasing the recorded warn-away.

"*Dutiful Passage*, Solcintra, Liad, Captain Priscilla Mendoza. Stand clear. Stand clear! We are on business of Korval and we are armed." The touch of a second key sent the Tree-and-Dragon roaring across the general band.

Silence on all bands for a heartbeat . . . three.

"This is Scout Commander Clonak ter'Meulen. The Scouts call the Department of the Interior to answer for acts of murder and mayhem. We subordinate our claim to the Captain and Korval."

Silence on the bands . . .

"Have you all run mad?" Solcintra Tower demanded. "There is no Department of the Interior!"

"On the contrary," Pat Rin said. "I advise the Tower that I am transmitting a ship's recording of an incident of attempted piracy which took place in the sovereign space of the world Surebleak.

You will note that the Department of the Interior claims to speak for Liad."

"Pirates, speaker-for-Korval," the Tower snapped. "Surely *you* know that pirates are not bound to speak the truth!"

Silence.

Aboard *Fortune's Reward*, Pat Rin laughed aloud, reached to the board—and froze.

Jump-flare distorted his screen. When the image was steady, there were six new ships in high orbit, their IDs stark and simple.

Juntavas.

Pat Rin bit his lip, remembering the courier who had departed at Natesa's word, leaving her partner to fly as part of this attack upon the homeworld.

In the screen, another flare, a sharp spike of static, and a ship's ID.

Implacable. High Judge. Juntavas.

The broad band crackled, fizzed, and produced a man's voice, speaking Liaden with a slight Terran accent.

"The Juntavas calls the Department of the Interior to answer for acts of murder and mayhem. We subordinate our claim to Tree-and-Dragon."

The lines were drawn, the orders given. Events were set in motion. There was the Plan and the end of the Plan—and the alternative plan, should, unthinkably, they fail.

Commander of Agents sat in his office, awaiting reports, and brooded upon Korval.

Perhaps it had been error, to allow them to continue so long. Perhaps they should have been weeded out quickly, at the very beginning of the Work.

For look at what Korval had cost . . .

First, the Scouts, backed by a ship piloted by a long-missing and presumed dead Korval elder, resist the Department's first open action on its way to fulfilling the Plan. Nor did the Scouts retreat to Liad, but withdrew entirely from the system . . .

Next, on what should have been little more than a routine pickup of the dismissible yos'Phelium ne'er-do-well, Departmental ships were lost in the discovery of a capable and disciplined fleet of war vessels flying the Tree-and-Dragon in Surebleak nearspace—a fleet led by none other than the supposed ne'er-do-well in a surprisingly well-armed pleasure yacht.

Then, as if unconnected, comes a ship full of mercenaries to Liad itself, claiming damage at the hands of the Department. Yet, in its many actions the Department had never dealt with the ship or its mercenaries.

In short order came a Korval battleship, several dozen openly Scout vessels—and who knew how many secret ones?—a Juntavas battleship and its escort—ah, and the Surebleak war fleet. All sitting in orbit, shouting Tree-and-Dragon to the universe, while here on the homeworld itself one Miri Robertson Tiazan publicly denounced the Department and described the location of several minor bases of operation, raising the citizenry to arms.

What more?

The Commander need not look at the charts that covered the desk. He need not look at the screens.

For, as difficult as they had been—as costly—Korval had in its actions against the Department revealed a weakness. There was a discernible pattern in their actions.

On Lytaxin, according to the intercepted mercenary reports, Val Con yos'Phelium had waited until action was in place and swept in with aircraft, sowing confusion and winning the battle and the war at once—all the while hiding behind the smoke-screen of his so-called Surebleak mercenary.

At Scout Headquarters, the same pattern—from nowhere came a ship to turn the tide of battle.

At Surebleak—a building of forces and then action by Pat Rin yos'Phelium . . .

An emergency buzzer went off, startlingly loud. He touched the comm button.

"Commander—Agent ter'Fendil. I report that the accountant is gone. There is a cat inside the facility. My error is that I pursued, but lost it. Upon my return to my post, I found the accountant gone."

Commander of Agents stared. A cat, inside the facility? Impossible. dea'Gauss, in his weakened and doubtless disoriented state, gone? Preposterous.

And yet . . .

Commander of Agents stood, automatically checking the position of his weapons.

"I will lead the search myself. Meet me in the infirmary lobby. Be wary—we may be facing a rogue Agent of Change."

"Yes, Commander," Agent ter'Fendil said.

The Commander cut the connection, walked across his office and put his hand against the plate set into the wall.

The scan crackled across his palm. He reached into the safe and removed a short, squat rod, which he slipped into his sleeve.

Kilon pel'Meret held tightly to Nev Art, her heart hammering with fear. Her son labored under no such affliction. *He* was enjoying one of the great days of his life. Not only had he spotted the soldiers walking in the park, but now came this parade of taxicabs, each stopping at the end of the placid dead-end street to allow even more soldiers to disembark. That these *were* soldiers was not in dispute; Kilon had no trouble identifying guns, missile launchers, backpacks.

Nev Art crowed as they dashed out of the cabs, forming into lines and units with bewildering speed as each cab roared away, to be replaced by another, and another, and . . .

"Excuse me, ma'am."

Kilon jumped back, staring up into the face of the sudden soldier. A Terran, dark-skinned and sober, carrying a rifle in her own streets, speaking to her in Trade. Why, she hardly ever—

"Ma'am?" he said again. "Please. We're holding a taxi for you and the boy."

"See, Thawla, I bet they're going after the Yxtrang I saw," Nev Art cried. And then, to the soldier, "Are you? Are you an admiral?"

"No." The man smiled as he answered, a slow smile. "I never do want to be an admiral, boy." He looked at Kilon, and pointed to the right, where indeed there was a taxicab, pulled slightly to one side of the street.

"I insist, ma'am. Please take the taxi. There's likely to be trouble and—"

"Ten'shun!" a large voice bellowed from the lines of soldiers. "Group One, double time, move out!"

Kilon looked about wildly. "Trouble? Trouble? Soldiers in the street are trouble!"

The soldiers did something—one moment they had been still as rocks; the next, one group was spread out and hurrying toward the park, while another group broke away, trotting down the street toward the office complex.

Their own soldier waved at one of his comrades, and said to

Kilon, "There's a good chance we'll be using weapons, ma'am. I'm sorry. You've got to leave!"

"I saw the Yxtrang!" Nev Art announced, tugging so hard against her hand that she almost lost him. "I want to talk to them!"

The second soldier had waved the taxi close, and opened the door.

"You've got good eyes, youngster, if you saw the 'trang," the first soldier said. "Just remember what they looked like, and get into the cab."

Behind them someone yelled, "Group Three, weapons check!" followed by a loud series of clicks and slaps, and, "Arm your weapons!"

Kilon flung back, found her arm caught, not ungently, by the dark-faced soldier. "Calm down . . ." he began, and was interrupted by the arrival of yet another man, much lighter of face.

He bowed, recognizably the bow of a ranking public servant to a person of unknown melant'i, and said in curiously accented Liaden, "I am Commander Higdon. This way, please, civilians must clear the area. I would not want to have to detain you."

He offered her a card, and automatically she took it, and was somehow gently pushed into the taxi, while her son was proclaiming, "Yxtrang and soldiers, can't we stay?"

The dark soldier handed the driver a twelfth-cantra piece.

"Take them wherever they want to go that's more than five minutes from here. If there's any change from that give it to the kid."

"Look!" Nev Art shouted in her ear. "*Big* guns, Thawla!"

The cab accelerated into a turn, flinging Kilon sideways in the back seat, so she never did see what her son was pointing at. She righted herself, glancing down at the card she still held in her hand, as the cab slewed 'round a corner.

Higdon's Howlers, the Trade words stated. *Military missions. Security to mayhem. Guaranteed service.*

The Department had long planned for this day. There was an undercurrent of expectation in the control room as the master switch was unshielded; the communications web checked; the technicians readied.

Before them the situation screen was clear; several orbiting stations would soon be under the direct control of the Department, and the destroyer *Heart of Solcintra*, long disguised as a freighter undergoing retrofitting, was already rising to orbit.

In the control room, they awaited the Commander's word. When it came, the flip of the master switch would shunt control of the planetary defense web from Solcintra port to the Department's control room, the power flowing from the selfsame uninterruptible source which supplied the portmaster's office.

The call came; the switch was activated. The screens came live; satellites and warning systems revealed their locations, weapon status, the locations of potential targets . . .

On the control board, an emergency light was blinking—not unexpected with so many ships coming in. An auxiliary monitor displayed the message *Captain's Emergency* in the lower left corner.

In the main screens, the stations, the destroyer, the satellites, the ships—

The master technician swore and leaned to her board.

Not a single Korval ship showed on the screens. *Dutiful Passage* was not there. Treacherous *Fortune's Reward* did not show. There was no range on Korval's four killer ships from Surebleak. . . .

But something *was* moving, near Station Three.

The master tech upped magnification, as the comm came alive with a shrill, "Danger! Danger! Hostile action on Station Three! Nine wounded, one dead . . ."

Ship ID came out: *Lifeboat A* off of *Jacksbucket Three*, Terraport. Somehow, it had escaped the Department's absorption of Station Three.

"Danger! Danger!" the Terran ship screamed, across all open bands, putting similar actions on the remainder of Liad's orbital stations at risk.

The merest touch of a dial and the proper blast-satellite was located. The master technician fed in the firing sequence.

Nothing happened.

The tech touched another switch, invoked a backup screen— Nothing.

"Check the lines," she snapped, to this aide. "Recycle the interface," to that one; and—"Rebooting . . ."

All for naught. The screen steadfastly refused to show any ship flying the Tree-and-Dragon. And the controls remained unresponsive.

Finally, an aide selected the flashing *Captain's Emergency* on the auxiliary monitor.

During a Captain's Emergency control of the planetary defense system is invested in the Captain or assigns. There will be a one minute warning when control is reassigned to the port office.

The master tech went to manual and ordered the nearest defensive device to use a pulse-beam against the fleeing escape pod.

Nothing happened.

"Alert *Heart of Solcintra*," she said to the comm-tech.

The most potent dramliza on the planet stood at bay, cornered in a corridor leading to the sealed rooms. She held in her arms a rather large gray cat. Behind her, leaning against the stainless steel wall for support, was dea'Gauss, shivering.

Agent ter'Fendil had alerted what few fellow Agents remained at headquarters. They'd spread out from the infirmary, in a circular search pattern, and had also triggered an automated rotating check of the internal sensors that had been turned off to conserve power—and which had ironically permitted the man responsible for the loss of power to escape. And quickly found him.

But not alone. It was obvious that the prisoner could not have risen from his bed without serious assistance from the woman holding the cat. It was equally obvious that, even with that assistance, his strength was fading, and would soon fail.

The woman was far more than the Commander had expected. Despite that she was dressed in the torn remnants of what had been formal Council attire, and that her face was dirty, she stood calm and alert before the not inconsiderable threat of three armed Agents.

She might well, the Commander thought, have a gun beneath the cat, or a bomb, or knife, or only her hands. The fact that she stood in this hallway at all meant that she was competent enough to make it past the outgoing attack teams without attracting notice. Worse, it meant that she had managed to avoid the carefully placed external sensors, and that she had slipped past guards on alert.

This was not someone to trifle with, despite her reported softness.

Without warning, the cat moved, flowing soundlessly out of the woman's arms—and fled away down the hall.

No one gave chase. They could take care of it later. The problem now was the woman, as she stood, catless, but holding a scout-issue pistol, pointed at the Commander's mid-section.

He inclined his head slightly in acknowledgment.

She said nothing; the gun remained steady.

"Danger! Danger! Hostile action on Station Three!"

Fortune's Reward located the source of the warning, and opened a window in the forward screen, showing Pat Rin an unarmed life pod, tumbling free of that same Station Three.

"Nine wounded, one dead! Hostile action on Station Three! Danger! Ho, the port!"

Tower came on-line, reciting coords for an emergency descent. Pat Rin watched the life pod move, clumsily, into compliance— and the glare of a beam weapon flashed across his screen.

"No!" he shouted, slapping up the magnification.

But, yes. The pod was gone, leaving a slight drift of debris along its descent path. Obligingly, *Fortune's Reward* redrew the detail window, tracing the path of the beam back to the originating vessel.

From the closed comm, Andy Mack's voice.

"I got a clear line to the bastid, Boss."

Pat Rin nodded. "Fire at will, Colonel."

Val Con led, now, Sheather and Nelirikk at his back. The lower service ways were empty, which was not surprising.

The Commander would surely have heard the *Passage* arrive in orbit, weapons hot and warn-away blaring. From it, he would have deduced Val Con's presence on-world. Being a bold man, he would have seen this circumstance as opportunity. If the Commander played well and audaciously now, the Department stood to win all: the extinction of Korval and the fruition of the Plan.

The goal was a man-high section of stainless steel access hatches built into the wall of a particular inner corridor. Behind those hatches were the cables, pipes, wires, and comm-fibers that connected and powered the facility and allowed the Commander to reach his hand out to the universe.

That the corridor in question was off one leading to the Commander's office was beside the point.

The hallway ahead was intersected by another. Val Con checked his inner map, and raised a hand. Behind him, Sheather and Nelirikk halted. Val Con proceeded at a crouch, hugging the wall, slipping his gun from its holster.

At the intersection of the hallways, he eased the safety off, and listened. He heard nothing but the hum of the air purification system, yet his hunch was that there was . . . something in the hall beyond.

Moving so slowly he scarcely seemed to be moving at all, he leaned forward, peering 'round the corner—

Directly into a pair of yellow eyes.

"Merlin?" Val Con breathed.

The yellow eyes blinked, happily, and Merlin burbled. Tail held high, he danced forward, stropped Val Con's leather-clad knee once, and strutted away importantly, pausing only once to look over his shoulder and be sure Val Con was paying attention. Since he was leading in the direction they needed to go, they followed, with Sheather drawing a long crystal blade as he hurried along.

The lifeboat was gone, vaporized.

Miri was bent over the schematic, swearing softly and continuously. She had an ID on the murderer—one *Heart of Solcintra*, claiming to be a freighter—but no clean shots. No shots at all, really, unless she wanted to go through a scout ship, a can carrier and a Juntavas courier to get her target, which did sorta seem a waste of allies and innocents.

A detail window blossomed in the corner of the situation screen—at least someone had a clear shot! The debris and gases of the lifepod lit in a lambent glow, and the destroyer itself was illuminated in a rush of scintillant brilliance. There was a flare then as the destroyer's shield went up and Miri could trace the beam to its source—one of the four monstrosities Jeeves assured her were nothing more exotic than asteroid miners.

There was sudden glare as the destroyer's shields were overwhelmed, and an odd coruscating flash as the mining beam oscillated the length and breadth of the target. The ship's hull expanded, peeled away, dissolved into a plasma of metal, evaporated before the beam, and then the seven decks could be seen clearly for a moment, as in some illustrator's cut-away of a slowly rotating warcraft. Multiple internal explosions speckled the obscuring mist and in one last flicker of the planet-killer ray—

Heart of Solcintra was gone.

• • •

"**Of** course you realize," the Commander said, "that this cannot last long. We are several, you are one—and time sides with us. We merely need wait until your qe'andra collapses."

"Perhaps you overestimate your advantages," Anthora yos'Galan said, and her voice was soft and husky.

"Commander!" The aide's voice preceded her around the corner—she stopped, amazed at the tableau before her.

"Report!" the Commander ordered.

She bowed, hastily, one eye on the woman with the gun. "The planetary defense grid has been subverted by Korval."

Of course. Commander of Agents pointed at Agent of Change bin'Tabor.

"Give the command for the air units to attack Jelaza Kazone at low level. Detach a ground force to—"

"Give no command," said Anthora yos'Galan, her voice firm and gentle.

The Agent stood as if rooted.

"*I* command it," Commander of Agents snapped, and saw the man stir. "Bring in the air units and—"

"Be still," said Anthora yos'Galan; and the Agent froze.

"I see," said Commander of Agents, and raised his gun.

There were voices ahead, and a better lit corridor. Merlin strolled on, unconcerned. The rest of the invasion force shrank back into the plentiful shadows.

Came the hurried clatter of someone who was not an Agent in the halls. They remained in the shadows, despite a complaining burble from Merlin—and then moved, cautiously, on.

"Commander!" came the call from the hallway they approached; the answering voice sent a thrill down Val Con's spine.

"Report!"

The words grew indistinct and the invaders, weapons ready, ghosted quickly to the intersection. Val Con spied 'round the corner, and swallowed hard against a surge of sheer horror.

His sister Anthora, trapped by two Agents and the Commander himself, using her body to shield one who could only be Mr. dea'-Gauss, but a dea'Gauss diminished and desperately ill. She held a gun, true enough, but so did her opponents. If all fired at once, even a dramliza—

The Commander raised his weapon. The Agents raised theirs. The aide gasped and bolted.

From the shadowed floor leapt a large gray cat, wrapping itself around the Commander's arm, pulling the gun down. A pellet whined by Val Con's ear as he jumped forward, his own gun out and up . . .

Training had prepared Agent ter'Fendil to face an opponent with a blade, a gun, or even a security dog. The apparition attacking the Commander bore no relationship to training—and he dared not fire again for fear of endangering the Commander. He reversed his gun, meaning to club the thing—

"Hold!" Anthora shouted, her voice a-glitter with power. "Do not move!"

Val Con kept moving, firing into the face of an Agent. Merlin snarled and dug his claws in the harder.

Everyone else in the hallway froze in place: ter'Fendil with his gun reversed, Sheather, his blade raised as if to behead him; Nelirikk, aim locked on the Commander.

The Commander struggled, as pain overrode the compulsion to stillness. But for Merlin's growls, there was silence in the hallway. The sound of dea'Gauss collapsing to the floor was loud—and so, too, was the sudden wail of alarms, and the sound of running feet.

Sheather shook himself, lowered his blade, and bowed in Anthora's direction.

"As you say."

The murderer was gone; destroyed at his word. For the second time in his life, he had killed a ship. Pat Rin touched a switch, opening the comm line between himself and those sworn to serve him.

"Well done, Colonel," he said calmly.

"Thank you, sir," Andy Mack replied formally.

"First class shooting," Dostie chimed in, just ahead of Bhupendra's satisfied, "We teach the enemy to fear us."

"Which ain't exactly," Cheever McFarland added, "an unmixed blessing." He paused. "How many of them ships out there can we count on as backup, Boss? The battlewagon?"

Dutiful Passage, that would be, and a question near to his own heart and peace. That it was captained by Priscilla Mendoza, Shan's first mate and longtime lover, was . . . disturbing. And yet . . .

Pat Rin leaned to the comm. "I shall attempt to ascertain, Mr.

McFarland. In the meanwhile, do me the kindness of speaking with the High Judge, as my deputy."

"Will do," Cheever said, as easily as if he spoke to such august persons daily, and signed off.

Pat Rin did the same, and sat for a moment, hands folded, as he gathered his courage—though what had he to fear? Priscilla Mendoza was well known to him as a kind and generous lady. He had no need nor reason to fear her. Indeed, he could be certain that she would tell him, at long last, the truth.

The truth.

He reached to the board once more, fingering the keys with care, accessing the most secret Korval band . . .

"Well met, kinsman!" Shan's voice flowed cheerily into the cabin, as clear as if his cousin sat in the co-pilot's chair. Pat Rin closed his eyes, fingers gripping the edge of the board.

"Well met," he answered, shakily, knowing Shan would hear the tears in his reply, and caring not at all. "How fares the clan?"

"As it happens, we thrive—the more so now that the one who had fallen off-grid is returned to us. You must tell me all about your holiday—later. For the moment—rest assured that the *Passage* stands at your back as you speak for Korval. Oh, and check in with Jeeves, will you?"

"Jeeves?" Pat Rin cleared his throat. "Yes, I will. Shan—"

"Softly," his cousin interrupted, not ungently. "We cannot know that the line remains secure."

"Of course." He drew a careful breath. "Until soon, cousin."

"Until soon, Pat Rin. Stay the course."

The connection light went out.

"How fare we, my brother?" Sheather inquired from his position as guard over the Commander, who lay unconscious, savaged hand hastily wrapped in a shirt.

Val Con was rapidly divesting Agent ter'Fendil of the tools of his trade: knives, smoke-gas pellets, garrotte, capsules filled with poison, cunning button-sized explosives; the wallet, with its generous destructive possibilities; the boots, the interesting little blade under the sock, various guns in a diversity of calibers . . .

They had concealed themselves in the Commander's office— a questionable solution, at best. The advantages of the situation included a door that would not yield to the searchers, and access to the Commander's files, computers and comms. That there was no easy escape was . . . annoying.

Val Con removed a selection of pins and wires from the seams of Agent ter'Fendil's vest.

"We are in some disarray, I fear," he said to Sheather. "Behind enemy lines, burdened by prisoners and casualties . . ." He glanced over his shoulder to the place where Anthora kept watch over their two injured—an old man and an ancient gray cat—and returned to his task.

"On the whole, it would be best if we simply melted away into the night . . ."

As if to underscore the whimsy of that expressed desire, the loudspeaker in the ceiling gave tongue: "Intruder alert! Multiple intruders on Level Seven . . ."

"Enough." Val Con pushed the Agent against the wall, under Sheather's watchful blade, and edged past Nelirikk, who was happily removing the travel packing from their supply of explosives.

At the Commander's desk, he sat, and reached for the comm.

The access codes changed frequently, according to a pattern imbedded in the Loop of every Agent. Val Con frowned at the comm, trying to reconstruct the barely-glimpsed pattern—and, suddenly, gently, in the space behind his eyes that had previously been reserved for Loop display, there hung an access code.

Something had gone terribly wrong.

Ren Zel felt himself a man of two separate but equal parts.

One part sat his board on the bridge of the *Dutiful Passage*, attending the minutia of piloting, monitoring the various bands that told of mayhem and dismay on the nearer stations, and minding his shields most closely.

The second part knelt next to Anthora on a cold metal floor, one hand on the chest of an old and fragile man, the other on the laboring side of a valiant gray cat.

"What's amiss?" he asked and felt her sigh.

"Mr. dea'Gauss must have a 'doc—and that soon. Merlin—he has been shot. I cannot—quite—understand how badly he is wounded. If I could but take both home . . . I have tried bespeaking the Tree, and there is no answer. We are trapped here."

"Are you?" He glanced around the cold metal room, seeing the golden lines running pure and true. "Perhaps not."

•　　•　　•

Fingers poised above the comm, Val Con considered the access code hanging just behind his eyes.

"Brother!" Anthora's voice was sharp with urgency.

He spun, heart clenched in fear of hearing the old man's death—but no. His sister was standing tall, face animated—even eager.

"I require aid," she said quickly. "Do you put dea'Gauss on my back and I shall take him to Jelaza Kazone."

He blinked. Anthora was a wizard of some note, true enough, but . . .

"Will you walk through walls?" he asked.

She nodded. "I will. Assist me."

In the end, it required Nelirikk to gently lift dea'Gauss onto Anthora's back. Val Con lashed the man's wrists together on her breast, and used a length of fuse to tie them both 'round the waist.

"If I am able to return, I will do so," she said, breathless with bearing the unaccustomed burden. "Merlin . . ."

"If you make it to safety, you will remain there," Val Con said firmly. "We shall care for Merlin—and ourselves." He stepped back, waving at Nelirikk to do the same.

"If you are able, now is the time," he murmured.

"Yes." Slowly, awkward with the added weight, she walked directly toward the wall.

There was a flash of golden light, and an instant when the metal went to fog—then Anthora, and Mr. dea'Gauss, were gone.

"Jela's blood produces many wonders," Nelirikk commented, and returned to the unpacking of explosives.

After a moment, Val Con went back to the comm, and tapped in the code he had been given.

The unit light went from red to green. Scarcely daring to breathe, Val Con punched in the code for Jeeves' private line.

"Jelaza Kazone."

Val Con sat down in the Commander's chair.

"This is Korval," he said, keeping his voice steady, despite his foolishly pounding heart. "Pray confirm my ID. Also, please put a tracer on this call. Let Miri know that we are well, at liberty, but . . . contained. How stands the action?"

"ID confirmed. Miri will be informed. Working. How wide a theater?"

"Entire."

A small pause.

"The planetary defense net is ours," Jeeves said. "We control near space. A warship of the Department of the Interior has been destroyed by one of Lord Pat Rin's vessels. *Dutiful Passage* has been pressed into service for backup and link duty. Scout and Juntavas forces are prepared to allow Tree-and-Dragon central command if action is necessary."

"Jeeves, forgive me—Lord Pat Rin's forces?"

"Yes, quite an elegant group of ships flying Tree-and-Dragon, perfect for a low key planetary embargo, insurrection control, or as siege ships. They are precisely disciplined and well-crewed."

Ah, are they? And how came Pat Rin by such ships? Val Con moved his shoulders, putting aside such questions in favor of those more pressing.

"Planetary?" he asked Jeeves.

"Much of the planet is calm; Solcintra Portmaster has issued a flight hiatus, incidentally warning Captain Mendoza that her license is in danger. Solcintra City is not calm. There are riots in strategic locations, and we have signs of enemy action in Low Port. Higdon's Howlers are active at your location and at the spaceport. Here, we have withstood several attempts at penetration and anticipate—pardon, working . . ."

Across the room, Sheather moved, knife flashing. There was a scream—of metal, as the blade sheared through the floor. "Brother, he has initiated a device!"

The Commander's hand was still wrapped in his shirt; Nelirikk sprang forward and jerked the covering off, forcing the clenched hand open . . .

"Scout." He threw the object; Val Con snatched it out of the air and stared down at it—a short and stubby wand, its surface studded with tiny buttons and switches . . .

Agent ter'Fendil shrank against the wall, staring at the Commander in horror.

"You've given them orders. But—"

". . . working!" Jeeves voice came out of the comm. "Alert! There has been a sixty thousand fold increase in neutrino emissions from Liad. Triangulation places the source at your location. Suggest immediate evacuation of all personnel."

Nelirikk had dragged the Commander up by the back of his collar. He shook him, as a dog shakes a rat. "Inform me!"

The Commander said nothing.

"The level of neutrino flux is consistent with old-style timonium powered armored units," Jeeves said. "Suggest immediate evacuation."

"Brother," Sheather said. "Something of much power is in motion. It moves strangely . . ." He turned and placed his three fingered hand flat against the wall.

"It comes . . ."

There was fighting on the stations, there was fighting in the streets. Status reports poured in steadily, until Miri felt like she was drowning in details.

The Department's base in the commercial district of Solcintra city had been taken by an angry mob, led, she strongly suspected, by scouts—a victory for the angels, except for the civilians dead, of course.

Closer to the port, the news wasn't so good—the mob there had been repelled, expensively. Word was that there was a regroup in process.

Low Port was the worry—there'd been a couple unanticipated explosions. There were scouts there, too, trying to organize an evacuation.

The wall of books to her left shimmered and went foggy, for all the world like Clutch drive effect.

Miri blinked and came half out of her chair, too tired to even swear at the pain in her arm.

The books solidified and suddenly she wasn't alone. A dark-haired woman with an old man tied across her back was swaying in front of the bookcase.

"Help," she said.

There was a crashing sound behind the wall, and another.

". . . Autonomous Semi-sentient Policing Systems," Jeeves said; "or ASPS. They were deployed a number of times on outworlds, for the most part disastrously, which resulted in public backlash against applications of such technology to civilian situations. I was once assigned as backup, and then lead control in a military operation designed to rid a world of the devices. . . . approximately seventeen million dead as a result of erroneous deployment . . ."

"You must define the enemy or they will destroy everything," Agent ter'Fendil said. He lurched to his feet, ignoring Sheather, his blade—and the Commander, who was all at once on his feet, a plain metal blade in his good hand, slashing at the unprotected back—

ter'Fendil spun, Agent-quick, slapped the knife away, closing and twisting, taking advantage of his adversary's momentum—

The Commander's neck broke with a *snap*. Agent ter'Fendil dropped the body and shrank back, staring.

"... do not draw attention to yourself in any circumstances ..." Jeeves was saying, over the clanking in the hallway.

Val Con slapped up the screen, accessed the hallway camera, and sucked in his breath.

The hall was blocked with objects—four objects, in fact. Each as large as Edger, all of deep green metal, all bearing large Terran numerals—Val Con saw numbers 1, 3, 15 . . .

"... energy spike entirely consistent with an intact ASPS unit . . ." the voice continued from the comm.

"Jeeves, I confirm such a unit. Options?"

"Evacuate immediately. General use explosives slow them down; the most effective resistance, aside from vaporization, is placing obstructions in their way or dropping things on them . . . When first mobilized they are methodical unless one triggers a self-defense program . . ."

"The control." Agent ter'Fendil was beside him. "They will destroy the planet. Give me the control."

Val Con looked at him, seeing honest fear in the Agent's eyes. "Can they be turned off?"

"There is a resting state, yes."

From the hallway outside, screams and the sounds of rending.

Val Con handed Agent ter'Fendil the control wand.

The old gent was settled in the autodoc. Miri leaned against the unit, feeling a kind of hum in her bones, which was probably the 'doc working, and which she shouldn't have noticed at all.

An arm's length away, Anthora yos'Galan slumped in a massively carved chair, eyes closed and voice low as she complied with Miri's request to be brought up to speed.

She was doing a good job, hitting the high points and not wasting any words, and Miri wasn't much liking what she heard.

"They're surrounded," she said, by way of a sum-up when the low, careful voice came to an end. "And trapped." She bit her lip. "We can bust them out, but we're gonna need coords for that room. Think you can work with Jeeves and figure it?"

Anthora shook her head. "Going in, the Tree provided the path. Ren Zel showed me the way out."

Right. The hum from the 'doc was making her twitchy. Miri straightened out of her lean and looked down at the kid in the chair, hating what she was about to ask.

"So, you can get the Tree to provide a path back in, right? And this time, we'll rig you up with a findme, and—"

Anthora opened her eyes. Silver-blue, like Shan's, wide-spaced and dreamy-looking—which Shan's weren't. "Val Con said, if I got to safety, to stay there."

Miri sighed. "Yeah, well. Val Con says a lot of stupid things, especially where it bears on somebody he cares about maybe getting hurt. Figures he's tough enough to take his licks and ours, too. Also figures he's fast enough to outrun most common trouble. Sometimes, he's right; sometimes, he's lucky. This time, he needs help. That's us."

"You don't understand," Anthora said. "Val Con *said*, if I got to safety, to stay there. I cannot return."

Miri closed her eyes, counted to ten, and tried it again. "Val Con's half of one good delm." She reached inside her shirt and brought the Ring up on its cord, so the kid could see it. "I'm the other half. I'll make it an order, if I have to."

Anthora shook her head. "You do not understand," she repeated. "Val Con—I am *forbidden*. He has this ability. I *cannot* return."

"I just saw you walk through a *wall*," Miri started—and blinked, as various memories from a young adulthood that was absolutely not hers unfolded, neatly, before her mind's eye.

"You're talking dramliza talent," she said to Anthora's soft silver eyes. "He can tell you no and make it stick."

"He can do it to Priscilla, too," Anthora offered helpfully.

"Great," Miri said, thinking that if there were one person in the universe who had to be a dramliza-brake, of *course* it would be—

"Miri." Jeeves' voice flowed out of the room speakers. "You are needed in the control room. A situation is developing."

The last charge was laid; the last timer set.

Val Con dropped out of the repair hatch to the floor below, counting in his head.

Six minutes before the charges blew, burying the ASPS unit in rubble. Three minutes from his location to the rendezvous point. Two minutes to the surface.

Plenty of time.

•   •   •

"**Lord** Pat Rin, your timing is impeccable, sir," Jeeves said—and surely, Pat Rin thought, it was an artifact of the transmission that yos'Galan's butler sounded breathless? "We have a situation. Stand by, of your goodness, while I ascertain . . ."

There was silence, though the connect light remained steady. Pat Rin recruited himself to patience which was very shortly rewarded.

"Working," Jeeves announced. "You will understand that control of the planetary defense net resides under the Captain's hand during this present time of emergency."

Pat Rin all but smiled. "Ah, does it? That will certainly expedite matters, should it become necessary to fire upon the planet. However—"

"Precisely," the robot said, cutting him off ruthlessly. "It is exactly the subject of firing upon the planet that must now be addressed. The nature of the fleet you chose to field dictates your task. It will shortly be necessary to fire upon Solcintra City. Coordinates and ranging will be supplied."

Necessary to fire upon Solcintra? Pat Rin closed his eyes. He had, of course, known that it might come to firing upon the homeworld—why else had he brought destroyers with him? Truth told, he had pinned his hope on the Council of Clans, that the all-too-public crying of Balance would flush the Department of the Interior onto the surface, where it might be dealt with as any other transgressor against the Code.

"Lord Pat Rin?"

"One moment," he managed, holding up a hand that the robot could not see. "Jeeves, how is it necessary that we fire upon Solcintra, now? There has been no time for the Council to speak, nor time for the Department of the Interior to make answer . . ."

"The Department has made answer," Jeeves said. "Certain intelligence reports, confirmed by direct observation of trusted parties, indicate that the Department of the Interior has deployed timonium powered weapons capable of overwhelming anything that Liad may bring against them on the ground. The planetary defense net is unable—by its nature—to effect an attack against a target situated upon the planet." There was a pause, then Jeeves continued, hurriedly.

"It is my estimate that a failure to destroy these weapons in short order will lead to planetary disaster. In fact, it is necessary to fire upon the planet, bringing destruction to a portion of the city, in order to preserve the greater part. Your vessels are uniquely fitted to this task. *Dutiful Passage*, for instance, may only deploy a broad beam—far more destructive than those precision cutting units borne by your fleet."

"There are *people* in that city!" Pat Rin snapped.

"There are. Evacuation has been sounded. I expect confirmation from teams shortly. In the meantime, steps are being taken to contain the targets." Another pause, then, with a gentleness a robot could certainly never feel—

"It is our intention to destroy as small an area as possible. However, we dare not err by the application of too little force. People will die, despite the call for evacuation and the best efforts of the teams. But more people will die, if the enemy is not destroyed."

Pat Rin bowed his head.

"I understand. I will require data."

"Uploading," Jeeves said promptly.

Diglon Rifle waited patiently for his next target. So far he had taken seven shots with this light rifle borrowed from Commander Carmody's troop; he felt confident of five hits.

Nearby, Commander Call-Me-Liz-Lizardi was speaking quietly into a comm unit. His duty was to guard her and to watch for breakouts at the door which was, by now, well shattered, and partly filled with bodies.

Their position was excellent—they had a large stone monument for cover when they stood, and a stone wall, half buried on the other side with soil, for cover when they sniped . . .

Hazenthull Explorer had not shot as much as he, but perhaps with more accuracy. The commander had told them to conserve their ammunition, and to be prepared to act as rearguard if need be—and to be rearguard with such as she, whose exploits were writ on books and worlds forever, such was a fate a soldier could embrace.

There came another one of those slight shakes of the ground, and a vibration that was longer. He was leaning against the monument, his face feeling the stone—and . . . there was a shake, a—

"Explorer!" he called. "Something happens here!"

Hazenthull gave an assent signal, indicated to the commander that she was moving his way . . .

"Feel," he whispered to her, pushing fingers to the stone. "Equipment!"

She looked at him in startlement, felt the stone herself, then leaned her ear against it.

Abruptly there was grinding noise close to hand and she jerked back, dragging Diglon with her.

A seam in the granite shivered, clunked, shrugged—and slid quietly into the rest of the monument, revealing a metal wall. Almost immediately that wall moved aside, and smoke billowed free, carrying the smell perhaps of burnt meat. From within the monument came the scout, Nelirikk Explorer, and another, with blood on his cheek—pushing the Honored One, guiding him into the light . . .

The scout was cradling something precious against his chest, gun held ready in his free hand. He looked around, caught Diglon's eye, smiled, and thrust the gray fur ball into his hands, saying in Troop, "Protect this hero from harm. Move away, move away!"

That quickly he was gone, dashing back to the monument, bending, making some unseen adjustment. There was a repeat of the clanking and grinding; the door shut, and the monument was as it had been.

"Medic! Medic!" yelled Commander Liz, and waved to him in his new troop-sign: *fast march that way* . . .

They all started running then, away from the monument and the fighting in the street, and when the ground rumbled and knocked them down, the monument swayed and great gouts of smoke and flame blew out of it, into the pale green sky.

The breeze was fairly stiff, blowing away from the city center and—by extrapolation—away from Jelaza Kazone and Korval's valley.

". . . not never meant for atmospheric work . . . damn, but look at that!" That was Andy Mack, muttering publicly under his breath.

Everyone else—including the usually irrepressible Cheever Mc-Farland—remained silent as rug mites, watching their separate screens and the results of their labors. There was fire—not all of Solcintra could be spared, no matter how precise the aiming Jeeves had contrived—and a black spout of soot and ash leaning away from the city. Already there was a darkening that was not mere shadow as the heaviest debris fell in a kind of non-volcanic pumice.

Pat Rin switched views quickly. Not all of the smoke above the city had its birth in their attack. Portions of Low Port and Mid Port were aflame, and elsewhere there were reports of scattered violence. The portmaster's jury-rigged comm was demanding answers, demanding control of the planetary net, demanding that the mercenary units vacate the planet, demanding Korval's surrender . . .

That last had brought a burst of laughter from several of his crew members; then Jeeves had once again brought their attention to the task at hand and they fired what Pat Rin hoped was the last blast at the city he'd called home.

Jeeves supplied them with several views of the target now. The beams, meant to slice and cut, had done just that, lancing through the atmosphere of Liad in unison from the four mining craft, each cutting its own edge of a box centered on a green park and then crisscrossing toward the center. The initial gout of reflective white smoke had given way quickly to a dense ash-filled swirl, and then when the interior of the buried domain was opened there had been explosions . . .

The while, Jeeves had spoken in the background, calmly instructing and coaxing minute beam corrections until at last, for good or for ill, the thing was finished.

Now, from above, Pat Rin saw the terminator on the planet clearly as his ship entered shadow. Soon, night would fall on Solcintra. He wondered if anyone there would be able to sleep.

DAY 56
STANDARD YEAR 1393

SOLCINTRA
LIAD

"Mr. McFarland, I thank you for your care, but I scarcely need *security* in the very heart of Solcintra."

The big Terran sighed. "Boss, use your head. Ships under your command fired on the planet not all that long ago." He held up a hand. "Yeah, we did it for a good reason and likely saved a buncha folks their hides, if not exactly their homes. And we can take it as given the evacuation missed somebody—probably more than a couple somebodies. *And* there's a big glassy hole in the planet where we beamed them 'bots into vapor.

"All of which says to me that there're some who ain't gonna be real pleased to see you."

Pat Rin closed his eyes. *True enough*, he thought. Nor would it do to deprive the delm of the honor of dealing appropriately with Korval's erring child Pat Rin by getting himself murdered beforehand.

"Besides," Cheever said. "Natesa'd chew me out good if I let somethin' happen to you."

Natesa.

"Your point is taken, Mr. McFarland."

He opened his eyes, checked the gun in its hidden pocket, pulled the jacket into seemliness—and paused, his fingers tightening on the leather. *Jacket*, he thought. *This jacket. Before Korval.*

Pat Rin yos'Phelium, you are a fool.

"Boss?"

He smoothed the sleeves, feigning a finicky lordling's care, buying time—a few moments, only; long enough for his heart to stop pounding so, and for his face to find the proper expression of cool neutrality. What, after all, was a pilot's jacket, when he already wore a ring?

"Something I oughta know?" Cheever McFarland asked.

Jacket settled, he looked up into the face of his oathsworn, seeing worry and . . . care in the strong lines. Gods, when had Cheever McFarland's face become as precious to him as kin?

He inclined his head.

"There is something you should know, yes," he said, deliberately cold. "When we are with my cousin Val Con, you will forget that you are armed. You will protest nothing that may happen while he and I . . . converse." He looked closely into the Terran's eyes. "I will not insult you by asking for your oath on this. I will merely remind you that—I am the boss. Is this understood?"

Cheever's face tightened, but—"Yessir," he said, mildly enough.

"Good," Pat Rin murmured.

•   •   •

Something was bad wrong, Cheever decided as Pat Rin bowed to the young buck from Binjali's who'd won the brief bowling ball game for the right to play taxi, and turned to look at the building where Val Con yos'Phelium had set up a temporary headquarters.

The slim shoulders rose and fell inside the leather jacket, then Pat Rin was gone, walking steadily across the street, head up, back straight. Cussing softly, Cheever went after him.

The door was flanked by two soldiers, male and female, each massing about as much as Cheever did. The male dropped his rifle across the door, barring the way.

"Name is?" the female asked, her Trade carrying a heavy accent that Cheever didn't quite place. "Business is?"

"My name is Pat Rin yos'Phelium Clan Korval. I have come to speak with my kinsman, Val Con yos'Phelium, on business of the clan."

"Hah." She snapped her fingers, the rifle was lifted away, and Pat Rin walked on, Cheever at his back.

They went down a short hallway, following the sound of voices to a room cluttered with people and equipment. Pat Rin hesitated on the threshold, scanning the crowd, maybe. A woman in working leathers pushed by, and ran down the hall. Still, Pat Rin stood there, oblivious to the jostling.

Suddenly, he moved, striding purposefully across the room toward a knot of people in leathers, uniforms, and Low Port motley. A dark-haired man in working leathers turned his head, said a quick word to the group and stepped forward, hands extended, smiling across a face so familiar that Cheever had to shake his head and look again—by which time Pat Rin was on his knees before the younger edition of himself, forehead on the floor, the back of his neck exposed and vulnerable.

Something moved across the busy room. Val Con glanced aside and saw two pilots approaching, the Liaden walking with purpose; the Terran—

"A moment," he said quickly to the cluster of scouts, and went forward, hands extended in welcome.

"Cousin, well-met!"

Pat Rin flung to his knees, face against the floor. Behind him, the Terran slammed to a halt, openly shocked.

Val Con looked down at the exposed neck, at the dark hair

curling softly, several fingers longer than its accustomed length, and the smooth, unmarred leather of the Jump pilot's jacket.

"As ill as that?" he murmured and bent forward, checking when he sensed the big man start.

Looking up, he met the man's eyes. "I will not hurt him."

The Terran nodded, brusquely. "Right."

Carefully, Val Con bent and put a hand on a bowed shoulder. The muscles were rock hard. "Come, cousin," he said softly. "You'd best tell me."

Nothing. Then, slowly, Pat Rin straightened. Val Con dropped lightly to one knee, putting them at the same level. Pat Rin, he saw, had lost weight; his face was chapped, as if he had spent too much time out in the cold; and there were new lines around his mouth and eyes.

"My lifemate and my oathsworn are blameless," he said, in the mode of transgressor to delm. "I claim all."

"Ever more terrifying," Val Con returned, lightly, deliberately, in the Low Tongue. "Pray reveal at once the horrific crimes of which they are innocent."

Pat Rin raised his left hand, on which gleamed Korval's—no.

"Ah, I see. Very prettily done, too. Though they should have been more careful about the emeralds."

The edge of a smile glimmered. "Just so." The smile faded, and he moved his hand again; light ran liquid over dragon scale and leaf.

"Using this, I have subjugated a world to my necessity. I have allied with the Juntavas. I have made promises in Korval's name. I have put things . . . into motion . . ."

"As well we all know, having seen that motion work wonders. Very well. And your necessity was—what? Usurpation of Korval?"

Pat Rin shuddered and closed his eyes. "They came to me," he whispered, and his voice was haunted. "They came to me and they said, *all your kin are dead.* They said, *Korval.* They expected that I would be *grateful* for their care of my interests—and that I would represent them to the Council."

"They were very foolish," Val Con said softly. "That was at Teriste? Where did you go after?"

The brown eyes opened. "First, to a Juntavas base. Then to Bazaar, to purchase stock. Finally to Surebleak, where I set up as a boss, and—and began my Balance—" the smile again, slightly more visible this time. "Among other necessary tasks."

"Ah." Val Con tipped his head. "And these are the crimes of which you alone are guilty?"

Pat Rin sighed. "I don't doubt there are others—impersonating a pilot comes to mind."

"Commander?" A voice called from behind. "We have word from the Low Port."

Val Con glanced over his shoulder. "A moment." He reached out and gripped Pat Rin's hand.

"Duty," he said. "Quickly now—tell me the name of your life-mate."

"Inas Bhar," Pat Rin said softly. "Called Juntavas Sector Judge Natesa the Assassin."

Val Con smiled. "The clan increases." He rose, pulling his cousin up, and embraced him, cheek to cheek.

"Bide," he murmured. "We will go home together."

DAY 59
STANDARD YEAR 1393

SOLCINTRA
LIAD

Speaker for Council was enjoying the show, Miri thought. Come to think of it, she'd be having a better time herself if she was sitting behind a high table, with a pretty silver bell to ring whenever she felt like hearing it, and a cup of her favorite brew to hand.

Unfortunately, Defenders Before Council had to stand on the low floor facing the paid seats stretching up to the ceiling, with the Speaker's high desk behind them. As far as Miri was concerned, the whole set-up was a melant'i trick designed to make the Defenders feel all humble and unworthy. What she mostly felt was annoyed—and she wasn't exactly getting humble-vibes from Val Con, either.

"Korval has been called before this Council to answer for the following crimes against the homeworld," Speaker said from behind them and considerably over their heads.

"Landing a hostile force comprised of Terran and Yxtrang soldiers at Solcintra Port.

"Leading a military action against Liad.

"Subverting the planetary defense net.

"Firing upon the homeworld."

She paused a nice, long while, to let the assembled delms get a good look at them. Miri ran a quick Rainbow and felt her shoulders relax under the ceremonial delm costume. From Val Con she caught a flutter of warmth, as if he had quickly kissed her cheek.

"Korval's answer, given before this Council, invokes the contract originally made between Captain Cantra yos'Phelium Clan Torvin and the Combined Houses of Planet Solcintra. The Council's attention was directed most particularly to the articles discussing the duty of the captain toward the passengers; the charge upon successor captains; and the term of contract.

"It is Korval's contention that this contract, made before the Exodus from Solcintra, remains in force, according to its conditions of termination. They provide evidence that a call for Captain's Justice was made in Standard Year 1061, which Justice was dealt by the delm of Korval in her melant'i as Captain Genetic in this very chamber."

There was a pause, and a small clink. Miri sighed inwardly. A cup of tea would taste good right now. Especially if she could have it in the back kitchen at Jelaza Kazone.

Another clink, as Speaker put her teacup down.

"Korval argues that their *contract of employment* burdens them with the duty of protecting the residents of the planet Liad, whom they are pleased to term 'the passengers.'

"Korval provides evidence of the existence and the crimes of an organization calling itself the *Department of the Interior*. The list of names of those allegedly impressed or murdered by this organization is particularly notable in that it includes many of those whom Korval has been charged with harming.

"Korval's conclusion and final answer to this Council is that the Captain Genetic, having ascertained the mortal danger presented to the passengers by the Department of the Interior, acted to remove this danger. For the best good of Liad."

She didn't, Miri thought, sound too impressed with all Nova's careful compilations and cross-checks.

"I must note, with some surprise, that various organizations and individuals have indicated a willingness—on the side of Korval—to file briefs and informational materials or have in fact filed briefs and such material sufficient to fill several warehouses. These organizations and individuals have, for the most part, a clear, well-known, and on-going relationship with Korval. I mention a few—the Scouts of Liad, the Accountants Guild, the Pilots Guild, the Solcintra Feline Appreciation Society, the Taxicab and Pedicab Association of Solcintra, Binjali's Repair Shop and Jalopy Garage," here there was a clear and distinctly disapproving pause, ". . . . the Juntavas."

That brought a murmur from the chamber and Miri raised her eyebrows Val Con-fashion as she glanced at him. He raised his back at her.

Robertson, she thought, *you ain't takin' this serious enough . . .*

"Also," Speaker continued, "University, the Defenders of the Code, the Little Festival Association, Tey Dor's Sporting Clubs— and the list is quite long, and will be appended to our decision which will be hung on the chamber door and published as required, with copies to all major parties. Given the seriousness and time-sensitive nature of the charges, the Council has decided to forego introduction of such material into the hearing process. We thank each of those who have offered assistance."

Hanging judge! Miri thought. *She don't want to be confused by the facts.*

A pause, the sound of a teacup being placed too close to the microphone.

"The Council will now render its judgment. Hedrede is called."

From the fifth row up came a stir and a rustle, and finally a man, decked out like they all were, in formal delm gear, arose and bowed toward the floor.

"As Korval will doubtless recall," he said, his voice about as warm as a Surebleak winter morning, "House Hedrede was among the signers of the contract with Captain Cantra yos'Phelium."

"Korval recalls," Val Con said from beside her.

"The Dragon's memory," someone said, loudly, from high near the ceiling, "is not in question."

There was a titter and a murmur of agreement through the hall.

"Mizel is found to be out of order," Speaker snapped. "Honored Hedrede, pray continue."

He inclined his head.

"The Council of Clans finds Korval in error," he stated coldly. "The contract between Captain yos'Phelium and the Houses of Solcintra was never intended to continue so long, or to place so much of a burden upon one clan. In undertaking the described actions against the so-called Department of the Interior, Korval has overstepped, to the endangerment and distress of the homeworld."

He paused, maybe expecting an answer from the floor. Miri preserved a dignified silence. Beside her, Val Con inclined his head slightly—courteous permission to continue.

"The Council of Clans likewise finds," Hedrede continued portentously, "that it has erred, in that it has not caused the contract in question to be terminated according to its articles, thereby removing the burden of captaincy from Korval." He bowed, employer to employee.

"The Council of Clans, successor to the Combined Houses of Solcintra, hereby terminates, closes, and declares fulfilled the contract of employment originally made between Cantra yos'Phelium Clan Torvin, captain-owner of the starship *Quick Passage*, and the Combined Houses of Solcintra."

From Val Con, a flare of joy so pure and so vivid, her breath caught in her throat.

"Korval hears," he said, his voice perfectly composed.

"This also means," said Hedrede, perhaps a bit testily, "that the defense of Liad shall no longer be the concern of Korval or its assigns. We require a timely transfer of the defense net to the duly constituted authority of the portmaster." Hedrede glanced up from the document he read from. "Is this clear?"

"To avoid potential conflicts of interest Korval relinquished control of the defense net to the Commander of the Liaden Scouts upon entering this chamber," Val Con murmured. "I am certain that the portmaster will contrive an orderly transfer."

There was a collective sigh in the hall.

Hedrede inclined his head. "We now come to the matter of Balance.

"It is the decision of this Council that Clan Korval is an active threat to the safety and security of this world. Therefore, Korval shall be cast out. No longer shall Korval have a voice in this

Council nor may Korval look to the assembled clans for justice, sustenance, or comfort.

"Korval is required to vacate Liad and Liaden space. All and any Korval properties or persons remaining within Liaden space on the one hundredth forty-fifth day following this judgment shall be forfeit to the Council of Clans."

Miri blinked.

The bright joy radiating from Val Con went incandescent.

In the fifth row, Hedrede bowed once more.

"Thus, the Council's judgment."

He sat. The room was real quiet; nobody shuffled papers; nobody coughed, or whispered, or dropped a stylus. Everybody was watching them, Miri realized, waiting to see what they'd do.

"Cha'trez?"

She turned, saw green eyes smiling at her, and a slim golden hand extended. Grinning, she wove her fingers with his. Together, they bowed to the assembled delms—*farewell*. Nothing else.

Hand-in-hand, not hurrying, but not wasting any time, either, they walked up the long ramp. The door swung open as they approached.

Neither one looked back.

"One hundred forty-four days to leave planet, lock, stock and piglet?" Shan repeated incredulously. "Have they lost their wits?"

"Certainly not," Val Con said drily. "They merely hope to hurry us sufficiently that we will leave a few things behind, to their benefit."

"Did the Council forbid sales?" inquired dea'Gauss—this the new dea'Gauss, a woman in her early middle years, with a serious face and unexpectedly merry eyes. Her father was yet with the Healers and he would be well, with time. Though his notes were before her, it was happily clear to Val Con that her course was her own.

Val Con shook his head. "The vote was close, as I counted. Close enough that those who most dearly wished us gone dared not risk their victory by burdening the issue with petty Balance."

The dea'Gauss inclined her head. "That is good, then. Allow me . . ." She bent to her keyboard.

"Even supposing we can pack everything of importance," Shan continued, "how the devil are we going to ship it? Worse, where will we go? Somehow, I don't believe Erob would be willing to have us."

Miri laughed, and Merlin, who was curled up on her lap, muttered a sleepy protest.

"Bad idea, anyway," she said. "Given the family tendency to force things into our own mold."

"There's that. We might try for New Dublin, I suppose . . ."

"Or Surebleak," Pat Rin said quietly from his place next to Shan.

"Surebleak's at the back end of nowhere—and it's cold," Miri said, and then shook her head, with a half-grin. "Why'm I telling you that, Boss?"

"In fact, Surebleak is not so ill-placed as it first appears," Pat Rin replied, earnestly. "Certainly, the presence of trade and an upgraded port would be more than enough to overcome any difficulty of location. As to the weather—" He moved his shoulders. "The portmaster has specs for climate satellites on file. It does not need to remain cold."

There was a brief pause, then—

"He's right," Shan said. "There aren't any major trade routes close, but there are three solid mid-level routes through that sector. If there was any reason for ships to stop at Surebleak—"

"They would stop," Val Con concluded. He glanced aside. "Cha'trez?"

She sighed. "Well, it'll give us a base. Hafta buy up a buncha real estate and do some heavy renovating . . ."

"There is land beyond the city, which is only lightly lived in," Pat Rin said, looking at Val Con. "We might be situated as we have been here, near enough to port and city, with easy access at need."

"And thus be invested in keeping the Port Road open." Val Con grinned. "Well-played, cousin."

"If we liquidate all holdings," the dea'Gauss said abruptly, "over a period of one hundred forty-two days, we may be able to prevent the Exchange from collapse, assuming we get and give value." She looked up.

"Unless your lordship wishes to incept a market collapse?"

"It is not necessary. We prefer to sell at fair value, however."

"Certainly," she said. "We have a list of off-world investors who have previously expressed interest in various acquisitions." She paused, touched a key.

"The accounts currently held at the Bank of Solcintra must be moved. Shall I query the Bank of Terra?"

"Why not transfer everything equally among our existing accounts," Shan suggested, "and sort that out once we're settled? I have a feeling that the Council of Clans may find themselves able to overlook Korval investments in Liad, after a suitable period of uncertainty."

"That's a point," said Miri. "Can't really do banking on Surebleak." She looked at Pat Rin. "Unless you fixed that, too?"

"Not yet," he said, and she shook her head.

"The dies, your lordship?"

Val Con frowned. "How much longer on the current term?"

"Less than a Standard."

"If we close the treasury, that *will* crash the market," Miri protested.

"Yet the dies are ours," Val Con said. "How if we—"

Across the room, the door opened, admitting Nelirikk.

"Captain, the elder scout is returned."

"That was quick," Miri commented. "Let him in, Beautiful. We need all the heads we can get."

"Captain." He stepped aside and Daav strolled in, pausing half-a-dozen steps inside the room to bow casually to the delm's honor.

"Good afternoon, Father," Val Con said mildly. "I confess that we had not looked for you so soon."

"I rather expected that you hadn't," Daav retorted. "However, the Clutch Elders have the ability to act rapidly, when they see the need—much like Clutch ships. Of which more anon. I hear on the port that we are unemployed, outlawed, and homeless, all in one canny throw."

"Indeed we are. The Council chose to see us as a danger to Liad."

"All hail the Council, wise at last," Daav murmured, and tipped his head. "Is that Pat Rin? I'm delighted to see you, child."

"Uncle Daav . . ." His voice failed him and he inclined his head, taking a hard breath. "I am all joy to see you."

"So what did the Elders say?" Miri asked. "No dice?"

"Entirely the opposite," Daav said, favoring her with one of his edged smiles. "They are eager to assist us in any way they can—and have detached one of their larger vessels for Korval's use. It is understood that this use will include transporting the Tree, but no limit of service was set."

"A ship large enough to move Jelaza Kazone?" Pat Rin asked.

"Oh, easily. In fact, if you would care to step outside, you may see for yourself."

It rode on the horizon like a moon, glass smooth and subtly glowing.

Miri took a hard breath against the sudden tightness in her chest and slid her hand into Val Con's. He squeezed her fingers gently, his attention focused on the moon-ship.

"Volume?" he murmured.

"Sufficient to contain those portions of Solcintra City still standing," Daav replied. "Or the Tree, and most of the valley."

Behind them, Shan sighed. "Brother, we have our transportation problems solved. But is Surebleak ready for that?"

"All the more reason to set down in the country," Pat Rin said unsteadily.

"Edger professes himself ready to commence immediately," Daav continued. "He is accompanied by several of his kin. If the delm wishes to remove all that is ours . . ."

"Yes," Miri and Val Con said—and abruptly laughed.

"Yes!" Miri said again.

DAY 201
STANDARD YEAR 1393

SOLCINTRA
LIAD

"Tomorrow is the day," Edger boomed, one three-fingered hand splayed flat against the trunk of the Tree. "The ship of the Elders shall descend with sample bay open and the lift active; it will be but a matter of a few hundred moments to adjust for Jelaza Kazone's necessity. We have spoken somewhat—the elder tree and I—and the vessel is ready to respectfully receive all into its interior."

Edger paused a short pause, thinking or watching or perhaps merely staring into the distance for some Clutch-required moment—and then continued in apparent haste.

"We have the coordinates for the new nesting place. There is no need for apprehension as Aelli has done the calculations. My brothers and I have consulted together, the boss kinsman of my brother and my sister has returned to put all into readiness. Thus, the work goes forth; art incarnate. Ephemeral and multi-stranded, it wends through time, space, and song, altering the very fabric of the universe. As I see, each day brings a new thread."

Miri stirred and squeezed Val Con's fingers. "Altering the fabric of the universe?" she whispered.

"Hyperbole," Val Con whispered back.

"Right."

There was a sound, somewhere beneath Edger's oration. Miri looked over her shoulder, and then turned—Val Con with her—staring at the apparition walking, none-too-steady, across the grass toward them, wary eyes on Edger.

She wasn't much more than a kid: undergrown, sharp-faced, and pale; her hair an uncertain sort of yellow, unruly rather than curly; dark eyes smudged by lack of sleep.

She stopped a couple paces away and bowed—out of mode and out of time, but, hell, the kid was dead on her feet. Her jacket told the story of how she'd gotten passed by security: Jump pilot.

"It is necessary that I speak to the delm of Korval, on business of the clan," she said, and her High Liaden was even worse than her bow.

Miri nodded—and blinked, feeling a rush of recognition from Val Con.

"*Another* one?" she complained, looking up at him.

"Shall you like odds?" he answered, and then nodded easily at the kid.

"You are addressing the delm of Korval," he said in Terran. "May we know your name?"

The kid frowned, equal parts irritation, exhaustion, and relief at not having to do the rest of the conversation in Liaden.

"Theo Waitley," she said.

Apparently realizing that the name alone was a little scant, she added, "I'm here because my father's missing and he told me—

he *always* told me to go to the delm of Korval, if ever there was really bad trouble."

She paused, running one hand through her thoroughly draggled hair.

"My father's name is Jen Sar Kiladi. He teaches—"

"He teaches cultural genetics," Val Con interrupted, gently.

"Right. I mean, you might not think it was a big problem, if your father wasn't where you left him—"

"No, acquit me—I would think it a very large problem, indeed."

Theo might not have heard him; she swept on, caught up in the tide of her explanation. "But, he's never done anything like this before—just up and left, in the middle of the term and—" Her mouth tightened.

"I got trouble," she finished, "and since I can't find him . . ."

"Well," Val Con murmured, eyes pointed over Theo's head.

Miri looked where he was looking, saw the tall shadow moving toward them from the house, and sighed.

"Theo," Val Con said, "please look behind you."

She blinked at him, then did what she was told.

"Father!" she shouted and leapt forward, slamming Daav into a full body hug.

"Father, where the *hell* have you been?"

Daav tousled the Jump pilot's hair, looking suddenly old.

"I have been busy, child," he said, returning the hug. "Very busy."

He paused, and shook his head, Terran-style.

"I can't tell you how glad I am to see you, Theo. And sorry, as well."

"Sorry!" She looked startled—and afraid.

"Gently, child," Daav said, touching her cheek. "Sorry, because you would not be here if there wasn't really bad trouble."

She nodded. "It's kind of complicated," she started . . .

ABOUT THE AUTHORS

Sharon Lee and Steve Miller live in the rolling hills of Central Maine. Born and raised in Baltimore, Maryland, in the early '50s, they met several times before taking the hint and formalizing the team, in 1979. They moved to Maine with cats, books, and music following the completion of *Carpe Diem*, their third novel.

Their short fiction, written both jointly and singly, has appeared or will appear in *Absolute Magnitude*, *Catfantastic*, *Such a Pretty Face*, *Dreams of Decadence*, *Fantasy Book*, and several former incarnations of *Amazing*. Meisha Merlin Publishing has or will be publishing seven books set in the Liaden Universe: *Plan B*, *Partners in Necessity*, *Pilots Choice*, *I Dare*, *Balance of Trade*, and two untitled—and *The Tomorrow Log*.

Both Sharon and Steve have seen their nonfiction work and reviews published in a variety of newspapers and magazines. Steve is the founding curator of the University of Maryland's Kuhn Library Science Fiction Research Collection. Sharon is the president of the Science Fiction and Fantasy Writers of America.

Sharon's interests include music, pine cone collecting, and seashores. Steve also enjoys music, plays chess, and collects cat whiskers. Both spend way too much time playing on the internet, and even have a website at:

www.korval.com